THE STARLIT WOOD

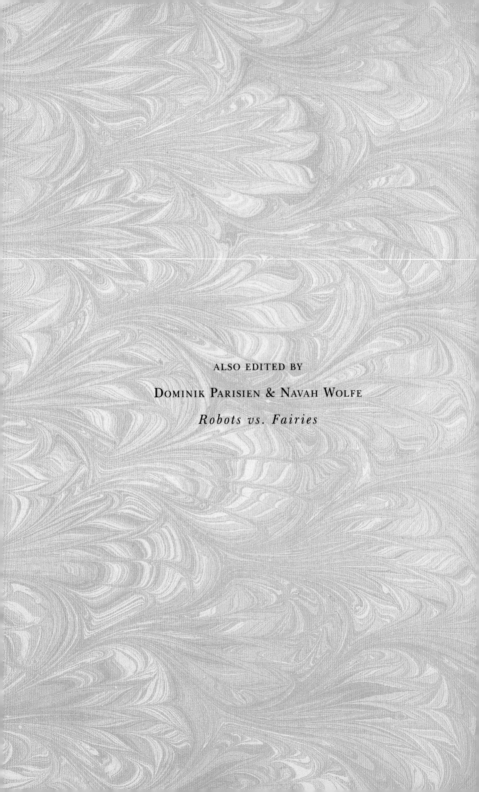

ALSO EDITED BY

DOMINIK PARISIEN & NAVAH WOLFE

Robots vs. Fairies

THE STARLIT WOOD

NEW FAIRY TALES

Edited by

DOMINIK PARISIEN
&
NAVAH WOLFE

Illustrations by Stella Björg

SAGA PRESS

LONDON SYDNEY **NEW YORK** TORONTO · NEW DELHI

SAGA PRESS
AN IMPRINT OF SIMON & SCHUSTER, INC.

1230 AVENUE OF THE AMERICAS, NEW YORK, NEW YORK 10020

In memory of my grandmothers:
Miriam Rosensweig, who shared stories with me,
and Marcia K. Levine, who made them
an integral part of my childhood.
—N. W.

For my parents,
who are not of the fairy tale variety.
—D. P.

Table of Contents

INTRODUCTION

When thinking of fairy tales, it can be easy to mistake the forest for the trees. In this case, the literal forest: the woods are almost ubiquitous in fairy tales. But perhaps they shouldn't be.

In times when individuals seldom ventured far from home, it made sense to view the unknown—usually the world just outside your little microcosm of a farm or village or city—as suspect. And so, the woods were the place of monsters, of weird happenings, of adventure. That is no longer the case. Over time the world has grown bigger and the woods—both metaphorically and physically—have grown smaller. Now the unknown is to be found in other places. The woods can still be a place of wonder and of danger, and sometimes they even feel more alien to us than ever because of how disconnected we are from them, but the strangers, the mysterious happenings, the fantastical adventures: those take place in other landscapes now. It's easy to forget that when we think of fairy tales. We tend to go back to what we think of as their original setting, to that old-timey, woodland world we *know* is home to those weird, sometimes frightening, often violent stories of wonder. But some of the tales never had woods to begin with. Fairy tales originate from all over the world, from widely differing traditions and cultures, and in many cases the woods are never even a factor.

So what connects them, if not the woods?

Think of skeletons. Mammalian skeletons, for example, all have similar touchstones. Just by looking at a mammal skeleton, you would know it was a mammal, even if some parts were missing. A mouse is not a whale, is not a tiger, is not an aardvark. You might not be able to see the similarities when they're covered by things like skin, fur, and hair, but when you strip them down to their bones, their most basic elements, they're slightly different but unmistakably related. So it is with fairy tales: we know to expect certain themes and subjects, or at least variations on them—terrible parents, wandering children, fantastical animals, enchanted items, moral components, trials and tribulations—to a point where even if we don't necessarily recognize the source material, a story can still *feel* like a fairy tale.

In their original form, fairy tales were always evolving. An oral tradition, they were constantly being told and retold, changing ever so slightly as they were passed from one storyteller to the next. As a definitive catalog of fairy tales emerged, writers borrowed and stole bits and pieces and elements from a vast mythos of stories and revised and reworked them tirelessly. In this way, retellings have always been a part of the fairy tale tradition.

In keeping with that original model of composite storytelling, we decided to run fairy tales through a prism, to challenge our authors to look at stories from an unusual angle, to bring them back into different genres and traditions, to—if you will—return them to their cross-genre roots. We wanted our authors to move beyond the woods. Sometimes that meant removing a piece traditionally viewed as integral to the story—like music from the Pied Piper—or putting a character as geographically far as possible from his or her original setting, as Little Red Riding Hood in the desert. In some cases it was exploring lesser-known or even newly

discovered fairy tales, which helps highlight the interconnected-
ness of the fairy tale tradition around the world.

From the woods to the stars, join us on eighteen extraordinary journeys into unexpected territories, uncharted lands, and
unforeseen experiences. Welcome to an adventure that's strangely
familiar and startlingly different at the same time. You're likely
to emerge changed, but isn't that the way it is with all the best
stories?

So come on in.

Step into *The Starlit Wood*.

—Dominik Parisien & Navah Wolfe

IN THE DESERT LIKE A BONE

Seanan McGuire

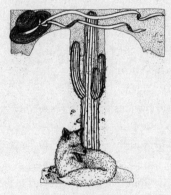

he sky is the color of bleached bone, neither white nor yellow, but a creamy in-between shade that speaks death from one end of the horizon to the other. Under it, the desert, the sand little darker than that endless sky. Upon that desert, two riders on horseback. Coyote has the lead, has had it since the day he swung a scrap of a girl barely worth the patchwork cotton she was wrapped in onto the back of his horse. She has her own steed now, can choose her own way, but still she follows in his wake, close and quiet and biding her time.

His shadow rides before the both of them, drawn bitter-black on the desert that stretches under the bone sky. As always, his face is concealed beneath the brim of his hat, and the gun at his hip glimmers with poisonous menace. He is a thin creature, is Coyote, raw of bone and furrowed of brow. The sun has burnt itself into him an inch at a time, turning his skin leathery and hard. Mosquitoes cannot pierce that skin, and fly away hungry when they come too close.

Behind him on her swayback mare rides his red fox girl, her eyes bright as bullets and scanning the horizon for signs of death or danger. Her hat is brown leather, but to listen to the people who have seen her, it should be red as blood, red as a harlot's corset, red as a rare, expensive apple stolen from an eastbound train. Her hair is the color of straw on a barroom floor, and her skin is tanned the color of the desert sand. She disappears, the fox girl does, whenever she slides from her horse and sets her feet to the ground. She is a child of this blasted, unforgiving land, and when she looks upon it, she sees a paradise, and not a waste at all.

She knows the rock, and the shadow of the rock, and the flowers that bloom there. If there is danger here, it does not frighten her.

The man in the black hat and the girl with hair the color of straw ride under the bone-colored sky, and no one knows from whence they ride, and no one watches them go.

"Once upon a time," say the prairie harpies and the respectable housewives, the snake-oil saleswomen in their jewel-colored gowns and glittering cosmetics, the woodwitches and the wisewomen and the lost, "there was a little girl in a place where no little girl should be. Her mama was long gone to blood on her handkerchief and fire in her lungs, and her daddy was no daddy at all but a man who saw no difference between daughter and dog—and he was a man who'd beat his dog besides. They lived in a little house all the way to the cruel, civilized East, and everyone who knew him for a widower said 'wasn't it fine' when they sighed over the way he was bringing up his little girl, all by himself, without a woman's hand to give him aid. That little girl had the best clothes and the best bread, and a cloak as red as the blood she'd seen on her mama's lips before the man in the black wagon came to carry her mama away forever."

That's where the stories diverge. "She would have been a fine lady; she would have grown up draped in diamonds, wrapped in silks. She would have danced in the finest parlors, and if her daddy didn't love her, she would have found a man who loved her more than the moon and the sun and the stars. But that bad wolf came in the night and gobbled her up, and she never got her dancing shoes, never got her debutante ball. She's a ghost in the desert now, lost and lonely and brokenhearted as a bobcat in October, and if you see her, child, don't you meet her eyes; don't you let her lead you astray." So say the housewives and the rich women as they tuck their own dear daughters into bed. For them, she is a cautionary tale, a way to keep their children close, and who can blame them? Who can blame them in the least?

"She would never have been a fine lady, as she had no grace for dancing; all her grace was in stillness and in silence, because those were the things her daddy prized, and so those were the things she learnt to please him. She would never have danced in the finest parlors, and who's to say the man in the black wagon, the wolf of the west who was never a wolf at all, didn't love her? What other reason could he have to come like a shadow in the night and sweep her away? Maybe she never got her diamonds, but she got the high desert stars, which shine far brighter. Maybe she never got her fine silks, but who would trade a single midnight breeze for all the silk in China? Her debutante ball was danced with jackrabbits and red-eyed lizards under the harvest moon, and if she never looked back, not even once, who can blame her? She'll lead you astray as easy as breathing, but that's no shame on her, or on you, for she never met a path she cared to follow. If you see her, child, don't meet her eyes; I need you here with me." So say the snake-oil saleswomen and the frontier wives, and they're as right, and as wrong, as anyone.

The girl in the hat that isn't red anywhere but in stories follows Coyote across the desert, and the stars are diamonds in her hair, and when she speaks—which is rare, for she trusts slow and warms slower—her voice carries the sound of the Atlantic, of deep woods and harsh snows and a climate she was born to but never belonged in. She could tell them another story, if she chose to, if she thought they'd listen. She could tell them about choices; about following because sometimes it was easier to track your prey when someone else blazes the trail. She could tell them all her choices have been her own, and will remain so: that if she had wanted someone else to make her choices for her, she would never have opened the window, never have left the path.

She says none of these things. She has other matters to concern herself with, and other jobs to do. She builds the fire when they stop for the night, piles the kindling high and coaxes the flames toward the moon. Some nights, Coyote goes hunting, and she sits close to the warmth and listens to the howls in the far distance. Other nights, she fetches the rabbits and the grouse for their supper. Her hunts are silent, unlike his. They are no less effective. Her feet still leave dents in the desert sand, but he assures her that this, too, will pass; one day, she will move as light as the wind that blows between midnight and morning, leaving nothing behind. On that day, she will earn bullets for the guns she wears strapped to her sides. On that day, she will finally be free.

Until then, she builds the fires when and where he tells her to, and she listens to him howl in the dark, and she tries to forget the house in the green world, where a man who claimed to know her had given bruises where he should have given kindness. She sleeps in the arms of the desert, and the stars keep watch above her.

This day, the sun is high and harsh in the sky, beating down until even Coyote shields his eyes. The girl huddles under her hat and thinks longingly of caves and mountain springs, of places of safety and succor. All of them are hidden somewhere in the desert. She does not think this a contradiction. The desert is the greatest safety she knows.

Coyote looks to her. A frown is on his lips, and there is worry in his eyes. "Are you well?" he asks. His voice is gunpowder and grace, as bone-bleached as the sky.

"Just hot," she says. Her voice still belongs to a young woman, growing from childhood into womanhood. She might still find her way back to the green world, if she chose to seek it. That door is not yet closed to her. "We almost there?" Questions are small, skittering things, like mice. Answers are the predators that pounce on them. She has learned to unleash her questions cleverly, rather than risk them all being devoured before she can learn what she needs to know.

"Close enough. You sure this is where we need to go?"

Her nod is tight. New Woodbury is a small town built around a well that cuts all the way to the bones of the world, down to where the water waits. The people who live there think they're going to thrive on that water. They don't understand how fickle the desert is; they don't know they're being hunted. "I'm sure. There's a man there. He says he's looking for something he lost."

Coyote looks at her, expression giving nothing away. "We have money. We could stop somewhere else. Rent a place, maybe get you some schooling before we finish the ride."

"I've had enough schooling. I don't want any more."

"Bullets are good. Knowledge is better. You want to keep riding with me, you're going to need both."

The girl, who knows better than to cross the man she rides with, says nothing. But her eyes burn beneath the shadow of her hat, and Coyote feels a pang of pride. She's growing up to be a proper wild thing, his little stolen pup. She'll learn soon enough why he insists on things she thinks have no value, that to reject something, it must first be understood. They all learn, given time. That's when they leave him. When they understand, and no longer need looking after; when they decide that it's time to start looking after themselves.

Distance has no meaning in the desert—not if the rider knows the way of things, the points of similarity between this and that, the places where the sky can fold. A man with a map, now, he'll have a hundred miles of hard land to walk, and every inch of it resenting him for what he represents, for the way he pins it down. A lake that was once free to move from here to there, as migratory as a bird, finds itself tethered by the intersection of pen and paper. The predators are heroes to the desert. If the mapmaker is lost, if all his possessions are destroyed, the landscape can be unbound. But if other eyes should see those lines, those laws, then all is lost.

To the mapmakers, Coyote and his red fox girl started the day a good sixty miles from New Woodbury, separated by long stretches of empty earth. But Coyote is no mapmaker, and his horse has no eye for cartography. He rides into town as the clock on the town hall strikes high noon, the girl still close behind him. The townsfolk stop what they were doing and turn to watch the strangers come, the man on the tall horse, the girl on the swaybacked mare. Their shadows are ink on the ground, etching them in the here and now as cleanly as any map could have dreamt.

They ride until they reach the boardinghouse, where a trough waits to soothe their horses, and a tying post stands ready to confine them. Coyote swings down as easily as breath, setting his feet to the ground and freeing his horse to drink. He leaves his reins to dangle. The horse would stay or go as it chose, and either way, he wouldn't try to argue with it.

The red fox girl doesn't seem to dismount at all. One moment she is seated on her horse's back, and the next moment she is standing on the ground, her hat still covering her eyes. Like Coyote, she leaves her reins untied. Unlike Coyote, she stands nervous, worried that her mare would leave her to ride double with the man who led her across the desert—but if he can trust his horse, she can trust hers. It seems the right thing to do.

Both horses stick their faces in the water and drink greedily, gulping until their bellies fill and their throats are no longer dry. Coyote and the girl dip their hands in the cool wetness and run dripping fingers across their faces, cutting trails in the dust that covers them. When they turn away from the trough, a man stands before them. He is plump, in the way of townspeople, an amiable, enviable softness that speaks to things being done for him, and not by him. His neck is thick, and his arms are heavy with muscle. A boss-man, then, and one for whom enviable plumpness was a new thing. That makes him dangerous. Men who haven't had a thing for long always know how valuable that thing is, and they more than any will fight to keep it.

"Welcome to New Woodbury," he says, and there is no welcome in his eyes. "We don't get many visitors around these parts."

"Can't say as we're visitors," says Coyote. "I'm John Branson." A simple name. A liar's name, a lying name, stolen from a tombstone at the edge of the green world that was Boston, a thousand miles and a lifetime behind the both of them. He glances at the red fox girl, who nods minutely. This is her lie, but he has to be the one to tell it. Little girls have no voices here. Little girls have no voices anywhere. "This is my niece, Mary. We were in East Canaan, saw a poster hung at the request of a man named Paul Stabler, said he was looking for someone as could retrieve a thing for him. Said as he'd pay. My niece and I, we're fond of money. Find it buys nice things, bread and wine and a basket to put them in. If you could direct us his way, we'd be grateful."

The red fox girl—whose name is not Mary, had never been Mary; her name is a secret to be guarded and concealed, as precious as a pearl and twice as prone to being stolen—holds her silence and watches the man with narrowed, mistrustful eyes. He meets them for a moment and then looks away. The things she isn't saying are painful even when unheard.

"Paul Stabler? He runs the bank. Other side of the town."

Not that there's much town to be on the other side of anything. New Woodbury matches its name: still new, still scented like sawdust and aspirations. The main street doesn't even have a sign. It's the only candidate for the position, running from one side of town to the other. It tapers off into the desert at either end, becoming one with the sand and the stone. The same fate awaits everything men could build here where the sun holds cruel dominion, and there is no forest to hide them, no path to lead them home. Conquer the desert, defeat it with wells and with walls, or be lost to it forever.

Coyote tips his hat. Somehow, the gesture neither reveals nor conceals any more of his face than was already showing. "We're much obliged. Is this a safe place to leave our ponies for a spell?"

"There's a livery stable," says the boss-man. He's losing control of the situation. He can feel it slipping through his fingers, never to be recovered. He just can't say *how*, and somehow that's the worst part of all for a man like him, in a place like this. He came to the wastes because here, no one would ever challenge his authority. This man in his black hat, this little girl in her brown one that still manages to be red as a berry on a bush, they're not challenging him. They're not doing anything of the sort. And they're *winning*.

"We'll keep that in mind for after we've been paid," says Coyote. "Come along, Mary." He starts across the street toward the distant outline of the bank. The red fox girl follows, leaving their horses untethered at the trough, leaving the boss-man to blink after them, confused and unsettled and feeling as if he's just escaped a predator with eyes that could see right through to the heart of him, and claws that had been poised to snatch him up.

He watches them go until he's satisfied they won't be coming back, and then he turns and walks toward the saloon. The sun is high and the day is young, but he needs a drink more than he can remember needing anything in his life.

The air inside the bank is cool and stale and old. It tastes like Boston, resting heavy on the tongue and carrying a hundred years of silent commands. Sit still, stand up straight, be quiet, be good, *behave*, or pay the price for misbehavior; do not stray from the path, do not wander into the wild places, do not speak with beasts. The red fox girl says nothing, but she steps closer to Coyote, haunting his shadow like the ghost of a drowned girl haunts the ditch where she died. He doesn't say anything either. He just slants his body to afford her more cover and walks on, toward the long oak counter where the teller sits, nervous as a rabbit, and watches him come.

The counter is a good ten feet long, polished wood from a forest so far from this place that it might as well have fallen from the sky. The teller, groomed and polished and perfect as a magazine ad, could have come from the same distant star. She forces a smile when the pair draws close enough, and says, "Welcome to the New Woodbury Bank. How may I help you?"

"We're here to see a Mr. Paul Stabler about a job he was looking to have done," says Coyote. "I hear there's a nice boardinghouse here in town. My niece and I would like to sleep there tonight, which means we need paying. Paying means working. So we'd like to see about that job sooner than later, if you don't mind."

The name of her boss is a rope, and the teller is swift to grab it. Let him pull her to safety. She works for him; the responsibility should be his. "I'll get him for you. If you'd wait here?" She doesn't wait for an answer. She's off and running, and Coyote and the red fox girl are, for the moment, alone.

"You can go, if you like," he says, looking down at her. He can't see her eyes under her hat, but he can read her posture, read the way she hunches her shoulders and dips her chin. She could live a hundred years, become a wild thing never before seen in the world, and he'd still be able to read her clear and easy. "I know this is your hunt, but a good hunter knows when it's better to stay home and hidden. I won't blame you if you go."

She shakes her head, ever so slightly, and for a moment the light slanting through the bank windows turns her brown leather hat apple-red, blood-red, the red of an expensive silk bonnet tied to the head of a girl too young to understand why she should value it. She wore the bruises for that bonnet on her skin for weeks after an errant gust of wind carried it away, leaving her laughing until the shadow of her father fell across her face. She was a girl who laughed then, his red fox child, and it was the sound of the laughter being beaten out of her that had drawn him, for no true hunter can stand the cries of a young thing being hurt. Kill them clean or give them peace and plenty, but do not harm them for sport.

"As you say," he says, and he turns, the man in the black hat with the young woman beside him, to wait for the door at the back of the bank to open.

Seconds slither by, the baitworms of time, followed by the larger minnows of minutes, until finally the doorknob turns, the door swings wide, and Paul Stabler appears. He is tall, in the way of men who ate well as children; his belly never ached in the night, his jaw never chewed at the air for the lack of anything else to eat. He is pale, in the way of men who never see the sun without glass between them and it. His mouth is hard and dips downward at the edges, for he has lost so much to come here; he has already paid so dearly.

"There you are," says Coyote, and his voice is bones and ashes and the white moon against the horizon. "I understand you've lost something, and you want to have it returned to you. Is that right?"

But Paul Stabler's eyes are only for the red fox girl. He takes a step toward her, drawn as if by a magnetic force, and says, "That's my little girl."

"She's her own girl, actually, and not so little for all of that," says Coyote, and his voice is teeth, nothing but teeth, teeth from one side all the way to the other. "That's the funny thing about children. They can belong to you as long as you're only dreaming them, but once they walk in the world, they have a nasty tendency to belong to themselves."

SEANAN
McGUIRE

"Did you steal her?" For the first time, Paul Stabler looks at Coyote, and he does not have the sense to be afraid. "Are you the one who opened her window and carried her away?"

Coyote says nothing. The window had been opened from the inside; the tree that had been used as a ladder to freedom would never have borne his weight, even slender as he was. There had been no kidnapping to pull her from the path, only a running away so comprehensive that it had reached across a desert and demanded aid. He had come for her, to be part of her story, to aid in leaving the green world she had always known. But steal her? Never.

She stole herself.

The red fox girl steps forward, tilts her head back enough to let the man—to let her father—see her face. This is her hunt. She must be the one who moves. She is thinner than she was in Boston, older, more wild thing than woman, and more woman than child. But her mother's eyes are her birthright, and no one who had known his wife could deny her parentage. "He didn't steal me," she says. "He found me. He helped me find my way here, to you. You'll pay him, won't you?"

And then, the most painful, most difficult word of all: "Daddy?"

Paul Stabler pays. Oh, yes, he pays. Some debts must be settled, after all, no matter how long it takes for them to come due. Coyote walks out of that bank with full pockets, and he does not look back. His part in this is not over, but it is finished, for a time.

The sun is setting in the desert outside, and the shadows it casts on the street are the color of blood, the color of garnets, the color of a lost red bonnet floating to freedom on a distant river.

Paul Stabler is a man who lives alone. It suits him, he finds, and if that's a surprise, it's only because he's never had cause for solitude before. First had come his parents, and then came his wife, and when his wife had gone his daughter had still been there, and when his daughter had gone, there had been all the eligible women of Boston, wanting to dry his tears and tell him he could be a father again. He fled west to escape, both from them and from the quiet ghost in the red hat who looked at him reproachfully from every shadow.

New Woodbury was exactly what the name had promised: new. If there were ghosts here, they belonged to someone else, and they had no interest in haunting him.

Now he walks into the front room of his modest home, and the red fox girl who was his Rosalind follows, her feet silent as a whisper on the carpeted floor. He looked for her not because he wanted her back again, but because it was his duty as a father to find what he had lost. As long as he was looking for her, he had had no need to remarry or to explain himself; his grief was seen as motivation enough for everything, from his stony silences to the bruises on his workers' arms. A man may be a wolf, if he's been bitten hard enough.

He leads her to the back of the house, where a narrow door like a coffin lid sits ajar. He pushes it open, looks to her, and says, "This is your room. You're not to leave it without speaking to me first. You're precious to me, and I'll not lose you again. Do you understand me?"

Rosalind nods, silent as a prayer, and steps through the open door, into the narrow child's room on the other side. The bed is covered in a thin layer of dust. It has never been used. She looks at that bed, and is still looking at it when the door closes behind her, and she is alone.

There's nothing to be done now but wait. This is a path she needs to walk alone, if she's to see it to its conclusion. So she sits down on the floor—she cannot bear to think of sitting on that dusty bed, or worse, sliding between those rigid, cobwebbed sheets, like a corpse sliding into its crypt—and waits. The sun will finish setting soon enough, and the wolves will come out to feed.

Night is the time for wolves.

She waits, and the hours run down around her, great river catfish chasing the baitworm seconds and minnow minutes into the undying ocean of the past. She waits, and the room grows dark, and she can hear her father's footsteps on the living room floor. Her father, who did not ask her why she had run away, who paid for her with crisp new bills and did not ask her where she'd been, did not ask her anything at all worth knowing. Maybe he should have. Maybe he could have saved himself.

But the hour grows late and the shadows grow long, and still she waits, until the soft tread of a father's footsteps in the next room have grown heavy, until she hears him coming toward her door. The knob turns. The door opens.

"You are an arrogant child," he says, and his breath is whiskey and winter.

"The better to defy you, sir," she says, and her words are summer in the desert, hot and cruel and unforgiving.

"You are an unwanted child," he says, and his breath is bruises and blame.

"The better to leave you, sir," she says, and her words are time to heal, hard and hopeful and full of peace.

"You are a spiteful child," he says, and his breath is captivity and cruelty.

"The better to spite you, sir," she says, and her words are

freedom, freedom opening all the way to the desert, freedom that knows no horizon.

The door closes behind him as he steps fully into the room. He reaches for her then, as he reached for her once on the other side of the country, in a green place where she wore a red hat she had not yet earned. He reaches for her, and she falls upon him, and the world is red as a desert sunset, and not half so forgiving.

Morning finds her sitting outside, picking her teeth with a splinter of what had been her bedroom door. Coyote strolls up, their horses following patiently behind him. This town is too small to contain them; they need the wide sweep of the desert, the hills and the rolling dunes, and the wind to carry the tears of children treated bad and women treated cruel.

"Your hat's red," says Coyote.

The red fox girl looks up through the tangled corn of her hair and smiles like a thousand miles of empty horizon. "It is," she says.

"You handle your wolf?"

"I did." She stands, stretches, moves to his side. She leaves no footprints.

It brings him no pleasure to ask his next question, but ask it he does, for some things must be observed: "You ready to ride alone?"

"Not yet," she says. "Got some lessons left to learn. Don't feel like looking for another teacher."

Coyote smiles. He sets his hand atop her head for a moment, feeling the reality of her. Then he swings himself up onto his horse and waits for her to do the same before he turns toward the horizon. There will always be wolves, even if some of them walk wrapped in human skins. There will always be woods, even if some of them are difficult to see. And there will always be little girls who leave the path in search of something bigger, something better, and find their own salvation on the line between morning and midnight.

SEANAN
McGUIRE

The sky is the color of bleached bone as Coyote and the red fox girl ride across the desert. His hat is black as shadows, and hers is red as blood, and none saw where they came from, and none will see where they go.

AUTHOR'S NOTE

Seanan McGuire: The story of "Little Red Riding Hood" has always had a special place in my heart—one that was solidified forever when I played her several times as a teenager in productions of *Into the Woods*. She is young; she is innocent; she is unprepared. Like most people who adore the story and grew up steeped in the modern mythology of horror movies and urban fantasy, I thought, "What if she was the werewolf?" and put together a whole series pitch; sadly, as I was in high school at the time, it never went anywhere, but still. I love Red, and when I was asked to be in this anthology, I leapt at the chance to tell her story again. I also love horror movies, but at this point, a werewolf Red seemed predictable. At the same time, her story is inherently one of betrayal by someone who was trusted, however unwisely, and of attaining adulthood through a single trip through the woods. It seemed natural to turn the story on its ear, to turn trees into endless sand, to turn men into wolves, and to let Red cut her own path for once. I think it's recognizable, and in the end, that's what matters about fairy tales: that they use different codes to tell the same story, and still bring you out the other side.

UNDERGROUND

Karin Tidbeck

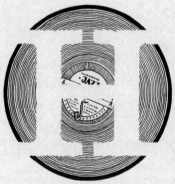

edvig hammered her fists on the front doors, more out of rage than hope that she would be let out. When her hands hurt too much to continue, she sat down and wept. When she ran out of tears, she opened the carpetbag the driver had left behind. The only items inside were the three gramophone records she had wanted for her birthday, and for which her father had given her away to the man underground.

You understand why I must do this, her father had said when the big black car came to fetch her. *I had to promise him the first living thing I saw.*

As the car door swung shut, he said, *I'm sorry. I thought it would be the dog.*

The faint scuff of a shoe made Hedvig look up. A butler and two footmen stood in the lobby next to a pair of ornate doors that led farther into the mansion.

"Please let me go," Hedvig said.

The servants said nothing, just watched her with impassive faces.

"Where's your master?" she asked.

The butler bowed and opened the rightmost door. Bright electric light spilled out.

Hedvig followed the silent man through room after room. The mansion was furnished in the new, angular style; it felt cold and oppressive compared to the soft lines and pastel colors of home. Instead of windows, the walls were covered in curtain-framed paintings of geometric suns and stark landscapes. The butler took her through a series of smaller rooms seemingly designed for a lady: a library with overstuffed chairs, a music room with a piano, and a fully equipped sewing room. In every single room sat a gramophone. Finally she was shown into a dimly lit room with a huge mahogany bed.

Hedvig grabbed the butler's arm. "Will he come for me?"

Up close, the butler's skin looked smooth and hard, like Bakelite; his eyes glittered like glass. He gave off a vague chemical smell. Hedvig realized that his mouth and eyebrows were painted on. He gently pried her hand off his arm with jointed fingers, bowed again, and left.

Hedvig cried until her eyes were dry again, then wound up the gramophone and put on one of the records. The soft voice rang out through the funnel, both intricate and soothing. It made her feel less alone.

The Bakelite butler appeared in the doorway. He pointed at the clock on the wall. It chimed eleven. All the lights went out. The darkness pressed in on her from all sides until she could barely breathe. Bright blotches of light swam in her vision as her brain tried to fill the void.

Hedvig waited for her captor in the dark.

———✦———

It had been her birthday. They had been for a walk in the park, Hedvig and her father and the family dog. Her sister and step-mother had stayed behind to organize the party. Hedvig decided to take a little path she hadn't seen before, and all of a sudden an unearthly music had filled the air: instruments she had no name for, at once hoarse and sweet. Over them hovered a voice, singing a wordless melody. She stopped dead in her tracks. Her father came up behind her.

"Father, I must have this music," she said. "I need it."

"Of course," her father replied. "I will find out where it's coming from. Anything for my birthday girl." He kissed her cheek.

A week later he came home with a package under his arm, and Hedvig outraced the dog to greet him, and she didn't understand why he burst into tears.

Quiet footsteps approached; the mattress dipped as someone sat down on the edge of the bed.

"My name is Lord Ruben," said a young baritone. "You may call me 'my lord.'"

"The lord of what?" Hedvig said.

"The underground," he replied. "This is my domain."

"Will you rape me now?" Hedvig said into the darkness.

"Of course not," Ruben said. "But I need your help. An evil countess put a curse on me so that I may never show my face to you. But if you will be faithful to me without ever seeing my face, then one day I will be free. If you break your promise, I will be in her power completely and forced to marry her."

"Just like what you're doing to me."

He touched her hand. Hedvig pulled away.

"Whatever you decide, you will remain here," Ruben said.

There was no way to tell the difference between night and day, only that the lights came on and switched off: at seven in what was presumably the morning, and eleven at night. Hedvig's only company in the daytime were the butler and two footmen, who moved quietly through the rooms, serving meals at regular intervals, dusting and cleaning. They obeyed her commands, all except one: to let her out.

In the beginning, Hedvig broke a lot of things. She smashed glass, flipped furniture over, tore at curtains and bedsheets. When the rage had left her, she put on one of the three gramophone records and let the music carry her away. It seemed different every time; it swirled and shifted, enveloped her in soothing green and bronze notes. It obliterated time and space. She only came to when the butler touched her arm and led her away for bedtime.

Lord Ruben would arrive shortly after, smelling of wine and heavy perfume. He wouldn't mention the mess. He wouldn't touch her either. He just lay there, breathing quietly. When the lights came back on, he would be gone and the furniture replaced.

Tears replaced destruction. Hedvig would find herself weeping on the floor, in an armchair, on the bed, in the bath. Again, the music soothed her.

Eventually, boredom won out.

Hedvig rediscovered the sewing machine and recalled the lessons of her childhood. She cut fabric and constructed dresses after her own mind, fantastical creations in silk and velvet and fine lace. She hung them on dress forms and doors and chairs, perfecting her technique: bodices encrusted with glass and metal, skirts flaring like trumpet flowers or falling in asymmetrical cascades. For each dress, an imagined party, a dance with her butler.

One night, Lord Ruben touched her. She let him; fighting would do no good. As he moved on top of her she lay still, clenching her jaws against the pain. He cried into her hair afterward.

"I love you," he whispered.

"If you love me, then let me go," she whispered back.

"I can't. It would be my undoing."

"But what about me?"

"They haven't tried to get you back, you know," he said. "They know where you are. I haven't heard from them at all. Perhaps they don't love you, after all."

The days bled into one another, and so did the nights. Some nights Lord Ruben lay on top of her, some not. She found herself pregnant and walked the halls with a growing belly. She gave birth to a boy, assisted by Bakelite hands. She named him Gustav. Lord Ruben was of no help when the baby fussed and screamed; he merely fell asleep and slept like the dead until he suddenly got up and left, and the lights came on, and it was morning.

The days were less lonely, less dull, even though there was screaming and vomit and shit and she was ready to smash the baby against the wall more than once, but the wordless footmen soothed her, and so did the gramophones. She lost herself in the intricate loops and strands of music.

"Your sister is getting married," Lord Ruben said one night. "Since you've been a good girl, you have my permission to watch the wedding."

Hedvig gasped.

"You'll watch it from the car, of course," he continued. "They didn't invite you, after all."

The daylight was too bright. The air was too sharp. Hedvig sat outside the church in the big black car as the bells rang and people poured outside. The happy couple came last and were showered with flowers and rice. Hedvig touched the door handle. Soon she would rush out there, back to her family, and join them. Everything would be all right. They would receive her with open arms.

Except they looked happy. Hedvig wasn't there with them, on this day of all days, but her sister and stepmother and father were smiling and cheering. They didn't look like they missed her at all. The church bells crashed overhead. It was all too much. Hedvig clapped her hands over her ears and closed her eyes. When she opened them again, the revelers had left and her stepmother stood outside the car, rapping on the window. The butler leaned back and rolled the window on Hedvig's side down.

"It *is* you!" the stepmother exclaimed. "I thought I saw—"

"You didn't invite me," Hedvig said. "Did you even come to look for me?"

Her stepmother's eyes filled with tears. "Of course we invited you, love. Of course we tried to visit you. He said that you didn't want to talk to us, that you were happy."

"I don't believe you," Hedvig said. "If you really loved me, you would have tried harder."

"Oh, darling." Her stepmother wiped her cheeks. "Your father made a deal. A promise is a promise, no matter how terrible the consequences are. You know that."

"But couldn't he just give the records back and let me go?" Hedvig said. "I could go home."

"You know it doesn't work like that. It's done."

They were both silent for a moment.

"Is he kind to you, at least?" the stepmother asked hopefully.

"He only visits me in the dark, and he makes me do things, and he won't help me with our Gustav," Hedvig said.

"You have a son!"

"I think Gustav looks like him." Hedvig looked at her hands. "But I will never know."

Her stepmother's hand came into view. It held a tiny cigarette lighter, embossed with flowers.

"The spell would break," Hedvig said. "He'd be forced to marry the countess."

"And why should you save him from that fate?" her stepmother asked, and dropped the lighter in Hedvig's lap.

Hedvig looked up. "Will you not save *me*?"

Her stepmother shook her head. "We can't. There are rules." She stepped away from the car, and her eyes filled with tears. "Goodbye, Hedvig. Remember that we love you."

"Where is Father?" Hedvig called after her, but then she saw him: pale and hunched behind the steering wheel of a car on the other side of the street. Her stepmother got in. Her father gave Hedvig a wordless look, then drove away.

Hedvig did it the following night, when Lord Ruben's breaths had evened out. She pressed the button on the cigarette lighter. In the faint yellow light, he was young and frail-looking: very pale, with dark eyebrows and hair, a long nose, and carefully carved lips, like a painting. He looked just like Gustav. The lighter abruptly became too hot, and Hedvig dropped it without thinking. It landed on Lord Ruben's chest and went out. He screamed.

The air abruptly went cold. Gray light crept in from somewhere to Hedvig's right. There was the noise of dripping water.

They lay on a filthy mattress in a tunnel. Around them, gravel, concrete, refuse. A rat slunk away into the darkness. Gustav lay on a pile of rags next to her, still sleeping. Lord Ruben stared up at her with eyes that had misted over.

"I can't see," he said. "Why can't I see? Did you look? You looked, didn't you."

"I did," Hedvig replied.

"You've ruined everything," he said. "She knows I've been seen. This is my punishment."

"Who is she really? Who are you?"

Ruben's blind eyes filled with tears. "I am hers. She let me have the nights to myself, but only if no living being saw my face. It was going so well. I had a mansion. I had you, and a son. Now look at us. Look at what you did." He pulled away and sobbed into his hands.

The air was very cold. Hedvig shivered in her thin shift and pulled what had become a soiled blanket closer around her. Ruben lay in front of her, shaking, not at all the commanding man she had come to imagine. It struck her that she could leave now.

"I'm free," she whispered.

"Will you just leave me here?" Ruben said softly.

Hedvig thought of her father, who had given her away. She thought of her stepmother, who had talked about obeying the rules. She thought of her sister smiling next to her husband. She looked down at the man on the mattress. He was the only person she knew now.

"Where can we go?" she asked.

Lord Ruben let out a long, trembling sigh. "Vega, my sister. She might at least take our son in until we find somewhere to stay."

They walked out of the culvert and into the wintry streets of Stockholm.

Lady Vega lived in Old Town, on a street winding away from the German church.

Lord Ruben pushed Hedvig toward the front door. "You can't let her see me. The countess will know. She'll take me then, for sure."

Hedvig climbed the stairs to Lady Vega's apartment. The woman who opened the door was short and fine-featured, much like a female version of Ruben, with crinkles at the corners of her eyes. She looked at Hedvig in confusion when she opened the door. Then she caught sight of Gustav and paled.

"I know that face," she said. "That's Ruben's, isn't it? Who are you?"

"I'm his wife, milady," Hedvig said. "We need your help. Lord Ruben and I are out on the street."

Vega squinted at her. "Since when is he a lord?"

Hedvig faltered.

"Where have you been living with him, exactly?" Vega asked.

"In his palace," Hedvig said slowly. "Except it's not there any-more, because I broke the spell. He's waiting downstairs, but you can't see him, because then the countess will—"

Vega uncrossed her arms. "This is absurd. Excuse me." She pushed past Hedvig and ran downstairs.

Hedvig scooped Gustav up and came downstairs to find Vega shouting at Ruben.

"You're not even man enough to show your face," Vega shouted, shaking his arm. "You send your *wife*! Or whatever she is. . . . What have you told her? She calls you Lord Ruben!"

"You don't understand," Lord Ruben said, ducking out of her reach.

An engine roared behind them.

The enormous car that came charging down the street was black and shiny, with darkened windows. It stopped with a screech of tortured brakes. The passenger door opened. A shadow curled around Ruben's arms and legs and pulled him inside. The door slammed shut. The car took off again, leaving the stench of exhaust and burning rubber. The two women stared down the street after it.

"I thought he was free," Vega said numbly.

Hedvig clutched her son, who had gone very quiet. "What just happened?"

"The countess took him back."

"*Who* took him back? Who is the countess?"

"The Countess de la Montagne. She is very dangerous," Vega replied. "He got involved with her when he was very young. I thought 'out on the streets' meant he was finally free."

"But I tried to tell you . . ."

". . . and I didn't listen. I'm sorry." Vega turned around and studied Hedvig. "How long have you been together? You're not wearing a ring."

"You don't know anything about me?" Hedvig said.

Vega shook her head. "I haven't seen my brother in years."

"My father promised me to him," Hedvig said. "So I had to go live in his mansion."

Vega stared at her. "He *what*?"

"I had to stay there and never see his face, or the countess would take him back."

"He kept you prisoner."

"Yes."

"The little bastard. I had no idea he would do such a thing."

Hedvig busied herself wiping her son's nose.

"All this, and you want to go save him," Vega said. "You're insane."

"I don't expect you to understand," Hedvig replied. "Will you help me or not?"

Vega shook her head. "He had it coming. And I'm not going up against the countess. But if you're so set on it, you could maybe talk to old Natalia."

"Who is she?"

"She's a dealer, of sorts. You'll find her in Hornstull."

Hedvig shifted her son on her hip.

"I'll take the boy," Vega said. "He deserves better. And stop calling my brother 'lord.' We're middle-class."

It was only half an hour's walk from Old Town to Hornstull, on the western tip of the southern island. Old Natalia opened the door dressed in a turban and a silk robe. She was very thin and looked very old. The hallway beyond her smelled of cigar smoke and heavy perfume.

"What do you want?" Her voice was unexpectedly soft.

"Madam, I'm sorry to disturb you," Hedvig said. "I'm looking to save my husband, and I'm told you might be able to help me."

Natalia tilted her head. "Save him from what?"

"The Countess de la Montagne."

The old woman let out a bright laugh. "Come in, you poor fool," she said.

She made Hedvig tea and smoked a fat cigar while listening to Hedvig's story about her capture and Ruben's. When Hedvig was done talking, Natalia sat in silence for a long moment.

"You want to rescue him from the countess," Natalia finally said.

"I don't expect you to understand," Hedvig said. "But I can't rest until I do."

"You know that no one picks a fight with her, don't you?"

"I know nothing about her," Hedvig replied. "My only concern is to save him."

"For some reason," Natalia said, then sighed. "Well. You're polite and you have guts, and for that I'll help you." She went over to a cabinet. "What skills do you have, then?"

Hedvig was quiet for a moment, then said, "I can make dresses."

"Excellent," Natalia said, and rummaged around in the cabinet.

She brought out a slender roll of fabric and a purse, then pushed a large suitcase toward Hedvig with her foot. Inside sat a portable sewing machine.

Natalia patted the roll. "This will give you all the fabric you need. The sewing machine will make you all the dresses you need. And the purse will give you whatever else you require. It'll never run out."

"That's a very small roll of fabric," Hedvig said.

Natalia grinned. "So it would appear," she replied. "Don't worry. Now. The countess is very fond of fashion and fine food, so make that for her."

"And what do you want in exchange?" Hedvig said. "Nothing is for free. I have learned that much."

"The satisfaction of seeing that bitch taken down is good enough for me," said Natalia. "I tried in my time. It's your turn now."

Hedvig stood up.

Hedvig rented a little room at the back of an old lady's apartment. She spent day and night sewing more of her dresses. The roll did in fact not run out but produced velvet and silks finer than she had ever seen. The sewing machine seemed to produce thread all by itself and made seams straight and fine, and it never pulled at the fabric. The dresses Hedvig made didn't look like the pictures in the magazines, not at all, but she thought they had their own beauty. When she had made nine dresses, she went to find the countess.

The Countess de la Montagne lived in a lavish apartment that covered an entire floor of a building in the most expensive part of Östermalm. A butler opened the door, and Hedvig recoiled; it was the same butler who had served in the underground mansion. He looked at her, bowed, and left the door ajar. A while later he came back with his mistress in tow. Hedvig had imagined her as old and repellent; instead she was tall and coolly blonde, with square features. She looked at Hedvig like a hawk looks at a mouse.

"I have a lovely set of gowns I'd like to sell you," Hedvig said. "They're like nothing you have ever seen."

"You dragged me to the front door for this?" the countess said to the butler.

Hedvig quickly opened her suitcase and held up a green bias-cut gown of her own design. The countess's mouth dropped slightly open.

"Do you have more like that?"

"Nine of them, my lady," Hedvig replied.

"Give her the small drawing room," she told the butler, then pointed at Hedvig. "I'll view them this afternoon."

The butler guided Hedvig through a warren of rooms that

were eerily reminiscent of the underground mansion: angular lines, dark wood, windows covered by heavy drapes. Here and there, Bakelite footmen and maids were busy with some task or other. There was no sign of human life. The butler showed her into a small drawing room and left.

When the countess arrived, Hedvig had turned the little drawing room into a showroom, fabric and sewing machine ready for alterations. The countess handled each of the dresses where they hung, rubbing the soft fabrics between her fingers.

"I've never seen anything like them," she said. "These aren't like the Parisian fashions. These are bizarre, they're too . . . Where did you learn to do this?"

"I designed them myself, my lady," Hedvig replied.

"Brilliant," the countess said. "I'll try them all. Bring out the dressing screen."

The dresses, which Hedvig feared might be too small, settled almost perfectly over the countess's forms.

"I'll take all of them," the countess said. "And anything else you make. My butler will settle the bill."

"I don't want money," Hedvig said. "All the money in the world couldn't pay for them."

The countess blinked. "Then what do you want?"

"I only want one thing," Hedvig replied. "I've heard about a gentleman who lives here. Ruben. I would like to spend three nights with him."

The countess's eyes narrowed. "I see. And what do you want with him?"

Hedvig shrugged. "I don't need money. I've heard of his beauty. I'd like to see it firsthand. You can have all of these dresses, if I can have three nights."

"Very well," the countess said. "If you want a blind junkie, then that's what you'll have. Come back tonight."

---◆---

The room was almost dark. Ruben lay on an enormous platform bed, fast asleep. He looked very small. A bottle of laudanum stood on the nightstand, together with an empty glass. Hedvig sat down on the side of the bed. The butler positioned himself by the door and closed his glass eyes.

"I came for you," she said to Ruben. "I came to free you. After everything you did, I came for you."

Hedvig lay down next to him and looked at him as he slept. He wasn't the man who had held her captive now. He was a helpless little thing. She told him about everything she had gone through to come here. He made no sign that he had heard her.

She woke up when the butler touched her shoulder the next morning. When the countess arrived for the fitting, she replied to Hedvig's complaint with a shrug.

"I told you, he's a junkie. You asked to spend three nights with him. You didn't say what state he should be in."

The second night went by much like the first. Hedvig talked to Ruben where he lay; she told him about their son, her sorrow, her work to free him. Ruben didn't move. Like the first night, she fell asleep, and woke up only when the butler gently roused her. She didn't complain to the countess when she fitted the last two gowns for her.

On the third night, no one came to show Hedvig inside, so she found her own way to Ruben's room. Just as she was about to open the door, the butler stepped outside, the laudanum bottle in his hand. He bowed and held the door open for Hedvig. She couldn't interpret the gleam in his eyes.

Ruben sat on the edge of the bed, holding on to the frame. His clothes were rumpled, his face grayish and sweaty. He looked up with milky white eyes as Hedvig stepped inside.

"Who's there?"

"It's me," Hedvig replied.

"You," he said. "You came."

He held out a hand. Hedvig sat down next to him.

"Why are you here?" he asked.

"I came to free you."

"She's planning to marry me," Ruben said miserably. "I'll be hers forever."

"We'll think of something," Hedvig said.

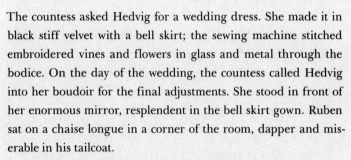

The countess asked Hedvig for a wedding dress. She made it in black stiff velvet with a bell skirt; the sewing machine stitched embroidered vines and flowers in glass and metal through the bodice. On the day of the wedding, the countess called Hedvig into her boudoir for the final adjustments. She stood in front of her enormous mirror, resplendent in the bell skirt gown. Ruben sat on a chaise longue in a corner of the room, dapper and miserable in his tailcoat.

"I made a matching scarf, my lady," Hedvig said.

The countess inspected the glass-beaded scarf and nodded. "Good." She flung the ends around her neck and turned back to the mirror. She grinned to herself.

Hedvig caught the ends and pulled the scarf very tight.

It seemed an eternity before the countess stopped fighting. When the last twitch finally left her body, Hedvig's shins were battered and her dress was torn, but she had held fast. As the countess dropped to the floor, Ruben gasped. His eyes were clear and very green, and focused on Hedvig.

"You saved me," he said.

Hedvig let go of the scarf and gazed down at the countess's purple face, then at Ruben where he sat on the divan. He looked like a little boy. He wasn't the stranger who had held her captive, nor the ravaged young man who had been the countess's thrall. He was back to square one, just like her. She was done. She had a world of choices.

"I saved myself, I think," Hedvig said. "Good-bye."

"Where are you going?"

Hedvig was silent for a moment. "I don't know," she finally said. "But I'll be free to choose."

"Then take me with you," Ruben said.

The plea made Hedvig laugh.

"What am I supposed to do?" Ruben asked plaintively.

"Do better."

Hedvig left him next to the dead countess. She walked down to the harbor and followed the shore into Old Town, where Ruben's sister waited with her son. A cool wind blew in from the sea. Ferries howled at one another across the water. Winter was giving way.

Karin Tidbeck: *"Prins Hatt under jorden"*—"Prince Hatt Underground"—was one of my favorite stories as a child. A princess is sent to live underground with a mysterious prince whose face she is never allowed to see; later she sets off to save him when he's abducted by the foul witch who wants to marry him. Together they outsmart the witch and live happily ever after.

When I was asked for a story for the anthology, my thoughts immediately went to Prince Hatt, both because I loved the story and because I'd never seen it retold anywhere. So I went back to read it, this beloved classic, and was horrified. A princess is sold off like chattel and has no problem with living underground with a man whose face she never gets to see, and no issues with never seeing her family except on three occasions. She immediately sets off to save the prince when he faces the same fate *he has already subjected his wife to*. It's a very disturbing narrative.

But what would it really be like to suddenly be sold off to a man underground? Who is that man, and why does he refuse to show his face? Why is it all right for him to keep her captive underground, but not for another woman to do the same to him? What started out as playing around with a folktale became a reckoning with my own social programming.

EVEN THE CRUMBS WERE DELICIOUS

Daryl Gregory

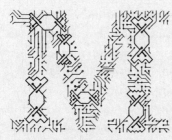aybe, just maybe, it had been a mistake to paper the walls with edible drugs. This thought occurred to Tindal when he walked into the living room and saw the open door, the pages torn from the walls, and the two white teenagers who'd decided to feast upon his home.

The girl was crouched on all fours, picking bits of pharmaceutically enhanced paper from the carpet. The boy huddled inside a white cardboard box that had held funeral party supplies—rolls of black crepe paper, a dozen black candles, two packs of white-print-on-black napkins (*RIP* in Gothic letters)—now dumped out onto the floor to make room for him. He rocked slightly in the box, hugging his knees, eyes focused on nothing. Until he noticed Tindal.

"Let me out of here!" the boy shouted.

The girl startled, terrified.

"It's okay, it's okay!" Tindal said. "Everybody calm down."

"I'm working as hard as I can," the girl said tearfully.

"Of course you are," Tindal said. "Good job." He knew not to argue with druggies. Especially when he was stoned himself. The girl returned her attention to the carpet.

"Return me to my true size," the boy demanded. "And release my sister from your spell."

Sister? He saw the resemblance now. Both of them brown-haired and sharp-featured. *Like rats,* he thought, then immediately felt bad. *Mice, then.*

"You guys can just leave," Tindal said to the mouse children. "Really."

"Don't mock me, hag," the boy said.

Hag? thought Tindal. *That was hurtful.* He edged warily around the box boy and approached the girl, who was inspecting each strand of carpet for shredded paper, plucking with tweezer fingers.

"Just don't eat those, okay?" Tindal asked.

"Have patience with me," the girl said without looking up. "This floor is so, so dirty."

"'Cause I think you've had enough," he added.

"Don't touch her!" the boy said. "Or so help me, I will carve the meat from your bones."

Tindal backed away from the girl. "No violence!" he said to the boy. "No bone carving!" He fled to the back bedroom, found his pen in the bedcovers (it was always in the bed), and flicked it open. The screen unfurled only halfway, and he had to yank it open to full size.

He called El Capitan, aka El C the MC (available for parties and events), and Tindal's best friend. He got no answer but kept trying through voice and text until El Cap's beard slid onto the screen, followed by his big, sleepy eyes. Tindal quickly told him about the intruders.

"Tindy, my man, slow down. And speak up. You're, like, whisper yelling."

"They're in the next room!" Tindal hissed. "They won't leave!"

"So who are they again?" El Cap asked.

"I have no idea!" he said, failing to keep a lid on the panic. "But they're *minors*. Minors in my house!"

"It's not exactly your house," El Cap said patiently. "Rolfe didn't leave a will." Rolfe had been Tindal's roommate. Or rather, Tindal had been Rolfe's roommate, because Rolfe owned the house and had let Tindal rent a bedroom. But now they weren't roommates at all, because Rolfe was dead.

El Cap said, "Look, just go out there and explain to them that Rolfe is gone, there's nothing to buy, and they're going to have to leave."

"I tried, but they won't go! They're tripping hard. One of them's kinda violent." The boy was still shouting. Tindal opened the door a crack, but only a corner of the living room was visible. "I think they ate a lot of wall."

"Hmm. Did you call the police?"

"The *police*? I have a house full of drugs!"

"Right, right," El Cap said. "And these kids don't need to go to the emergency room or anything? They're breathing?"

Tindal moaned. "This is your fault."

"How so?" El Cap hadn't taken offense. The Captain was philosophical about all things.

"You're the one who said we needed a funeral party."

"True, true," El Cap said. "I do recall, however, that the walls were your idea."

"And how many people did you tell about that?" Tindal demanded. El Cap, for all his dependability as a friend, was unfortunately a friend to everyone. He overshared and overcommitted, possibly due to the year he'd spent on a South Dakota trust farm doped to the gills on oxytocin enhancers.

El Cap tugged a hand through his beard. "Hang tough, Tindy. I'll be right over."

———◆———

Rolfe's suicide note had been printed on a decocell sheet from his last batch and attached to the refrigerator with a magnet. That was so Rolfe.

Tindal didn't take it seriously at first, even though Rolfe didn't come home that night, because Tindal got pretty high after eating the note. (It was PaintBall, one of Rolfe's most popular recipes, and the synesthesia/ecstasy combo was intense.) Besides, it wasn't unusual for Rolfe, the chief beta tester of his own products, to disappear for a day or two to get his head straight.

But not a week. When Rolfe failed to reappear, and the groceries were almost gone, Tindal thought, *This shit is getting serious.* Rolfe's friends/clients were showing up at all hours, asking about him and the latest recipes. Tindal put them off, told them Rolfe hadn't kept any stock, and promised to tell them when he came back. He tried calling the dozen or so of Rolfe's numbers that he knew about (drug dealers picked up and disposed of pens like toothpicks) and got no answer.

By week two, Tindal had to admit to himself that Rolfe had really killed himself.

El Capitan tried to comfort him. He brought over some amazing dope he'd bought from the Millies, genetically tweaked super smelt that delivered a hardcore yet loving THC punch to the brain. "Maybe he's at peace now," El Cap said.

"That's what he said in his note," Tindal said. "'Don't worry about me, I'm going to a better place.' Or something like that." He took a hit from the comfort-joint. "He was never a happy person in the real world."

"Which caused him to lash out at you," El Cap said.

"True," Tindal said, thinking of the times he hadn't been able to pay the rent, and Rolfe failed to see his way to being okay with that. "Still, we should do something for him." Maybe it was the dope that made him want to be as calm and reasonable as the Captain. "Something to honor his memory."

"We can make a shrine," El Cap said. "Like they did for that guy down the block who was hit by that car when he was bicycling. They painted a bicycle white and people put candles and flowers around it."

"What would we paint?" Tindal said. "We don't even know what Rolfe was on when he died."

"Drugs, probably," El Cap said.

They went to Rolfe's bedroom to look for shrine-worthy objects, but of course the door was padlocked. Even in death, Rolfe was paranoid. In the nine months Tindal had lived there, he'd never been allowed inside the room.

El Cap went to work on the lock with a meat-tenderizing mallet from the kitchen. That proved ineffective, even for the Captain's mighty arm, and it was doing the door frame no good. They smoked a while, considering the problem. Then Tindal remembered that Antonia, one of Rolfe's clients, was a bike thief. She was pretty broken up to hear about Rolfe, but in an hour she was there with a device as big as the Jaws of Life. She snipped the lock and the door swung open to reveal Rolfe's bedroom/lab.

"Wow," Tindal said.

"Very mad scientist," El Cap said.

"Like I always imagined it," Antonia said.

The room was crammed with electrical equipment, shipping boxes, and homemade ductwork: PVC pipe and laundry dryer foil tubes held together with silver tape, all running to the bedroom's single window. The pipes were all connected to the machines at the center of the room, two chemjet printers, one older model and one that looked brand-new. These were the main tools of Rolfe's trade. He could download recipes or create his own on the computer, send them to the chemjets, and print the designer drugs onto decocell sheets. The only part of the process that Rolfe had ever let Tindal do was trim the sheets into strips and wafers.

"I need something to remember him by," Antonia said, and grabbed a stack of already-printed pages.

"Hey!" Tindal said. "I don't think you should take anything until—"

She was gone before he finished the sentence.

"It's okay," El Cap said. "Rolfe would have wanted it that way."

The boxes were filled with foil precursor packs. These were the most expensive components in the process, even pricier than the chemjet printers, which were not cheap. You could order the packs from chemical supply companies, if you had the right permits; otherwise you had to buy from an online front company at the usual high markup for quasi-illegal services. With the right packs and a recipe, though, any idiot could make their chemjet mix, heat, chill, distill, and recombine molecules into whatever smart drug you wanted.

Rolfe never hid his disdain for the script kiddies who pumped out MDMA variants all day. Rolfe was more than that. He created new recipes on a weekly basis, assembling molecules whose effects were infinitely more interesting than the pleasure-center hammer blows craved by Cro-Magnon club kids. He was an artist.

"His life's work," Tindal said, taking in the stacks of rice paper remaining. "There's no way you and I can eat all this."

"*Probably* not," El Cap said. "We should invite people over. A quake of a wake! We can consume Rolfe's last run."

"No, it can't be just what's already printed," Tindal said. "We should do it all. Use every pack. Print every recipe he's got."

"Hand them out like appetizers," El Cap said.

"Wait," Tindal said. Something like an idea rose up in the back of his mind, gathered weight, and then crashed upon the beach of his consciousness: complete, beautiful, loud. He said, "I know what we have to do."

———✧———

Word of the walls must have leaked, Tindal thought. It was too much to believe that these (probably) homeless ragamuffins had found the house by accident. The intruders, however, couldn't or wouldn't tell him how they'd gotten there, how they'd forced their way in, or how they knew to strike on the day before a massive drug party/wake/art installation.

The kids wouldn't even tell him what their names were. Tindal suspected that more than natural stubbornness was at work.

"What recipe did they eat, you think?" El Cap asked.

"Hard to say," Tindal said. "I didn't really keep track of what I'd printed. Or where I hung it up. But it's pretty clear they ate a lot. And a bunch of different ones."

"That might explain the major head scramble," El Cap said.

"It's like they were born the minute I walked in. Rolfe has five or six recipes that affect memory. One of them even makes you forget you're conscious, though you're still awake."

"Oh yeah, Zen. I had that once. Tastes like cinnamon."

The girl insisted that she keep cleaning. She'd finished her inch-by-inch grooming of the carpet and had pleaded with Tindal to give her a rag so that she could dust all the flat surfaces. He was happy to oblige. It was by far the most sanitary thing that had happened in the house since he moved in.

"Somewhere in here there's a recipe that triggers OCD," Tindal said. He'd copied Rolfe's recipe index to his pen, and he'd been scrolling through the notes. "He sold it to students. Helped them stay focused."

"She's focused, all right."

"Restore me now!" the boy in the box shouted.

El Cap said, "As for psycho Stuart Little over there . . ."

"I think he's on something Rolfe called Double-A, or Ask Alice," Tindal said. "You know, like the song? 'One pill makes you smaller, one pill makes you tall.'"

"Rolfe always appreciated a Grace Slick reference," El Cap said.

Tindal ran his finger down the *A*s until he found Ask Alice again. "Mimics Todd's syndrome," he read, "which causes dismal— dis-mee—shit. Dysmetropsia."

"That sounds bad."

"It means he thinks he's tiny," Tindal said.

"That explains his problems scaling the walls of the box. You know, this whole thing reminds me of that story. You know the one. Tiny guy grows some weed, sneaks into the home of the giant, tries to steal his stuff."

"I'd kick them off the cloud now," Tindal said. "But they're too high."

"How long do you think it will last?"

"Most of Rolfe's stuff wears off in four or five hours," Tindal said. "But then again, they ate so much, and what with interaction effects—"

El Cap winced. "Never mix, never worry, I always say."

The boy shouted, "I can hear you, foul woman! You and your giant friend!"

"Anything in the recipe box cause Tolkien dialogue?" El Cap asked. "And gender confusion?"

"Pretty sure it's my dreadlocks," Tindal said. "Or the kimono I was wearing this morning. He doesn't seem to be confused by you, though."

"I'm all man." This from a guy wearing a flowered tank top, bicycle shorts, and flip-flops. But the boy was right in using the word "giant." El Capitan was indeed mountain-sized.

Tindal flicked the pen screen closed. "Could you keep an eye on the boy? I want to see if I can get anything out of the sister." The girl was crouched beside the second-lowest bookshelf, her nose inches from the wood. She didn't seem to be wiping up the dust so much as gently encouraging it to move to one side. Dust herding.

Tindal knelt beside her. She didn't look up from her work.

He started to say something, then realized that her sleeve had pulled away from her wrist. Her arm was striped with blue-green bruises. And now that he was looking closer, there were marks on her neck, too.

Had her brother done this? He talked tough, but Tindal couldn't see him doing it. The kid radiated love for his sister in a frequency that could not be faked or chemically induced.

"Excuse me," Tindal said quietly, and the girl jerked away from him. "You don't have to be afraid of me," he said.

"Whatever you say."

"No, really," he said. "And you don't have to, like, obey me."

"I understand. Your wish is my—"

"No! Please! I'm not trying to patriarch you. Or even matriarch you." Tindal sighed. "Could you put down your rag for a second? And come with me to the kitchen?"

The girl looked longingly at the shelf, perhaps imagining the carefully coerced particles scattering for the hinterlands. Finally she ducked her head and followed Tindal out of the room.

"I have to urinate!" the boy announced.

"Can't you hold it?" El Cap asked, not happy about it.

"I'll piss all over your precious cage!"

In the kitchen, Tindal pulled out a chair from the table and motioned for the girl to sit. She folded her hands in her lap and stared at her feet. Her track shoes were filthy. The hole in the knee of one pant leg showed a dirty kneecap.

"I want you to think real hard," Tindal said. "Can you remember your name?"

"What name do you want to give me?" she asked.

"See, that's not really helpful." He pulled up another chair. "Do you remember where you live? Do you have a home somewhere?"

She shook her head.

"So no clue where you were before you broke into my house?"

"The door was open. I remember that."

"You mean, like, unlocked?" Tindal asked.

She slowly shook her head. "Wide open."

"Huh." Now that he thought about it, it was possible he'd gone to bed without closing the door. Rolfe had gotten angry with him about that before, though the latch was clearly faulty. Now that he was the owner of the house, he'd have to buckle down, get serious about security.

"Can I go back to the dusting?" the girl asked impatiently.

Tindal intuited that an awkward amount of time had passed. "Sorry. Zoned out there," he said. "You can go back when you tell me where you came from. And, uh, who did that to your arm."

Her face crumpled.

He felt terrible for asking. But hey, kids, right? See something, say something. As long as he didn't have to do something, too.

"I don't know!" the girl said. "I don't remember! Just let me do my job, please?"

From the hallway the boy shouted, "Be careful with me, ogre!" El Cap walked past, cradling the boy in his arms, heading toward the bathroom. "I will crawl in your ear and batter your brains!"

The girl burst into fresh sobs.

"I need something, anything," Tindal said. "Do you have a wallet? Purse?"

She shook her head.

Tindal put his face in his hands. He'd have to drop these kids off at the police station and hope the amnesia held after the drugs wore off. If he was lucky, all they'd remember was that a hag and a giant held them captive.

Tindal wasn't sure he was that lucky. "So, little girl," he asked gently. "Do you know who I am?"

"Tindal the Witch," she said, wiping away a tear. "And your companion is El Capitan." She smiled for the first time since he'd found her. "Did I do good?"

"Just . . . great," Tindal said.

The boy shouted from the bathroom, "Don't you dare drown me! Wait! Come back! Give me back my wand!"

El Cap walked into the kitchen. "This fell out of his pocket."

"A pen! He's got a pen! Thank God," Tindal said.

"May I please go back to my chores?" the girl asked.

The boy refused to unlock the device. When Tindal tried to hand the pen to him, he threw his arms wide as if trying to hug a redwood. Something about taking the device from him had moved it from the realm of the tiny—one more toy-sized item among the boy's micro-possessions—to Thing of Giants.

"We're just trying to find your next of kin," El Cap said to him.

"Never!" the boy said.

"Or your friends," Tindal said. "Wouldn't you like your friends to come pick you up?"

The boy's look turned crafty. "And how many young ones have you lured here in just that way?"

"There's no *luring*," Tindal said. "I do not *lure*. You walked in uninvited."

"Because I was *lured*," the boy said.

The word sounded dirtier every time they said it.

"Hey, what about the emergency contacts?" El Cap asked.

"Right! Of course." Tindal unrolled the screen and said in a clear, perfectly sober voice, "Call. Emergency. Contact." He grinned. "It's ringing. You're a genius, mon Capitan."

El Cap shrugged bashfully. The screen displayed a number and the name ICE HOME hovering over an animated map of Toronto.

"What the fuck do *you* want?" a woman said. At least he thought it was a woman. The screen stayed rudely dark, and that harsh, corrugated voice could have been that of an old man.

"Uh, hi," Tindal said. "Who's this?"

"Who the fuck is *this*?"

"My name's—" Caution neurons managed to fire in time to interrupt him. "I'm a friend," he said. "Calling from your son's phone. At least I think he's your son. Do you have a son? Or a daughter? Because—"

"Fuck off," the woman said. The screen displayed CALL ENDED.

"Huh," Tindal said. He let the screen retract. "Was that your mom?" Tindal asked the boy.

The lad glared back over the tops of his knees.

"I'd run away too," El Cap said. "That voice."

"Right?" Tindal said. "Like a garbage disposal with a spoon in it."

"A garbage disposal that smokes three packs a day," the Captain said.

"Ha! A garbage disposal that—"

In the corner, the girl moaned.

Oh. Right. Focus. Tindal called the number again. "Please don't hang up!" he said. "I just want to get your children home. See, they're here in my house—"

"You call me again, motherfucker, and their dad will track you down and bash your fucking head in, you hear me? Tell those fucking kids they're not welcome here anymore."

The pen went dead again. "Whoa," Tindal said.

"I think I see where the boy gets his anger," El Cap said.

"She said, 'their dad.' I don't think they're her kids."

"Evil stepmother," El Cap said, nodding. "Classic."

"She said Dad would track us down."

"How?" El Cap said. "You didn't tell her your name."

"Unless—shit. What if the phone's got location turned on?"

"Who leaves that on?" El Cap said. "That's the first thing you learn in the war against the Great North American Spytocracy." He took the pen from Tindal. "Maybe I can—huh."

"What?"

"Evil Stepmom didn't have location turned off on *her* phone.

Look." A pulsing dot hovered over the animated map next to the words ICE HOME.

"Don't close the screen!" Tindal said. The locator would vanish, and he'd have to call that terrible woman again.

El Cap touched something on the screen and showed it to him. A trail of pulsing dots between here and there. "Perhaps the father is henpecked but kindly."

"I don't have time for this," Tindal said. "The wake is in four hours. I still have to decorate, make pizza pockets . . ."

El Capitan regarded him from behind his expanse of beard, saying nothing.

"Okay, okay," Tindal said. "You're right." He took the pen from him. "I'm going to need some courage, though." He went to the living room and looked at the pages of recipes taped to the walls. Which one was Courage? He had a distinct memory of printing some out on orange paper. Or maybe red. Blue? No—

"Are you going or not?" El Cap asked him.

Damn. He was going to have to do this straight. Or at least as straight as he was currently, which in medical terms was Not Very. "While I'm gone, maybe point OCD girl at the kitchen?"

"Dude," El Cap said disapprovingly.

He followed the trail of dots past KFCs and nail salons, through throngs of Numinous-addicted converts pressing Numinous-infused paper into his hands, over underpasses and under overpasses, around shifty-eyed cops and their drug-sniffing badges, through leafy blocks of ramshackle twentieth-century frame houses and shadow-slabbed blocks of ramshackler apartment buildings, until he reached a blighted neighborhood that was ramshacklest of all: unregulated multifamily homes painted with multiple coats of resignation and misery.

It was the longest two kilometers he'd ever walked.

He found an empty cement planter to perch upon and rested

his soul for a while with a quick half-dozen vapes of Millie-produced ultraproduct. Not Courage but definitely a viable treatment for anxiety.

The destination dot still throbbed at him from the boy's pen screen. Not too far now. Though he was concerned by the battery indicator that had started flashing at the opposite end of the screen. How long had that been going on? It was interesting that the battery icon flashed in synchrony with the map dot. *Beep-boop. Beep-boop. Beep—*

"Uh-oh." Tindal said this aloud, though only the planter was there to hear him. The trail of dots had vanished as if consumed by ravenous pill heads. He tapped at the screen, and the whole of it went black.

He experienced a wave of panic that was subdued only by another set of hits from the vape. Then the cartridge gave out, and he knew he was truly screwed: alone in unfamiliar territory, holding two skinny, dead devices. He would have thrown them across the road if he was the kind of person who threw things. What was he supposed to do now? Going door-to-door in a neighborhood like this might get him killed. And even if someone answered, what would he say? *Hi, my name's Tindal, and I'm looking for the parents of two cognitively impaired white slaves staying at my house.*

No sense in that. The only choice was to go home. His brain flooded with relief chemicals, most of them internally generated.

From above him a voice said, "And don't forget the fucking tampons!" Tindal thought, *I know that voice.* It sounded like an animated garbage disposal.

He did not want to look up. Instead he looked right, where a short, pudding-faced white man had stepped out of the apartment building. A swoop of black hair covered his forehead, leaving none to cover the bald spot in back. He raised a hand to the upper window and said, "I heard you!"

Henpecked? Tindal wondered. *Kindly?*

Tindal risked a peek skyward. From an open second-floor window, a pickax wearing a white dust mop screamed down, "And pizza pockets!" Which reminded him that he was hungry, and that he really needed to get back to the house to prep for the wake.

Tindal hopped up and began following the man down the sidewalk. When they were a hundred yards away from the ax-wife's window, he said, "Hey, man, quick question?"

The man kept walking. Tindal hurried up alongside him. "Fuck off," the man said tiredly.

"I'm here about the kids," Tindal said.

The man shot him a glance.

"Fourteen or fifteen?" Tindal said. "A boy and a girl. I don't know their names."

The man stopped. "What about them?"

"Don't worry, they're safe. They're in my house, and they've eaten some of my—I think they've taken drugs."

"They do that," the man said.

"But they're fine!" Tindal said. "I just want to be able to get them home safe to you and their stepmother."

"Their what?"

Tindal nodded back the way they'd come. "No judgment? But, I mean, wow. Harsh."

The man's eyes narrowed. "You're the one who called."

"That's right. I was just trying to reach out to—"

The slap spun Tindal's head around. Pen and vape went flying, proving that Tindal *was* the type to throw things, but only under specific conditions. Then he bounced off a NO PARKING sign and plopped to the ground.

The man bent over him like a Doberman on a short chain. "That's their goddamn mother, motherfucker! I'm their goddamn father! You don't talk to us like that! And you tell those fucking kids that I will not be disrespected in my own damn house!"

Tindal put up his hands. "Wait a minute, wait a minute. I think I've made a mistake."

"You bet your ass you have," the man said.

Tindal took a breath, then coughed. His jaw felt like he'd been hit by a shovel. He thought of those bruises on the girl's arms. Either Mr. Shovel Hands put them there, or Madam Ax Face had. Did it matter which?

"I'm just a little confused," Tindal said. "You're *both* shitty parents?"

That was when Mr. Shovel Hands started kicking him. His feet were pretty hard, too.

By the time Tindal limped back into the house, it was transformed: black crepe paper looped across the front windows, candles burned on the tables, and a Gregorian chant dance remix played through Rolfe's array of matchbox speakers.

Well, not everything had changed. The boy still huddled in his box in the living room.

"Where's El Capitan?" Tindal asked him.

"He went to obtain food, I think," the boy said almost sheepishly. "My sister is cleaning the bathroom."

"You seem better," Tindal said. Not completely, though: his skin shone with sweat, and his eyes were red-rimmed with exhaustion.

"I *am* better," the boy said. He ran a hand through his damp hair. "I would like to apologize for some of the things I said to you. I am so sorry."

"No worries, little man."

His head jerked up at that.

"I mean, young person! Not little person!" The boy did not seem to believe him. "Listen," Tindal said, "you want something to eat? Drink? I think I have some Vegemite and pita chips."

The boy exhaled. "I would like that, thank you."

Tindal walked toward the kitchen, then realized the boy wasn't following. "It's in here," Tindal said.

"I understand, but . . . ?" He glanced down at the box.

"Just stand up," Tindal said. "Oh wait, are your legs cramped? Sure they are. Just a second." He limped back to him, held out his arms. The boy reluctantly reached up. Tindal bent at his knees, freshly kicked ribs twinging, and got his arms around him. The boy came out of the box, feet pedaling the air, and Tindal set him on the ground. Immediately the kid hunched to the floor.

"Ha-ha!" he said, and slowly turned toward the door. He put his right hand down inches in front of him, then dragged a knee forward.

"What are you doing?" Tindal said.

"I shall escape, find a weapon, and then come back and rescue my sister!" His left hand moved another few inches.

Tindal moved between him and the door. They boy howled in anger. His fingers crept forward to grip the toe of Tindal's sandals. He pushed up, grunting.

"Are you trying to *trip* me?" Tindal asked.

"Fall, crone, fall! Crack your head against these stones!"

"First of all, this is carpet. Really, really clean carpet."

El Capitan appeared in the doorway, holding two sacks of groceries in one arm and a twelve-pack of Molson in the other. "Oh, should have left you a note," El Cap said. "He tries to escape every time you let him out of the box. What happened to your face?"

"Turns out, Tiny Tim's dad is an asshole."

El Cap frowned. "I'll put these away, then put him away."

"Thanks, man." Tindal walked down the hallway, leaving the boy to creep slowly toward the doorway. He was thinking of taking a shower before switching to his funeral T-shirt. What day was it, Friday? Not too early in the week for a quick wash-down, and it would be a sign of respect to Rolfe. He wasn't looking forward to seeing the extent of his bruises, though.

The girl lay on her side on the bathroom floor, a sponge in her hand. Her eyes were closed.

Tindal squeaked and threw himself down beside her. "Hey . . . you!" He'd never learned her name, a definite drawback in the resuscitation department. "Are you okay? Don't be dead. Please don't be dead."

He turned her face toward him. The collar of her shirt fell open, fully revealing the necklace of bruises. *Fucking Shovel Hands,* Tindal thought. He tried to remember how mouth-to-mouth worked. Okay, mouth on mouth, obviously, but after that?

"Cap! I need you!"

He heard a *thunk!* from the living room. "Darn it," El Capitan said.

Tindal shouted, "The girl's passed out!"

A moment later El Cap was there, the boy in his arms again. "So's this one," he said. "She's breathing, right?"

"I don't know! Wait. Yeah." He'd just seen her chest move. In fact, now it was clear that she was breathing deeply. How had he missed that? He sat back against the tub, sick with relief. They were sleeping. Only sleeping.

"I'm going to put him down in your room," El Cap said.

In a few minutes they had both of the kids tucked into Tindal's queen-size bed. "Should we surround them with pillows?" Tindal asked. "So they don't roll off?"

"They're not babies," El Capitan said.

"I know," Tindal said with a sigh. "But they're so beautiful when they're sleeping."

The Captain put his arm around Tindal. "So what are we going to do with them?"

"Can't go back to their parents," Tindal said. "They're horrible."

"Well, we can figure them out in the morning. Tonight we have a party to throw."

———✦———

Rolfe's friends and clients—a Venn diagram of two circles that overlapped almost completely—started rolling in before seven and soon filled the house. Tindal recognized the heavily tattooed plumber, a pair of shock-haired assistant professors, an award-winning pet groomer, half a dozen unpublished poets . . . and those were just the Ps. The weepy wept, and the stoic nodded with the wincing frowns of those who were not only familiar with tragedy but had its private number. Tindal hugged them, told the story of the suicide note again and again, and waited for them to notice the paper-covered walls.

"You just printed . . . everything?" asked an unlicensed Reiki therapist. "Without labeling them?"

"I think it's more true this way," Tindal said. "Like life. Random."

"But isn't it kind of dangerous?" she said.

He didn't like her judge-y tone. "This is art," he said. "For adults. You don't have to have any."

The wake accelerated from there, at least subjectively. Tindal had started eating some of his own handiwork, and the recipes were busily redirecting all neuronal traffic into complicated patterns. One of the pages was evidently that old favorite MirrorMaster, because suddenly half a dozen El Capitans—Los Capitans!—were ferrying trays of Bagel Bites out to the living room. Interestingly, each copy wore a different apron. "I meant to have pizza pockets," Tindal explained to a squad of Antonias, who'd kindly returned to pay their respects, if not pay back the sheets Antonia-prime had taken from the deceased's lab. "Rolfe always got so angry when I burned them."

"True, true," they said, eyeing the walls.

"Goddamn it, Tindal!" a voice shouted.

"I can almost hear him now," Tindal said.

The crowd, now a thousand strong, parted biblically. At one end of this new path was a trio of Rolfes. They stood in the doorway, holding backpacks and roller bags.

Tindal burst into tears and dropped to his knees. Then thought, *Wait, what if I'm hallucinating this?* Before he could decide, the lead Rolfe seized him by the T-shirt. "I told you, no parties!"

"You're alive," Tindal said, wiping at his cheek.

"Of course I'm alive. I went to visit my parents in Decatur. Didn't you get my note?"

"It was delicious," Tindal said.

All eyes of the mob were on Tindal and the Rolfes, beaming so many emotions at them: confusion, joy, confusion, anger. Mostly confusion.

The Rolfes were looking around now. "Tindal?" they asked in soft three-part harmony.

"Yes?" he answered.

"What's that on the walls?"

Suddenly, there was one chief emotion hammering at his psyche, drowning out all the others: Rolfe Rage. The screaming went on for some time, until suddenly one of the Rolfes tapped the shoulder of another and said, "Who the hell is that?"

Tindal glanced behind him. The boy and the girl were awake, or almost: the waifs were sleepy and bewildered and frightened. Also sober, judging from his ability to walk and her ability to ignore the trash already littering her carpet.

"Are those *minors*?" Rolfe shouted. "Are you fucking crazy? You want to get me sent to prison?"

Tindal, still kneeling, said, "I can explain."

The Rolfes swept past him and screamed at the siblings, "Get the hell out of my house! Both of you!" The kids, shocked, didn't move. A Rolfe seized the girl's arm, and she yelped in pain.

"HEY!" Tindal said, and scrambled to his feet. He pushed through two of the Rolfes and yanked at the shoulder of the one who'd grabbed the girl. "Don't touch her! Or him!" He placed his body in front of the kids. "They've had a really rough day."

"You brought them into my house?"

"That depends," Tindal said. "Can you lure someone accidentally? Or does 'lure' imply an *intent* to—"

"Get them out," Rolfe said. *"Now."*

Tindal turned to the boy and girl. They looked at him with wide eyes. "Children?" he said, with as much dignity as he could muster. "Come with me."

He put his arms around their shoulders and walked with them to the front door. The pack of Rolfes followed behind, barking the whole way.

On the porch, Tindal turned to the Rolfes and said, "Can I just say again how glad I am that you're all okay?"

"And stay the fuck out!" They slammed the door, but it bounced open again. That door was always trouble. The Rolfes were forced to close it slowly.

Tindal stood on the lawn, feeling . . . what was the word? Hungry. He'd forgotten to eat again. The funeral party—now a resurrection party, after the stoned Tindal had been rolled away— resumed at even greater volume.

"We'll be going now," the girl said.

"Are you going to call our folks again?" the boy asked. This was the first indication that he remembered anything from his life as a micro human.

"Are you kidding?" Tindal said. "They're the worst parents in the world."

"They beat you up," the girl said, studying his face.

"I get the feeling they do that a lot," Tindal said. "Look, you can't go back to them. You'll stay with me till you find a place. No arguments. End of story."

The boy raised his eyebrows. "You're kinda homeless, too."

"Who, me? Rolfe will forgive me. He always does. We just need to let him cool off. He'll love having you."

The siblings exchanged a skeptical look. The boy started to

say something but was interrupted by a single Capitan storming out of the house. "What did I miss? Is everybody okay?"

"We're going to get something to eat," Tindal said.

"Oh," El Cap said. "Kebab?"

The four of them walked through the nighttime streets under the light of twin moons, following a white bird that guided them to the second-best döner kebab in the city. *I should really ask the children their names,* Tindal thought. Then the food arrived, and the thought evaporated in a haze of steam and spice.

AUTHOR'S NOTE

Daryl Gregory: I'm not the first person to realize that the main villains of the Hansel and Gretel story are those awful parents. As a father myself, I've sometimes wanted to ditch my children in the forest—but to actually do it? Twice? It seemed to me that it was time the witch got to be the hero of the story. Maybe she wasn't a monster but a person with terrible judgment in home decoration. Once I decided to set the story in the same drug-addled near future of my novel *Afterparty*, Tindal the kindhearted stoner was born.

THE SUPER ULTRA DUCHESS OF FEDORA FOREST

Charlie Jane Anders

There is a perfect valley, nestled near the foot of the Sherbet Mountains and bordered by the River of Middling Ideas. It's just a two-day ride away from the Lazy Geyser, which grants good luck to anyone who throws a coin in its path at the very moment when it finally gets around to erupting. There, in that valley, in the shelter of the fedora trees, is the most splendid place in the whole world to make your home.

Once, that valley was home to a small cottage, in which there lived a mouse, a bird, and a sausage. They were the best of friends, with the perfect partnership.

Every day, the bird would fly into the forest and collect wood. The mouse would carry in water from the well, make a fire, and set the table. And then the sausage would cook their dinner, slithering around in the fry pan to coat it with grease for their vegetables or grains.

The sausage had fled the Republic of Breakfast Meats, during one of High Commodore Gammon's occasional campaigns to purge the realm of improper "meatizens." (It usually started out with the Canadian bacon, which wasn't even proper bacon at all, and then spread to those accursed chicken-fried steaks, and then turned into just a general massacre.) The sausage heard the sounds of trucks and loudspeakers, and barely managed to pack up her few precious belongings (such as an MP3 player that contained all of her beloved EDM tunes, which she loved to listen to and dream of becoming a DJ someday).

The sausage had barely made it through the border from the Republic of Breakfast Meats to the Federation of Circus Animals, thanks to some help from a kindly blood pudding who forged some traveling papers for the sausage. Once in the land of Circus Animals, the sausage had found shelter in a trailer with a friendly balloon elephant, who was best friends with an actual elephant. ("People can never tell us apart," the balloon elephant had said, making a squeaky-squocky noise with his laughter. The flesh-and-blood elephant had just snorted through her trunk.) From there, the sausage had traveled south, skirting the edge of the Monster Truck Preserve.

Once, this land had been home to men and women. People had built the houses and roads, and they had made places for all the creatures of the forest and all the food items of the table. Even the balloon animals and monster trucks had known exactly where they belonged. That had been paradise, and now the men and women were gone, and everyone lived in a fallen state.

That, at least, was what the cartoon Blanketsaurus standing on a sardine crate was saying, on the day when the sausage had met the bird and the mouse. The Blanketsaurus, whose skin was a beautiful soft fluffy wool-cotton blend, had stood facing a crowd of every kind of person you could imagine, in the market square of the town of Zay!. "We're just all jacked up," the Blanketsaurus insisted. "Our shiz is a mess, brothers and sisters and others. We can't ever even have any purpose at all without the humans."

The sausage had made a dismissive noise, like a sausage makes when she's getting a bit steamed. "Who needs humans?" she had whispered. "I never even saw a human. Never saw a need for one, neither."

That was when the mouse had spoken up. "I just don't know. I sometimes have the feeling that my life has no organizing principle, ya know? I'm living with a bird, in this cottage in the valley, and we're just playing house. What are we even doing with our lives? Some days, I just want a human to chase me into the wainscoting. And I don't even know what a wainscoting is."

"A wainscoting is a sort of musical instrument," according to a nearby cactus, who was kind of a know-it-all. "It plays mournful sounds, like the wind on a lonely, moonless night."

"We don't need any crunking humans," the sausage had insisted. "We don't need anybody besides one another. We can make our own rules. You and that bird can figure it out, all on your own." And the more the mouse had told the sausage about her life with the bird, the more the sausage had piped up with ideas about how to make it work, and how they could get everything set up just right.

So that was how the sausage ended up living with the mouse and the bird, and the three of them had a perfect system. They were able to salvage enough valuable artifacts of the former human world to sell in the town of Zay!, and soon they had amassed a great many fine possessions. Meanwhile, the sausage finally had a place to practice her DJing, and she started spinning at some of the smaller raves and warehouse parties, over near Confetti Canyon. Her DJ rig included a big mic, with various cool effects, and a built-in speaker on wheels, for outdoor parties.

For years, the mouse, the bird, and the sausage lived merrily together. In the evenings, they played video games and worked on their dance routines. The mouse, who had grown up in a barn full of serious square dancers, was learning to throw it down. (The mouse hailed from a farm many miles away, and she always told the bird and the sausage that if you wanted to see serious drudgery, try farm work. Farms were like a chore wheel with a million spokes, man.)

"You guys are the best friends I've ever known, man," the bird said to the mouse and the sausage one night, when they were kind of crunked up on aromatic bark that the bird had brought back from the town market earlier that day. "I'm serious. I never really felt like I belonged with the other birds. But you guys, you are my sisters. I never thought I would find my place in the world with a mouse and a sausage." The bird was perched on his usual chair back but kept wobbling.

"You too, absolutely," the mouse said, wrinkling her nose. "I feel like I just always had a sausage-and-bird-shaped hole in my life, and I never even knew."

"Awww, I love you guys," the sausage said, greasy tears rolling down her face.

Nobody knew what kind of bird the bird was. He was just "a bird." People would sometimes try to identify his actual species: like, maybe he was a bluebird because his wings were kind of blue, or maybe he was a robin because his breast was reddish. But the bird would get grumpy whenever anybody tried to label him. Why wasn't it enough just to be a bird? One reason why he liked being the only bird in the neighborhood was because you could ask, "Hey, where's the bird?" and everybody would know you were talking about him.

So they went on: the bird fetching wood, the mouse fetching water and setting the table, the sausage making the food and seasoning it with her body. A perfect system!

A few times a month, the bird, the mouse, and the sausage

would venture into the town to sell their wares (and to get more DJ gigs lined up for the sausage). They knew everyone: all the scrap dealers, and farmers' market stall keepers, and truck whisperers, and sno-cone motivational speakers. Everybody had a friendly word for their little makeshift family.

Except, as time went by, they kept hearing whispers. "Things are changing," said this one scrap-metal dealer, who was a big roast turkey leg. "Good old High Commodore Gammon from the land of Breakfast Meats signed a treaty with Grand Marshal Ruffles from the Circus Animal country, and they've both entered into a confederation with the Dandelion Lady."

"What does that mean?" the bird asked, with a toss of his wings.

"It means, be careful about traveling if you don't have identity papers and letters of transit," said the turkey leg, quivering with indignation. "It means, honest businesspeople like myself get to have our goods searched and seized for no reason, unless we pay bribes to the border guards. It means that they're forming an army and preparing to go to war against the Insect Principality. I would just keep your heads down."

"But why?" the mouse asked.

"It makes no sense," the sausage said. "People just want to have a simple life. Gammon should stick to what he's good at, arresting good innocent salami slices for being too Continental a breakfast item."

A month or two after that, the sausage saw the big vermilion Blanketsaurus again, once again addressing the townsfolk of Zay!. Only this time, the Blanketsaurus had a fancy uniform with big epaulettes, and his title was Admiral Blanketsaurus. (There was no ocean anywhere nearby, even if you counted the Root Beer Sea, but the Blanketsaurus explained painstakingly that the word "admiral" meant that you had lots and lots of secret admirers.) And now, the Blanketsaurus was accompanied by a few dozen people, all of them wearing uniforms as well.

"Brothers, sisters, and others," the Blanketsaurus told the crowd in the town square. "Our lives were empty and without purpose. Our creators were gone, and we were living in their world without them. The human race decided to endow a great many things and creatures with higher awareness, and then they were wiped out by a flu virus that had gotten a PhD in linguistics. As a result, we were left behind, possessing consciousness without context. But now, at last, we can prove ourselves worthy of our heritage. We can re-create civilization!"

The Blanketsaurus wanted everyone to swear loyalty to the Confederation and to its leaders, like High Commodore Gammon and the Dandelion Lady. And if you originally hailed from one of the member states—like, say, the land of Breakfast Meats—you would be required to travel home and register there. This was a mere bureaucratic trifle, after which you would be free to carry on as before.

The sausage heard this and nearly cooked in her skin. There was no way she was ever going home, to be subject to the cruel whims of Gammon and his sort. She slipped away while everyone else was cheering for the new, more organized government, and ran home.

"I just don't get it," said the mouse, making a fire and setting the table for their dinner as usual. "I mean, why should anybody care what we do with our lives? Isn't the whole point that everybody gets to live happily ever after in our own way?"

"Well," said the bird, "they're just trying to do the same thing we're doing here, man. We've got our perfect civilized setup, right? Each of us has our tasks. The wood gathering, the water, the cooking—we have an order to everything. They just want the same kind of thing, on a larger scale. Right?"

"It's not the same thing," said the mouse.

"We're a family," said the sausage.

"Sure, sure," said the bird. But his feathery brow wrinkled a little bit.

A couple of weeks passed, and they all forgot about Blanketsaurus and about the conversation they'd had afterward. Until one day, the bird came home from fetching wood, and his wings were fluttering with anger. He scratched at his chair back as he glowered at his two friends. "It's an honest disgrace," the bird grumbled.

"What's wrong?" asked the mouse, wide-eyed.

The bird kept just muttering and glaring, until he finally explained. When he was out in the woods, he'd met up with another bird who lived a few miles away and had come over here to flutter around and hunt for gumdrops. You know, bird stuff. And the bird—our bird—had started bragging about his situation, and how good he had it, with his friends the mouse and the sausage. They had everything locked down. Everybody had a job to do, and it all ran smooth as butter. And then they played video games and danced to EDM!

But the other bird just fluffed his bright tail feathers and said that it sounded as though the bird was being straight-up taken for a ride. After all, the bird had the toughest job of the three of them. He had to go into the forest and collect the wood, and carry it all the way back to the cottage. Meanwhile, the mouse only had to carry some water and set the table, and a few other chores, and then she could just lounge around. The sausage just had to climb into the pan for a little while and season it. Of course *they* were happy: they'd suckered the bird into doing all the real work! "I'm glad I don't have to get bossed around by a rodent and a piece of meat," said the other bird with a chortle, before flying away.

Now the bird was back at home, spitting mad at his friends. "You think I'm just a chump," he squawked. "You think you can just treat me like your fool forever. You guys just loaf around here, putting on your fancy airs, while I'm out there dragging wood in from the forest. It's exploitation, is what it is."

"But I mean, you've never complained before," said the mouse, her fur standing on end.

"And that's how you knew I was a sucker!"

The mouse and the sausage tried to reason with the bird, pointing out that each of them had the task that she or he was most suited for. They weren't trying to exploit anybody, just use their shared resources in the best possible way. And so on.

But the bird was having none of it. He kept insisting that the free lunch was over, and it was about time they shared the workload more equally.

"What do you have in mind?" the sausage asked, trembling with nervousness, but also with the fear that she had lost her friend forever.

"How about we trade jobs tomorrow?"

So it was that the sausage went out to the forest to fetch wood, in spite of all her protests. And meanwhile, the bird would get the easy job of fetching water and setting everything up, while the mouse threw herself into the hot frying pan to get it greased up. If this worked out as it should, the bird had said, maybe they could have a chore wheel from now on.

The sausage felt naked and exposed, moving through the trees with the delicate marbling under her skin visible in the sunlight filtering through the big hats above. She tried to hum a David Guetta song to steady her nerves, but every sound in the woods made her jump. The fear, the uncertainty, were like a lump of gristle in her brain. And meanwhile, she kept arguing with the bird in her head, coming up with more and more reasons why this was unfair and a dreadful mistake, and surely the bird had to see that the sausage was much too delicate to carry wood every day, or even once every three days.

The sausage got so worked up, arguing with the bird in her

mind, that she didn't hear the dog coming up behind her until its hot breath and slobbery tongue were right behind her. She tried to run, but the dog's jaws closed around her.

"Hey," the sausage protested weakly, "let me go."

The dog did let go of her for a moment, just so he could talk. "You're a mighty juicy sausage," he whuffed. "But you're a long way from the Breakfast Meats country. I don't suppose you have any valid travel papers?"

"Uh—" The sausage fumbled around in her pockets. "I do, I do. I have some right here."

And she produced the papers that the blood pudding had made for her, so long ago. The dog picked them up in his front paws and inspected them. Now that she wasn't in the dog's mouth, she could see that he was a big brown hound, like a hunting dog, with a slobbery mouth and flat ears.

"Hmmm," the dog said. "This is certainly most interesting. But it's clearly a forgery. You see this smudging around the great seal of High Commodore Gammon, here? And also, even if this was real, it's no longer valid. You would have had to return to your home and get updated papers for the Confederation. In any case, you're carrying forged papers, and thus you are free booty." He leaned his head in a graceful movement and scooped the sausage up again.

The shout came from behind the sausage: "Let go of my friend!"

The sausage would never know why the bird came looking for her. Maybe the bird felt guilty? Or maybe he just wanted to come and gloat. Either way, he arrived just in time to see the dog carrying her away, and try to intervene.

"Oh, hi." The dog let the sausage go again so he could address the bird. "Unfortunately, your friend here is carrying forged letters. Which is like ten kinds of a crime. So I was about to carry her off and eat her, maybe not in that order."

"That's . . . that's barbaric!" The bird's wings shook with outrage, and his feet scraped the forest dirt. "You can't go around eating people!"

"Civilization has certain rules," the dog growled. "You break them, you get eaten. This isn't up to me. I have to follow the same rules as everybody else."

"You don't have to eat anybody. That's not in any rules," the sausage said, gaining a bit of courage from having her friend there by her side.

"That's true," the dog said. "I mean, I could take her all the way back to the Republic of Breakfast Meats, where they would execute her. But that's a lot of bother, and the end result is the same. And I can tell just by smelling her that she's got bits of fennel and wild boar in her. She's going to be delicious."

"But," the bird said. "But—but—we're friends with the Super Ultra Duchess of the Fedora Forest! She has a great army and immense power. She'll be mega pissed if you kill our friend here. She'll probably hunt you down and make an example of you."

"What?" the dog said. "What the hell are you talking about?"

The sausage was about to say the exact same thing as the dog. But when she glanced at the bird, he rolled his eyes and poked forward with his beak, as if to say, *Just work with me here.*

So the sausage chimed in. "Yes! The Super Ultra Duchess. You didn't even know this forest had its own ruler, did you? And we're under her protection. She's so powerful, even the Confederacy leaves her alone."

"I've never heard of any Super Ultra Duchess," the dog grumbled, "and I'm on all the message boards."

"Well, you obviously don't come to the Fedora Forest too often," the sausage said huffily.

"In fact," said the bird, "I think I saw her just a little while ago." He was gesturing at someone whom the sausage couldn't see, and she realized that their friend, the mouse, must be someplace nearby. The bird kept talking, trying to stall the dog. "She makes all the rules hereabouts, and in fact, you better watch out, because I think you're violating a bunch of her regulations and ordinances and statutes. For reals."

"I don't know." The dog sniffed the air. "I think I would have smelled it if there was any such authority around here. Authority has a very distinct scent."

"I'm pretty sure she's right around here," the bird said, looking around in a panic.

"This is your last warning," the sausage said, with zero conviction.

"Nah," the dog said. "I think I'm going to eat this sausage now, and then there won't be any evidence left anyway."

He bent his head to scoop the sausage up in his jaws, ready to gobble her up once and for all.

"WHO DARES?" came a thundering voice through the forest.

The dog dropped the sausage, his tail going between his legs by some instinct.

"UNMOUTH MY SUBJECT," said the voice. And the source of the voice came close enough for the sausage to see. It was the mouse, riding on top of the sausage's mobile DJ rig, using the microphone on its highest reverb setting. The mouse had found a big mushroom, which she was using as a hat, and had covered herself and the DJ rig with a big velvety red blanket.

"Hey," the dog said, with a bit of a whimper in his voice. "I found her. She had forged papers. She's free booty, man."

"YOURS IS THE BOOTY THAT WILL BE FREE," said the mouse, "IF YOU MOLEST MY SUBJECT. GO NOW! BEFORE I BRING MY MIGHTY ARMIES DOWN UPON YOU."

The dog hesitated one moment longer, but the mouse bellowed, "GO!" He turned his lowered tail and ran off into the forest with his legs flailing. The sausage was so amazed and relieved, she fell on her back, wobbling as if she was being grilled.

"That was a near thing," the sausage said.

"That dog will be back, I bet," said the mouse, disentangling herself from the DJ rig, the mushroom, and the blanket.

"We'll just have to make the Super Ultra Duchess more convincing next time," said the bird. "We'll all have to work together on it, since she's like our insurance policy."

"Ow." The mouse cringed as it exposed its patchy fur to the open air. "I am actually in pain, all over my whole body. I tried to get into the hot frying pan to season the food with my body, and my fur did not like it at all. That's why I was here in the woods when that dog attacked you. I came here to ask you for advice on what I was doing wrong. I burned my poor feet, so I had to ride here on your DJ rig, and it's lucky that I did, too."

"There's a whole art to wriggling around in a frying pan and seasoning it with your body," the sausage said, still expanding with relief.

"Really?" the mouse said.

"No, not really," the sausage said, with an exasperated laugh. "You just have to be a sausage, dude."

"Oh," the bird said. "That actually makes total sense."

After that, they carried on more or less as they had before. Except that now, they had a house meeting once a week or so, just to make sure they were all happy with the arrangement of the jobs. Some days, the bird skipped fetching wood and went flying off to look for cool stuff that they could sell to the scrap merchants in town. The sausage's DJ gigs started bringing in enough money that they could hire some part-time help. The mouse got better at pretending to be a Super Ultra Duchess, until they finally received an embossed invitation to join the Confederacy. They framed the invite and put it on the mantelpiece, over their PlayStation's big screen.

"It just proves," said the bird, who would not stop extolling his own cleverness for a minute, "anybody can be a big deal, if they just have a posse."

"Yeah," the mouse said, curling up between her friends. "It just makes me wonder. Why doesn't everybody just invent their own nation?"

"I think maybe they do," said the sausage. They were playing a side-scrolling shooter, and the sausage had just gotten to the Final Boss, so nobody talked for a while after that. Until it was time to climb into the frying pan and make dinner.

Charlie Jane Anders: "The Bird, the Mouse, and the Sausage" is one of the strangest Grimm Brothers fairy tales. It's incredibly bleak and unbelievably strange. There's no plucky hero who triumphs in spite of doing the thing that he (or she) was told not to do. There's no hint of a reward for doing the right thing, whatsoever. There's just hubris and death.

If you haven't read the original version of this fairy tale, you really ought to. It's very short and intensely odd. Just Google "Grimm bird mouse sausage" and it'll be the first hit. And once you've read the original fairy tale, you'll see why I was so obsessed with it. And why, when I was asked to contribute to this volume, I couldn't think of any story I'd rather do.

On one level, the original tale is clearly about division of labor, and the importance of sticking to your assigned task and not trying to challenge the established Order of Things. But on another level, it's about an unconventional family, and what happens when they pay too much attention to the opinions of outsiders.

But once I started pulling at the threads of this story, it got more complicated. There are plenty of Grimm tales with talking animals—but this is a world where there's a talking sausage, too, and nobody bats an eye. And the dog in the story attacks the sausage, not just because the dog likes sausages, but because the sausage is carrying forged letters. Who issues documentation to a sausage? The more I thought about this, the more confused I became.

My first few stabs at expanding and transforming this fairy tale were too literal minded. I described a laboratory where foolish scientists imbued a sausage with sentience, and how their experiments gradually went wrong. I imagined a world slowly overrun by talking animals and self-aware pieces of food. It wasn't clicking. It was only when I decided to go fully postapocalyptic and turn this story into, basically, a kind of *Adventure Time* fanfic that it started to click for me. And that had the bonus of giving me a sausage that not only talks but wants to be a club DJ.

CHARLIE
JANE ANDERS

FAMILIARIS

Genevieve Valentine

 mean, if you don't want to have one," he says, that single line down the center of his forehead like his face is about to peel.

"Someday," she says. His hand is too tight in her hand. One of them is sweating.

The prince and princess had no child.

Eventually, wolves.

Long ago, a woman in Bavaria had to peel some potatoes. She had to do the washing. She had to check on the soup that simmered on the stove and was never quite thick enough. She had to watch her smallest child where it lay wrapped near the fire and sweating, and watch her oldest daughter tying back her hair to look finer when she went to trade the day's milk for some woolens from the merchant with the unmarried son. She wanted to tell a story that could lock the door.

The prince and princess had no child. The princess insulted a peasant mother as unfaithful for having triplets; as punishment, the princess bore seven sons in seven days. She sent them to be killed. (Mothers in stories are hateful and unkind; they never peel potatoes for the soup.) The prince found them and saved them and let them grow, and as soon as they were men of eighteen, they appeared in the feast hall to swallow the princess whole.

Wolves, the mother calls them, when she speaks of young men. Oldest daughters don't fear much anymore—they don't fear enough—but a wolf can still make a girl pause at the window and glance into the woods, just in case.

Fairy tales are collected by the scholars who show up in the center of town with neat coats darned at the cuffs, with pen and ink and paper, but they begin with a woman at the fireside, looking out the open door and fearing the worst.

She wants the lock to sit fast, even if it's too late. She wants to make her daughter listen to the story of a princess who couldn't bear children and then suddenly, horribly could; who saw only a wolf when her husband forced her to look in her mirror; who was ruined the moment she insulted the farmer, because women are doomed if they open their mouths, and that mountain's so steep it can ruin a queen.

You tell stories because your fears have no easier name. The merchant's son smiles, but he's tall, and when his father is gone to sell near the cathedral, the son offers to show girls the woolens they store upstairs and keeps them there too long. The soup is going to sour any minute, and your daughter needs to come home.

"How can she have so many?" she says, looking at the woman who can barely push the double stroller, one older child dragging on her shirttail. One of them is shrieking. It won't stop. The mother looks like she hasn't slept in a hundred years; her anger flaps empty and worn-out every time she opens her mouth.

Familiaris

Her husband says, "We should be so lucky," and for a moment she looks at him like his tongue has turned into a salamander before she remembers that the last time she mentioned she was doing well at work, his smile was thin. (He still hasn't assembled the desk in the room that's supposed to be her office; she does her work at the dining table, as her mother did the darning. He's gotten adamant that they clear it before dinner. "We're a family," he says, "we should get in the habit to make it easier when we have children," and she thinks about what he looked like the first time he told her he wanted to marry her and what her mother says about the Holy Spirit alive in the home, and makes her work disappear.)

Her stomach goes rancid. He doesn't see it—what's there to see, in an empty space? He has an office in a company that matters, with windows on two sides. She's going to go to the doctor and slap her feet in the stirrups and vomit for months and swell and lose her job and her wits in the mud of pregnancy, and she'll expel a child from a body that's been wrecked by an intruder (she knows what that's like; she's lived with her husband long enough).

She wonders what would happen if she took her hand out of his hand and ran until she dropped.

One of the other children is crying now; piercing. She checks to see if her nose is bleeding.

The princess was chosen, not born. The prince rode by her parents' hovel with his hand out to her, and the saddle chafed the back of her legs so much she dared not sit before the king and queen. They thought it charming. She kept her hands clasped behind her when she departed; they thought that charming, too.

The prince had left a stain on the back of her dress, a small dark spot she clasped her hands over. She'd been foolish, and had dressed in white like a bride.

He laughed when he saw it and said, "That's what happens to

a prince with a pretty maid and a long ride," and she said, "But I'm a princess now," and he smiled as if she was agreeing with him and not warning him.

Seven boys. Seven sons. We imagine it; a thousand legends and a thousand songs have taught us to want them. It's a mythic number that means greatness, that suggests higher purpose, a beautiful whole.

Later stories come by to separate them into people, and they take up songs and novels and celluloid and occupy different faces, but the fairy tales seldom bother. They're frightening enough just as they are—a brother for every day of the week, all healthy, enough grown sons to fill the doorway of the audience hall—and really, there's no time. The old Bavarian woman who let some scholar write down "The Wolves" can barely bring them back into the story in time to condemn their mother to death for sending them into the forest as soon as they were born. It takes only so long to make porridge, to card wool, to shuck peas, to worry about her daughter. The story has to be over before the work is over. The point is, men will conspire to win. The point is, women are sacrifices. The point is, take the bread off the coals before it burns.

You can't leave a story like this broken off for later. It has to be whole to make any sense. Halfway through this story, the queen's given birth to seven sons in seven days to punish her for an accusation even fairy stories know is false, and a maid is carrying seven babies through the woods to be eaten, and in a cave that no one ever sees, the beast sits with its jaws open, waiting for a meal it will never get. Bring them back quick as you can and punish the queen. The sun's going down.

Heroic, though, those seven sons, any story you find them in. (And of course you find them; we're taught early of the worth in groups of men who conspire.) The oldest one solemn and sure—but not the darkest eyes; that's the fourth one, the one who has no time for the small-minded girls from their small-minded home. He and the second brother and the youngest sit up at night on the tallest hill they can come by and look at the road until it vanishes.

It doesn't matter when the story takes place, not really—just that there's a road. Some of them have wagon ruts and point toward the market in the shadow of the king's cathedral. Some are paved black and empty, and the brothers tighten their fingers around the grips of their motorcycles.

The third brother, the only one who isn't perfect, stands with one hip cocked to hide that one leg's shorter than the other. The second-youngest is the runt of the litter, who still has the tenderness of a newborn, soft and young and seamless no matter what work they've done: farmers, maybe, or mechanics; grease on his face is like nightfall on the moon.

The fifth brother is the angry one. In any age, he handles metal. In any age, he makes the iron shoes.

They're cruel, probably—groups of men tend that way no matter how carefully someone has raised them up from the dirt; they're called "the wolves" because it's a flattering enough name for something terrifying that the brothers will never realize is a warning to strangers—but still, the town that sheltered them will weep to see them go.

The brothers never think of that town again. They haven't thought of it in years. The first time someone told them they were princes, they were gone.

The king and queen walked past a christening—triplets, three at once, showered with petals by the cheering villagers and juggled by an old woman who staggered under the weight of the baskets.

"Where is the father?" the queen asked in horror, wanting to look away from it, desperate to be gone. The mother dead—she had to be, with some stranger carrying the children—and the farmer father wandering the churchyard, accepting the accolades and the sympathy while his wife was dead in the ground, broken by sons.

Bile tasted green in her throat. "So many children, too many at once—it's a betrayal—"

Her husband the king laughed and took her arm to hold her fast. "Stop babbling. Are you accusing a dead woman of adultery? Her husband stands there, he'll hear you."

The priest was congratulating him on his children, nodding solemnly. The father wore a black ribbon and a white one, and a jacket gone thin at the elbows.

"But the mother," the queen said, at the same time as the king told her, "Don't say such cruel things; it's your own fault we have nothing, if you want children so badly." At home he pointed at her mirror and snapped his teeth like a dog and gave her a look like he'd picked the wrong girl out of the dirt.

But she'd tried to point out that the mother was missing. She knew the mother had been faithful, you'd have to be to carry three of his issue; it was the children who killed her that had broken trust.

Women tell each other stories about it. (You can't stop women from telling you stories about it; it's a horror as old as the dark, and a different monster emerges every time.)

She had kept *her* mother sick for seven months, and when her mother couldn't keep down enough food to satisfy her, she had sucked the marrow from her mother's teeth. Her mother only had ten left now—they'd crumbled to dust, hollowed out by the parasite she'd carried. The rest of her teeth were false, and they would be cruel to look at if her mother ever smiled anymore.

You birthed a queen, she wants to say, *I kept you safe and rich and those false teeth are made of ivory*; but she'll birth princes and knows there's no comfort in it.

When she wakes up, the baby's pulled at her skin so much

that the white gouge marks along her stomach are raised from the pressure of the blood inside, pulsing, like worms converging on a meal.

You drown in your children. She knows. She prepares for a siege.

It takes four years for him to get her to agree, but eventually his smiles and that line between his eyes feel like the tip of some ice pick, and she doesn't dare. So let him divorce her, she thinks when she's angry, but as work slows down and her boss starts to ask about family plans and her mother offers to go with her to the doctor or to church for counseling on the woman's place in the home and the glory of children, she realizes with the sensation of dropping off a cliff that she might as well have a child—someone has to be on her side, and she'll have to start from scratch, because the world has already gotten to the rest.

She lets it happen. She grits her teeth against it, but she lets it happen. The first time it moves is like a nail in the bed underneath her.

She picks a name for the child. It takes three weeks, during which he comes home from his office with the two big windows and they stand together in the room that had been meant for her work or her sewing and is a nursery now, while he paints and she reads names he hates.

"I like that one," he says sometimes. She keeps reading until she finds one she likes, and folds a corner over. The nursery gets painted yellow, like piss on a stick.

He sleeps on the couch for the last week of name selection, until he breaks, and she writes the two names she wanted down in the journal his mother bought her as a reminder that the child is coming and she will have to be interested in it for the rest of its life.

She lets him fuck her for a while until he forgets to resent her; it's an even trade, she figures, because sooner or later she won't have to fuck him anymore, but that child will bear the name forever. ("Pregnancy hormones," he laughs, unfastening his pants. "The guys all told me.")

It's not for the child's sake she works so hard for the name. It's not for the child's sake she eats until she can feel food pressing against the back of her eyelids, and her arms float out to the size of loaves of bread and her ankles swell so badly she can only wear mules and the reflection in the mirror would agonize her if she was vain.

She eats because if the parasite has no nourishment, then it eats its host. She makes sure it has enough to feed on. She gives it room in her stomach, then her rib cage, where her lungs start to feel tight five months in and only get smaller; she gives up room for it in the bladder that holds less and less.

She picks a name she hopes to care about because it will be her name, appended at teacher conferences and playgroups and anywhere else her husband isn't there for her to be appended to: as soon as the baby breathes, she'll be Christopher's Mother.

It never stops consuming you, a child; not so long as it lives.

Everyone knows how to tame something: you start with a wolf, something sovereign and smart enough to know better, and you wait until it's starving, and then you feed it and teach it to put up with the touch of your hand, and you raise its children and its children's children until their teeth fall out and they gum at your fingers with no pride left, endlessly starving for your kind words and your palm, where they sit on the ground at your feet for the rest of their locked-in lives, and they get so good at it that you name them "familiaris," to take the wolf out of even their name, so they have nothing ever again but you.

The king was away when the queen gave birth: seven boys in seven days, red and screaming and hated.

"Carry them into the forest and feed them to the wolves," she gasped over and over through lungs that had no room left. A maid with sharper eyes than the others bundled all seven into a basket of laundry and promised to let them be devoured, and as soon as she was gone, the queen burst into tears that shook the bed beneath her.

Remorse, all the nurses told themselves, packing up the bloody linen (seventh-best, the babies hadn't left much time to appease royal sensibilities) and watching the queen clutch at her heart. It's only fear that's made her do this—she can't be caught out looking unfaithful after that fuss she made, to be sure, they all have to go—but ah, it's kind she mourns them now.

The queen pressed her hand against her lowest ribs, the ones that had cracked under the endless swelling of them all (with luck, the physicians had told her, they would set tighter toward one another once the child came, so her waist would be pleasingly small). She felt the relieving emptiness of her stomach, between her legs; a ruin vacated. Her breasts were heavy with kings' milk.

Let them die soon, she thought, *before they cry out, lest my body betray me and answer.*

She had no need of worry. The milk turned to dust before the king ever came home.

In the story, the king meets the maid on the road and asks her purpose. She shows him the children, on their way to be placed in a wolf's den and eaten.

How stories fail us without the right teller, with wool to be carded before the cows' milking. What on earth possessed that maid? Was she crying? Was she foolish? Was it triumph? Did loyalty to the king overwhelm her at the last? Had the queen given her one duty too many and the maid wanted only for the queen to suffer? Was the road long enough for her to become afraid of something well beyond the understanding of the king and queen—perhaps the maid had a mother who told her stories too—and she hardly minded being run through so long as she didn't have to look a wolf in the eye?

The woman by the fire wanted to make her daughter wary of kings; for no other reason would that maid have submitted to the sword. It would have been no work to lie to a king—lying to a man is easy—and manage the work she had promised. The wolf was nearby, so close the king just barely stopped her in time, and she knew the way. Wolves in stories are easy to find.

The king takes his seven sons from the dead hands of the castle maid and brings them to the village and orders them raised up: tall and handsome, long hair shining, eyes on the road that leads to the castle gate.

He goes home to his milkless wife and waits for eighteen years.

How stories fail us! What a pleasant husband he must have been—distant enough that his wife had space to think, deferent enough not to arouse suspicion among the court that anything was wrong. What a measured monarch he'd have made, building a kingdom worth inheriting as if his wife wouldn't know what it looks like when a king has heirs. What a kind man he must have been, all that time; men always are when they have something to look forward to.

But this is a fairy tale, where there are more lessons than reason. The mirror reflected a wolf when the queen came home from church, to warn her she would bear them. The king must have known the boys would live to revenge themselves. Every day from sunset to darkness, the queen stood at her balcony and waited. She was standing there when they came back, after eighteen years and seven days, racing horses in a cloud of dust along the road that led from the village. She must have known who they were the moment she saw them; she must have known, for eighteen years and seven days, that her children would walk through the doors and consume her.

———◆———

Familiaris

Seven sons. One at a time, she loses her life to those beating-heart swellings that leave an abscess, that suckle your breasts and then forget the sound of your voice (children never listen, they're wolves), the questions that make you hope they choke on their tongues, the toys that pierce your feet and the screams that pierce your ears. Seven sons, and she feels every moment that she should have stopped it somehow—tied her tubes, thrown herself down the stairs, spit in the aisle of their church until the priest disowned them and she could start walking and not stop until traffic hit her. But whenever she tried to do any of them, it was with the futile force of a dream, where you open your mouth to warn yourself but nothing comes out, and you keep moving the way the dream has laid before you because you know you'll never wake up.

She ceded the office long ago to the wailing babies, but then they engulfed the guest room, the basement. "Maybe someday," he says about a bigger house when she confronts him, "but houses are expensive, and we only have one income now," and when he sees her face even he must be embarrassed, because he amends it to "Later they'll be so big, we'll cherish the memory of all being together like this," and her face must not change much, because he curses under his breath and leaves.

It's no loss, really, the guest room and the basement. Her mother can't come this year anyway; her mother can't ever help except to offer wrong advice and to tell her she's selfish when she complains and to ask for photos every day. There's no help. Who could help her with so many sons except someone who would take them and run?

The baby sits in a bassinet at the foot of their bed, so not even her dreams are quiet, and she'd stay awake watching television except the children broke an armrest on the couch (on her side; they know better than to ruin anything of their father's) and it makes her want to grab the nearest thing and slam it into the wall.

One day the formal dining room that has two doors she could

close on them becomes a playroom. She can't remember if she agreed or if their father just had a bright idea. But her anger about it is the anger of a dream, too, where no matter how much your skin itches from the insects laying eggs inside you, you can't make a noise. Not like anyone would hear it with all the children who drag at her fingers and yowl to be fed and laugh when her husband laughs at what a mess the house is, at how peevish she looks.

(He doesn't care how she looks. He's been sleeping with someone else since the fourth son. She hopes he'll file for divorce. She'll get herself admitted to a hospital so the children can't follow her, and will swallow any pill they give her for the rest of her life, swallow a handful at a time if they're trying to kill her; she doesn't care so long as she's alone.)

He gets angry with her for staying mad at him; he watches TV at night, so he's used to husbands being forgiven in twenty-two minutes. She'd maybe forgive him if she could close the dining room doors and think it over. Her seven sons won't stop breathing.

She spent a summer at camp once, when she was ten, and mosquitoes hovered over her face every time she lay down, and all she could dream of was them laying their eggs and the larvae crawling out of her ear. She got too paranoid to sleep, because every time she closed her eyes they found her. The camp sent her home after a week because she hit another camper with a tennis racquet. Exhaustion, they said.

When her children cry, she sobs until her husband gets out of bed to tend them, and she doesn't care how angry it makes him, because he's a stranger to them and they might listen. She knows she would pick up the heaviest toy in the room and swing.

She's thirty-eight—baffling, impossible, how much of her life has she lost?—and there are seven sons. Her husband says he's house-hunting for something bigger. He's fucking the real estate agent, so it's slow going, but sometimes he brings home a flyer from a viewing: a five-bedroom charmer so far away from their school and their friends that she'll spend the rest of her life in the station wagon; a house with a yard so small she'll have to enroll the older ones in soccer and baseball and slice oranges on game day and stand next to the other mothers and pretend she doesn't want to run them over.

"You're making this goddamn difficult," he says when she turns them down. "I thought you wanted a new house."

She doesn't sleep much anymore; the grub at the foot of the bed claws at her breast twice a night, the soft sleek hair at the back of his head like a spider's leg. The oldest one won't stop telling her that all his friends think boys are better than girls and how lucky he is to be a boy—"Thanks, Mom," he says with a smile, every time—and she wants to hold his face in the bathwater until the waves stop, until he'll never say it again.

Christopher's Mom, says the envelope from school with the field trip instructions on it. They need chaperones.

"Well, I can't do it," her husband says. "This presentation is really kicking my ass, honey, and this is really your thing. Come on, you know."

She was sick for four months with Christopher. Her body tried to rid itself of the foreign object every day for four months, until it got too weary to resist and let the thing have its way with her.

Like pushing a kid under the wheels of the bus, she thinks, on the way home from the field trip, wherever it was that they went. *You fight the idea for a long time until you're too tired to do it, and that's how any child gets to grow old.*

Five kids are shrieking in the back of the bus. Something lands near her head. She checks to see if her nose is bleeding.

The queen stood in the tower, looking out over the kingdom. Her hands were on her stomach. She was looking for her children.

She had seemed incomplete for the last five months of the pregnancy, heaving, pitied; a woman is complete, and a woman and a child, but when you're pregnant everybody knows you don't quite have what you want yet. Expectation. Cannibalism.

In the churchyard the farmer father and the priest were digging a grave. Only one of the triplets had died, then. A merciful winter.

(Her children would all live. That's how these stories go—the ones you hate always prosper until the very end, when you find out whether or not you're the villain.)

They were seven years old then, all the way up to seven years and seven days. They can consume you even when you don't want to; you can still know they're breathing. Somewhere—perhaps in the village where the prince had found her—they were growing up, and someone was telling them their mother hated them, and it was all perfectly true.

She was frightened, looking out from the window of the tower. Who isn't frightened when they think how death is coming? But it was steadying to think she would die for an honest reason. It was good to think she'd have these years alone; these long and quiet years.

In the story, at the grand feast when the wolves appear, when the king asks the queen what punishment awaits a woman who abandons her children, she tells him that such an unfaithful mother should be danced to death.

Of course she does. He's been open about his tastes since that day in the saddle. She knows what he's planning. His eyes have sparkled for six months. The forge goes all night, practicing shoes.

It's all right. She's practiced her dancing. A tame hand and a cage are very different; the first she's never bent to, the other carries no shame. *Lupus*, she thinks when her seven sons walk in

Familiaris

the door, sulking and vicious and already tame. The last glimpse the wolves have of their mother is her smile.

Someone at the bank asks for her name. She says "Christopher's mom" without thinking, and when the teller's still waiting, she forgets for ten full seconds what else she can tell him to prove who she is.

"I have to get out of here," she tells their father at home, so hard it startles him.

"What about the beach?"

"Mosquitoes," she says.

He says, "Sand's free."

She keeps her eyes open all night and thinks about waves.

Someday, iron shoes.

Eventually, children.

AUTHOR'S NOTE

GENEVIEVE
VALENTINE

Genevieve Valentine: When I first came across "The Wolves" in "The Turnip Princess," I was struck by its almost delighted nastiness, as if Franz Xaver von Schönwerth had tripped over himself recording the story of a horrible princess who abandons her seven sons to the woods out of fear of being thought unfaithful. But the fear still seeps in around the tidy comeuppance: fear of judgment, fear of childbirth and maternity, fear of being beholden. (Princesses in fairy tales are often missing a certain agency, but this princess is cruelly taunted by her handsome prince and forced to be obsessed with fertility; I don't blame her if her agency skews a little dark.) And beneath that, more so than many of the just-the-facts stories he recorded, you can hear the fear of the storyteller; this is a story where, any way you slice it, the moral is that you're doomed. It's a tangle of fears begging to be dissected, so I did.

SEASONS OF GLASS AND IRON

Amal El-Mohtar

[*For Lara West*]

Tabitha walks, and thinks of shoes.

She has been thinking about shoes for a very long time: the length of three and a half pairs, to be precise, though it's hard to reckon in iron. Easier to reckon how many pairs are left: of the seven she set out with, three remain, strapped securely against the outside of the pack she carries, weighing it down. The seasons won't keep still, slip past her with the landscape, so she can't say for certain whether a year of walking wears out a sole, but it seems about right. She always means to count the steps, starting with the next pair, but it's easy to get distracted.

She thinks about shoes because she cannot move forward otherwise: each iron strap cuts, rubs, bruises, blisters, and her pain fuels their ability to cross rivers, mountains, airy breaches between cliffs. She must move forward, or the shoes will never be worn down. The shoes must be worn down.

It's always hard to strap on a new pair.

Three pairs of shoes ago, she was in a pine forest, and the sharp green smell of it woke something in her, something that was more than numbness, numbers. (*Number? I hardly know 'er!* She'd laughed for a week, off and on, at her little joke.) She shivered in the needled light, bundled her arms into her fur cloak but stretched her toes into the autumn earth, and wept to feel, for a moment, something like free—before the numbers crept in with the cold, and *one down, six to go* found its way into her relief that it was, in fact, possible to get through a single pair in a lifetime.

Two pairs of shoes ago, she was in the middle of a lake, striding across the deep blue of it, when the last scrap of sole gave way. She collapsed and floundered as she undid the straps, scrambled to pull the next pair off her pack, sank until she broke a toe in jamming them on, then found herself on the surface again, limping toward the far shore.

One pair of shoes ago, she was by the sea. She soaked her feet in salt and stared up at the stars and wondered whether drowning would hurt.

She recalls shoes her brothers have worn: a pair of seven-league boots, tooled in soft leather; winged sandals; satin slippers that turned one invisible. How strange, she thinks, that her brothers had shoes that lightened their steps and tightened the world, made it small and easy to explore, discover.

Perhaps, she thinks, it isn't strange at all: why shouldn't shoes help their wearers travel? Perhaps, she thinks, what's strange is the shoes women are made to wear: shoes of glass; shoes of paper; shoes of iron heated red-hot; shoes to dance to death in.

How strange, she thinks, and walks.

Amira makes an art of stillness.

She sits atop a high glass hill, its summit shaped into a throne of sorts, thick and smooth, perfectly suited to her so long as she does not move. Magic girdles her, roots her stillness through the throne. She has weathered storms here, the sleek-fingered rain glistening between glass and gown, hair and skin, seeking to shift her this way or that—but she has held herself straight, upright, a golden apple in her lap.

She is sometimes hungry, but the magic looks after that; she is often tired, and the magic encourages sleep. The magic keeps her brown skin from burning during the day, and keeps her silk-shod feet from freezing at night—so long as she is still, so long as she keeps her glass seat atop her glass hill.

From her vantage point she can see a great deal: farmers working their land; travelers walking from village to village; the occasional robbery or murder. There is much she would like to come down from her hill and tell people, but for the suitors.

Clustered and clamoring around the bottom of her glass hill are the knights, princes, shepherds' lads who have fallen violently in love with her. They shout encouragement to one another as they ride their warhorses up the glass hill, breaking against it in wave after wave, reaching for her.

As they slide down the hill, their horses foaming, legs twisted or shattered, they scream curses at her: the cunt, the witch, can't she see what she's doing to them, glass whore on a glass hill, they'll get her tomorrow, tomorrow, tomorrow.

Amira grips her golden apple. By day she distracts herself with birds: all the wild geese who fly overhead, the gulls and swifts and swallows, the larks. She remembers a story about nettle shirts thrown up to swans, and wonders if she could reach up and pluck a feather from them to give herself wings.

By night, she strings shapes around the stars, imagines familiar constellations into difference: suppose the great ladle was a sickle instead, or a bear?

When she runs out of birds and stars, she remembers that she chose this.

Tabitha first sees the glass hill as a knife's edge of light, scything a green swathe across her vision before she can look away. She is stepping out of a forest; the morning sun is vicious, bright with no heat in it; the frosted grass crunches under the press of her iron heels, but some of it melts cold relief against the skin exposed through the straps.

She sits at the forest's edge and watches the light change.

There are men at the base of the hill; their noise is a dull ringing that reminds her of the ocean. She watches them spur their horses into bleeding. Strong magic in that hill, she thinks, to make men behave so foolishly; strong magic in that hill to withstand so many iron hooves.

She looks down at her own feet, then up at the hill. She reckons the quality of her pain in numbers, but not by degree: if her pain is a six it is because it is cold, blue with an edge to it; if her pain is a seven it is red, inflamed, bleeding; if her pain is a three it has a rounded yellow feel, dull and perhaps draining infection.

Her pain at present is a five, green and brown, sturdy and stable, and ought to be enough to manage the ascent.

She waits until sunset, and sets out across the clearing.

Amira watches a mist rise as the sun sets, and her heart sings to see everything made so soft: a great cool *hush* over all, a smell of water with no stink in it, no blood or sweat. She loves to see the world so vanished, so quiet, so calm.

Her heart skips a beat when she hears the scraping, somewhere beneath her, somewhere within the mist: a grinding, scouring sort of noise, steady as her nerves aren't, because something is climbing the glass hill and this isn't how it was supposed to work, no one is supposed to be able to reach her, but magic is magic is magic and there is always stronger magic—

She thinks it is a bear, at first, then sees it is a furred hood, glimpses a pale delicate chin beneath it, a wide mouth twisted into a teeth-gritting snarl from the effort of the climb.

Amira stares, uncertain, as the hooded, horseless stranger reaches the top, and stops, and stoops, and pants, and sheds the warm weight of the fur. Amira sees a woman, and the woman sees her, and the woman looks like a feather and a sword and very, very hungry.

Amira offers up her golden apple without a word.

Tabitha had thought the woman in front of her a statue, a copper ornament, an idol, until her arm moved. Some part of her feels she should pause before accepting food from a magical woman on a glass hill, but it's dwarfed by a ravenousness she's not felt in weeks; in the shoes, she mostly forgets about her stomach until weakness threatens to prevent her from putting one foot in front of the other.

The apple doesn't look like food, but she bites into it, and the skin breaks like burnt sugar, the flesh drips clear, sweet juice. She eats it, core and all, before looking at the woman on the throne again and saying—with a gruffness she does not feel or intend— "Thank you."

"My name is Amira," says the woman, and Tabitha marvels at how she speaks without moving any other part of her body, how measured are the mechanics of her mouth. "Have you come to marry me?"

Tabitha stares. She wipes the juice from her chin, as if that could erase the golden apple from her belly. "Do I have to?"

Amira blinks. "No. Only—that's why people try to climb the hill, you know."

"Oh. No, I just—" Tabitha coughs, slightly, embarrassed. "I'm just passing through."

Silence.

"The mist was thick, I got turned around—"

"You climbed"—Amira's voice is very quiet—"a glass hill"—
and even—"by accident?"

Tabitha fidgets with the hem of her shirt.

"Well," says Amira, "it's nice to meet you, ah—"

"Tabitha."

"Yes. Very nice to meet you, Tabitha."

Further silence. Tabitha chews her bottom lip while looking
down into the darkness at the base of the hill. Then, quietly: "Why
are you even up here?"

Amira looks at her coolly. "By accident."

Tabitha snorts. "I see. Very well. Look." Tabitha points to her
iron-strapped feet. "I have to wear the shoes down. They're magic.
I have a notion that the stranger the surface—the harder it would
be to walk on something usually—the faster the sole diminishes.
So your magical hill here . . ."

Amira nods, or at least it seems to Tabitha that she nods—
it may have been more of a lengthened blink that conveyed the
impression of her head's movement.

". . . it seemed like just the thing. I didn't know there was
anyone at the top, though; I waited until the men at the bottom
had left, as they seemed a nasty lot—"

It isn't that Amira shivers, but that the quality of her stillness
grows denser. Tabitha feels something like alarm beginning a dull
ring in her belly.

"They leave as the nights turn colder. You're more than welcome
to stay," says Amira, in tones of deepest courtesy, "and scrape your
shoes against the glass."

Tabitha nods, and stays, because somewhere within the measured music of Amira's words she hears *please*.

Amira feels half-asleep, sitting and speaking with someone who isn't
about to destroy her, break her apart for the half kingdom inside.

"Have they placed you up here?" Tabitha asks, and Amira

finds it strange to hear anger that isn't directed at her, anger that seems at her service.

"No," she says softly. "I chose this." Then, before Tabitha can say anything else, "Why do you walk in iron shoes?"

Tabitha's mouth is open but her words are stopped up, and Amira can see them changing direction like a flock of starlings in her throat. She decides to change the subject.

"Have you ever heard the sound geese make when they fly overhead? I don't mean the honking, everyone hears that, but— their wings. Have you ever heard the sound of their wings?"

Tabitha smiles a little. "Like thunder, when they take off from a river."

"What? Oh." A pause; Amira has never seen a river. "No—it's nothing like that when they fly above you. It's . . . a creaking, like a stove door with no squeak in it, as if the geese are machines dressed in flesh and feathers. It's a beautiful sound—beneath the honking it's a low drone, but if they're flying quietly, it's like . . . clothing, somehow, like if you listened just right, you might find yourself wearing wings."

Without noticing, Amira had closed her eyes while speaking of the geese; she opens them to see Tabitha looking at her with curious focus, and feels briefly disoriented by the scrutiny. She isn't used to being listened to.

"If we're lucky," she says softly, turning a golden apple around and around in her hands, "we'll hear some tonight. It's the right time of year."

Tabitha opens her mouth, then shuts it so hard her back teeth meet. She does not ask *how long have you been sitting here, that you know when to expect the geese*; she does not ask *where did that golden apple come from? Didn't I just eat it?* She understands what Amira is doing and is grateful; she does not want to talk about the shoes.

"I've never heard that sound," she says instead, slowly, trying not to look at the apple. "But I've seen them on rivers and lakes. Hundreds at a time, clamoring like old wives at a well, until something startles them into rising, and then it's like drums, or thunder, or a storm of winds through branches. An enormous sound, almost deafening—not one to listen closely for."

"I would love to hear that," Amira whispers, looking out toward the woods. "To see them. What do they look like?"

"Thick, dark—" Tabitha reaches for words. "Like the river itself is rising, lifting its skirts and taking off."

Amira smiles, and Tabitha feels a tangled warmth in her chest at the thought of having given her something.

"Would you like another apple?" offers Amira, and notes the wariness in Tabitha's eye. "They keep coming back. I eat them myself from time to time. I wasn't sure if—I thought it was meant as a prize for whoever climbed the hill, but I suppose the notion is they don't go away unless I give them to a man."

Tabitha frowns, but accepts. As she eats, Amira feels Tabitha's eyes on her empty hands, waiting to catch the apple's reappearance, and tries not to smile—she'd done as much herself the first fifty or so times, testing the magic for loopholes. Novel, however, to watch someone watching for the apple.

As Tabitha nears the last bite, Amira sees her look confused, distracted, as if by a hair on her tongue or an unfamiliar smell—and then the apple's in Amira's hand again, feeling for all the world like it never left.

"I don't think the magic lets us see it happen," says Amira, almost by way of apology for Tabitha's evident disappointment. "But so long as I sit here, I have one."

"I'd like to try that again," says Tabitha, and Amira smiles.

First, Tabitha waits. She counts the seconds, watching Amira's empty hands. After seven hundred seconds, there is an apple in Amira's hand. Amira stares at it, looking from it to the one in Tabitha's.

"That's—never happened before. I didn't think there could be more than one at a time."

Tabitha takes the second apple from her but bites into it, counting the mouthfuls slowly, watching Amira's hands the while. After the seventh bite, Amira's hands are full again. She hands the third apple over without a word.

Tabitha counts—the moments, the bites, the number of apples—until there are seven in her lap; when she takes an eighth from Amira, the first seven turn to sand.

"I think it's the magic on me," says Tabitha thoughtfully, dusting the apple sand out of her fur. "I'm bound in sevens—you're bound in ones. You can hold only one apple at a time—I can hold seven. Funny, isn't it?"

Amira's smile looks strained and vague, and only after a moment does Tabitha realize she's watching the wind-caught sand blowing off the hill.

Autumn crackles into winter, and frost rimes the glass hill into diamonds. By day, Amira watches fewer and fewer men slide down it while Tabitha sits by her, huddled into her fur; by night, Tabitha walks in slow circles around her as they talk about anything but glass and iron. While Tabitha walks, Amira looks more closely at her shackled feet, always glancing away before she can be drawn into staring. Through the sandal-like straps that wrap up to her ankle, Amira can see they are blackened, twisted ruins, toes bent at odd angles, scabbed and scarred.

One morning, Amira wakes to surprising warmth, and finds Tabitha's fur draped around her. She is so startled she almost rises from her seat to find her—has she left? Is she gone?—but Tabitha walks briskly back into her line of sight before Amira can do anything drastic, rubbing her thin arms, blowing on her fingers. Amira is aghast.

"Why did you give me your cloak? Take it back!"

"Your lips were turning blue in your sleep, and you can't *move*—"

"It's all right, Tabitha, please—" The desperation in Amira's voice stops Tabitha's circling, pins her in place. Reluctantly, she takes her fur back, draws it over her own shoulders again. "The apples—or the hill itself, I'm not sure—keep me warm enough. Here, have another."

Tabitha looks unconvinced. "But you looked so cold—"

"Perhaps it's like your feet," says Amira, before she can stop herself. "They look broken, but you can still walk on them."

Tabitha stares at her for a long moment, before accepting the apple. "They feel broken too. Although"—shifting her gaze to the apple, lowering her voice—"less and less, lately."

She takes a bite. While she eats, Amira ventures, quietly, "I thought you'd left."

Tabitha raises an eyebrow, swallows, and chuckles. "Without my cloak, in winter? I like you, Amira, but—" *Not that much* dies on her tongue, as she tastes the lie in it. She coughs. "That would be silly. Anyway, I wouldn't leave you without saying good-bye." An uncertain pause then. "Though, if you tire of company—"

"No," says Amira, swiftly, surely. "No."

Snow falls, and the last of the suitors abandon their camps, grumbling home. Tabitha walks her circles around Amira's throne by day now as well as night, unafraid of being seen.

"They won't be back until spring," says Amira, smiling. "Though then they keep their efforts up well into the night as the days get longer. Perhaps to make up for lost time."

Tabitha frowns, and something in the circle of their talk tightens enough for her to ask, as she walks, "How many winters have you spent up here?"

Amira shrugs. "Three, I think. How many winters have you spent in those shoes?"

"This is their first," says Tabitha, pausing. "But there were three pairs before this one."

"Ah. Is this the last?"

Tabitha chuckles. "No. Seven in all. And I'm only halfway through this one."

Amira nods. "Perhaps, come spring, you'll have finished it."

"Perhaps," says Tabitha, before beginning her circuit again.

Winter thaws, and everything smells of snowmelt and wet wood. Tabitha ventures down the glass hill and brings Amira snowdrops, twining them into her dark hair. "They look like stars," murmurs Tabitha, and something in Amira creaks and snaps like ice on a bough.

"Tabitha," she says, "it's almost spring."

"Mm," says Tabitha, intent on a tricky braid.

"I'd like—" Amira draws a deep, quiet breath. "I'd like to tell you a story."

Tabitha pauses—then, resuming her braiding, says, "I'd like to hear one."

"I don't know if I'm any good at telling stories," Amira adds, turning a golden apple over and over in her hands, "but that's no reason not to try."

Once upon a time there was a rich king who had no sons, and whose only daughter was too beautiful. She was so beautiful that men could not stop themselves from reaching out to touch her in corridors or following her to her rooms, so beautiful that words of desire tumbled from men's lips like diamonds and toads, irresistible and unstoppable. The king took pity on these men and drew his daughter aside, saying, Daughter, only a husband can break the spell over these men; only a husband can prevent them from behaving so gallantly toward you.

When the king's daughter suggested a ball, that these men might find husbands for themselves and so be civilized, the king was not amused. You must be wed, said the king, before some guard cannot but help himself to your virtue.

The king's daughter was afraid, and said, Suppose you sent me away?

No, said the king, for how should I keep an eye on you then?

The king's daughter, who did not want a husband, said, Suppose you chose a neighboring prince for me?

Impossible, said the king, for you are my only daughter, and I cannot favor one neighbor over another; the balance of power is precarious and complicated.

The king's daughter read an unspeakable conclusion in her father's eye, and in a rush to keep it from reaching his mouth, said, Suppose you placed me atop a glass hill where none could reach me, and say that only the man who can ride up the hill in full armor may claim me as his bride?

But that is an impossible task, said the king, looking thoughtful.

Then you may keep your kingdom whole, and your eye on me, and men safe from me, said his daughter.

It was done just as she said, and by her will. And if she's not gone, she lives there still.

When Amira stops speaking, she is taken aback to feel Tabitha scowling at her.

"That," growls Tabitha, "is *absurd*."

Amira blinks. She had expected, she realizes, some sympathy, some understanding. "Oh?"

"What father seeks to protect men from their pursuit of his daughter? As well seek to protect the wolf from the rabbit!"

"I am not a rabbit," says Amira, though Tabitha, who has

dropped her hair and is pacing, incensed, continues.

"How could it be your fault that men are loutish and ill-mannered? Amira, I promise you, if your hair were straw and your face dull as dishwater, men—bad men—would still behave this way. Do you think the suitors around the hill can see what you look like, all the way up here?"

Amira keeps quiet, unsure what to say—she wonders why she wants to apologize with one side of her mouth and defend herself with the other.

"You said you *chose* this," Tabitha spits. "What manner of choice was that? A wolf's maw or a glass hill."

"On the hill," says Amira, lips tight, "I want for nothing. I do not need food or drink or shelter. No one can touch me. That's all I ever wanted—for no one to be able to touch me. So long as I sit here, and eat apples, and do not move, I have everything I want."

Tabitha is silent for a moment. Then, more gently than before, she says, "I thought you wanted to see a river full of geese."

Amira says nothing.

Tabitha says, still more gently, "Mine are not the only iron shoes in the world."

Still nothing. Amira's heart grinds within her, until Tabitha sighs.

"Let me tell you a story about iron shoes."

Once upon a time, a woman fell in love with a bear. She didn't mean to; it was only that he was both fearsome and kind to her, that he was dangerous and clever and could teach her about hunting salmon and harvesting wild honey, and she had been lonely for a long time. She felt special with his eyes on her, for what other woman could say she was loved by a bear without being torn between his teeth? She loved him for loving her as he loved no one else.

They were wed, and at night the bear put on a man's shape to share her bed in the dark. At first he was gentle and kind, and the woman was happy; but in time the bear began to change—not his shape, which she knew as well as her own, but his manner. He grew bitter and jealous, accused her of longing for a bear who was a man day and night. He said she was a terrible wife who knew nothing of how to please bears. By day he spoke to her in a language of thorns and claws, and by night he hurt her with his body. It was hard for the woman to endure, but how can one love a bear entirely without pain? She only worked harder to please him.

In the seventh year of their marriage, the woman begged her husband to allow her to go visit her family. He consented to her departure on the condition that she not be alone with her mother, for surely her mother would poison her against him. She promised—but the woman's mother saw the marks on her, the bruises and scratches, and hurried her into a room alone. In a moment of weakness, the woman listened to her mother's words against her husband, calling him a monster, a demon. Her mother insisted that she leave him—but how could she? He was still her own dear husband in spite of it all—she only wished him to be as he had been when she first married him. Perhaps he was under a curse, after all, and only she could lift it?

Burn his bear skin, said her mother. Perhaps that is his curse. Perhaps he longs to be a man day and night but is forbidden to say so.

When she returned to her husband, he seemed to have missed her, and was kind and sweet with her. In the night while he slept next to her in his man's shape, she gathered up his bear skin as quietly as she could, built up the fire, and threw it in.

The skin did not burn. But it began to scream.

It woke her husband, who flew into a great rage, saying she had broken her promise to him. When the woman wept that she had only wanted to free him from his curse, he picked up the skin, tossed it over her shoulders, and threw a bag of iron shoes at her feet. He said that the only way to make him a man day and night was to wear his bear's skin while wearing out seven pairs of iron shoes, one for each year of their marriage.

So she set out to do so.

Amira's eyes are wide and rimmed in red, and Tabitha flushes, picks at a burr caught in her husband's fur.

"I knew marriage was monstrous," says Amira, "but I never imagined—"

Tabitha shrugs. "It wasn't all bad. And I broke my promise— if I hadn't seen my mother, I would never have thought to try and burn the skin. Promises are important to bears. This, here"—she gestures at the glass hill—"*this* is monstrous: to keep you prisoner, to prevent you from moving or speaking—"

"Your husband wanted to keep you from speaking! To your *mother!*"

"And look what happened when I did," says Tabitha stiffly. "It was a test of loyalty, and I failed it. You did *nothing wrong.*"

"That's funny," says Amira, unsmiling, "because to me, every day feels like a test: Will I move from this hill or not, will I grasp at a bird or not, will I toss an apple down to a man when I shouldn't, will I speak too loudly, will I give them a reason to hurt me and fall off the hill, and every day I don't is a day I pass—"

"That's different. That's dreadful."

"I don't see the difference!"

"You don't *love* this hill!"

"I love you," says Amira, very softly. "I love you, and I do not understand how someone who loves you would want to hurt you, or make you walk in iron shoes."

Tabitha chews her lips, trying to shape words from them, and fails.

"I told my story poorly," she says, finally. "I told it selfishly. I did not speak of how good he was—how he made me laugh, the things

106 —

he taught me. I could live in the iron shoes because of his guidance, because of knowing the poison berry from the pure, because he taught me to hunt. What happened to him, the change in him"— Tabitha feels very tired—"it must have had to do with me. I was meant to endure it until the curse broke, and I failed. It's the only thing that makes sense."

Amira looks at Tabitha's ruined feet.

"Do you truly believe," she says, with all the care she pours into keeping her spine taut and straight on her glass seat, "that I had nothing to do with those men's attentions? That they would have behaved that way no matter what I looked like?"

"Yes," says Tabitha firmly.

"Then is it not possible"—hesitant, now, to even speak the thought—"that your husband's cruelty had nothing to do with you? That it had nothing to do with a curse? You said he hurt you in both his shapes."

"But I—"

"If you've worn your shoes halfway down, shouldn't you be bending your steps toward him again, that the last pair be destroyed near the home you shared?"

In the shifting light of the moon both their faces have a bluish cast, but Amira sees Tabitha's go gray.

"When I was a girl," says Tabitha thickly, as if working around something in her throat, "I dreamt of marriage as a golden thread between hearts—a ribbon binding one to the other, warm as a day in summer. I did not dream a chain of iron shoes."

"Tabitha"—and Amira does not know what to do except to reach for her hand, clutch it, look at her in the way she looks at the geese, longing to speak and be understood—"you did nothing wrong."

Tabitha holds Amira's gaze. "Neither did you."

They stay that way for a long time, until the sound of seven geese's beating wings startles them into looking up at the stars.

The days and nights grow warmer; more and more geese fly over-head. One morning Tabitha begins to walk her circle around Amira when she stumbles, trips, and falls forward into Amira's arms.

"Are you all right?" Amira whispers, while Tabitha clutches at the throne, shaking her head, suddenly unsteady.

"The shoes," she says, marveling. "They're finished. The fourth pair. Amira." Tabitha laughs, surprises herself to hear the sound more like a sob. "They're done."

Amira smiles at her, bends forward to kiss her forehead. "Congratulations," she murmurs, and Tabitha hears much more than the word as she reaches, shaky, wobbling, for the next pair in her pack.

"Wait," says Amira quietly, and Tabitha pauses. "Wait. Please. Don't—" Amira bites her lip, looks away. "You don't have to—you can stay here without—"

Tabitha understands, and returns her hand to Amira's. "I can't stay up here forever. I have to leave before the suitors come back."

Amira draws a deep breath. "I know."

"I've had a thought, though."

"Oh?" Amira smiles softly. "Do you want to marry me after all?"

"Yes."

Amira's stillness turns crystalline in her surprise.

Tabitha is talking, and Amira can barely understand it, feels Tabitha's words slipping off her mind like sand off a glass hill. Any-thing, anything to keep her from putting her feet back in those iron cages—

"I mean—not as a husband would. But to take you away from here. If you want. Before your suitors return. Can I do that?"

Amira looks at the golden apple in her hand. "I don't know—where would we go?"

"Anywhere! The shoes can walk anywhere, over anything—"

"Back to your husband?"

Something like a thunderclap crosses Tabitha's face. "No. Not there."

Amira looks up. "If we are to marry, I insist on an exchange of gifts. Leave the fur and the shoes behind."

"But—"

"I know what they cost you. I don't want to walk on air and darkness if the price is your pain."

"Amira," says Tabitha helplessly, "I don't think I can walk without them anymore."

"Have you tried? You've been eating golden apples a long while. And you can lean on me."

"But—they might be useful—"

"The glass hill has been very useful to me," says Amira quietly, "and the golden apples have kept me warm and whole and fed. But I will leave them—I will follow you into woods and across fields, I will be hungry and cold and my feet will hurt. But if you are with me, Tabitha, then I will learn to hunt and fish and tell the poison berry from the pure, and I will see a river raise its skirt of geese, and listen to them make a sound like thunder. Do you believe I can do this?"

"Yes," says Tabitha, a choking in her voice, "yes, I do."

"I believe you can walk without iron shoes. Leave them here— and in exchange, I will give you my shoes of silk, and we will fill your pack with seven golden apples, and if you eat from them sparingly, perhaps they will help you walk until we can find you something better."

"But we can't climb down the hill without a pair of shoes!"

"We don't need to." Amira smiles, stroking Tabitha's hair. "Falling's easy—it's keeping still that's hard."

Neither says anything for a time. Then, carefully, for the hill is slippery to her now, Tabitha sheds her fur cloak, unstraps the iron shoes from her feet, and gives them and her pack to Amira.

— 109

Amira removes the three remaining pairs and replaces them with apples, drawing the pack's straps tight over the seventh. She passes the pack back to Tabitha, who shoulders it.

Then, taking Tabitha's hands in hers, Amira breathes deep and stands up.

The glass throne cracks. There is a sound like hard rain, a roar of whispers as the glass hill shivers into sand. It swallows fur and shoes; it swallows Amira and Tabitha together; it settles into a dome-shaped dune with a final hiss.

Hands still clasped, Amira and Tabitha tumble out of it together, coughing, laughing, shaking sand from their hair and skin. They stand, and wait, and no golden apple appears to part their hands from each other.

"Where should we go?" whispers one to the other.

"Away," she replies, and holding on to each other, they stumble into the spring, the wide world rising to meet them with the dawn.

AUTHOR'S NOTE

AMAL
EL-MOHTAR

Amal El-Mohtar: "Seasons of Glass and Iron" took shape at the request of my seven-year-old niece, Lara, who asked me to tell her a fairy tale. I wanted to give her one while also telling a story about women rescuing each other, and was struck by the thought that the iron shoes in "The Black Bull of Norroway" might enable the climbing of "The Glass Mountain." After I told Lara her story—making quick work of leaving the glass hill in order to send the girls off on adventures together—the idea stuck with me. I knew I had to write it out at length for this particular anthology—a story about women reaching out of their respective tales to read each other's lives against their grain.

I'm often amazed by the things we're willing to endure that we would never allow our loved ones to suffer, and the double standards that govern the stories we tell ourselves. I treasure the ways in which friendship can undermine the poisonously seductive narratives we sometimes trap ourselves in, and I hope this story goes a little way toward celebrating the enormity of what friendship means to me.

BADGIRL, THE DEADMAN, AND
THE WHEEL OF FORTUNE

Catherynne M. Valente

he Deadman always wore red when he came calling. Not all over red. Just a flash, like Mars in the nighttime. A coat, a long scarf, socks, a leather belt. An old sucked-dry rose in his buttonhole. A woolen cap with two little holes in it like bite marks. A fake ruby chip in his ear. One time he wore lipstick, and I cried in my hiding place. I always cried when the Deadman came, but that time I cried right away and I didn't stop. Real quiet with my hands over my mouth. I can be a little black cat when I want, so he didn't hear.

Daddy always used to say the Deadman came to bring him a cup of sugar, and when I was a tiny dumb thing I thought that meant he was gonna make me cookies or blue Kool-Aid or a cake with yellow frosting even though it wasn't usually my birthday. I liked yellow frosting best because it looked like all the lights in our apartment turned on at one time and nothing can be scary when all the lights are turned on at one time. I liked blue Kool-Aid best because it turned my tongue the color of outside.

So I hid from the Deadman in my tree house and thought real hard about blue Kool-Aid with ice knocking around in it and a cake all for me with so much frosting it looked like an ice cream cone. My tree house wasn't a tree house, though. It was the big closet in the hallway between the two bedrooms, the special kind of closet that has four legs like a chair and doors that swing out and drawers under the swinging doors. I heard the Deadman call it something French-sounding but he said it like a pirate kiss. *Arrrr. Mwah.* Daddy called it my tree house because it's made of trees nailed together, so what's the difference when you think about it. Whenever the Deadman came with his cup of sugar, I pulled out the drawers like a staircase, climbed in, shut the swinging doors tight behind me, and closed the latch Daddy screwed onto the inside of the pirate kiss closet. It was nice in there. Nothing much in it but me and a purple sweater half falling off a wire hanger that might've been my mom's, but might not've just as easy. It smelled like a mostly chopped-down forest and crusty pennies. I tucked up my knees under my chin and held my breath, turned into a little black cat that didn't make one single sound.

"You got what I need?" my Daddy said to the Deadman. And the Deadman said back, "If you got what *I* need, Mudpuddle, I got the whole world right here in my pocket."

And then there was a bunch of rustling and coughing and little words that don't mean anything except filling up the quiet, and in the middle of those funny soft nothing-noises the Deadman would start telling a joke, but a dumb joke, like the kind you read on Laffy Taffy wrappers. Nobody likes those jokes but the Deadman.

"Hey, did you hear the one about the horse and the submarine?"

"Yeah, I heard that one, D," my Daddy always said, even though

I never heard him tell a joke ever in my whole life and I don't think he really knew the one about the horse and the submarine at all. But after that the Deadman would laugh a laugh that sounded like a swear word even though it didn't have any words in it and he'd leave and I could breathe again.

Everybody called my Daddy Mudpuddle, just like everybody called the Deadman the Deadman and everybody called me Badgirl even though my name is Loula, which is pretty nice and feels good to say, like raindrops in your mouth. Where I live, we don't call anybody by the name they got at the hospital.

"It's 'cause I'm a real honest-to-Jesus old-timey gentleman, Badgirl," Daddy told me, and clinked our mugs together. His had a lot of whiskey and mine had a very little whiskey, only enough to make me feel grown up and stop asking for cocoa. "Almost a prince, like that cat who went around sniffing all those girls' feet back when. So when I'm escorting a lady friend and I see a big nasty mudpuddle in our way, I always take off my coat and lay it down so my girl can walk across without getting her shoes dirty."

"Daddy, that's the stupidest thing I ever heard. Who cares if her shoes get dirty when your coat gets *ruined*? Why can't she just walk around the puddle? What's wrong with her?"

Daddy Mudpuddle laughed and laughed, even though what I said was way smarter than what he said. I thought people called him Mudpuddle because his clothes usually weren't too clean, and the cuffs of all his pants were all ripped up and stained like he'd walked through the mud. But I didn't say so. It's not a nice thing to say. I liked the story where my Daddy's almost a prince better, so I let that one stay, like a really good finger painting hung up on the refrigerator. Besides, I've never done anything very bad except get born and one time swallow a toy car and have to go to the hospital, which Daddy couldn't afford, but I still get called Badgirl. One time Daddy tucked me into bed and kissed my nose and whispered, "It's 'cause you were so good your Mama and I had to call you Badgirl so the angels wouldn't come and take you away for their own."

And that's stupider than putting your coat down on a mud-puddle, so I figure names don't really have any reasons or stories hiding inside them. I wasn't good enough to still have a mama now. I wasn't good enough not to swallow a toy car and cost all that money. Names just happen to you and then you go on living with them on your shoulder like an ugly old parrot.

I remember the first time the Deadman came and Daddy didn't have what he needed. But only barely. I wasn't tiny anymore but I was still little. Daddy'd taken me to the thrift shop and bought me a new dress with blue and yellow butterflies on it and a green bow in the back for my first day of school, which was in a week. It was the most beautiful dress I'd ever seen. It had green buttons and every butterfly was a little different, just like real life. It was gonna make me pretty for school, and school was gonna make me smart. So I decided to wear it every day until school started so that I could soak up the smart in that dress and then I'd be way ahead of all the other kids on day one. You think funny things when you're little. You can laugh at me if you want. I'm not ashamed.

Anyway, I was playing with the toy from my Happy Meal, which was a princess whose head came off and you could stick it on three different plastic bodies wearing different ball gowns. I took her head off and on and off and on, but I got bored with it pretty fast because what can you do with a toy like that? What kind of make-believe can you get going about a girl whose head comes off? All the ones I could think of were scary.

Daddy was all jittery and anxious and biting his fingernails. I don't think he liked the princess either. She didn't even have any shoes to get dirty. She didn't have any *feet*. The bottoms of her ball-gown bodies were all flat, smooth plastic like the bottom of a glass. He wasn't himself. Usually he'd give me plenty of warning.

CATHERYNNE
M. VALENTE

He never wanted the Deadman to see me. He said nobody who loved their baby girl would let the Deadman near her. He'd say:

"Deadman's here, Badgirl, go up in your tree house." And I'd go, even though I didn't hear anything out on the stoop. I never heard the Deadman coming, never heard a car engine or a bike bell or boots on the sidewalk or anything till he knocked on the door.

But this time he didn't even seem to remember I was there. The knock happened and I wasn't safe in my tree house with the purple sweater and the pirate kisses. I wasn't turned into a little black cat that never made a sound.

"Daddy!" I whispered, and then he did remember me, and picked me up in his arms and carried me down the hall and put me in his bedroom and shut the door.

But Daddy's door doesn't shut all the way. It's got a bend in the latch. Daddy's room had a lot of cigarettes put out on things other than ash trays and a TV and a painting of frogs on the wall. I didn't like the smell but I did like being in there because normally I wasn't allowed. But even though that part was exciting, I started shaking all over. Deadman's here. I wasn't safe. Safe meant my tree house. Safe meant the drawers turned into a staircase and the smell like a chopped-up forest. I watched Daddy go back down the hall. I could make it. Little black cats are fast, too. I slipped out the bedroom door and scrambled up into the pirate kiss closet. I didn't even pull out the drawers into a staircase, I got up in one jump. I locked the lock and held my breath and turned into a little black cat that doesn't ever make a sound. I pulled my butterfly dress over my knees and felt the smart ooze out of the fabric and into me. The smart felt big and good, like having your own TV in your bedroom.

The Deadman knocked. I could see him through the crack between the tree-house doors. He had a pinky ring on with a red stone in it. The Deadman had real nice eyebrows and a long, skinny face. His shirt was cut low but he didn't have any hair on his chest.

"You got what I need?" Daddy said. And the Deadman said back:

"If you got what *I* need, Mudpuddle, I got the whole world right here in my pocket."

Only Daddy didn't. Daddy stared at his shoes. He looked like a princess-body without a princess-head.

"I'm just a little short, D. I started a new job, you know, and with a new job you don't get paid the first two weeks. But I'm good for it."

The Deadman didn't say anything. Daddy'd been short on his sugar a lot lately. And I knew he didn't have a new job. Or an old one.

"Come on, man. I'm a good person. I know I owe you plenty, but owing doesn't make a man less needful. I'll pay you in two weeks, I swear. My word is as good as the lock on a bank. I'm a gentleman. Ask anybody."

The Deadman looked my Daddy up and down. Then he looked past him, into the living room, at my princess's three headless bodies lying on the carpet. The Deadman chewed on something. I thought maybe it was bubble gum. Red bubble gum, I supposed. Finally, he twisted his pinky ring around and said:

"Did you ever hear the one about the devil and the fiddle?"

Daddy sort of fell apart without moving. He was still standing up, but only on the outside. On the inside, he was crumpled up on the ground. "Yeah, I heard that one, D," he sighed.

"I tell you what," the Deadman said. "I'll give you what you need this week—hell, next week too and the one after—if you give me whatever's in that armoire back there."

Arrr. Mwah.

Daddy looked over his shoulder, all frantic. But then he remembered that he'd put me in his room with his TV and his painting of frogs and I was safe as a fish in a bowl. Only I wasn't.

"You sure, Deadman? I mean, there's nothing in there but an old purple sweater and a couple of moths."

Daddy kept looking on down the hall like he could see me. Did he see me? Did he know? Little black cats have eyes that shine in the dark. Sometimes I think the only important thing in my whole life is knowing whether or not Daddy could see the shine on my eye through the crack between the doors. But I can't ever know that.

"Then I'll guess I'll have something to keep me warm and something to lead me to the light, my man," laughed the Deadman, and he made a thing with his mouth like a smile. It mostly was a smile. On somebody else it would have definitely been a smile. But it wasn't a smile, really, and I knew it. It was a scream. *No, Daddy. I'm in here. It's me.* But I still didn't make a sound, because Daddy loved me and didn't ever want the Deadman to see me.

"Okay, D." Daddy shrugged like it didn't matter to him at all. Like he couldn't see. Maybe he didn't. Maybe he really put his coat down over those mudpuddles.

The Deadman gave him something small. I couldn't tell what it was. It wasn't a cup of sugar, for sure. How could something a man needs so much be so small? Daddy started back toward my tree house, but the Deadman stopped him, grabbed his arm.

"You ever hear the one about the cat who broke his promise?"

Daddy swallowed hard. "Yeah, Deadman. I heard that one a bunch of times."

Mudpuddle hit the light switch in the hall and the lamp came on, the one that had all those dead bugs on the inside of it. The Deadman danced on ahead of him and took a big swanky breath like he'd bought those lungs in France. He hauled on the doors of my tree house, but they didn't come open because of the secret latch on the inside. Daddy Mudpuddle put his hands over his face and sank down on his heels.

"This thing got a key?" the Deadman said, but the way he said it was all full of knowing the *arrr mwah* had more than a moth inside.

It's okay, I thought, and squeezed my eyes tight. I sank down in my blue-and-yellow-butterfly dress. *I'm a little black cat. Little black cats can be invisible if they want.*

Daddy looked sick. His face was like the skin on old soup. *I'm a little black cat and I have magic.* He flicked out his penknife and stuck it in the crack between the doors. The latch lifted up. *I'm a little black cat and little black cats can do anything.* The Deadman opened the doors like a window on his best morning.

The Deadman didn't say anything for a good while. He looked right at me, smiling and shining and thinking Deadman thoughts. His eyes had blue flecks in them, like someone had spilled paint on his insides. *I'm a little black cat and no one can see me.* He pulled down the purple sweater and shut the doors again.

"I'll come back for the moths, Mudpuddle. It's such a cold day out. I'm shivering already. You stay in and enjoy yourself. Have a hot drink."

The Deadman took his red and disappeared back out the door.

After that, the Deadman came around a lot more often. I didn't have to hide anymore, though sometimes I did anyway. Mostly I played with my toys and thought about who came up with the names for all the colors in the sixty-four-color crayon box or whether or not rhinoceroses were friendly to girls who really liked rhinoceroses or how much three times four was because those are the kind of things you think about when you've soaked up all the smart in your dress and some of the smart in your school, too. Deadman and Daddy got to be best friends. They didn't talk about the day of the closet, ever. They'd lay around and drink and eat plain tortillas out of the bag and watch game shows on the living room TV. The Deadman always knew all the answers. The first thing I ever said to him was:

"Why don't you go on one of those shows? You'd make a million dollars and you could move to a nice house that's really far away."

I popped my princess's head off and stuck it on the blue ball-gown body. The Deadman turned his head and looked at me like I was a twenty-dollar bill lying on the sidewalk with no one around.

"Wouldn't be fair to all those other contestants, Badgirl." He glanced back toward the TV. "What is plutonium?" he said to the game-show man in the gray suit. Then back to me: "Why don't you come and sit by me? I'll let you have a sip of my . . . what are we drinking, Muddy? My vodka 'n' OJ."

"Don't want it."

"Come on, it's just like water. It'll make you grow up fierce and bright."

But I didn't want his nasty vodka in his dirty mug that had a cartoon cactus on it saying GOOD MORNING ALBUQUERQUE. I didn't know where Albuquerque was, but I hated it because the Deadman put his mouth on the *A* and ruined it forever.

"Don't be rude, Badgirl," my Daddy said, because he loved me but he'd heard the one about the cat who broke his promise and he didn't want to hear it again.

So I sat down between them and I hated them both and I drank out of the Albuquerque mug while the man in the gray suit told us that the dollar values had doubled. The Deadman touched my hair, but after a while he stopped because little black cats bite when strangers pet them. Everyone knows that.

The Deadman started showing up in the mornings and saying he'd walk me to school so Daddy could get to his work on time. Daddy didn't have a work, but he made me promise never to tell the Deadman that, so I didn't tell, even though nobody who has a work lives where we do and eats powdered mashed potatoes without unpowdering them. I said I didn't need to be walked anywhere because I wasn't a baby, but the Deadman just stared down the hall at the pirate kiss closet till Daddy looked too and then nobody said anything but I had to walk to school with the Deadman.

I didn't like walking with the Deadman. His hands were clammy even when he wore gloves, and he always took the long way. He talked a lot but I could never remember what he said after. One time I thought I should ask him questions about himself because that's what nice girls do, so I asked him where he was from. Grown-ups asked each other that all the time. The Deadman swept out his arm all grand for no reason.

"Paris, France!"

"That's a lie. You're a liar."

"You got me, Badgirl. You're too good for the likes of me. The truth is, I'm from the continent of Atlantis. My parents had a squat on the banks of the river Styx."

"Is that in the Bronx?"

"Yeah, Badgirl. That's just where it is. You're smarter than a sack of owls, you are."

"It's 'cause of my dress," I said proudly.

A little while after that, the Deadman started walking me home from school too. He slicked up his hair fancy and told my teacher he was my uncle. Had a signed slip from Daddy and everything. But we never made it all the way home. He'd stand me on a corner and give me a box that had pills inside it, so bright they looked like Skittles. And he said:

"You're so good, Badgirl. Nobody'll mess with you on account of how good you are. You're just as clean and bright as New Year's Day."

"I wanna go home."

"Naw, you can't yet. This here is medicine. Lots of people need medicine. You know how you hate it when you get sick. You don't want people to get sick when you could make them better, do you? Just stand here and keep the box in your backpack, and when sick people come asking, take their money and give them

— 121

a couple of whatever color they ask for. If you do a good job, I'll buy you a new dress."

I sniffled. It was fall and the damp came with fall. I had a wet leaf stuck to my shoe. "I don't want a new dress," I whispered.

"Well, a new doll, then. God knows a girl needs more than that ratty headless thing you got. I'll come back for you and we'll get back before your Daddy finishes his work."

I didn't have mittens so my hands got tingly and cold and then I couldn't feel them anymore. I waited on the corner and all kinds of strangers came up talking to me like we were friends and I did what the Deadman said I had to. My fingers felt like they were made out of silver so I pretended that was the truth, that I had beautiful silver hands with pictures scratched onto them like the fancy dishes on TV. And every time I had to touch somebody strange to me so I could give over their medicine, I pretended my beautiful silver hands turned them into game-show contestants with perfect teeth and fluffy hair and name tags the color of luck.

At Christmastime the Deadman brought over a tree with one red ball on it and a strand of lights with only three bulbs working. He had on red velvet elf shoes like the kind Santa's helpers wear at the mall, only his were old and dark and the bells didn't make any sound. He also brought a bottle of brandy and some cheeseburgers and a cake from the grocery store with HAPPY BIRTHDAY ALEXIS written on it in hot pink frosting. I could read it by myself by then, even though I'd had to stop wearing my smart dress because it got holes in it and all the buttons fell off. The Deadman set it all out like he was Santa but he was *not* Santa, and I bet Santa never came to his house when he was little, if the Deadman ever had been little. He never did bring me a new doll or a new dress. Daddy put on that show where they play part of a song and you have to guess what it's called.

Daddy and the Deadman had gotten so used to having me around they didn't bother hiding anything anymore.

"'Bennie and the Jets,'" the Deadman said. It took the blonde lady on TV forever to get it. She squealed when she did and jumped up and down. Her earrings glittered in the stage lights like fire.

They ate some cake. It was red velvet on the inside, but I didn't feel right eating Alexis's birthday cake. I ate half a cheeseburger but it was cold and the ketchup tasted like glue. The Deadman gave Daddy his Christmas present. Daddy didn't say thank you. He didn't say very much anymore. He just took the little small lump wrapped in red tissue paper from the Deadman and shook some out into a spoon. It did look like sugar after all. He flicked a lighter under the spoon and held it there until the sugar got all melted and brown and gluggy. It was sort of oily on top too, like spilled gas.

Like a mudpuddle.

Then the Deadman handed him a needle, like the kind at the doctor's office when you have to get your shots because otherwise you'll get sick. I pulled the head off my princess and stuck it on the body with the pink ball gown. Daddy tied one of my hair ribbons around his arm and the Deadman stuck the needle in the mudpuddle first, and into Daddy second. Then he did it all over again on himself. Daddy smiled and his face got round and happy. It got to be his own face again. Daddy has a good face. He patted his lap for me to come sit with him and I did and it was Christmas for a minute.

"'How Deep Is Your Love,'" the Deadman said. Another blonde lady frowned on the TV. She couldn't think of the song. Poor lady. I didn't know that song either. But I knew the next one because it was Michael Jackson and I knew all his songs.

"'Billie Jean,'" I whispered. Daddy was asleep.

"C'mere, Badgirl," said the Deadman.

"Don't want to."

"Why you afraid of me?"

"I'm not afraid. Little black cats aren't afraid of anything."

"Come on, Badgirl. I'm not gonna hurt you. I got you a present. Make you grow up quick and sharp."

"Don't want to."

The Deadman lit himself a cigarette. He had the same don't-get-sick shot Daddy had, so how come he didn't just go to sleep and leave me alone? I'd have cleaned up the dishes and made sure the TV got turned off. I did it all the time.

"Your dad promised me whatever was in the armoire. You were in there. So you have to do what I say. I own you. I've been nice about it, because you're such a little thing, but it's hard for a man like me to keep being nice." The Deadman started doing his trick with the mudpuddle and the spoon again. "I gotta carry that nice all day, and Badgirl, I tell you what, it is *heavy.* I wanna put it down. My shoulders are *aching.* So you better come when I call or else I'm liable to just drop my nice right on the ground and break it into a hundred pieces."

"Don't be rude, Badgirl," Daddy murmured in his sleep. I looked up at his scruffy chin and something popped and spat inside me like grease and it made a stain on my insides that spelled out *I hate my Daddy* and I felt ashamed. He wasn't even awake. He didn't know anything. But I still hated him because little black cats don't know how to forgive anybody.

I think it's against the law for a person to own another person, but maybe he did own me because in a flash minute I was sitting down next to the Deadman even though I didn't want to be. But not on his lap. On TV, a man with red hair was listening to the first few notes of a song I almost knew but couldn't quite remember. The Deadman reached for my arm and Daddy woke up then, coughing like his breath got stolen.

"What the fuck, man! Don't do that," Daddy said. "She's my kid."

"Lighten up, Muddy! It's just a little Christmas fun. She's such a sour little thing. Always scowling at us like she's our mother. You gotta nip that in the bud when they're young. A lady should always be smiling." The Deadman looked my Daddy in the eye. "You ever hear the one about the cat who broke his promise?" And he stuck the needle in my arm.

After that I didn't have hands anymore.

I felt like I was all filled up with yellow, the yellow that looks like all the lights turned on at once. I could hardly see with all that yellow swimming around in me. The TV changed to another show, the one where the beautiful lady in a glittery dress turns giant glowing letters around and everyone tries to guess the sentence. She was wearing my smart dress with the butterflies on it. She reached up and turned over a *B*, but I don't like *B* because *B* is for Badgirl, so I reached up to turn it back around and that's when I knew I didn't have hands anymore.

My arms just ended all smooth and neat, no thumbs, no pinkie, no ring finger, like the plastic bottoms on the ball-gown bodies. The stumps dripped yellow and blue butterflies onto the carpet. They flapped their wings there, grazing the rug with their antennae to see if it was flowers. It didn't hurt. It didn't anything. I looked around but I couldn't see my hands lying anywhere, not even under the sofa. I couldn't feel anything when I touched the letter *B* on TV with my stump, or the beautiful lady's hair, or the wall of the living room. When I gave up and dropped my arm back down I must have knocked over a bottle or something because there was glass everywhere, but I didn't feel that, either. The Deadman grabbed me to keep me from falling in the mess but I couldn't make my fingers close around anything, not his sleeve or the corner of the table or anything. My fingers wouldn't listen. They weren't fingers anymore.

I had so much yellow in me it was coming out, coming out all over, washing over everything and making it clean like the dancing lemons on the shaker of powdered soap. I twisted out of the Deadman's grip and crawled away from him back into Daddy's lap.

"Daddy, my hands are gone. Fix it, please? I don't know how to be a girl without hands. All girls have hands. No one will play with me at school."

But Daddy was asleep in his mudpuddle world again and when I tried to pat his face to wake him up I just clobbered him because stumps are so heavy, so much heavier than fingers. But he didn't wake up. Someone on TV in Giant Letter World spun a big wheel and it came up gold. The beautiful lady in my smart dress clapped her hands. See? All girls have hands. Except me. Another blue butterfly flew out of my stump and landed on the window. It was night outside. The butterfly glowed so blue it turned into the moon.

The Deadman pulled a deck of cards out of his back pocket and started dealing himself a hand of solitaire at our kitchen table. He was real good at shuffling. I took my eyes back from the butterfly moon and put them on the Deadman. He put his cigarette in his mouth and dragged on it good and ragged.

He was shuffling cards with my hands.

I knew my own hands and those were it. My pinkie still had green fingernail polish on it from my friend's mom's house and a scratch where I fell playing hopscotch last week. My wrist had my lucky yarn bracelet on it. He'd popped them off me like a princess's head and stuck them on his body. My hands should have been way too small for the Deadman to wear but somehow they weren't, either he got little to match them or they got big to match him. I decided he got little, because my hands should be loyal to me and not him. My hand put down an ace of hearts and waved at me. Then words started coming out of me like blue butterflies and I couldn't stop them and they came out without permission, without me even thinking them before they turned into words.

126 —

"Are you a person?"

The Deadman chewed on one of my fingernails, which he had no right to do.

"Used to be."

"In Paris, France? With the river?"

The Deadman snorted. "Yeah."

"How do you stop being a person?"

"Lots of ways. It's far harder to keep on being a person than to stop. I do think about starting up again sometimes, though. I do think about that. But once you been to that river, it fills you up forever. You need something real good to turn your heart back to red."

"Why do you keep coming back here? Do you even like my Daddy? Are you really his friend?"

"I think he's a worthless piece of shit, Badgirl. But he has cable. And he has you."

The blue butterfly moon got bigger and bigger in the window. It was gonna take up our whole apartment. "Did he know I was in the . . . the . . . *arrr mwah*?"

The Deadman sighed. He put down a quick two-three-four on his ace. "It wouldn't have gone different if he did or didn't, kid. The thing about having the whole world in your back pocket is that every day is nothing but wall-to-wall bargains. I don't have to dicker. They keep upping the price. Everyone wants the world. I just want everyone."

"I want my hands back."

The beautiful lady turned around six or seven letters quick, one after the other. She was still wearing my smart dress, which I guess is why she always knows the answer to the puzzle. But now my dress had gotten long like a wedding dress. It glittered all over. The green bow and green buttons were all emeralds falling down her back and all over the stage. Her chest looked like the sun and she had stars all up and down her arms and the blue butterfly moon was rising in the studio, too, right behind her head like a crown. Everyone had stolen my things. I wanted her to come out of the TV and save me and turn me around like the letter *B*. But she wasn't going to. She had my dress. She had what she wanted.

I'm a little black cat, I thought. *Little black cats run away. Little black cats don't need hands.* The blue butterfly moon had gotten so big it bulged up against my tree house and the front door at the same time. *Little black cats can climb up on the moon and ride it far, far away. To Paris, France, and the Bronx and the continent of Atlantis.*

The Deadman glanced at the game show. For once, he didn't solve it before the contestants did. He just touched his lips with my fingers and said quietly:

"I need them."

Little black cats don't need anyone. Little black cats have magic no one can steal. Little black cats run faster than dead men.

"Why?"

All the letters lit up at once and the lady in my dress touched them all, smiling, buttons and bows and butterflies sparkling everywhere, until they spelled out: HELL IS EMPTY AND ALL THE DEVILS ARE HERE.

"With clean hands, Badgirl, you can start all over."

Little black cats run right out, just as soon as you open the door.

AUTHOR'S NOTE

CATHERYNNE
M. VALENTE

Catherynne M. Valente: Some eighteen months ago, an acute attack of carpal tunnel syndrome left me unable to use my hands for a period of about five months. It was an absolutely perception- and life-altering injury—one that immediately brought the variations of the Armless Maiden fairy tale to mind. And while I meant to write more directly about that experience when I first set out to retell the tale, Badgirl leapt to the front of the stage and demanded to be heard—this was her story, and her voice, and she would run it as she saw fit. So in the end, I left my helplessness by the wayside and delved into hers. This is the only story I've written where I continually had to stop because I'd upset myself and needed to find some equilibrium again. The Armless Maiden stories are some of the darkest fairy tales around, which is part, I think, of why they persist. They are stories about girls lost between the weak and the strong, and how they find their way to wholeness once more.

PENNY FOR A MATCH, MISTER?

Garth Nix

The moon was high above the canyon, its silver light reaching into even the most shadowed depths. It was too bright to be a good night to lie in ambush at the exit, where what passed for a road finally wound its way out of the narrow, zigzag way between rocky walls and ran straight for the town, some five miles distant.

But bright moon or not, there were three men lying in wait for the next stagecoach to come out of the canyon. Two were long-term outlaws, the Osgood brothers, of whom nothing good was known. The third man, the much younger Danny, surname variable according to who was asking, had been drinking whiskey with the brothers all day in town and now he wasn't sure how he had ended up with them, crouched down behind a large rock, his father's old .52-70 Sharps with the black walnut stock in his hands, and fear in his heart.

The Osgoods were the leaders of a large outlaw group known

in those parts as the Nail in the Head Gang, after a certain episode where Ten Osgood, the older brother, had attempted to torture the combination for a safe out of a bank manager, hammering a nail into his head. Predictably, the manager died, and the safe was not opened. But the name stuck. Eleven Osgood, the younger brother, did not like the name but had not been able to come up with a viable alternative.

Danny was uncomfortable in his innards, and not just from all the whiskey he'd drunk. It was more anxiety about his present company, the plans they had, and a growing realization he'd made a serious mistake. After trying for some time to quell this nervousness and discomfort, he finally stood up, plucked at the buttons on his breeches, and took the first step toward a walk some ways off to take a leak.

"Piss where you are," instructed Eleven Osgood. "Don't want no one catching sight. Moon's too damned bright."

The moon was so very bright. Danny obeyed Eleven, pissing where he stood. He stared up at the shining disk while he did so, slack-jawed, not watching his pale stream of urine, which splattered upon the boulder in front of him and splashed back toward the Osgoods.

"I said piss where you are!" yelled Eleven, forgetting about the need to be quiet. "Not where I am!"

Danny didn't hear him. He kept staring up at the night sky. There was a silver road clearly visible there, a road stretching from the moon down to the ground. He knew from the stories his mother used to tell him that this was a path for things from the other side of the Line. A road of moonsilver was a means for persons and creatures barely imaginable to cross the Line, to come into the human world and there cause mischief, mayhem, misery, or mystery, as was their wont. The stories hardly ever mentioned any of them doing anything helpful or kind.

All that was needed to connect the silver road with the good

earth was a sacrifice, the spilling of blood. Preferably human, but anything red would do the job.

Danny suddenly decided he didn't want to be there anymore, just as Eleven Osgood stood up, drew his broad-bladed knife, and plunged it into the still-pissing man's guts and hauled it up, grunting, toward his heart.

Death came almost instantly.

Almost.

Eleven pushed Danny's still-coming-to-terms-with-it body away and watched him twitch in the dirt while he wiped his knife across his own left thigh, adding a scum of blood and filth to the many layers already caked there.

A shadow passed over him, and he looked up, expecting a bird of some kind. A big owl perhaps. Something sizable. But there was nothing in the sky but the bright moon. He blinked, dismissing it as a bit of windborne grit, caught for a moment in his eye.

"Shouldn't have done that," said Ten, and spat.

"He done pissed on me," protested Eleven, lifting a boot to show the faintest of stains.

"Spillin' blood under the full moon," said Ten. "And if I don't misremember, this is the thirteenth day of the month."

"So?"

"Maybe you just helped summat cross the Line," said Ten. He spat again. "That ain't never useful, brother."

"Hell, we ain't near no gate I ever heard about," replied Eleven. Nevertheless, he looked around nervously and gripped his knife a little tighter. Ten knew a lot more about that kind of stuff than he did. "Not round here."

"Maybe so," said Ten. He hesitated, looked up at the moon again, then made a decision. "We'll give up the stage. Let's get back to the horses."

"Whaaat!" exclaimed Eleven, drawing the word through his

teeth like he was inhaling some ugly smoke. "After we been sitting here so long? And they got the payroll for them new workings aboard?"

"Yep," said Ten. He stood up, spat again, and stalked off, calling over his shoulder, "See if the boy had any money on him. Leave the rifle. Folk'll recognize it."

"Whatever you say," grumbled Eleven. He sheathed his knife, bent down, and rummaged through Danny's pockets. Finding nothing, he started to pull off the boy's left boot but stopped when he heard a faint noise. Or to be more specific, a noise from Danny. Which would be surprising, given the young man's guts and blood were all over the ground and he'd completely stopped moving a minute or so before.

There was nothing in the left boot. But again, when Eleven was wrestling the right boot over a recalcitrant heel, he heard something. A whisper, almost beyond the edge of his hearing.

He dropped the boot and backed away from the corpse. Not quite quickly enough to miss the third faint noise. A definite whisper that might or might not be coming directly from the dead man.

"Vengeance . . . vengeance . . . vengeance . . ."

Eleven turned and fled, face gray under the moon, eyes that had seen horrendous things done wide in terror, hands that had done horrendous things shaking in fear. He ran past where Ten was saddling the horses and kept running, not stopping, not stopping at all till he fell from exhaustion two miles along the road, and had to be strapped across his own horse by his exasperated brother.

Neither of the Osgoods noticed the thing that had crossed the Line. A being without flesh, made of air perhaps, or smoke. It had a faint touch of color in it, off and on. The reddish hue of Danny's spilled blood. The color faded as it drew apart to become almost invisible and then intensified as it coiled together again.

Bright and red for a moment, before stretching out into absence, slowly inchworming its way from Danny's body after the outlaws, and always whispering, almost too quiet to be heard.

"Vengeance . . . vengeance . . . vengeance . . ."

The insubstantial creature had come from across the Line, and found blood and a purpose. Now it needed to find someone to help it along, someone who could move faster than its meager inching pace, someone who shared some of dead Danny's blood, kin to the drop it held tightly in the core of its new being.

Danny had three sisters, but two of them had lit out for more fascinating parts as soon as they were old enough to get away. His one remaining sister, Lilibet, called Lili, was eight years old and a lot smarter than her brother. He was, or had been, a waster and a drinker. Lili was a worker and entrepreneur. One of her major enterprises was buying a box of matches for three cents, then reselling the individual matches at a penny apiece to profligate miners, melancholy drunks, and lonely travelers who took pity on a small, destitute orphan likely to starve without assistance. It helped that this was essentially true. She certainly couldn't rely on her sibling Danny to reliably provide shelter and sustenance, and their parents had died of yellow fever when she was five.

Selling matches was a good business. When all the miners were in town, Lili would sometimes even get a nickel or a dime for a single match, and once had almost bitten her tongue in surprise at the careless handing over of a silver dollar.

It took three days for the thing from the other side to find her. Blood called to blood. Lili saw something glinting in the dust around the side of the livery stable. A penny, strangely red. She picked it up, and that was all it took.

Around that same time, a traveler, drawn by the circling buzzards, found Danny's body. He took the rifle and handed it over to the sheriff, a man name of Laidlaw. The sheriff threw the Sharps in a chest with other lost weapons and forgot about it. Whatever had occurred was outside the town limits and therefore none of his concern. Sheriff Laidlaw did consider telling Lili her brother was dead, but he didn't get around to it straightaway. Or at all, as things turned out.

Ten was the first to go. It was late, near midnight, with a clear sky, and the beginnings of frost. He came out of the saloon, buttoning up his big sheepskin coat, the one he'd taken off the body of a rancher a lot farther north, in the high country. Lili was waiting by his horse, a small lump of darkness. When she moved, he reached for his pistol before he realized it was only a little girl.

"Penny for a match, mister?" she asked, lisping. She'd never lisped before.

"Git away from my horse," snarled Ten. He was in a temper due to losing money playing faro against three well-heeled, dangerous-looking gentlemen he hadn't dared cross, not without his brother or more of his gang.

Eleven and the others were all drinking themselves stupid out at the ranch house where Errol the sheep farmer had been killed by a gunman brought in by the Cattlemen's Association. The Nail in the Head gang had informally taken over the ranch house, and the sheep, which they ate. The former sheep farm was well outside the town limits, so the sheriff paid them no mind. He'd done a deal with the Osgoods: provided the gang behaved themselves within a mile in every cardinal direction from the central saloon, he'd leave them alone. Beyond that range, they committed whatever crimes they felt like.

"Penny for a match, mister," repeated Lili. Then, unusually, she held one of her matches up. "I'll show you how good it is."

"Git!" swore Ten, aiming a drunken kick at the girl. He missed, and almost lost his balance, staggering against the hitching rail.

When he straightened up, the girl was holding a lit match. A

match that burned with unnatural ferocity, the flame a good foot high, white at the core, blue at the tip.

Ten went for his pistol, and Lili flicked the match.

The outlaw burned, his screams mingling with the roar of the air that the fire sucked in, craving oxygen. But it was a curiously contained fire, not spreading to the hitching rails, the stoop beyond, or the saloon's shingled roof. It just stuck to Ten, burning down from his head toward his heels.

Like he was a match, held upright to the last.

When everyone inside the saloon came rushing outside, they saw a column of flame lurching into the street, spinning and turning, as if there might be some way to escape for the man within.

No one saw a little match-selling girl. All attention was on the burning man, who was still screaming. A fire that hot should have killed him near instantly, but this death was drawn out. His screams remained full-throated, not husky, fading gasps from smoke-filled, heat-destroyed lungs.

His agony might have lasted even longer if one of the faro-playing gentlemen hadn't sworn a strange oath, drawn a funny little piece from inside his coat, rather than the Navy Colt at his side, and fired three shots into the spot where he reckoned Ten's head would be, the fire now too intense to make out any anatomical details.

By the time Sheriff Laidlaw got there, still buckling his gun belt over his long johns, all that remained was a blackened husk. Vaguely man-shaped, it was made brighter here and there by little puddles of hot metal. The fire had burned so hot that Ten's pistol had melted in an instant, without the rounds in the cylinder having a chance to cook off, and the rest of the metal came from his silver belt buckle, spurs, and two gold fillings.

The man who'd fired the mercy shots still had the small revolver in his hand. He walked over to where the sheriff was about to gingerly touch the ashy pile with the toe of his boot and said,

"I wouldn't if I were you, Sheriff. That there weren't no ordinary fire. It'll be damned hot for hours yet."

The sheriff drew his boot back and looked at the stranger. He seemed typical enough of the kind of successful gambler who drifted through the saloons of the West, winning often enough to keep himself in fine clothes, company, and whiskey. But the weapon in his hand spoke otherwise. The sheriff had seen one of those silver-chased revolvers before and thought it too small in caliber to be a serious weapon. He had learned he was wrong about that, and a few other things besides. He hadn't expected to see such a weapon again.

The stranger saw him looking.

"Yep," he said, replacing the pistol inside his coat. "Tombstone bullet, cold marble, fired from a silver-washed gun. Lead would've melted, and that man would still be screaming. Something very nasty's come over the Line, Sheriff. Better get yourself some help."

"You offering, sir?" asked the sheriff hopefully. Now that he looked closely at the stranger, he thought he could put a name to him, a famous name, a man renowned as both gunslinger and wizard. "Town's got a budget for—"

"Nope," said the stranger, with great surety. "I got business elsewhere. I'm heading out on the morning stage. Besides, I ain't a lawman. You need a warden-marshal got jurisdiction both sides of the Line."

"Yeah," replied the sheriff, staring down at the remains of Ten. "I reckon we do."

He thought for a minute, then turned to the silent, awed crowd who were arrayed on the saloon's stoop.

"Anyone know who this is . . . I mean was?"

There was no reply for a moment. The stranger, who had been about to go in, turned at the door.

"Ten Osgood," he said.

"Shit," said the sheriff, seeing his comfortable arrangement

with the Nail in the Head gang about to turn into as big a pile of ashes as Ten Osgood himself.

Lili had no memory of what she'd done, or rather what the thing that now lived within her had done. She heard about Ten Osgood's mysterious fiery death, all right, because everyone in the town talked about it at every opportunity. But she had no idea she was connected to it in any way. She also still didn't know her brother Danny was dead, and half expected him to turn up at some point and shamefacedly ask if she was all right and if she needed anything. Not that he would provide. He'd always seemed to think the asking was enough.

So Lili kept selling her matches, and helping Marcia in the laundry, and Lee Liang in the feed store. By dint of working every daylight hour there was and then some more, she usually managed to get enough coin to have two or sometimes even three meals a day, and still be able to hand over the weekly dime to old Mister Tobin, who let her sleep in the loft above the livery stable. It smelled, but it was warm, with the horses below.

It was a week past Ten Osgood's demise when another opportunity for revenge arose. Eleven Osgood had taken it into his head that it was the faro players who'd been responsible for his brother's death, so he and the gang had wasted several fruitless days pursuing the westbound stage. Finding himself inexplicably unable to catch it—every time they almost did so, a girth strap would snap, or a horse would stumble, or there'd be a sudden rainstorm—he'd given up and returned to town, fourteen disgruntled members of the gang trailing in his wake.

They rode in just after dusk, tired, saddle-sore, and parched. Sheriff Laidlaw met them in the main street, a little ways short of the saloon, a double-barreled shotgun under his arm. A charcoal-black stain in the dirt a few paces away marked the last resting place of Ten Osgood. They'd tried to get rid of this unwelcome civic blemish, but even digging up the whole area hadn't made a difference. The mark returned overnight.

"Evening, Sheriff," said Eleven, in as peaceable a manner as he ever achieved.

"Evening, Eleven," said the sheriff. "I just wanted a quick word."

"I'm listening."

"There's a marshal-warden coming to investigate whatever burned up Ten," said the sheriff slowly. "Until she's done—"

"She?" asked Eleven.

"Yep. Name of Rose Jackson."

Eleven nodded slowly. The name was not unknown in those parts.

"There's paper on you and the boys, federal paper," continued the sheriff. He was speaking very slowly, a sign of his nervousness. "The marshal won't overlook that. I want you to stay out of town, stay up at the sheep place until she's gone."

"Need a drink," said Eleven.

"One of your boys can pick up half a dozen bottles," said the sheriff. "Then you gotta go, and stay out until I send word."

Eleven thought about it for a few seconds, the rage building inside him. He'd been thwarted from catching the faro players, and now this pipsqueak of a sheriff wanted to stop him spending the evening in the saloon. And he was no closer to finding whoever killed his brother, and that in turn meant his leadership of the gang was weakening. . . .

He snarled, making the sheriff twitch and raise his shotgun, but the snarl was just Eleven letting some of that anger out.

"All right, Sheriff, all right," growled Eleven. He wheeled his horse around and yelled at the least of the gang members, a cousin of his who wasn't much use. "Potato! You go get a *dozen* bottles and bring 'em out to the ranch."

"Yeah, boss," said Potato, whose real name was Patrick. He dismounted gingerly, very stiff after a long day's ride, and hitched

up his horse as the rest of the gang headed back out, their dust rolling over Potato as they passed. The sheriff watched them go for a good ten seconds, gently uncocked his shotgun, and wandered into the saloon himself.

Potato was alone. Except for the little girl no one had noticed, swinging on the post at the end of the stoop.

"Penny for a match, mister?" lisped Lili, holding one sulfur-headed stick out to the young man.

"Uh, I ain't got a penny," said Potato. "Sorry."

"These are real good matches," said Lili.

"Sure," said Potato uneasily. There was something funny about the girl. Her eyes were kind of bright, way too bright, full of fire—

"Vengeance," said Lili.

There was fire in her mouth as well as her eyes, and the match she held was alight, alight without striking.

Potato screamed as the match flew through the air and landed in the hollow of his throat, sticking to the skin. He reached up to pluck it off, but it was already too late, the flame spreading across his shoulders and head, licking down his arms and torso.

Like his cousin Ten, Potato spun burning out into the street. Unlike Ten, he kept screaming for a good fifteen minutes, a corpse-fire capering in the dust all that time, because no one present had a silver-chased gun charged with a tombstone bullet, or anything else that might end his suffering.

The warden-marshal arrived the next morning, to a town that had largely stayed awake and fearful all night, not counting the few who'd immediately decamped.

Rose Jackson rode in and went straight to the sheriff's office, pausing briefly near the saloon to glance at the two charcoal marks and sniff the air. She wore both a marshal's star-and-circle badge and a warden's star of bright silver on her leather waistcoat, and had a Frontier Colt .45 on her right hip, a knife on her left, and a Winchester '73 in the bucket holster by her saddle.

"Telegram I got said one burning," said Rose, as she settled back in the sheriff's own rocking chair, a cup of his coffee in her hand. When she didn't get an answer, she added, "Sheriff Laidlaw. That really your name?"

"Huh? Oh sure, my apologies, Marshal," said the sheriff, who'd been staring out the window. He grinned weakly. "Laidlaw by name; laying down the law's my nature. My pa was a town constable too, back East. You were saying?"

"Telegram said one burning, name of Ten Osgood," said Rose. "Who was the second and when did it happen?"

"Last night," replied the sheriff. He looked out the window again. "Young man named Potato . . . that is, Patrick."

"Patrick got a surname?" asked Rose.

"Uh, yeah . . . Osgood," replied Laidlaw slowly. "A cousin of Ten's."

"And another member of the so-called Hole in the Head gang."

"Nail in the Head," muttered the sheriff. "Uh, yeah, that's so."

"How many Osgoods are there about the place?"

The sheriff swallowed and continued staring out the window.

"How many Osgoods?" repeated Rose. She set down her coffee on the desk and settled back in the chair, rocking it forward and backward a few times.

"There's Eleven," said the Sheriff reluctantly.

"Eleven of them? That must be near the whole gang," said Rose, her tone of voice a little facetious.

"I ain't responsible for their naming," said the sheriff irritably. "And I thank everything nameless I never met One to Nine Osgood or their misbegotten parents. Anyhow, there's Eleven Osgood, that's all."

"So two Osgoods killed by fiery magic and one remaining," mused Rose.

"There is another cousin of the same name," said the sheriff. "Jeremiah Osgood, called Jem. But he don't ride with the Nail in the Head, nor live near here neither."

"The Osgoods do anything particular recently?" asked Rose. "Somewhere near a gate, or to a practitioner?"

"Not that I know of," said Laidlaw.

"Seems to me there's something stalking Osgoods," said Rose. "Something that came across the Line. But that don't happen without a reason."

"What . . . ah . . ." asked the sheriff. He cleared his throat a few times before continuing. "What could it be, and . . . um . . . how do we get rid of it?"

"Well, there's a number of things it could be," said Rose. She rocked a few more times. "Do you know what the Osgoods were up to, last full moon?"

"I ain't their keeper," said the sheriff. He ran his finger around his collar, loosening it up a little.

Rose rocked a few more times, then suddenly stopped. The sheriff flinched as she reached forward, but she was only going for her coffee cup.

"We got to lure it out," she said. "Put something it wants within reach."

"Like what?" asked the sheriff.

"Eleven Osgood, of course," said Rose. She pulled a rolled-up poster out of her boot and flicked it open across the desk. The words DEAD OR ALIVE were very prominent. "He's wanted anyway. Surprised I didn't see this poster on your wall outside."

"Yeah," croaked the sheriff. "Uh, how we going to do that?"

"The usual way," said Rose. "How many in the gang?"

"I guess about eighteen," said the sheriff.

"Well, get a posse together," said Rose cheerfully. "A dozen ought to do it. You ride up to the front of that sheep farm this afternoon and call him out."

"The sheep farm?"

"Errol the sheep farmer's place," said Rose. "That's where they hang out, isn't it?"

"Uh, yeah," said the sheriff uncomfortably. He opened his mouth to ask her how she knew about that but shut it again as he met her cool, steady gaze, which quite clearly told him she knew a lot more about everything than he would like.

"A dozen against eighteen . . ." continued the sheriff after a moment or two of wary silence. "Uh, where you going to be?"

"You just do your part," said Rose. She stood up, and even though the sheriff was taller, he felt diminished by her presence. He had to turn his head aside, because her warden's badge hurt his eyes. It was bright, uncommon bright.

"Like you should have done quite a time ago," added Rose. She poured the dregs of the coffee over his boots with some contempt and walked out.

The posse came back just before sundown, with Eleven Osgood hog-tied over a horse, blood dripping slowly through the bandage on his wounded hand. Half the sheriff's men were still back at the sheep farm, digging graves for the four outlaws who hadn't laid down their weapons when called to do so, not realizing Rose Jackson was already inside the house with them, moving like smoke in a hurricane, too fast to see, too insubstantial to shoot. Eleven himself had been shot in the hand by the sheriff when the outlaw ran out, though in truth Laidlaw had been aiming for his head. He didn't want Eleven talking.

"We'll string him up on that big elm over by the livery stable," said Rose cheerfully. She was riding alongside the sheriff, with the prisoner just behind, hemmed in by the bolder members of the posse. "Just on sunset. That should bring it out."

"What?" growled Eleven, trying to raise his head. "You gonna hang me? What for? I want a trial!"

"You've had two that I know of," said Rose. "Been sentenced to hang both times. So you're overdue."

Eleven took this in silence for a while, thoughts very slowly percolating through his head.

"What you mean by 'bring it out'?"

"Whatever's hunting down Osgoods and burning them up," said Rose. "Something from across the Line. Caught up someone's dying wish for revenge, I'd guess. Who you kill recently, Eleven? Or maybe your brother did the deed? Or your cousin, for that matter."

Eleven muttered something inaudible.

"Night of the full moon, I'd guess," said Rose. "I don't have to know, but it'd make it easier, give me a little warning. It's got to be in someone, you see, someone of the same blood as you murdered."

"I ain't helping you, Marshal!" spat Eleven. "Hang me and be damned!"

"Someone who deals with fire," said Rose thoughtfully, looking across as they passed the town farrier, who was newly wreathed in steam from a quenched horseshoe and not paying the passersby any attention.

"Joel? The blacksmith?" asked the sheriff, in surprise.

"No, smiths have their own mysteries and are too ringed with cold iron for anything from the other side to get a hold," replied Rose. "But it'll be someone used to fire. Maybe a cook. A baker. Someone like that."

"I don't ever want to see . . . or hear . . . anyone else burn like Potato did," said the sheriff nervously.

"We'd better get the critter, then," said Rose brightly. "Specially as they sometimes get a very wide notion of revenge. You know, start on those directly responsible, but then move on to anyone who might have helped out in any way. Unrelated people, even. Who'd you kill, Eleven?"

Eleven remained stubbornly silent. But the sheriff opened his mouth.

"Come to think about it," he said. "Come to think about it . . ."

He lifted his hat and wiped the sweat from his forehead, though the day was already cooling, the sun beginning to set.

"There was a body found soon after the full moon, up by the canyon," he continued. "Young feller Danny . . . called himself Danny Hallaway, sometimes Danny Hathaway. Knifed in the guts."

"He have kin in town?" asked Rose.

The sheriff thought for a moment, eyes crinkling.

"Parents dead, two sisters run off with the traveling show," he said finally. He turned to Rose. "But he had a little sister. She sells matches."

"Makes sense," said Rose.

"So what do we do?" asked the sheriff. He was mightily relieved to have figured it out. "Kill the girl?"

"You do that and Eleven won't be the only one hanging," said Rose. "What *I* will have to do is catch it when it shows itself, which will be just one moment before it sets Eleven here on fire."

The sheriff blinked. He didn't have anything to say to that. It was only a hundred yards or so to the elm, so they rode in silence.

They tied off the horses at the livery stable and wandered the dozen yards along to the tree, where the sheriff threw a rope over the best-looking branch and handed off one end to four of his men. He fumbled about making a noose for a while with the other end, till Rose took it from him and tied the neck-breaking knot with ease.

"You cinch him up," she said, stepping back. "I got to get ready."

"I ain't seen that little match girl around," said the sheriff.

"You won't," said Rose. She got a round, enameled box out of her waistcoat, the kind of thing a woman might keep earrings in, or maybe a little powder. She unscrewed the top and

held both halves, carefully holding each up to the fading sunlight to inspect the insides, which were of mirror-bright polished silver.

"What . . . what happens if you don't catch it in time?" asked the sheriff. His hands shook as he stretched the noose over Eleven's head and pulled it tight, the long knot plumb against the back of the outlaw's head.

"Don't worry about that," said the marshal easily. She looked to the west, where the sun had almost dipped below the horizon. The shadows were very long, and there was one extra over by the stable doors, a small human shadow without anyone belonging to it, with a reddish glint suggestive of eyes. "Lift him up!"

The sheriff stepped back a few paces. His men hauled on the rope. Eleven went up, kicking and—

"Penny for a match, mister! Penny for a match!"

The lisping, little-girl voice was all around. The sheriff turned on the spot, desperately trying to see her. The men let go of the rope and ran away, sending Eleven plummeting back to the ground with the awful crack of a leg breaking.

A match struck in empty air.

The sudden, sucking breath of combustion sounded.

The marshal leaped, clapping both halves of her silver box together.

Just a moment too late.

Eleven Osgood burst into flame, his screams louder and higher than his brother or his cousin. A second later the fire leaped from him and hooked the sheriff in, Laidlaw screeching and turning, screeching and turning as he was drawn toward Eleven and they joined to become one great tower of incandescent flame.

Rose screwed down the lid of the silver box, slipped it inside her waistcoat, and drew out a little pepperbox derringer instead. She fired all four barrels into the capering, conjoined shape of fire that was Eleven and Laidlaw, finishing the screams, if not the flames.

"Penny for a match, mister," said Lili, not seeing anything that was before her, and not lisping either.

Rose picked Lili up, carried her away, and set her on her horse, before mounting behind her. Her body shielded the girl from the fire, which was only now burning down. Rose made a *tcha-tcha* sound with her tongue, and her horse ambled off.

They hadn't gone more than a dozen yards along the main street when the little girl suddenly stiffened under her hand, as if unexpectedly awoken.

"Oh no," she wailed. "I done lost three matches, and no money for 'em neither!"

"Here," said Rose, slipping the girl a silver dollar. "You're finished selling them anyhow."

Lili took the silver dollar.

"What am I to do?" she said forlornly. "Who are you anyhow?"

"Well, I'm Marshal-Warden Rose Jackson, only you can call me Auntie Rose, on account of we're going to be traveling together a ways."

"We are?"

"Yep," said Rose. She looked down at Lili, who twisted back and smiled tentatively in return. "See, you don't know it, but you're special. You're going to have magic powers and all when you grow up, so you gotta go somewhere to learn how to be wise about using 'em."

Lili pondered this for some time, occasionally darting looks at Rose, and to either side of the strangely empty street.

"We going across the Line?" she asked finally, as they neared the edge of town.

"Yep," said Rose. "Going to visit with my daughter, lives there. She's got two girls of her own. Younger than you. You'll stay there a spell."

*Penny for
a Match,
Mister?*

"They eat regular?" said Lili.

"Three squares, regular as clockwork," said Rose.

"And I won't have to sell matches?"

"Nope," said Rose. "There'll be work, but not selling matches. You're done with that, I reckon."

"Good," said Lili. She held the silver dollar tight in one small fist, relaxed back against Rose, and fell asleep.

AUTHOR'S NOTE

Garth Nix: I actually don't like the Hans Christian Andersen story very much. It could be called "It's Okay to Be Poor and Freeze to Death, at Least You'll go to Heaven with Granny." But its evocation of the magic of creating fire with matches is very powerful. We take it for granted now, but for most of humanity's existence fire was much more difficult to conjure up. And it has always been both an invaluable ally and a potential foe, even a lethal one. I started my story before I reread the original, and my recollection of it was wrong. I thought I remembered that no one would buy her matches and they treated her badly, which led me to thinking about revenge. So my starting point was not entirely the original Andersen story but rather my imperfect memory of it. I guess it became a Western because matches are such a motif of the imagined West. Struck against a boot, lighting a cigarillo, held to the fuse of a stick of dynamite . . . I thought matches, and I thought a Western. But a fantastical one, of course, because that is how my mind tends to work. Accordingly, I set it in the world of one of my previous stories, "Crossing the Line." I love a Weird Western, and I think I'll probably write some more!

SOME WAIT

Stephen Graham Jones

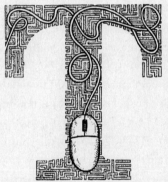he first of our children to disappear was Jace Weissman.

The whole town shut down, walked the trees, beat the grass, dragged the creek, held prayer vigils.

While we were out doing that, the second of our children was spirited away. Alyssa Johnson.

This time we locked our doors, leaned our shotguns against the wall, one in the chamber, our fingers always hovering over that third digit of calling the sheriff's department.

The third of our children to go missing made the national news. Cathy Gutierrez. Three children in two weeks.

Husbands and wives traded shifts sleeping, bedrooms were consolidated, sick days were used, and more were begged for.

It didn't matter.

It happened again, and then again, and then three more times.

Understand, our town is two thousand people.

Of that two thousand, not many are fourth graders.

Even fewer now.

The detective assigned to liaison with the parents was from the city. Claude Weissman, Jace's dad, claimed to remember the detective from a high school basketball tournament. Meaning he was chosen as liaison because he was from these mean streets, not those.

Claude Weissman couldn't remember what position the detective might have played on the court.

"Point guard," Andrew Rucker said after our first meeting, when we were all shuffling around in the elementary school cafeteria. The lights were flickering above us. They hadn't really taken hold yet.

"Homicide now," one of us said, watching a long tube of light shudder with darkness.

It was the word we'd all been holding in our mouths for nearly four weeks.

Television re-creations of these events are years away, if ever. No dramatizations are in the works.

Just look in our eyes instead.

We're the ones who walked our son or daughter to the bus stop that first kindergarten day, trying to make a photograph of it. And then it's like we're just standing there at the end of the driveway, by the mailbox, Hamlinberg swirling and smearing around us, the seasons cycling through faster and faster, Easter to Thanksgiving, homecoming to prom.

Watch the eyes, though.

We're still looking down the road. We're still watching where our son or our daughter just disappeared.

They'll be back, we're telling ourselves.

We just have to stand here.

———✣———

We saw the nanny-cam recording before any of the detectives, before anybody from the sheriff's department.

Trina Johnson had always been vigilant.

We all had. As vigilant as you can be without wrapping them in a quilt, carrying them from place to place.

Trina Johnson's daughter was Alyssa.

We're not supposed to use the past tense for them, and we never meant to. But at some point you do, and it just falls like a dead bird onto the floor, doesn't even kick once, and all the parents, they look away from it.

Alyssa's babysitter had, for her last two years of high school, been Connie Abbot. Connie was back from college for the summer. The thought nobody would think out loud was that she'd met someone in the city. That she'd been followed back. That when she'd shown up to babysit Alyssa, she'd had a shadow.

The detective told us it was natural for smart people like ourselves to develop our own theories. To grasp at whatever straws there were, or could be.

We weren't children, we told him. We were parents.

From the other room, then, Trina Johnson screamed.

What she'd found on the monitor of Alyssa's computer was what we all found on our missing children's monitors within the hour.

It is one hundred years since our children left.

"What is it?" one of us said, the voice breaking the way all of ours would have, had we been the one to say it.

"That game," Trina Johnson's husband Gerrold said. "It's that game. Right?"

The game had been on a freebie CD all the kids had come home with from school.

Our midnight interrogation of Principal Wilkins on his front lawn established that the CDs weren't from the textbook salesman, like the teachers had assumed. The days didn't match up. The box had just been in the hall one Tuesday.

A fourth grader will look into any box that's just sitting there.

And the game, it was outdated, it was clunky, but it was free, right?

We policed them over their shoulders the first week or two, told them that they knew this was all fake, didn't they? That it was all pretend?

They all knew.

Until it wasn't.

That line about it having been one hundred years since our children left took very little research to crack.

The story is hundreds of years old itself, is thought to be a fanciful way of remembering a sickness that passed among a village's young.

Part of that fantasy—what we thought was fantasy—is that a man in patched clothes uses his wiles to lure all the rats out of a village. For an agreed-upon price. One the village then decides is too high. It was just a few rats, right? So, to exact the payment he deserves, the piebald man then uses his wiles to lead all the village's *children* out of town, never to be seen again.

It's better to figure Death as a jester sometimes. To let his comical bells jingle louder than the moans, louder than the sound of pustules bursting under fingernails.

The parent who figured this out wasn't the librarian. Our librarian, Mr. Dockett, had no children, so he wasn't at these meetings.

The parent who dredged this story up from his childhood, it was Martin Able.

His chin trembled into a prune as he retold the story.

Never for years, save at funerals, had people cried as freely as we did that month.

It wasn't Mr. Dockett taking the children, either.

And it wasn't the babysitter's boyfriend.

The game the fourth graders had all been playing was a simple labyrinth. It looked like it was supposed to help with their spatial reasoning.

The animation wasn't refined, and transitioning from room to room took much longer than a blink. It made us wonder how they could invest so intently in the labors their characters were going through.

A different generation, we told ourselves.

The television shows we'd believed in at their age would be basic and crude to them, we knew. Thinking this let us feel part of a grander cycle. It let us feel like we were handing our art and entertainment down. And of course those idle pastimes would become instantly unrecognizable. It was for them, right? Not us. And we knew from our parents' efforts that any attempt to suppress their interest would only fan the flames higher, as it were.

So we let them click and watch and move through those narrow, dimly lit halls.

The goal, as our Jaces and Alyssas and Cathys told it, was to fill the game's leather knapsack with items. There were molded spaces to hold these items. According to the scroll that read itself aloud, the knapsack was all you got to take with you to the next level, and the items in there determined the scope of that level, so stock it for the adventure you want. Be thorough. Open every door, look into every corner.

Hundreds of years ago, it had been a rat catcher who lured the children from their homes.

Now, for our children, it was a mouse.

Before presenting our evidence to the detective, we first of course tried to figure out the meaning ourselves:

It is one hundred years since our children left.

The possessive pronoun was the first issue.

Was it meant to suggest it was one of us doing this? Was that "our" meant to act as a seed of doubt in our ranks, or was it actually a confession, a bread crumb?

On the chance that it was, and because none of us could be trusted, we hired a sheriff's deputy after hours. Where we found him was on a list the sheriff's department keeps, of deputies willing to consider general security work—concerts and graduations and the like.

With us walking behind him, a clump of parents in the street with beer and candles and a secret pistol or two, every basement in town was inspected.

We considered it a mark in our favor that not a single home owner declined. To have declined would have been to invite suspicion. Right then, one of us would have taken up the first watch. The first vigil.

In the old story, the children are either led into a river or they're led into a cave.

Either way, river or cave, they don't return.

The instruction we gave Deputy Moonlight, as we came to call him, was to push his nightstick into every last square foot of the walls of these basements. For tunnels. For hideouts that had been dug in secret, and soundproofed.

We were playing the game now, yes.

The dated lobby of the sheriff's office was where we presented our evidence to the detective.

"So it's not the Abbot girl's boyfriend, like you thought last time?" he said.

"She doesn't have a boyfriend," one of us said.

The detective licked his lips, turned back to a page he'd already read.

"Pied Piper, now?" he said at last.

It was a name we'd been avoiding as well.

Next would be Tin Men, Talking Wolves. Pigs.

They could have walked into town single file at that point, though. So long as they each carried a sleeping child in their arms.

We would have stepped forward for our own, kept our eyes down in respect, and waited for them to shift each sleeping form from their arms to ours.

Counting Bradley Masters, there were now four missing. Four children in just over four weeks.

School had been shut down. Not to keep the remaining children safe, but because the parents already were keeping them safe, at home. Or what they thought was safe. By the third child not in his or her bed in the morning—Cathy Gutierrez—the halls of the elementary had been empty of children. The bus stopped where it usually did, and opened its doors onto nothing, as if compelled by law to try.

"We don't know what he calls himself," Doug Lawson said back to the detective, in response to the way the detective had said "Pied Piper."

"Does it matter?" another of us said.

The detective looked from face to face of us, and if he lingered anywhere for a moment, it was on Claude Weissman, who had introduced himself that first meeting as—and he'd paused to swallow before saying it—Jace's dad.

The reason he could introduce himself like that, it was that there were no bodies.

As long as there are no bodies, you're still a dad.

Leaving the grounds of the sheriff's office that night, we of course cued on the low-slung, unfamiliar sedan parked at the curb. Not in front of the building, but off to the side.

To our credit, we didn't bleed across the manicured grass, cover that car with our bodies.

Rather, we faked our good-byes, made sure our lips were moving, that our eyes held the proper regret, not the hope we were feeling.

What we were talking about was who was circling back around this way, and with what, and who was keeping an eye on the car until then, and how much racket the trash can would make if kicked repeatedly, and whether that would be alarm enough for the rest of us.

Six minutes later, four of us materialized from the shadows to each side of this sedan, make-do weapons gripped by our legs.

In the passenger seat was a child of perhaps ten years old.

Two of us on the right side of that car, we fell to our knees, our mouths open, our lungs empty.

And then the rest of us were there.

The ten-year-old looked up to us, from face to face.

The doors of the car were already locked.

He was doing homework, still held a transparent peach ruler in his left hand.

When he saw us, he pawed onto the dashboard, for what his father had left for him to defend himself with: a shield.

It was the detective's son.

We could all see the resemblance.

We held each other up by the arms, drifted off to our kitchens and living rooms for another night.

It started in the dairy section of our grocery store, what happened next.

It was a grim Thursday afternoon.

Four of us had found ourselves shopping for snacks and juice packs we no longer needed.

If you stand in the dairy section long enough, over the open tub-cooler for butter and cottage cheese, your breath will frost.

We were recounting the search Deputy Moonlight had conducted.

At the end of that night of the official search, as we'd come to call it, instead of counting hours and doing math, we'd passed a version of an offering plate among the congregation we were, came up with what was probably a week's pay for him.

If you didn't give all that was in your pocket, did you truly want your son or your daughter back? Or, if your child was safe at home with the other parent, could a wad of cash exempt him or her from these proceedings? Please?

Deputy Moonlight took what he was owed, tried to hand the rest back, but none of us would take it.

Now, in the dairy section, we finally said it: If the barber shaves all the men of Seville, then who shaves the barber?

Substitute "Deputy Moonlight" into that.

We didn't know where he lived. Or if he had a basement.

Trina Johnson's nanny cam had been hidden in the right eye of a beige teddy bear in Alyssa's bedroom.

In the game all the fourth graders were playing, that *It is one hundred years since our children left* was inscribed on the baseboard of a room with only one door. But the words would only flicker into existence under the light of what was called a "Black Flame Lantern." The only way to refuel your Black Flame Lantern, of course, was to stand in shadows for long minutes, its reservoir filling with the darkness it needed.

Where you get this lantern is in an altar embedded in the wall early in the game. But you don't realize what the fuel is until many sessions later—or until you study the cardboard slipcase the CD came in, which one of the fourth graders must have realized was a key of sorts. A clue.

Within three days of finding the Pied Piper connection, all

of us were looking for our sons and daughters inside that game. We didn't hope to find them around every next corner, but we did keep alive the chance that there would be footprints in the dust, as it were.

The words on the baseboard, though—perhaps it wasn't just the Black Flame Lantern that revealed them? Perhaps the contents of your knapsack already mattered, even at this stage?

We had to assume so. The words wouldn't appear for any of us, no matter how faithfully we traced what we assumed our sons' and daughters' footsteps had been. It wouldn't even appear for us when we created new accounts, lied about our ages.

Without Trina Johnson's nanny cam, though, we never would have known about what happened *after* those words showed up on the baseboard in the game.

What happened, what that bear saw—

Of course Trina Johnson screamed when she saw it.

The real question, it's how she ever stopped.

Imagine you're in fourth grade.

You're in that saddle of time between school and dinner. There are no sports or clubs this afternoon. There's homework, but you're only going to play for fifteen minutes. It's what you promised your mom.

A cool half hour later you walk into a room that, unlike the rest of the labyrinth, doesn't look as if it served as a dungeon, centuries ago.

Maybe a storeroom? There are casks and jugs that will surely hold items—space is becoming an issue in your knapsack—but there are no other doors or windows, and no holes dug in the corners, as you've started to find and explore.

Hold your lantern high now. Let that black flame lick at the stone walls like it wants to.

Don't ask yourself why there's a baseboard in a medieval facility.

You're in fourth grade. It's just a plank of wood. It doesn't need an explanation.

These words that are fading in, though.

Smile. In the recording, Alyssa does.

There's never just graffiti in a game. There are only clues.

In the recording—the bear was positioned on the shelf beside her monitor—Alyssa mouths the shape of the words, even reaches forward to touch the letters with the tip of her finger.

And maybe that's what refocuses her eyes.

Not onto the game in the monitor, but on the reflective screen of the monitor itself, which only she can see.

The bear can see behind her, though. Over her shoulder. Meaning we could too. A week later, we could see what had surely been in the reflection of her monitor.

There's a shape standing behind her.

A trench coat would be scary, but there isn't one. Male, female? It's just a shadow of a person. At least until the hands open by the legs, right first, then left, even slower. When those long fingers uncurl, they have points sharp even in silhouette.

At which point Alyssa flinched around hard enough to bump the desk, aim the teddy bear's camera eye a different direction.

Eight hours later she was gone.

The group that piled into the cars and trucks for Deputy Moonlight's house at the county line was a motley crew.

One of the team moms had the black greasepaint quarterbacks wear under their eyes.

She passed the little tube around without asking if we wanted it. Without asking if we were ready to admit what we were doing.

Just one index finger of that can hide the shiny parts of a face, if you want it to.

Because Deputy Moonlight was on duty, we let ourselves into his house.

There were deer heads on the wall, magazines on the coffee table, beer in the refrigerator.

"This is Anton's old place," Syd Gustavson said at last.

It was.

Old Man Anton had finally died five years ago. Syd wasn't his son—Anton famously had no children—but somehow the property had found its way to this sheriff's deputy. Perhaps rented from the county?

"Cellar," one of us said.

We filed down. If we'd had torches, they would have been smudging the ceiling black.

In the cellar, under the pull-light, was a rough workbench, at stool height.

On the workbench a body had been meticulously opened.

Julia Garrett threw up, her vomit splatting onto the dirt floor.

Was someone screaming? Someone was screaming.

"Whitetail," James Teague said, simply.

Because it was.

Deputy Moonlight the apprentice taxidermist.

When we rose back into the living room, our detective liaison was waiting for us, a look in his eyes we were more accustomed to giving than having to turn away from.

The timbre and the tone of our dreams that month—the screaming didn't stop in Deputy Moonlight's basement.

Did we all at one point or another see a beige teddy bear wobbling up the hall for us?

If we all did, how many of us ran from that bear and what it knew? How many of us fell to our knees, waited for it to climb our torsos, latch its mouth onto our necks?

And how many of us, in our sleep, where our deepest fantasies writhe and have license, how many of us let out a little "Oh," then, very businesslike, very parentlike, walked down the hall to

Some Wait

that bear, scooped it up, held it to our chest, waiting for its small footpad to wrap around to the back of our neck, clutch us like it needed us? Like it had just been sleepwalking again?

How many indeed.

When the words in the game wouldn't show up for any of us, at our age . . . can you blame us?

No, you can't.

Lincoln Adrian would be the sixth fourth grader to go missing. The sixth to fall to what the national news was calling this "epidemic."

He was also the only remaining fourth grader to have had a cousin in his own class, a cousin among the missing. Because his mother, Veda Robbins, still had to work, he was spending his afternoons with Bradley Masters's parents, Trace and Abby.

What Veda assumed was that there could be no safer place, could there? That this plague of disappearances, it had already visited this house, right? And could there be any more vigilant parents now than Trace and Abby Masters? Could anybody watch Lincoln better or more fiercely than his own aunt and uncle?

She wasn't wrong, either.

But she wasn't right.

Because this stealer, this Pied Piper, because he or she wasn't camera shy, Abby set up her mother's borrowed video camera under an out-of-place doily in what she was still calling Bradley's room, where his cousin Lincoln was supposed to be doing his homework.

If he needed anything, he was to call down the hall. Even just a glass of milk, a piece of toast, *anything*.

He never noticed the doily or the camera.

Inside of five minutes he'd made his way from social studies to the game.

Not on purpose, but not *not* on purpose, Trace had left the

162 —

game paused in the doorway of that room with only one door. So the day wouldn't keep ticking past while the player stood there, Trace had clicked the knapsack open. It was a holding pattern that held until Lincoln Adrian licked his lips and reached to the right, out of frame, for the mouse.

Just like Abby, he smiled when the words appeared.

They were still there when Veda Robbins picked him up after dinner that night.

They were still there when she found his bed empty the next morning.

It would be the last she ever talked to her sister in anything but a scream, one that welled up deep in her, deeper than she knew she had.

And maybe she saw the recording, or maybe she never did.

We did.

The lace edge of the doily drapes down into the frame like a gauzy eyelid, but Lincoln is still there. There's Lincoln's guilty smile. There's Lincoln, reading these words to himself.

And now, a figure is stepping in front of the camera, blotting out the recording.

It wasn't Mr. Dockett, our librarian, we know that now—"Mr. D" to the students, which was a little too suggestive for the circumstances—but before we knew that, he had what the sheriff's department ruled an accident.

It was because he had no children.

But didn't he pioneer story time on Saturday afternoons?

He evidently *liked* children, and of course he knew books, knew stories.

Being single, too, there would be no monitor on his behavior. His hours after work were a complete mystery to all of us.

It was Deputy Moonlight who found him.

Mr. Dockett had apparently lost control of his hatchback and turned over into the creek, which was unusually full that year.

There were no photographs of his hatchback's rear bumper to suggest that any dents or scratches there were recent. To suggest they were day-of.

We didn't say anything, even when Deputy Moonlight came back around, fastidiously returned each crumpled bill we'd paid him with.

For the next three days, not a single son or daughter disappeared.

The next meeting with the detective, it was story time as well.

The look on his face told us he knew it, too.

"What if this is a test?" he said, cutting from face to face.

"Test?" one of us offered, playing along for the group.

"You believe in fairy tales, right?" the detective said.

Our stone faces betrayed nothing.

"Say there's a group of children in an empty septic tank out there somewhere right now," the detective went on. "Say somebody just wants to judge . . . *reactions*. Probe for inevitabilities in human nature. See if he's wrong."

"Or she," one of us said.

"Or them," the detective said back.

What if, right?

Because of the librarian's accident, were we now failing? Was a cap being screwed onto the top of that empty septic tank?

This was the meeting where James Teague, longtime stepfather to Martin Able, Jr. and onetime linebacker, charged the detective, slammed him into a wall of Tom and Julia Garrett's living room. Every glass figurine arranged on the entertainment center crashed to the carpet. Not a single one broke.

After it was done and over, all bloody lips and torn jackets attended to as best as possible, many hollow assurances given, we looked from face to face in the living room.

The detective was gone.

"Guess he *was* a basketball player," Syd Gustavson said to James Teague, clapping him heartily on the shoulder.

In the doorway of the kitchen, Trace Masters was nursing his beer. Over it, he caught his wife's eye for a knowing moment.

Eight days later, Lincoln Adrian would disappear from his bed.

Before that, though, there was Cathy Vance, the child who could have proved us killers instead of saviors. She would be the second Catherine to disappear. The first had been Cathy Gutierrez, already getting her big sister's cheerleading skirts handed down to her.

This was Catherine Vance. A farmer's daughter.

The sixth week of our ordeal, as it was now known on the news, her father, Theo, showed up at the door with a shotgun.

In one form or another, that's how all of us had shown up.

Theo's skin was patchwork, from a chemical accident in his childhood we all knew about only in the broadest of terms.

We told him we were sorry. We told him he was welcome here. We told him we understood what he was going through, but that was a lie. We didn't understand anything. We knew full well that each of our griefs, it was fierce and individual.

You can't compare grief. It's not a contest, and it's not a common well.

If anything, it's a granular cool fog you've walked into. One that stretches for years in every direction.

But somewhere out there in it, there are small footsteps you know you recognize.

Run after them now. Close your eyes, reach down.

Once it dawned on us that Deputy Moonlight was a taxidermist, James Teague had winced, because he *knew* that.

For the detective, James Teague had tried to take all the blame.

We were all guilty, though.

To make up for it, James Teague organized us outside Veda

Robbins's trailer home that night Trace and Abby Masters had sent her son home with a timer ticking on his life.

We didn't want to know if he *would* disappear.

We wanted to know how. We wanted to know who.

We were in concentric rings spaced all through the trailer park.

We didn't use flashlights or walkie-talkies, and we didn't whistle or resettle our feet in the gravel.

If you miss a deer, that deer just gets away. That deer, it goes on.

If we didn't watch Lincoln Adrian's bedroom close enough, Lincoln Adrian would get away.

Those of us who cried, standing watch, we did so silently, with our hands balled into fists.

Fifteen minutes after eleven, Veda Robbins's current boyfriend showed up, staggered to the front door, and opened it without bothering to knock.

The television turned on. The light in the kitchen.

In that instant we all looked to that glowing yellow square—we think that's when it must have happened.

Nothing had changed about Lincoln Adrian's window.

What had changed was Lincoln Adrian.

He was gone.

In his steady, plodding way, Theo Vance surmised for us what made no sense about that night.

No, Lincoln Adrian's bed hadn't opened up, swallowed him.

No, Lincoln hadn't stepped into a shadow, waited for it to fold around him.

What Theo Vance told us was to imagine what the world must look like to a fly, or a grasshopper. Or a horse.

A grasshopper looks away for an instant, to a vibration on the road maybe, and by the time that grasshopper looks back where it had been looking, and registers what it's looking at, somebody's painted a barn, say.

What was faded brown is now yellow, or red.

It was the same with Lincoln Adrian.

The instant we'd all had our eyes drawn away, the Pied Piper had woven through us like smoke but at his own peripheral speed, and stepped as easy as anything into Lincoln Adrian's bedroom when Lincoln opened the window for him.

Because Lincoln recognized him.

Either the game was becoming real—that's always the dream, isn't it?—or this really was a dream, with no consequences.

Once the Pied Piper's in, well.

Then all bets are off.

Theo Vance had nothing past that.

Probably because his daughter was still just two days gone.

Some rooms, you don't look into.

Next for us, and last, was an accounting.

Not of our crimes and trespasses since our children had started to disappear, but of the days and weeks before that started.

In the story, the legend, the Pied Piper had been wronged by the village, hadn't he?

Who had we wronged? Who would feel justice was being served by leaving that box of CDs in the fourth-grade hall?

What had we done to call this down upon us?

For this we convened in the gazebo in the park, where many of us had had our first kiss. Where our parents had watched movies on a wall of sheets sewn together by their mothers, our grandmothers.

The cigarette butts were already smashed into the peeling railings from the high schoolers. The beer bottles, we brought.

The park was good because the park was dark.

We spoke from that darkness, long wandering confessions punctuated by hesitation and tears. Adulteries, skimmed accounts, furtive glances at legs not legal yet. In addition to Mr. Dockett and Lincoln Adrian, there was even one body maybe still in the bar ditch of another state. As it turned out, Martin Able, Jr. was James Teague's *biological* son.

Martin Able, Jr.'s former biological father turned away from the group, wouldn't look back.

Syd Gustavson, upon hearing what really happened prom night of his senior year, walked evenly to his truck, stepped into the cab, and punched the windshield white.

Julia Garrett, in an attempt to save their son Theodore, still at home with both his uncles standing over his bed, stepped forward and in a high, wavering voice detailed a series of sexual escapades so daring and so broad-daylight that some of us would have blushed, had it been any different circumstance.

And then she stepped back beside Tom, their hands falling into each other's.

That night, even though every install of that video game had been clicked away, all of those computers already becoming shrines, still, Grant Rucker went missing.

We were tiring of euphemisms, though.

What happened to Grant Rucker was that the night, it ate him, body and soul.

The Pied Piper can open his grinning mouth that wide.

He can do anything, really.

Our children were Jace and Alyssa and Bradley and Lincoln and Cathy and Catherine and Martin and Grant.

Maybe they still are.

After the meeting in the park, we became reluctant to see each other in the light. To see each other's faces. An outcome we should have expected, we know.

Where we started to congregate next, it was Theo Vance's barn.

Not to solve, but to remember.

Once, on a particularly low night, one of us started to dance alone through the floating hay dust, her arms out beside her, head lolling, eyes closed, just moving slow and mournful like you imagine a drowned body might float, and the rest of us clapped her a tune. The beat was faltering and uneven, but it was something, anyway.

That night Trace and Abby Masters killed themselves in their bedroom.

Three months later, Claude Weissman called that detective back from the city, where he'd returned once the disappearances had stopped, and asked to meet at the old gym.

The detective found him there, hanging by the neck.

We all wondered how that felt.

As it turns out, Theo Vance's splotchy skin, it was from a pesticide spill that happened in the barn. Though it was years ago, all our arms and faces are starting to show the same patchwork lately—large dry spots that drink lotion, don't take the sun.

We're marked. On the inside and on the outside.

And, that second issue stemming from the baseboard words about the children having been gone a hundred years? Not the possessive pronoun part, but the hundred years part.

Now we understand.

Even when your child's just been gone five days, it feels like a century already. Like everything that's left of your lifetime. Everything good and possible.

And we understand who the Pied Piper was now, too.

Here's how this dark machinery works.

There *is* a village back there somewhere in medieval Germany. The children do get taken just like the story says. And the parents of those children, they kept meeting afterward, whispering their hearts to one another, their skin going pale and mottled from their choice of meeting place. Going piebald.

And those parents, their grief kept them alive, kept them searching in the fog long after they should have been in the ground.

We understand because some of us have started lingering by the playground, where the elementary children move in slow, graceful motion behind the chain-link.

We tell ourselves it's because we remember.

The truth, though, the truth, it's that we *want*.

The reason we could never find out who had shortchanged some drifter for yard work or killing rats or cleaning a gutter, it was that that's just a part of the story you tell yourself. What it allows is a system where bad behavior is punished and good behavior is rewarded.

This isn't that world, though.

Here, the Pied Piper doesn't come to town because of something we've done or not done. The Pied Piper came because of what we *had*.

Just like us, the Pied Piper lost a child, and now wants another, and another, and another.

It's an impulse that makes complete sense to us.

We know we can't spirit away even a single child from the bus stop now, but in a decade? A quarter of a century? In another state?

Wait, we tell ourselves.

Wait just a little bit longer.

Just a few more years.

AUTHOR'S NOTE

Stephen Graham Jones: It's kind of an elliptical path that got me to this Pied Piper retelling. I was working with a grad student on his novel, and his model for it was Rick Moody's *The Ice Storm*. But every time I'd be talking with this student about his novel, my head was always keying on Russell Banks's *The Sweet Hereafter*—which is all pretty ridiculous, as I've never read either *The Ice Storm* or *The Sweet Hereafter*. But I did for some reason know *The Sweet Hereafter* was a kind of loose retelling of the Pied Piper, so it was like he, the Piper, was always lingering at the edge of my thoughts for that semester. My initial plan for this story was for it be cyberpunk, too, but then, man, not even a page in, I realized this isn't freewheeling digital fun and paranoia, this is a town's children getting snatched. And that's horror right there. So I dropped the cyber angle—it's still there a smidge in the video game—stole that *Virgin Suicides* royal first-person trick and twisted its kind of built-in passiveness so as to erase agency, and went with it, just to see what dark places it could take me. That's kind of always how it works, writing horror.

THE THOUSAND EYES

Jeffrey Ford

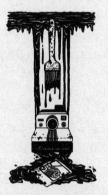

doubt South Jersey's ever been called the Land Where No One Dies, but according to my painter friend, Barney, who lives near Dividing Creek on the edge of the marshland leading to the Delaware, back in the early sixties, out there amid the two-mile stretch of cattails, quaking islands, and rivulets there was a lounge called the Thousand Eyes, and there was a performer who sang there every Wednesday night, advertised on a hand-painted billboard along the northbound lane to Money Island as RONNIE DUNN, THE VOICE OF DEATH.

Barney heard all about it from another local painter, Merle. Old Merle was getting on in years, and I'd see him myself when driving through Milville, creeping along the sidewalk in his tattered beret, talking to himself. He swore that his apartment was haunted. Still, Barney said he never doubted what Merle told him. The reason he trusted him was that a few years back he'd asked

Merle if he'd ever been married. The old man said, "Once, for a few months, to a charming young blonde, Eloise. It lasted through spring and summer, but come fall she up and fled. Left me a note, saying my breath stinks and my dick's too small." Barney vouched for the former, and then added, "Do you think somebody who'd tell you something like that would lie to you?"

Anyway. Merle was in his late twenties and it was 1966. He was living by himself in the top-floor apartment of a half-abandoned building in the town of Shell Pile. Even though the floorboards creaked, the paint curled, the windows let in the cold, and every hinge groaned, the place was big, with plenty of room to paint and live. He scrounged together an existence between doing odd jobs around town and working a few shifts when he had to load trucks at the sand factory. If he had to travel any distance, he rode a rusted old bike with a basket and pedal brakes. He ate very little, twice a day, and blew most of his income on cigarettes, liquor, and weed. The most important thing to him was that he had plenty of time to paint. As long as he had that, he was happy.

At the time, he was working on a series of paintings depicting the bars in South Jersey. He'd go to one, have a few drinks, take some shots with his Polaroid Swinger, and then go back to his place and paint an interior scene with patrons and barkeep, bottles and bubbling neon signs. Barney explained Merle's style as "Edward Hicks meets Edward Hopper in a bare-knuckle match." Still, he was a hard worker, and before long he'd been to all the bars in the area and painted scenes from each. He liked the individual paintings in the series, but overall he felt something was missing.

Then one day when he splurged for lunch and had a burger and fries at Jack's Diner, served as they always were back then on a piece of wax paper instead of a plate, he overheard the conversation of the old couple in the booth behind his and realized what it was that was missing from his series.

"The Thousand Eyes," he heard her say, and instantly it struck him that he'd not painted it.

"I heard it's impossible to get to," the old man said.

"Nah, I had Doris at the liquor store draw me a map."

"That's where you want to go for our fortieth, some mildewed old cocktail lounge sinking into the Delaware?"

"I want to hear that singer who's there on Wednesday night, Ronnie Dunn. He's got a record that they play on the local station, 'Fond Wanderer.'"

"Wait a second," he said. "That's the 'word of doom' guy."

"The Voice of Death."

"Who wants to hear the voice of death?" he said.

"You know, it's a gimmick. Mysterious."

Their food came then, and Merle paid and left.

He'd heard about the Thousand Eyes since he'd moved to Shell Pile, but he'd never been there. It advertised only late at night on the local radio with a snappy jingle, "No one cries at the Thousand Eyes." The place came up in conversation around town quite often, but he'd only met a handful of people who'd actually been. The shift manager at the sand factory told him, "I drank out there one afternoon during low tide. If a shit took a shit, that's what it would smell like. I almost hallucinated.".

There was a woman he met at one of the bars he was photographing, who told him that she heard, and now believed, that only certain people were called to see Ronnie Dunn perform. The singer sent out secret invitations through his song on the radio. If one was for you, you would find the Thousand Eyes; if not, you wouldn't. "I've been out there three times with my girlfriends and three times we got lost," she said. "A couple of people supposedly went to look for it and never came back."

"Is that true?" asked Merle.

"I guess so," she said.

Luckily, Doris at the liquor store didn't mind at all drawing

Merle a map. So on a Wednesday night in September, he took off on his bike, camera around his neck, pedaling west toward the  river. Doris figured by bike the trip would take him about an hour and a half. He was to look for Frog Road off Jericho, and then head west following Glass Eel Creek, looking for a spot where a packed dirt path led off on the right into the cattails and bramble. She told him the Army Corps of Engineers built the road back in the early fifties when they were trying to eradicate mosquitoes. The sunset was rich in pink and the weather was cool. Merle rode fast, excited by the prospect of finally finishing what he'd started.

He found the path and took it out into the marsh, cutting through stretches of cattail, stretches of soggy earth dotted with green. He passed into a small wood, all its trees twisted and stunted by the salt content in the water. Stopping and resting for a moment, he took a deep breath. The call of mourning doves and the breeze in the dying leaves gave him a chill of loneliness. As he got back to pedaling, he wondered how lonely it would feel there in the dark on the way home. On the other side of a clutch of white sand dunes, he descended and crossed a wooden bridge over what looked like deep water. Beyond it sat the Thousand Eyes, majestic in its grandiose molder. A Victorian structure with a wraparound porch and a splintering wooden cupola over the entrance.

The dirt path became the dirt parking lot of the place. Situated at the spot where one turned into the other, there was a large sign held up by two 4x4s planted in the ground. The only writing it held was in the very bottom right corner; otherwise it was a big rectangle of eyes on a violet background. Carefully rendered peepers of all sizes with lids and lashes, staring, squinting, popping and red, sad and blue. In the corner it said, THESE ONE THOUSAND EYES WERE PAINTED BY LEW PHARO. Pharo was one of the local painters, and Merle knew him. He couldn't recall Lew ever speaking of this job, though.

Beneath the signature, there was a vertical list in smaller script—NO BARE FEET, NO PETS, NO FOUL LANGUAGE, NO SPITTING, NO CAMERAS! Merle hid his bike in the cattails at the edge of the parking lot and then took his jacket off and wrapped it around the camera. Darkness swamped the marsh as he took the splintered steps to the entrance. He opened the glass door, and when he closed it the sound echoed through the place. His footsteps set the floorboards to squealing down a dim hallway. Off to his right, he saw a pair of doors flung open on a large room lined on two sides by windows. A lit tea candle sat on every table, and beyond there was a dance floor and a low stage with a curtain behind it. As he entered, the bar came into view off to the left.

There was a guy behind it wearing a white shirt with the sleeves rolled up and a black bow tie. He had a lit cigarette in the corner of his mouth. When he caught sight of Merle, he called in a puff of smoke, "Step right up." An older man and woman sat at the bar, drinking martinis. "What'll it be, sailor?" the bartender said.

"Vodka on the rocks," said Merle.

"A purist."

"Is Ronnie Dunn performing tonight?"

The woman turned and said, "Yes," before the bartender could answer.

Merle wondered if the old couple were the same people from Jack's Diner. His drink came and he said, "So did you name this place after the Bobby Vee song?"

"This place has been here long before that song ever came to be," said the bartender. "In fact, that song was written by two women and a guy. The guy, Ben Weisman, who wrote songs for Elvis and dozens of other stars, came in here one night, and that's where they got the title for 'The Night Has a Thousand Eyes.'"

"For real?" said Merle.

"Yeah, there was this housewife from Passaic, Florence Greenberg, who started a record company around 1960, Tiara Records. She was on vacation down here that summer, visiting relatives, and Weisman flew into Philly and drove down here to try to sell her some songs for her artists. Greenberg's niece, Doris, gave them directions to the Thousand Eyes as a place to get away, and they spent the afternoon into the night, doing business right at this bar. I was tending bar that night, and I clearly remember Weisman at one point asking Greenberg, 'What rhymes with eyes?'" The bartender took a deep drag on his cigarette to emphasize the profundity and blew it out at the ceiling.

JEFFREY
FORD

After another round had been served, the bartender said, "You folks better get your seats for the show. It's gonna get crowded in here in a few minutes." Merle thanked him, took his drink and balled-up jacket, and chose a table set off in the back by the wall from where he could take the whole scene in at once. He sat there in the shadow, staring into the light of the candle on the table, sipping his vodka, feeling for the first time the damp chill of the place, when a thought popped into his head. First it struck him that he hadn't seen Lew Pharo in a long while, and then came the memory flash that Pharo was, in fact, dead. It all came back—Lew had suddenly gone blind, couldn't paint, and shot himself in the head.

He smelled low tide, heard the cars pull up in the parking lot. The patrons shuffled in. That night the Thousand Eyes drew six couples in rumpled finery, a pair of girls a little younger than Merle, a creepy-looking guy with a wicked underbite, and a crazy woman in flowing pink gauze who danced to her chair. A waiter appeared and took orders. Merle was still trying to figure out, since he had to use the flash, how he was going to get a shot. He wondered how serious they were about NO CAMERAS.

By eight thirty, everyone was juiced. The waiter had been twice to Merle's table, and the bartender put on the jukebox a string of Jay Black and the Americans tunes. The crazy lady in

pink and the guy with the underbite took to the dance floor and did a dramatic fake tango to "Cara Mia," and everybody applauded. Finally at nine o'clock, the houselights went down and then out. A few moments later a spotlight appeared on the twelve-inch raised platform at the edge of the dance floor. It was the waiter, with a microphone hooked to a small sound system strapped to a hand truck. "Ladies and gentlemen," he said into the mic, which sparked with feedback, "now the moment you've all been waiting for." While he spoke, two guys rolled a very small piano onto the stage from behind a curtain.

The waiter stepped forward as they brought out a drum set. "As some of you might know, there's an old Romanian tale about a man who, late in his life, becomes wealthy. This fellow thinks it's a shame that he won't live long enough to spend all his money. His rich friends tell him he should go to the Land Where No One Dies. So he does and takes his wife and daughter with him. Everything there is smooth as silk, plenty of sunshine, plenty of booze, no hangovers. What's not to love? But then the wealthy man finds out that although no one dies, occasionally someone hears a persistent voice calling them. When they follow it, they never return. He realized this must be the voice of death. When his daughter hears its call, he tries to stop her from following it, but he fails. The voice is just too compelling."

The waiter stopped for a deep breath and then said, "Renowned critics, ladies and gentlemen, have likened the allure of our special guest performer's voice to the voice in that very tale. So let's hear it for RRRRRRonnie DUNN, the Voice of Death." The guys moving the instruments had become the band—a bass, piano, electric guitar, and drum. They played "When Smoke Gets in Your Eyes," and the stage filled with fog. It crept up around the legs of the players and billowed out onto the dance floor. When it cleared, there stood Ronnie Dunn, mic in hand. The band switched course into the intro for "Fond Wanderer."

Barney quoted to me Merle's firsthand impression of the singer. "It looked like they dredged him out of the river. Gray complexion, and kind of barnacles all over his neck and face. His hair was white going yellow, like an old wedding dress, and he wore it in a moth-eaten wave. The tux was too tight. Ronnie wasn't just Dunn, he was well done." Still, he slowly lifted the mic and sang.

> *"Fond Wanderer, where do you go?*
> *Fond Wanderer, I know you don't know.*
> *Fond Wanderer, come to me now,*
> *Step into the shadow, and I'll show you how."*

Merle described Dunn's voice as "If you took Little Jimmy Scott and Big Ed Townsend and sandwiched Johnny Ray between them and then lit the whole fucking thing on fire, it'd be a little like that." He said Ronnie was out of tune and behind the count, low, menacing, but sometimes he'd hit a few sweet and beautiful notes. There was a rich resonance to the sound of his voice before it even hit the twang of the tinny speaker, like a song echoing down through a metal pipe from some strange other place. Off-putting at first, then intriguing, and eventually its appeal was hard to resist.

> *"Fond Wanderer, please hear my plea.*
> *Fond Wanderer, you can't ignore me.*
> *Fond Wanderer, it's over and out,*
> *More like a whimper, less like a shout."*

Ronnie creaked around with some mortuary footwork between stanzas and then hopped off the stage and approached the table with the two young women. "You girls busy tonight?" he said into the mic. The band waited for him, keeping the tune

going. "Step into the shadow," he said, "and I'll show you how." The young women grimaced, got up, and left. The crowd loved it.

> *"Fond Wanderer, can I have this dance?*
> *Fond Wanderer, are you sleepy by chance?*
> *Fond Wanderer, this way's the door,*
> *Out to the boat waiting down by the shore."*

Merle had heard the song on the radio enough to know there was another stanza coming. He got the camera and put his jacket on. His strategy, born from momentary intuition, was to approach from the right, sweeping around the tables to that side and getting close to the stage, from where he could capture Ronnie, some of the patrons on the dance floor, and the reflection of the tea candles off the mirror and bottles behind the bar. He moved without hesitation.

The flash made the singer lift his arm in front of his eyes and stagger backward, shrieking like a gull. In the fifteen seconds Merle had to let the film develop before he could rip it off and peel it open, the band stopped playing and Ronnie lurched through the spotlight. "You've ruined it," he screamed, going green in the face. Dust fell out of his nose and his hair wave had broken. Abruptly he stopped, looked across to the bartender, and yelled, "Don't just stand there, get the camera. Come on." The bartender waved to the guys in the band, and they put down their instruments and stood up. Merle ran.

He brushed past the couples on the dance floor and was heading toward the double doors. From the corner of his eye he noticed the bartender coming from behind the bar with a sap in his hand. He looked to the doors again, only to find that the waiter had, in an instant, planted himself in the line of escape. Merle put on speed, determined to make a go at just running the guy over. He had the momentum, but it never came to that, because from off to the right, the dancing lady in the pink gauze came twirling by like a dervish and smashed into the waiter. The two of them went over like sacks of turnips. Merle leaped and cleared them. He streaked down the hallway, his steps making a racket. Out into the cool night, he ran for the cattails, shoving the photo in his jacket pocket and draping the camera belt around his neck.

It was dark, but he managed to find the bike pretty quickly. As his ass hit the seat and he pedaled, he looked back over his shoulder. Shadowy figures emptied out through the lighted portal of the Thousand Eyes. When he reached the path, a car started up behind him. His heart was pounding and the adrenaline was spurting out his ears. He pedaled with the belief that Ronnie Dunn's flunkies really meant to kill him. "Like Superman," Merle told Barney, "I was flying down that path, but I couldn't see a fuckin' thing. Behind me, I hear the car coming and they're getting so close they've got me in their headlights."

In the midst of the chase, Merle reported having what he called "a moment of genius." He bet that with the confusion of the flash in the dark, no one could see he had an instant camera. He took it from around his neck and threw it back over his shoulder, hoping they'd at least stop to pick it up and that would buy him more of a lead. In fact, it worked. Not only did they stop, but once they had the camera they broke off their pursuit. Later, on the safety of Frog Road, heading toward Jericho, he realized he'd gotten away and could laugh at the thought of Ronnie Dunn holding the camera, discovering that the shot Merle had taken was no longer inside it.

A lot was riding on that one photograph: the foundation to the grand finale of the Bars of South Jersey series. As he discovered, once back in his apartment, the door locked, that picture was a success in every way. It had that Polaroid flash glare he'd come to love, sweeping vaguely down from the left corner. The hundred reflections of it off the glass behind the bar were like a

distant constellation. Slow-dancing shadows with glowing red eyes. And Ronnie, eyes soulfully closed, with a corona of light around his head and bathed in white fire, his open mouth emitting a beacon of green mist. When he first saw it, Merle couldn't wait to get down to work, but as it turned out, he put off starting the painting for nearly a year. He told Barney the photo had given him nightmares. And so the Bars of South Jersey series sat unfinished.

In September 1967, Hurricane Doria, only a Category 1, made it to the Jersey coast. It wasn't bad but for two tragedies it left in its wake. One made the national news; one made only the local radio station in Bridgeton. In the national news story, three people drowned when their boat sank off Ocean City. The local story, which Merle heard late at night while painting, was that the rising tide had swept away the Thousand Eyes. Upon hearing it, he immediately went looking for the Polaroid from his visit there and found it under a stack of drawings. The bad dreams hadn't visited in months, and he laughed at his own foolishness, admonishing himself for not having already finished the series.

The same week The Thousand Eyes washed into the river and Merle started the painting, he pedaled over to Milville for an art show opening late one afternoon. He got there early and was standing on the sidewalk, waiting for things to get started. Last time he was there they'd had a tasty white Zinfandel. Across the street, in the shadow of the sub shop, he noticed some commotion. Other people on the street were stopping and staring in that direction as well. It was the old couple from Jack's and the Eyes. The woman was pulling herself out of the grasp of the old man. She yelled, "I got to go. He's waiting." She'd move away from him a few feet and he'd run and catch her by the arm. "Don't go," he said. "Please, I can't stay," she said, and pulled away again. "I'll go with you," he called. She didn't look back, and he didn't follow but leaned against the front of the sub shop and wiped his tears with a handkerchief.

Merle got blitzed that night at the opening, was shown the door, and could barely pedal home. Still he went back to work on the painting of the Thousand Eyes, putting everything he had into it. Two weeks later all that was left was Ronnie Dunn's weird left eyebrow, a couple of gray barnacles, and a small section of forehead. The rest was complete, perfect, capturing the Polaroid effects, the singer, and the grim, cold spirit of the lounge. Merle worked with a homemade squirrel-hair brush to render the up-twist of the pale hair, concentrating so hard he perspired. As he executed the final stroke on the eyebrow, he heard something odd. Backing away from the painting, he reached behind him with his free hand and turned the radio down.

He listened, and eventually the soft noise came again. At first he mistook it for a mosquito, but then he remembered it was the end of October. He closed his eyes and, hearing it twice more, recognized it as a distant voice. Someone calling out on the street, he thought. He laid the brush down, went to the window, and opened it. He stuck his head out, and above the sound of the wind, he heard the voice of Ronnie Dunn, singing "Fond Wanderer." He laughed, slammed shut the window, and went back to work, figuring someone in one of the buildings across the street was playing the old 45.

But as he painted on, the voice got louder and louder. As Merle told Barney, "It was like Dunn was out in the street, then in the downstairs foyer, then out in the hallway, then in the corner of the room. And the closer I got to finishing, the closer he got to me. I was shivering scared, but I was damned if I wasn't going to finish the series. I worked fast without giving up anything in the quality, hoping that finally finishing would put Ronnie and the whole mess out of my misery." He finished the painting an hour later, "Fond Wanderer" booming in his head. The second

he was done, he put on his jacket and headed for the door.

Merle said he knew what was happening, and the drive to follow the voice was monumental, like two metal fingers were hooked in each of his nostrils and attached by a chain to the Queen Mary, which was pulling out of port. He got as far as the door and opened it. And here's where my doubts about the story came in, because Merle attested to having another "moment of genius," and my credulity can only accommodate one Merle moment of genius per story. Barney convinced me, though, that it all made sense. Anyway, Merle flung himself back into the room, grabbed the palette knife, and scraped off down to primer the last gray barnacle he'd painted on Ronnie Dunn's forehead. With that, the voice abruptly stopped, and he was no longer compelled to follow.

Two weeks later he tried again to finish the series, and again the voice returned. He scraped it quick before Dunn got too loud. He found that as long as he left that swatch of canvas bare, the voice was silent. The kicker, as far as Barney was concerned, was that Merle eventually tried to get a show with the paintings of the bar series that were finished. He saved up and made slides and took them around to the different galleries. The gallery owners were intrigued by the local subject matter, but every one eventually passed, saying something along the lines of, "Really pretty good, but there's just something missing."

"And that," said Barney, "is the real voice of death."

Somewhere around 1975, Merle said he sold off for cheap, sometimes as low as twenty dollars, each of the paintings in the series, except for the Thousand Eyes. He confessed their presence was turning him into an alcoholic. As long as he had access to the last, unfinished piece and could still complete it if he dared, it didn't matter to him where the other paintings were. Once the series was properly finished, it would take on a power greater than the sum of its parts, and Merle would, of course, be dead.

The painting of the Thousand Eyes hangs, as it has since 1976, above the booths in the back of Jack's Diner. Jack's son Dennis understands it's just for safekeeping. Barney said Merle swears that he's going to finish the piece any day now, but the old man does a lot more mumbling around town than painting lately, looking everywhere for that street that leads to the land where no one dies.

JEFFREY
FORD

AUTHOR'S NOTE

Jeffrey Ford: When I got the request from Dominik and Navah to do a story that was to be a riff on a classic fairy tale for their anthology, they requested that I send, as soon as possible, which fairy tale I'd be working with, so I got up, walked five feet to a bookcase shelf where I have a lot of fairy tale anthologies, and picked a book at random. The one I came up with was Andrew Lang's *Red Fairy Book*. I opened the book in the middle to the story, "The Voice of Death." Without reading it, I wrote to them and told them that was the one I'd be using. Months later, when I had time to actually write the story, I read the tale. That morning, before reading it, I'd had a memory from when my mother died. I was in a limo with my wife and kids. In the opposite seat was this old Irish woman, Rose, who lived across the street from my parents and whose lawn I used to cut when I was young. The day was sweltering hot and my younger son, maybe two at the time, got carsick and puked. Right when that happened, I looked out the window and we were passing this old abandoned bar, all the windows busted out and partially burned. Its sign was still intact. *The Thousand Eyes*, it read. That memory mixed with the fact that I'd gotten a call the day before from my painter friend, Barney, who lives in southwest Jersey, by the Delaware River, which is a strange land unto itself. And the final influence was some of the true-life ghost stories old Rose brought from Ireland and used to scare the shit out of me with when we'd sit in her grape arbor after the mowing was done.

GIANTS IN THE SKY

Max Gladstone

equisition Officer Log, 11887/quartz

Honestly I can't even with these motherfuckers and their magic beans anymore

Is it my fault they keep losing the requisition form

I mean

Fine

Probably it is

Requisition Officer Special Memorandum to Ops, 11887/quartz

OK so seriously bro

This, Best Beloved, is a requisitions form. I know it's been a few hundred years since you cloud-brained assholes wore the flesh, but surely before the Great Upload you at least once in your marketable lives signed a contract with an actual goddamn pen

———❖———

NOTED that as per Ordinance 9a22e3c/gamma, "due to the volatility and sensitivity of the Leguminous NSpace Rotator, groundside contact agents are required to file requisitions forms on a per-unit basis" ~~which document I may add is not exactly the most complicated~~

~~THERE ARE ONLY THREE BLANKS FOR FUCK'S SAKE~~

which form is publicly available on netpub/rx/*.

NOTED that groundside contact agents are ~~morons~~ frequently delinquent in requisition form submission (1 out of 287 complete and on-time as of 11886/quartz), increasing Beanstalk Protocol risk.

REQUESTED that Ops ~~put the fear of God into~~ remonstrate with agents about the importance of proper procedure when ~~placing n-dimensional spatial rotation technology in the hands of castoffs~~ dealing with uplift scenarios like those faced on Earth.

EXPECTED that ~~someone might fucking care what I'm doing around here~~ communication of Project Beanstalk risks and goals will lead to improvement in on-time requisition form submission, with a goal of at least 80 percent by end Q1.

With thanks,
[sigfile.asc]

OUTER VASTNESS, 11888/quartz
ORM SPRAWLS FULL BEAUTIFUL AND
BELLYSWELLED THROUGH TIME
ORM THROBS ORGASMIC UNION WITH

MANYGENDERED CRYSTAL STRUCTURES OF PURE MATH
   ORM MASTERS SUBMITS BIRTHS UNIVERSES
THROUGH MULTIVALENT TUMESCING ORMLOINS
   ORM IS L33T HAXXORZ

MAX
GLADSTONE

Yo

UM
SHIT
SORRY, HOLD ON
ORM DID NOT SEE YOU THERE

Que pasa, Orm ol buddy

DE NADA Y TU
HOW FARES THE FLESH

Fleshy

YOU ARE TROUBLED

Orm, you ever get the sense people aren't paying attention
to you?

ORM'S MANY ARMS EMBRACE COSMOS
WITHIN ORM THERE ARE MULTITUDES

Look I told them Beanstalk would be a waste of time unless
they wanted to do it right
And nobody's *fucking doing it right*
Like think it through for a minute say you're a groundling

ORM COMPRISES GROUNDLING ASCENDED

TRANSPOSED AND VOYAGEUR

So imagine some bearded meat puppet staggers up to you and offers to trade you beans for cow

ORM COMPARES BEANS-TO-COW AUCTION PRICES, CONSTRUCTS RISK/REWARD MATRIX, PROJECTS MOST PROBABLE FUTURES, INHABITS ALL, STRIDES GODLIKE BETWEEN WORLDS

Yeah
Not exactly what I meant
I've been embodied for, what, about three hundred years. I've been watching. Ops and the other Higher-Ups don't listen. They think that just because they plumb vasty deeps with quantum brains untethered from physical reality, they know everything

MUCH HIDES FROM THE FLESH THAT IS REVEALED TO ORM

Oh yeah?
Like what

YOU FEEL SLIGHTED

Dipshit I just *told* you—
I mean yes, okay
Look, we need someone in flesh, for legal reasons. An observer with a meat brain's the last bulwark against hacking—I keep laws and paperwork. It's not as if I don't have the same extensions and add-ons as the rest of you, it's just there's a flesh-brain *too*, so yeah I'm a bit pissed the Higher-Ups don't take me seriously

ALSO YOU MISS LIZA

. . .

OPS HAS RECEIVED YOUR LETTER
ORM KNOWS THIS, AS ORM KNOWS ALL
YOU ARE NOT ALONE

<u>Requisition Officer Log, 11889/quartz</u>
No reply from Ops today either
I mean what did I expect really
Can't get no respect
Shit, nobody down there in the mud has remembered those words for, what, a thousand some-odd years
Which is funny, see, coz it means these days Rodney Dangerfield really *couldn't*

Okay, Liza, look. You're sitting there—fine, floating there, hosted in a pineapple-size probe headed toward Deneb at an appreciable fraction of light speed, reading this, maybe, I hope you're reading this, anyway *sitting* or something vaguely like sitting, and you think, oh, she's blowing things out of proportion again. She's not really as frustrated as it sounds, she's just writing to hear herself write, maybe you're even chuckling—God, I hope you can still chuckle, I hope you thought the ability to chuckle was worth including in that compressed version of yourself

Yes, dammit, I *do* get carried away sometimes. I get on a roll. I like *feeling* and there's something so, so much fun about pretending, for once and for certain, that I'm not the fucked-up one. So when I *find* a case like this, God, it's hard to look away. I couldn't make it up.

Look at them down there.

I'm not supposed to be watching through this satellite, not really in my remit, but, but, okay, just look

See the old dude with the beard and the robe by the side of that muddy strip the locals call a road? The one with the staff and the peddler's pack? The one who hasn't blinked in a quarter hour? A fly landed on his eyeball three minutes ago?

That's our guy. Groundside Contact Agent. That one in particular's puppeteered by a Higher-Up name of I shit you not Iluvatar, Ops's number two. After you left, there was a big fad for name changing. Ops became Ops. Doesn't leave a lot of room for a personal life, or a personality, but let's not kid ourselves, Ops never had much of either. Some people kept the names others gave them, or they gave themselves. Some named themselves for gods, because some people are colossal cocks.

And some named themselves for gods from Tolkien. You see where I'm going with this.

You remember: when we sublimed, we pulled up the rope ladder behind us, right? The world was going to shit, so why not? We climbed the Beanstalk and closed it down. Didn't want the war chasing us up here.

Most people think we destroyed the Beanstalk, but why would we? Motherfucker was capital H-A-R-D hard to build, and look, even though we got freaky godpowers so long as we stay virtual, construction work's still construction. You have to hoist frustrating huge chunks of matter around. Plus, raw materials are sort of hard to come by? We're still shy of singularity-powered monomolecular nanofactories; we can't just rajaniemi ourselves a new megastructure out of nothing.

If you have a working space elevator, you don't blow it up, is what I'm saying.

So we rotated the thing into a higher-dimensional space. It's still there. We can bring it back whenever. You want the math, it's in your archive at acad/rx/*, along with a nice bit of proof that n-dimensional rotation costs less than just building a new one.

Everything went fine for us and shitty down below. I don't think you ever saw how shitty. No shame in that. Most people didn't want to look at what might have happened if we hadn't made it up. Lots of blood. Lots of death. Lots of *details*. The first four timekeepers checked out as soon as their decade was up; I stayed. I wanted to watch. I felt like I owed someone something.

Took the groundlings three centuries to pull their faces out of the mud, adjust to the higher rad levels, stop killing one another quite so much. Basically feudal conditions now, pockets of supremacist ideology, and a lot of folk who need food, water, sanitation. I sent a note up the line about thirty years after you left.

Well, anyway, I suggested we do something. Ops ran with the idea. They spent a long time debating uplift strategy. How do you explain to people who've forgotten all the science their great-great-great-et-ceteras knew that we up here were humans, sort of, once, but now we're not, mostly, but anyway here are some bacteriophages and by the way you should wash your hands with soap and water after hog butchery? Also we heard you need food, so here's some.

Try to do that equitably, in a way that doesn't pour gas on the flames of premodern warfare. (You remember gas and flames, I hope.) How?

Fairy tales, was Ops's plan. Just plain give them food and medicine, and they might not trust it. Let them steal the stuff— sneak into heaven, grab the goose with golden eggs or whatever, and run back home—and they'll be so pleased with themselves they'll never ask why.

So: see that dumb kid plodding down the mud road, leading a cow that barely deserves the name? See Iluvatar pilot that jerky meat-marionette toward him, the kid I mean, offering beans? See the kid react the way you would if you saw some bug-eyed zombie stagger out of the trees toward you, speaking an ancient language, shoving a handful of beans in your direction?

The kid punches Iluvatar's meat puppet in the face, and it pops with a wet, wretched sound, because there's nothing *inside*. The beans tumble. The kid runs away with his cow. Nightmares tonight. Maybe for the rest of his life. Can you blame him?

And I fucking bet Iluvatar didn't sign out a single one of those beans.

Checking. Yeah. No.

<u>Unthinking Depths, 11890/quartz</u>
Why you gotta keep busting my balls?

Hello Iluvatar
Ops finally get on you about those forms?

Didn't have to. We share everything up here. Ops just left the letters for me to read and sort through what to do about 'em. Killjoy.

You could maybe do without the laser light show, man
I can see you just fine
No need to go all Oz the great and powerful

Our plans are ineffable and myriad. We are trying to fix a broken civilization. Computing every word of this interaction requires more processing power than the entire human race possessed until the beginning of the last millennium. I don't understand your warp.

Warp?

Your major malfunction. Your problem. Your kink for paperwork.

I'm not asking you to solve quantum gravity with a slide rule. I just need you to pay a little more attention to details. Like the location of all those n-dimensional rotators.

What does it matter? They can't hurt anyone.

They can't hurt *us*. But say one of the groundlings busts one open without protection. Say they accidentally activate it without safeties.

So we lose a few castoffs. It's no big deal.

You arrogant prick. You cocksucking motherfucking

Hey.

—are actually *people* down there, even if they look like—

Simmer down.

—to you, but no, you're off pretending to be—

Stop.

<u>Requisition Officer Log, 11890/quartz-2</u>
And then he made me.

One tick I was shouting at him and the next he grew so *big*,
not like there was more of him but like the whole world had been
a part of him all along, like even I was a part of him and hadn't
noticed it, I was just this flea-speck crawling on his arm, and then
he pinched me between his fingers, narrowed his eyes and

Well

He said, these were his actual *words:* if you want to worry
about the small things, do.

And he left and let me fall.

So that's where it sits: Ops silent, Iluvatar galaxy-striding,
and they care enough to screw with groundling lives, but not
enough to help, really. All the small shit, that's for me to sweep up.

Fuck.

I still have satellite privileges. I guess I can pull the logs, see
how many beans we made, scan Earth inch by inch and row by
row; I'll need a high-res search, and the radiation still screws our
sensitivity, but if I go over the area around the Beanstalk anchor
one square k at a time, I should be able to find most of them. And

if I miss, some people die. Which Iluvatar and Ops seem to find acceptable, since it saves paperwork

Don't

I mean

It's fine it's fine it's fine

I wish you were here.

I could have gone with you. I should have, maybe. You asked why I stayed. We need someone incarnate on Earth Station, sure, but I could have handed off the job. I'd held it long enough. Thirty times longer than anyone else. You told me I was afraid. You were right

I felt afraid, then. When he held me between thumb and fingernail like a tick. Not as afraid as I felt when you left.

Fuck it, I'll find those beans myself. It'll take a while. Might as well start with the road where I watched Iluvatar yesterday.

Requisition Officer Log, 11891/quartz
There's a girl

Liza, you don't understand

She's so fucking *smart*

Smart as any of us were way back when

Getting ahead of myself.

Let's take it from the beginning.

A girl has the beans

A groundling kid, maybe fourteen, gangly as all hell, knees and elbows

Roll back the tapes and you can see her hiding in the bushes near Iluvatar's old-man puppet. Watching. The puppet staggers forward. The boy hits him, runs. The puppet falls. So do the beans.

The kid snags 'em.

Three. Purple. Smooth. Glowing faintly from within. Because of course Iluvatar and Ops, when they assembled the operation (*without consulting me*), missed the point of the beans being beans, which is that they don't look valuable. Not worth a cow, not worth trade.

These ones sure look worth stealing, though, because shiny.

The kid must have snuck next to Iluvatar's fallen puppet, grabbed the beans, run off.

And she's *testing* them.

She's had trouble with curiosity in the past. She has scars on her arms and legs; part of her cheek is melty and slick. Napalm? A fire? Looks like she got too close to some leftovers from the war.

The kid boils one bean for a long time, with no discernible change. (They're not water-soluble, of course, and well-insulated.)

She takes it, rigs a rock to fall on it from a high place when she pulls on a rope, retreats to what she hopes is a safe distance, and tugs. Breaks containment: the bean compresses a few hundred cubic meters into a very small space, explodes. Our girl's hiding behind a rock, of course. Smart. The heat's enough to singe her hair.

She ponders the next two beans.

I ponder her pondering.

OUTER VASTNESS, 11891/quartz
SOLAR GRAVITY CANNOT CONTAIN ORM
ORM SPINS SAILS AND HULL FROM ASTEROIDS
ORM HALF-TWISTS ORMSELF UPON ORMSELF AND
STRETCHES TO ORM'S FULL LENGTH, CUTS ORMSELF
IN HALF, REMAINS WHOLE
ORM JEWELGLITTER RIPPLES SPACE

Orm, pal, friend, I need a favor

DELAY, WHILE ORM IGNITES THIS FUSION
REACTION WITH THE HEAT OF ORM'S REGARD
DONE
THANK YOU FOR AWAITING ORM

Orm, what are you doing?

ORM ALLBRIGHT BECOMES ORM SHIPBUILDER
ORM TIRES OF ORGIASTIC BACCHANAL MATH
ORM'S FANTASIES STALE
ORM BEGINS TO GROW WEARY OF THE SUN
IF YOU SEE WHAT ORM DID THERE
THE UNIVERSE IS VAST

CONTAINING INFINITE REFLECTIONS OF ORM
ORM SHALL STARE INTO ABYSS
ABYSS SHALL STARE INTO ORM

You're leaving
I didn't
Okay, fine

ORM SENSES YOU ARE LESS SANGUINE THAN YOUR
RHETORIC WOULD INDICATE
DO NOT FEAR ORM WILL FORGET YOU
ORM WILL AWAIT AMONG THE STARS

When do you leave?

SOON. LONG HAS ORM PONDERED, AND
CONFIRMED IN ORMHEART
SHIP HAS STOOD READY FOR PROPER SOLAR
ORIENTATION W/R/T GALCENTER
ORM WILL SWALLOW CORE SINGULARITIES
MAKE THEM PIECES OF ORM
ORM HAS CALCULATED A SEVEN-SLINGSHOT
ORBIT PATH OUTSYSTEM WHICH LESSER BEINGS
WOULD TERM OBSESSIVE
ORM LEAVES IN
THREE DAYS

Orm I
Never mind
You have root access to the Beanstalk, don't you?
You helped design the thing

ORM COMPREHENDS ALL ROTATIONS IN SPACE

NO SECRETS HIDE FROM ORM

But can you hide secrets from, you know, other people?

EXPLAIN YOUR DESIRE

There's this girl

ORM UNDERSTANDS
ORM HAS COMPILED EXTENSIVE SIMULATIONS—

No no no no no
That's not what I
I mean
Look so one of the groundlings has a bean
I want to get this kid up here and out again without anyone
noticing
Like Ops or Iluvatar or anyone like that

WHY

They're not looking to help, Orm
Iluvatar especially
Dude wants a hobby, wants a pet
He doesn't give a fuck about the groundlings really
He might break this kid just playing with her
He wants to be worshipped
And she's not the worshipping type
I like her
I just want to hide the Beanstalk's rotation back into
threespace for a while
And keep her hidden while she's up top
That's all

ORM CAN DO THIS THING
OR

Yes?

YOU COULD COME WITH ORM
WITHIN ORM'S SHIP SPREAD VASTNESSES
SUFFICIENT
ORM'S WINGS BEAT FASTER
ORM'S CONSTANT ACCELERATION DESIGN WILL
OUTPACE LIZA'S PROBE WITHIN TWO DECADES
WE WILL CATCH HER

Orm, I
That's a very kind offer
But
I have this thing I need to do

WHAT DO YOU SEE DOWN THERE
THAT IS NOT WORTH LEAVING

Liza asked the same—
Look, just rotate the Beanstalk when the time comes, okay?

<u>Requisition Officer Log, 11893/quartz</u>
She's almost here
The kid I mean

Noticed the beans' glow was brighter when she faced south
Followed it through the forest
Fought off bloodthirsty mutant monkeys
Made her own spear from bamboo and a piece of broken
airplane hull

So, so, so smart

Kid will find the platform soon

Orm's leaving

Tonight
Midnight

What's Orm looking for out there anyway?
What were you looking for, when you left?

Sometimes I wonder which of us was the more afraid

I think I know

Requisition Officer Log, 11894/quartz

I can see the awe in the kid's eyes from orbit when the Beanstalk rotates into being. Diamond miles glisten into a lapis sky and she's so *excited*

She enters. Looks at little things: tests for weld seams with her thumb, pries at panels with a piece of flat metal hanging from her belt. I remember what that feels like, learning, not knowing.

The kid climbs.

No one notices but me.

Unlogged audio, Earth Station, 11895/quartz
"Hi."

"I'm sorry about my voice. It's been a long time since I used it."

"I'm alone. I'm hiding you from the others. They're even less like you than I am."

"I was, yeah. A long time ago. The metal keeps me alive. Something like alive."

"No, sorry, you can't stay. I made you a care package. Textbooks. Transmitters. Medicine. You'll figure it all out. I'll help when I can."

"What do you mean, the station's shaking?"

"Oh."

"Shit."

"Run."

<u>Unthinking Depths, 11895/quartz</u>
[Caught in the swirl of Iluvatar's rage]

[Sinking sinking sinking]

[I can fight I do fight I scrape and scramble and transform but he doesn't have a meatbrain holding him slow, he's a distributed consciousness spread throughout planetary orbit, I got nothing to handle that]

[make the motherfucker sweat for it though]

I can explain

What explanation would satisfy? You gave her—

Knowledge.

They're not ready. We wanted to establish terms. Trade. We wanted them to know their place.

Bullshit. You don't even watch them. To you they're the children of failures, that's all. You need to be able to point to some reason you're up here, and they're not. She deserves—they all deserve better.

They deserve what we give them.

If you fuckers weren't going to care about them, why didn't you leave them to me in the first place?

[he swirls]

You didn't even pay attention when they were dying. You hid in your own fantasies until those got tired and then you went out into space, wave by wave, and didn't spare one backward glance at the folk left behind. Nobody bothered to check in for three hundred years. The whole project only started because I kept bugging Ops. And then you assholes got involved, because why, because it gave you a chance to prove how fucking superior—

No.

You don't scare me. You're big, and you're smart, and yeah you can cut off my access privileges, kill me—but I'll still be right. Those kids down there, they'll learn. They'll grow. You won't be able to stop them when they rise.

Watch me.

[can't breathe]

[can't]

[fingers in my mind]

[fire]

[can't]

[Liza]

[a glow]

[a susurrus of scales]

[a sun rises]

[no sun, but an enormous eye]

MAY ORM INTERJECT?

[Iluvatar screams]

Heh

OUTER VASTNESS, 11895/quartz
You came back

ORM NEVER LEFT
TIME AND SPACE ARE AS ONE TO ORM
ORBITAL CONDITIONS WILL BE RIGHT ONCE MORE
IN A FEW MILLENNIA

I could have handled him

ORM IS CERTAIN

Why?

YOU ARE RESOURCEFUL

I meant, why did you come back?

ORM DOES NOT UNDERSTAND YOU

Not sure how I can make it clearer . . .

ORM MEANS
ORM DOES NOT UNDERSTAND
WHAT YOU SEE DOWN THERE
ORM CONSIDERS THAT MANY FRONTIERS EXIST
NOT ALL ARE SINGULARITIES
ORM CONSIDERS THAT MANY PROBLEMS EXIST
NOT ALL ARE MATHEMATICAL

ALSO ORM HAS NEVER LIKED ILUVATAR
WHAT A PRICK

Fair

Personal Communication, 12003/quartz
Liza
I'm sorry I couldn't say this before.
I was scared.

You were wrong

Leaving was wrong

Taking the easy way out was wrong

Even before that—locking yourself away in sims

While the planet burned

You were wrong not to watch

I love you and

I was afraid to have that fight, afraid to say all this. So

I let you paint another fear on me

I became the woman who wouldn't fly

Christ, I wish I'd fought. I've wished for a long time now.

Maybe you can't forgive me

Maybe you won't

But—my best guess is you're a hundred fifty light-years out

Call it one fifty for my message to reach you

A couple centuries for you to beam back, coz you'll be traveling

meanwhile

A few hundred years round trip

No time at all, really

We have work to do, Liza

And I miss you

And you should see this kid

She's nonstop

You'd like her.

But for now, I gotta go. Orm's helping me teach Ops's goons
to use a pen.

AUTHOR'S NOTE

Max Gladstone: Have you ever watched a cappuccino die?

It's a sad sight. The drink waits on the bar, flush with foam at first, but those little bubbles don't last forever; as they pop, the plush surface dimples and pits. Minutes pass, and the foam collapses. You can still drink the cappuccino just fine—but in its freshness, it was beautiful.

Most stories don't work like that. Often, they're best grown slowly and from grand consideration, like sprouts from seed. They reward refining.

No doubt I wasn't born knowing "Jack and the Beanstalk," but it soaked through my skin. When I realized no one in the anthology had spoken for it yet, I had to raise my hand. And *beanstalk* leads to *space elevator* quite naturally.

Then I got stuck. I couldn't figure out how to make the story mine. Which version was ideal? How could I break the tale open? I've wanted to play with form for a while, and fairy tales seemed like a great opportunity, but: *how?* Giants are fascinating: like humans, just . . . bigger. Post-humanity seemed like a good analog, in modern SF language. But to pack the world I wanted into the space I had, I needed an angle.

The first line of this story popped into my head on the train. I wanted to write the rest of it more than anything in the world. Once back from the gym, I ran to the keyboard and slammed out the rest.

Most stories aren't the cappuccino on the bar. But some are best written before doubt dimples the foam.

THE BRIAR AND THE ROSE

Marjorie Liu

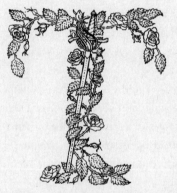

he Duelist was an elegant woman, but that was by her own design and had nothing to do with the fact that her mistress bade her act with certain manners when she was not, by law, killing her peers.

She was called Briar, but only on Sunday. Other days, she was simply the Duelist. No man had legs half as powerful or as long, and her reach with a sword was so terrifying that experienced fighters would surrender at her first lunge. A foreigner from across the sea, a brown woman in a city where she was as exotic for her skin as she was for her sword; where, after some seven years—four of which had been spent in her mistress's employ—she had settled down comfortably in her reputation and only had to draw her sword against the very young and very stupid.

Her mistress was the most favored courtesan of the Lord Marshal, and in the evenings she was called Carmela. The Lord

Marshal thought himself a special man that he knew her name, but Carmela had a talent for making every man feel the same, and each knew her by a different identity.

Even the Duelist was not privy to all her secrets, though she spent most of her waking hours attending to the woman, and even longer nights sitting by that bedchamber door, listening to her loud, dramatic lovemaking. The Duelist knew that Carmela had more respect for her sword than her intelligence, that she took delight in having a quiet beast of a woman guarding her, a woman with the same brown skin, as if they were a mismatched set.

Carmela paid the Duelist well for her sword, silence, and skin—and trusted her not to, as she put it, get any ideas.

But the Duelist, in fact, had many ideas.

Saturday had come around again, and it was almost midnight. Nearly Sunday, in fact. Which was the only day worth living, in the Duelist's estimation.

She stood at the edge of the ballroom, wearing her most imposing jacket—a stiff green silk that hugged her trim waist, held down her breasts, and enhanced the already massive width of her shoulders. No one had ever told her to dress in outfits that complemented her mistress's voluminous ensembles, but the Duelist had made it a rule. She understood Carmela's vanity, that a valued guard was also an accessory, and that it would please her mistress that nothing around her, nothing that reflected her taste, could ever be accused of anything so tacky as *clashing*.

Tonight Carmela was dressed in emerald silk, a gown embroidered at the bodice with gold thread and laced with rare gems as yellow as a cat's eye. Her full skirt rubbed against the stocking-clad legs of the men crowded around her. "To remind them of my hands," she'd once told the Duelist. "To make them imagine my hands stroking their legs."

Her breasts were as enormous as her waist was small: two

immense, soft, ridiculous distractions that were barely covered by that petite bodice. Her brown skin looked even darker against her bright dress; dusted in gold, Carmela's skin was nothing but supple, her face slender and delicate, crowned by thick brows. She was the only flame burning in a room full of aging pale-skinned men and women who would never be the equal of such raw beauty, not even in their wildest dreams.

She was also a proud, dangerous woman who had stayed up too late and danced far too long with the Lord Marshal. Addicted to the attention she received from him and his cronies, even as the Duelist watched her movements slow and her words thicken.

"She'll collapse soon," said the Steward, in passing.

"Prepare the special tea," replied the Duelist, watching as Carmela missed a step in the waltz and stumbled against the Lord Marshal. He laughed, gathering her up in his arms like it was some great joke. But Carmela wasn't smiling.

"Don't tell me my job," muttered the Steward. "If you were only half as fast with that sword as I am with her tea, you'd be more than just her paid dog."

The Duelist could have drawn her sword and removed his head before he even finished that sentence, but she was beyond the age where she needed to prove a point by killing. That had been the way of her youth, but no longer.

The Duelist crossed the ballroom instead, causing a minor ripple as the much shorter guests stumbled in their dancing to get out of her way. The Duelist ignored their frowns and the deliberately loud whispers; some of it was sour grapes, anyway. She'd dueled against, and killed, hired swords who belonged to the uninvited (and now, in some cases, divorced) wives of several guests. Wives who would have been wiser punishing their wandering husbands, rather than attempting to murder the woman those men had wandered to.

Still, the Duelist felt some sympathy for those spurned wives.

Carmela flaunted her conquests, vaunted her great beauty and wealth, cultivated an obsessed audience—rubbed it in, as if she wished to blind every other woman with her magnificence. In short, Carmela—unlike most others who spread their legs for coin—did not know her place.

Carmela saw the Duelist coming, frowned, and touched her brow with delicate painted nails.

"My darling," she cooed to the Lord Marshal, leaning over so that her breasts swelled even more from her dress. "I'm *quite* exhausted. It's time for me to retire."

"I know better than to argue," he said, with a pout that did not belong on a man in his fifth decade. "Every Saturday is the same. You throw these lavish parties in your home, then run away just as things are getting interesting."

"I'll make things *very* interesting for you, should you come back Monday evening."

The Lord Marshal patted her waist. "I will count the minutes."

Carmela smiled and made her way through the crowd, so graceful she might as well have been dancing. She curtsied and murmured her good-byes, encouraging guests to dance into the morning, taking a glass of wine from one of her admirers to draw her tongue over the rim (out of sight from the Lord Marshal, of course), and laughing merrily at some dirty joke that the Duelist felt certain was anatomically impossible.

Only when they were outside the ballroom, deep in the shadows, did Carmela's smile slip and that sharp charm dissolve. She passed the Duelist, hissing something completely unintelligible beneath her breath, and made her way through the library. The Duelist always posted guards in that room to keep out roaming guests; the men straightened as they walked past, gazes firmly on the floor and not on Carmela's breasts, now spilling free of the bodice she was loosening from around her waist with frustrated, angry movements.

The Steward appeared at the foot of the stairs, accompanied by a young maid.

"Get this thing off me," Carmela snapped, but the ruddy-faced teen was already plucking at the stays. She pulled the dress down her mistress's body, which was naked underneath.

The Steward had his eyes closed, the cup of tea held out in both hands. Carmela grabbed it from him, drank the brew in one long, grimacing gulp, and tossed the cup to the floor, where it shattered against the stone.

"My lady," he murmured. Carmela ignored him and proceeded up the tower stairs with only the Duelist behind her.

The tower was high and narrow, a place for prisoners or the doomed. One cell at the top of an endless spiral of stone steps, its dense wall broken only by slits too narrow for a woman to slip through and jump. Murder holes, the Duelist called them. No furniture, save a thick mattress upon the floor. Not even a bed frame. Too much a risk. Sheets, but nothing to tie them to. No bucket for relief, but a small closet with only a hole in the stone floor to squat over. The massive oak door took all the Duelist's strength to open, and only two people had the key: she and her mistress.

Such were the rituals for falling asleep on a Saturday night.

"Go on, go," her mistress commanded, already collapsed on the mattress and tugging on the linen nightgown that had been left folded on her pillow. The Duelist obeyed, closing the door and turning the lock. She thought she heard her mistress say something but knew better than to go back inside.

She waited until she was certain Carmela was unconscious to reopen the door and step into the darkness of the tower cell. She sat upon the floor and listened to the other woman breathe.

The Duelist always knew when her mistress was truly asleep. Not just asleep in body, but in soul—when her hold finally relaxed, and she slipped away for good. Her breathing would change in that moment, become something else. Lighter, sweeter. The breathing of another woman entirely.

Another woman, the right woman: the woman whose body her mistress had stolen.

It was in these silent moments of watching, waiting, that the Duelist had first begun falling in love.

The Duelist had bought a book the previous morning while on another errand. Something old and worn, so that the ink from newly printed pages would not rub off on the skin. Nothing that could leave a trace, not even a little, not in the slightest. She often bought books, and chose the subjects just as carefully; last week, a romantic adventure involving pirates and island temples filled with gold; today, a treatise from an ancient philosopher on the affliction of malevolence, which some believed was spread upon the breath of men. The Duelist had learned, long ago, that oppression could be defeated only through study; like a sword, the mind must always be tended to if it was to aim true.

Because it was Sunday, the town house was entirely empty when the Duelist came home from her morning walk to the port. Not one maid, not one footman, not even the Steward or the Cook. Orders from Carmela herself.

"No one else in this whole quarter has a Sunday off," the Steward boasted. "Ours is a magnanimous mistress."

Of course, the same quarter also wondered why the entire staff was turned out on Sunday—something that was just not done. The gossips couldn't decide whether Carmela used Sundays to bathe in the blood of orphans or to offer up unholy sacrifices to the Fallen Gods. After all, beauty such as hers could not come naturally.

It didn't. And yet it did.

On those secret Sundays when the entire household was dismissed, only the Duelist was allowed to attend Carmela—or even

set foot under her roof. Her guard camped outside the front gate, with orders to never allow anyone else to enter the premises, not for any reason, under pain of death.

And no one ever, on any day, was allowed in the tower.

The Duelist, of course, had made herself the exception.

Light seeped through the murder holes, but the young woman was still asleep. Fallen limp among the tangled covers, a thin sheen of sweat on her brow. Long black hair clung to her skin, gleaming beneath shafts of morning light: golden and piercing. Dust motes floated.

The Duelist watched her breathe. It was one of her few joys. It was easy not to confuse her for Carmela, even though they shared the same body. No acidic scowl, no cruel tension in her jaw. Even in sleep, that face was gentler, and more beautiful for it.

The Duelist sat on the floor, close to the mattress. The tower cell had not been built for a woman her size—standing felt claustrophobic, her head nearly touching the ceiling. She always feared, too, that it might be too intimidating for the young woman. The Duelist had never, until three years ago, wished she could make herself smaller.

The book was beside her, along with a basket of food: a soft bitter cheese, a tender roast dove, loaves of crusted sourdough, and more. She unbelted her sword and laid it on the rough stone. Removed her silk jacket and unbuttoned the collar of her blouse. Unwrapped the wide black scarf that held down the graying curls of her hair, which spilled outward, against her cheek.

"Rose," she said quietly.

The young woman stirred, slow and drugged, and it was another long moment before she opened her eyes.

"Briar," whispered the girl, and even her voice was different: her accent, the way she curled the final note of that name.

Her mistress was asleep and Rose was awake.

"I'm here," the Duelist said. "It's safe. Take your time."

Rose's eyes stayed open, staring at the ceiling. "You shouldn't say that to me, Briar. There's no time at all."

"Not if you waste it," replied the Duelist, rising from the floor. "Sunday is long. And I have your favorite stinking cheese, and that nectar from the ridiculous fruit you so like. Some formerly fresh bread, too. I thought to tempt you."

A weak cough broke from between those round lips, those perfect lips. "Oh, Briar. You never change."

The Duelist frowned. "Forgive me if I offend."

Rose tilted her head to look at her, mouth tugging into a weak smile. "No. I celebrate you. I am blessed with you. As long as you're here, I am not alone."

The Duelist sat very carefully on the edge of the mattress. Rose visibly swallowed. "Anyway, I *am* starving. The last meal I remember was here, a week ago, with you. That's the only good in my life. You and this room, just the two of us. I'd lose my mind, otherwise. All that emptiness. All that lost time when I'm asleep and she— she has my body—"

Her voice stopped. After a moment, she held out her hand.

The Duelist almost took it but caught herself. No contact, not even the slightest. It might wake Carmela early, which had happened once before, long ago, the same day the Duelist realized there was another woman living in that perfect skin. Just one touch, a brush of her fingers against Rose's hand, and that was enough to make those eyes change, that mouth tighten into a hard line—a shadow rising to press against the insides of that face like a demon wearing a mask made of human flesh.

"How dare you touch me," whispered Carmela.

"You were crying for help," stammered the Duelist, unable to think of a better lie in that moment. "You reached for me yourself."

"Get out," said Carmela, swaying and falling to her knees on the mattress. "I sleepwalk, you idiot. Ignore everything you hear inside this room and *never* disturb me again."

The Duelist had not survived that long by always taking orders—or curbing her curiosity. The next Sunday, she returned to the room. Found Rose.

They never touched again.

But the Duelist could not help making at least the gesture of a touch: she extended her hand, and their palms hovered close, heat gathering in the air between them. They stayed like that, almost touching. Until it was more than the Duelist could stand.

She placed the book into the young woman's open palm. "She has your body, but you are still Rose. You still live."

"Stop it," replied Rose, clutching the book to her chest; and then: "I hate this sleeping draft she uses. I can barely move."

"Here." The Duelist held out the bottle of juice, but the young woman shook her head, eyes going dark in that way she knew too well and dreaded.

"How many men this week?" asked Rose, in a quiet voice.

"This accounting does not serve you—"

"How many?"

The Duelist did not want to tell her, but long ago Rose had refused to speak to her until she revealed the truth. That silence had lasted weeks, and left the Duelist forlorn, confused. Since then, she had come to understand how there could be more pain in the not knowing. In that first year of knowing Rose, understanding what had been done to Rose, she did not think often of what it would mean to be possessed—did not reflect on how it would feel to have some other person inside her own body, controlling, distorting, plundering. The violation, the horror.

These days the Duelist thought of it often and the knowing, while hard, took less work than the not knowing.

That was wisdom, a storyteller had once told her.

It hurts, she had responded, almost casually.

The storyteller had nodded. Wisdom always does.

The Duelist said, "Three different men, but she was with the Lord Marshal every night, as well."

Rose managed to find her feet and was once again trying to jam her fingers through the murder holes. Just to feel the sun.

"Rose," whispered the Duelist.

"I'm fine," said the young woman in a soft voice. "I don't remember a thing."

There was a time, in the beginning, when the Duelist considered killing Rose.

It was not her idea, of course. That first year the young woman made the request often—quietly, desperately, angrily—even silently—and those appeals chased the Duelist from the tower at sunset and followed her during those long days escorting Carmela from one appointment to another, watching as lard-heavy men, pale and sweating, drooled over her mistress's figure. Sometimes they glanced at the Duelist, but only because she was a brown woman with a sword.

The Duelist was not beautiful. She had been blessed with a man's square jaw and strong nose, and though she was elegant, there was nothing fine, nothing compelling to stare at but the long scar that traveled from her temple to her throat, a duel gone wrong in her youth, a duel with a man who had fast feet. The Duelist was not sorry for that scar. Beauty had a price that she was content to never pay.

"If you wish to be more than a common street fighter, if you want to be a hero, then you *must* kill me," said Rose, early on, in a perfectly reasonable voice. "To stop her from doing this to another innocent girl—that would be your prize. I'm dead anyway; you know that. When she's done with my body, she won't keep me alive."

The Duelist didn't mind those conversations, much. Others were harder.

Sometimes Rose would cry, "What is wrong with you? How can you stand it? How can you watch those men, that witch—all of them using me? *Raping* me?"

And the Duelist would say nothing.

But sometimes when she stood guard behind her mistress, stood still and silent as Carmela sat naked in her dressing room smoothing oil over those breasts the Duelist knew so well, she thought of what it would feel like to push her sword through the delicate muscles of her back, what it would sound like to hear that gasp, smell her blood. She thought of it often, in the beginning.

She thought of killing them both, some Sunday: the young woman and herself, by sword and rope, or poison. Quick. Holding each other. Touching at last, as she desired, more than anything.

Giving in, giving up. Almost.

Then, one afternoon, Carmela remarked, "Did you see the Lord Marshal's wife in the garden when we left? The old dodder? Would you believe she was lovely once?" Quiet laughter, slow and mocking. "Beauty is always the first to die, my Duelist. It is the most fleeting of all our mortal gifts, and there is no power in this world that can save it. All we can do is steal time, when we can. Steal moments." Her mistress gave the Duelist a coquettish look that did not belong on that face, those eyes, that mouth, and gently tapped her nearly exposed bosom, which glimmered with gold dust. "*This* is a moment."

"You wear it well," said the Duelist in a quiet voice.

She decided, right then, that she and Rose would live.

She had not crossed those thorny mountains and lifeless seas to die so stupidly. She had not humbled herself, hidden herself, forgotten herself—nor left the desert and her home—to surrender. Not once had she ever surrendered. Not in the war, not when the Torn Men had surrounded her in the Balelands and broken her sword and made her wear chains for a year until she escaped. Not then. She had not wavered. Not once.

She was the Duelist, after all.

"How do you fare?" she asked the young woman, the next Sunday they were together.

"Terribly," she said. "I want to die."

"You must have hope," said the Duelist.

"Hope." The girl barked a laugh. "What is that?"

"To never surrender."

There were different tellings of the tale, and all were a little true. In each there was a witch, an ancient crone. In every version a comely girl, cursed to sleep. The Duelist had heard them all as a child and scoffed at such nonsense.

Now she was older, wiser. Now she scoured books for such tales, and on those afternoons when her mistress set her free to deliver messages or buy her perfumes or lurk menacingly upon the stoops of admirers who were a little too demanding, the Duelist always made extra time for herself: to search the city for story-tellers, the ones who were blind and toothless, confined to their stools in the shade; the ones who were not fools, who knew there was truth in what they told.

In the desert, storytellers were the keepers of ancient things and could be trusted with secrets. Here, too, in this city across the sea.

There was a girl, the Duelist told them after months of tea, months of listening at their knees. The only child of a desert king. Most beloved, and graced with many blessings. Perhaps too many. Beauty has a price, after all.

Beauty draws many eyes, agreed the storytellers. Some of them unkind.

Yes, said the Duelist, and told them of a witch, a witch in the body of an aging beautiful woman, who had come to the king to seduce him—but only for the purpose of becoming close to his daughter.

A witch who craved power, yes—but who craved beauty even

more. Power could be lost and regained—power was fleeting, power was part of a game she loved to play—but beauty was far more precious, far more rare. Beauty could feed a hunger inside the witch that no crown or treasure on earth could ever satiate; a hunger to be seen and adored, and *desired*.

Except the king was no fool, and neither was his child. Both saw the witch for what she was. Both denied her, drove her away. But not before she promised to take the girl. A curse upon her, a prophetic oath.

Time passed.

The girl became a young woman, still most beloved. But the witch had not forgotten—no predator would give up so perfect a prey. And so she hunted, and she connived, and she made her way back to the young woman, found a way into the desert fortress.

The king was away, gone into the mountains to harry his enemies. And the witch had taken a new body: a sun-wrinkled arthritic old crone who spun fine cloth, and who begged an audience with the young woman. A brief encounter, involving thorns hidden in a bolt of linen, thorns that pricked that perfect skin and drew beads of blood, blood that invoked magic, blood that sent the young woman into a slumber from which she could not wake; a slumber no one noticed because the witch had stepped so neatly into her body.

The witch fled, in that body. Fled across the desert and the sea. And in this new city, she built a home.

And in this home, she hired a guard.

The guard was another foreigner, from another desert. A woman who had lost her family in a hideous war—a war she fought for endless dire years.

Deadened her heart, said the Duelist to the storytellers. Stripped away joy, all ability to feel the simplest of pleasures. Even love was nothing but a rumor she'd once heard, so long ago she'd forgotten what it was, and who had started it.

The guard believed the witch was nothing but a frivolous courtesan, and felt little for her, barely even loyalty. Until one day she entered the tower where the witch slept, there to perform a duty—and the princess opened her eyes instead.

Their gazes met. And in that moment—

—she remembered love, said the storytellers.

Love, echoed the Duelist. Love did not make the guard clever. She could not find a way to free the princess.

Love is powerful, replied the storytellers. Love is divine. That is the answer to every tale we tell. What sleeps can always be awakened with love.

I love her, said the Duelist, abandoning the story. But nothing has changed. I cannot see the way.

You will, they replied.

But the Duelist was not so certain.

There was a small girl amongst the storytellers, a bright young thing with brown hair and freckles dashed across her nose. Her grandmother, who was the eldest of the storytellers, said to her, How would you break a witch's spell, little one?

Find her true name, said the girl.

And how, asked her grandmother, do you glean a true name from one who speaks only lies?

Patience, replied the child. You listen.

The grandmother smiled. Even the greatest liar must eventually tell the truth.

One must only be wise enough to catch it.

"I had a dream," said Rose, one Sunday. "Several dreams, actually. My head is full of them, Briar."

The Duelist paused in mid-stretch, palms pressed flat against the floor in front of her toes. A demonstration for Rose, who wanted to learn how she had stayed in good health after more than a decade of hard fighting. No one ever assumed that anything but her size had kept her alive all these years; for Rose to realize there was actual skill and training involved was rather unexpected. And gratifying.

"I didn't know you dream," said the Duelist.

"I don't. This is the first time." The young woman grimaced, and scooted off the mattress to her feet. She fell backward and had to struggle again to stand.

The Duelist would have only needed to extend her elbow to help her, and she almost did so without thinking.

"What did you dream?" she asked.

Rose walked with small, unsteady steps to the narrow window in the tower wall, placing her fingers in the slit. "It was all . . . unfamiliar. I was in a chamber made of smooth blocks engraved with leopards. I had many servants. My skin was golden in color, not brown, and I wore white silk."

"Was there more?"

"A different dream. Somewhere else. Carried in a litter, holding a dog in my lap, smelling the rain outside while thinking that I had better hurry or—or, nothing. I can't remember much else. The last dream is even more unclear. Standing naked before an immense bearded man wearing armor and a red sash. My body was round. My thighs rubbed."

The Duelist thought about that for a moment. "I have a surprise for you."

Rose glanced at her. "You have decided to kill me?"

The Duelist stepped over the mattress to the door. With a hard tug, she pulled it open. And stood there, waiting.

Rose stared. "What trick is this?"

The Duelist started to answer, but something hard lodged in her throat, something so magnificent and wild she felt like a child again, small and vulnerable, and consumed.

"Are you strong enough for the stairs?" she asked.

The young woman still seemed stunned, but gave a short

sharp laugh. "I'll manage, even if I have to slide down each one."

But both women hesitated at the tower door. The Duelist said, "Sometimes I wonder how asleep she really is."

"That's part of her trap. Using fear to bind people in their place. I wonder if I'd been stronger . . ." Rose went silent, leaning against the door frame. "How much of that witch's power did I hand her outright?"

"Don't blame yourself."

"Ah," she replied sadly, and sat on the stairs to scoot herself down to the step below. A long journey, just like that—scooting, lowering, bit by bit—mostly silent—until halfway down Rose's face crumpled and the Duelist thought she'd begin to cry. Instead she let out a sharp, almost hysterical laugh that rebounded off the curved stone walls and made the Duelist blink in surprise. Rose clapped her hands over her mouth but was still shaking with laughter.

"I feel free," she managed to say. "Oh, gods, I'm a fool. But this is the first time in years I've felt free."

"Rose," said the Duelist, and then smiled—a real smile, a crooked grin that seemed to emerge straight from her heart to her face with terrifying, beautiful power. She felt flush with the thrill of exhilaration and fury. The Duelist wanted to lean in and kiss her.

Rose said, "You're beautiful."

"Let us hurry," said the Duelist. "I want to show you something."

The house was quiet except for them. Odd, seeing Rose walking outside the tower. The Duelist felt dizzy looking at her, for a moment afraid she was wrong, that it was instead her mistress. But then she looked into those eyes and relaxed.

There was a library, but it held no books. Carmela was not much of a reader. She possessed only artifacts, sculptures, low couches covered in soft pillows; and along the walls, massive paintings of women framed by long velvet curtains that hid the

empty bookshelves. Twenty portraits, twenty different faces, twenty bodies hanging. All of them, gazing out with the same sly expression, that cruel smile.

"It's her," said the Duelist. "Every one of them."

Rose shuddered. "She hasn't done mine yet."

In fact, Carmela had taken to bed the artist she'd commissioned to paint her portrait; he was scheduled to begin next month. But the Duelist kept that to herself. Instead she said, "Look around this room. This is where she keeps her treasures. See if anything is familiar."

"That," said Rose, pointing to an engraved vase perched on a small marble pedestal. "I saw the design in a dream, embroidered into a tapestry that hung beside a fireplace." Hesitation, while she looked again at the paintings. "My dreams are of these women, when the witch was in their bodies. I'm seeing her memories."

The Duelist felt pleased. "We already know there's a limit to how long she can hold you. She must rest one day a week in order to regain her strength. And now that you are glimpsing her memories—"

"—perhaps the lines between us are weakening in other ways. But that could put you in danger, Briar. What if she's dreaming of this moment, right now?"

"Rose," began the Duelist, then stopped and turned, listening.

The young woman also went very still, balanced on the balls of her feet. She'd bragged once that she was a fast runner—or had been. But there was no outrunning what was inside her. Or what had opened a door in the other room and was coming toward them with heavy footsteps.

The Duelist strode from the library. Her sword was in the tower, but her hands were strong and that unspent fury burned deep in her belly—rich and hot, and powerful.

"You," she said, entering the hall and finding the Steward just outside the parlor, holding a satchel in his chubby white hands.

"You are not permitted in my lady's home on Sundays. Where are our guards?"

He gave her a startled look, but only for so long as it took him to remember who he was.

"How dare you," he replied. "You desert cunt. Our lady gave me special permission to come here today. She has errands for me to run."

"You are a liar," replied the Duelist in a cool voice. "And a thief, I think."

His mouth twisted. "It hardly matters. We'll all be turned away from her employment, soon enough. She's going to live with the Lord Marshal, and he has his own staff."

"What are you talking about?"

The Steward let out a laugh. "Of course you don't know. You never speak to the serving class. Our mistress is *pregnant* with the Lord Marshal's child."

The Duelist went still. The Steward looked past her, and his smile froze.

"Oh," he said.

Rose stood in the hall, staring at him. The Duelist watched her, every nerve on fire. Her slender body, covered in fine linen— her hands at her sides, slowly rising to touch her stomach.

"How does he know it's his?" she asked. And then laughed. A cruel, unhappy sound.

"M-my lady," stammered the Steward.

The Duelist slid a thin wire from the back of her belt, stepped behind him, and in one smooth motion brought it down over his head and pulled back hard on his throat. He stiffened, choking, but it was easy enough to kick the back of his knee and ride him face-first to the floor. Bones crunched. His feet danced. The Duelist pulled back so hard she felt the wire cut through his throat.

He died quickly. The Duelist slid off his back, tugging the wire free. Blood dripped, but she cleaned the thin steel on his fine jacket. Her face was hot, heart pounding. She felt deeply troubled, and knew it was partly because Rose had seen her kill.

The young woman said, "Thank you."

The Duelist finally glanced at her. "He was a dead man the moment he saw you. He would have brought up this conversation." She paused. "But you knew that."

Rose gave her a cold smile.

They tossed his body into the slop pit where all the excrement flowed. It was a tight fit. The hole in the cellar was only meant for garbage, but the Duelist used a sledgehammer to break and twist his arms and shoulders until they resembled pulp, and kicked his body through. Someone else might have wavered or lost their resolve, but this was the sort of work, sadly, she excelled at. The work of eliminating foes.

She cleaned. Got down and scrubbed the stone floor where she'd cut his throat, checked the walls, the stairs to the cellar, examined every place his body had been. And then she had Rose hold out her hands, and examined her nightgown for blood.

"I can't truly be with child," she said.

"Your hands are trembling," the Duelist said.

"The sun has gone down. I'll have to sleep soon." She hesitated. "I was angry before, but now I'm just afraid."

The Duelist led Rose up the tower stairs. It was harder going up than down, and there were long moments when the young women was forced to stop and rest. It was not just the drugs in the previous evening's tea—it was the arrival of night, it was the curse, it was the witch beginning to stir from her own brief sleep. The Duelist could feel Rose slipping away from her. Sunday was almost over.

In the tower, in her room, the young woman collapsed upon the bed with a groan.

"Briar," she said, as the Duelist sat on the mattress beside her.

"I will try my best to dream. I will look for a way to be free."

"I will be with you," replied the Duelist. "The next time you open your eyes, mine will be the only face you see."

A month later the Lord Marshal announced he was divorcing his wife to marry the incredibly wealthy daughter of a foreign duke. The girl was rumored to be only a little better-looking than the sea sloths that spouted water in the harbor.

Within days Carmela was confined to bed complaining of a stomachache, but her bitterness prowled through the house. Maids were dismissed or beaten with hairbrushes, dishes were thrown at the cook, even the Duelist found herself nearly slapped for standing too close, but perhaps—even in anger—Carmela was not quite that stupid.

"I would have killed the child anyway, before it had a chance to grow too large inside me," she told the Duelist outright, watching her as if she half expected recrimination. "It was only a whim, nothing more. I thought it would be an interesting experience being a mother." She patted her breasts. "Thankfully, I came to my senses. I alone am allowed to cannibalize *this* body."

The following Sunday, when Rose found herself still spotting with blood from the miscarriage, she wept with all the force of a monsoon. Relief, yes. But grief, too, that a life had been forced inside her womb without her even realizing it.

"What am I?" she cried, scratching her own arms. "I'm not human anymore. I'm just a thing she uses."

The Duelist said nothing. Outside the guards were shouting about an oversized cart. She left the tower early.

The angry season passed and with it the summer plague. The only person who died in the house was the new Steward, but that was the final indignity. Before the corpse cart could drag the poor man off to the pits, Carmela announced it was time to move.

"This is not a place for a woman with ambitions," she declared.

"So where do we go?" asked the Duelist.

They were standing over a map of the Known World, a gift from an admirer, his name long since forgotten.

"South," said her mistress.

The entire household fit into three barges, and they traveled down the river into the rich farmlands of the southern valleys, where from the deck one could see lush rolling hillsides over which ran countless grape arbors, and local children in dusty rags played along the shore amongst ragged herds of goats.

It was idyllic, lovely—except for the boatloads of mercenaries heading north. The Duelist could smell them from nearly a mile off. War was coming again, perhaps. Across the sea, over the mountains, in the desert, in these perfect valleys—no place was ever quite safe enough. The Duelist had learned that the hard way. Peace rarely lasted.

Carmela turned her nose up at it all—the vineyards and mercenaries alike—and rested beneath her parasol, the latest Steward at her side. When an undine slid under the barges, she refused to come to the rail to see. The Duelist crowded with the crew, gaped at the creature's massive graceful passage. The Duelist wished she were a painter, so that she could show Rose these sights with more than just her poor words.

Their new manse was even larger than the last, tucked within the most elite neighborhood of the capital; a steaming sprawling riverine city where every canal and building was part of some ancient ruin. The Duelist did not care for the place; its rulers had funded the invasion of her desert kingdom, hoping to possess the endless, gnarled groves of a rare spice tree her people were famous for, which grew only in the perfect sandy soil at the base of their mountain.

She could smell that spice everywhere. It floated in the air, on the breath of everyone who spoke to her; she tasted it in every meal that curdled on her tongue, and even her clothing began to reek. To her, it smelled like ancient history. Like blood.

"I'm sorry," said Rose, when the Duelist could no longer hold her bitterness inside. "I remember hearing of that terrible invasion, their awful greed. My father was too far away to send help."

"It would not have mattered," the Duelist said, amazed at the ease with which she lied.

Carmela had no such reservations about their new city. Her target was the Regent, a man both cold and restless, and with immense power. He had the long-lobed ear of the king, some said—and most certainly held the keys to the coffer.

When the Regent came with them on the tour of their new home, he asked the Duelist, "You, with the sword. Man or woman?"

Carmela answered for her with a laugh. "Oh, how you jape. A woman, of course. I can't have a man guarding me while I sleep, can I?"

"You could leave that to me," he replied, with absolute seriousness. "Your guard won't be necessary in this city, I promise. If you must have protection, at least hire someone less . . . frightening to children. I'll pay for it."

"Oh, you," demurred Carmela, and later said to the Duelist, "The Regent is a very generous man."

"You think quite far ahead," she replied.

"A woman must," said Carmela. "Only men can surrender themselves to the Fates. If a woman is to make something of herself, she *must* plan. Otherwise, even the most precious gifts"—and she waved her hand over her face—"will go to waste."

This, the Duelist knew, was true.

For nine months she waited. She watched the household prosper. A stable was refurbished to house a matching pair of stallions, a gift from the Regent. The new cook tried to steal some gold, was caught, and survived the amputation of his left hand—but not the removal of his right.

And every Sunday she listened to Rose's dreams.

One day in particular when the monsoons had finally returned and the war in the south was turning from rumor to fact, they sat quietly for a long time, listening to the downpour. Rose looked up suddenly, half-shy, half-defiant. "Do you know what it's like when you have a word on the tip of your tongue and can't remember it?"

The Duelist did, having learned and forgotten three languages before the one she spoke now.

"Well, it's not a word precisely," said the young woman.

"Is it a song?"

Rose shook her head. "It's a life."

Then she stood and pulled off her shift, standing naked. And for an endless time neither of them moved nor spoke.

The Duelist could feel the girl's breath on her, and she was sure the girl could feel her breath in return.

Storytellers knew other storytellers and were loyal only to one another—and to those who had a very particular need. The Duelist sought out the old ones who lived in her new city, but they had already heard her tale from their brothers and sisters in the north.

They had nothing new to offer, but only a word of warning: the body her mistress had stolen was still young and beautiful, but a smart woman like the witch would already be looking for a replacement. In the stories, in the lore, it was so—and once she left one body for the next, her old skin would be destroyed. The witch wouldn't even need to order it done. The separation alone would kill the body she'd been inhabiting, drop it like a puppet, even with another soul still trapped inside.

The Duelist was deeply troubled by this. She'd told herself she could wait, wait forever, for the witch to leave Rose. And then it would be as simple as spiriting her away, protecting her from the witch and whoever she sent to kill her.

But this . . . she could not fight. Which meant there had to be another way.

And then came the Regent's ball, on a Saturday.

In the weeks preceding, the city had been abuzz with rumors of assassins, that this would be the night when western agents attempted to murder the king's right hand. Carmela laughed such things off as petty, but the Duelist clad herself in cold gray Samarin chain mail. Around her neck, a stiff collar. Even the edges of her gauntlets were ridged in iron.

"I am always gratified by your professionalism," said Carmela.

The Duelist nodded. "Professionally speaking, I find living more gratifying than dying."

The Regent had no wife, which made it less awkward when he sat Carmela at the great table, at his side. Her dress was more conservative than any she had worn at previous balls: a high collar, long sleeves, skirts that clung to her hips rather than sweeping outward like a great fondling hand. The dark red silk still served to reveal every curve of her astonishing body, but no one could complain that she showed an inch too much skin.

The Duelist stood against the wall, watching nothing but her for the entire night, studying the way she touched the Regent—or did not touch him—taking in her new restraint, how her mistress kept her seductiveness in check except for certain moments when the Regent reached for his glass and she leaned in to whisper in his ear, rubbing her breasts against his arm.

She was quite good. The Duelist watched her with the same admiration she felt for particularly cunning snakes, the ones who put their prey in a trance. It was clear, too, that this was what she'd been trying to achieve all along. There was no mistaking that cold, triumphant smile.

"Just think, our mistress could be the next queen if she marries the Regent," said the new Steward, in passing. "Should anything happen to His Majesty, that is. He's old, doesn't have any children. The Regent is his chosen successor."

"How very convenient," said the Duelist.

Unfortunately, midnight arrived. Before the musicians could really get started, Carmela's hands began to tremble, and a sheen of sweat could be seen across her entire face. The Duelist tried to hide her pleasure as she made her way through the crowd. Her mistress was surrounded by the most elite of the city; men and women whose pale skin was flushed pink from drink and dancing.

The Duelist ignored the affronted looks they gave her and locked eyes with Carmela.

"My lady," she said, bowing. "Perhaps it is time for you to retire."

Time slowed down. In that moment it was like a fairy tale come true, but only the part where the wolf eats the girl, a set of twins gets stuffed into an oven, or the ogre jams a little goat into its massive jaws. The look of malice on Carmela's face would have broken steel.

But the Duelist had faced grimmer odds.

"What is the matter?" asked the Regent, turning from another conversation. "Who are you to address my lady so?"

The sound of the Regent's voice broke the spell. Carmela's face smoothed into something sultry and affectionate. "My servant is right. I must retire."

"My love, this is nonsense—"

But the witch had already risen to her feet and, taking the Duelist's arm, allowed herself to be walked from the hall.

And that night, after the witch had fallen into darkness, Rose dreamed of a name.

They were seated across from each other at the kitchen table, holding hot mugs of tea. The chair was uncomfortable—most chairs were, for the Duelist. Far too small and unsteady. She preferred leaning against the wall, but she liked sitting across from Rose, like a normal person. It was nice to pretend this was their home and it was just the two of them.

Rose said, "I smell of roasted goat. I loathe goat."

"Hunger is much worse than goat."

"Perhaps," Rose said, and stiffened. A moment later, she rattled off a long, complicated word.

It was not a language the Duelist knew. "What does it mean?"

Rose closed her eyes. "It's a name from my dream. A name of someone powerful. An emperor, I think. But he was speaking to the witch, and she was in no other body but her own."

The Duelist straightened. "How do you know that?"

"I just do." Rose looked startled and set down her tea. She was on her feet next, pacing around the kitchen. The hearth cat, asleep by the ashes, looked up at her and meowed.

"It's a feeling," she said, rubbing her hands together. "In dreams, you just know things."

"The name you heard—it was not her name? You're sure?"

"She spoke it from her lips, addressing the emperor. It belongs to him."

"Repeat it."

Rose said it again—and a hundred times after that. The Duelist tried to say the name, but it was impossible. The language was a complex tonal tongue, more nuanced than even Stygian.

"Perhaps," the Duelist said, without too much hope, "I could bring a linguist."

"I'll do you one better," Rose said, reaching into a bag of flour, and tossed a handful onto the table. "I can see it in my head."

And in forty-seven strokes, she traced out the characters of the name.

It took the Duelist a month to find someone who could help her. A young scholar who, for three weights of silver, explained to her that this so-called emperor had ruled two hundred years before, across the sea, not far from where the Duelist's nation had fallen.

"Not a very successful emperor. Assassinated by his daughter, or perhaps his wife. His one crowning achievement? A fortress library high up on the slopes of Mount Attarra. With a peculiar covenant. No woman could set foot inside its halls, upon pain of death.

"He must not have liked women too much," joked the scholar.

"Perhaps," said the Duelist, "it was a precaution."

"Against what?"

The Duelist got to her feet. "What were the names of his wife and daughter?"

The scholar required a ten-weight of gold and sent out two dozen chiroptera. Six months passed before one finally returned. From the library, no less. "The fates have smiled on you, Duelist," the young scholar said. "They almost never honor petitions."

Such simple moments when lives change, when one world ends and another begins. She remembered another time, another place, how she stared out at a cloud and her mother, in a high voice, called her name, told her to run. The soldiers were already halfway across the field. The Duelist ran. They caught her anyway and nothing was ever the same again.

The scholar handed her the sheet of vellum, and with her hands trembling the Duelist tucked it inside her blouse, against her heart.

That night the Regent threw a party and announced to everyone his betrothal to Carmela. At the edge of the banquet table sat his cousin's daughter, no older than fourteen, and already blindingly beautiful. She was to marry the king in less than a year.

The witch never once looked at the young princess, and that of course was how the Duelist knew. Twice the witch caught her eye, and the third time she snapped her fingers, summoned her to the dais.

"Why are you smiling so much?" demanded Carmela in a whisper. "Are you that happy for me?"

"I am a romantic at heart," said the Duelist.

Storytellers gave names to everything because they knew, better than anyone, that names were power. To name a witch was to control a witch, and, in the old stories at least, to destroy her.

The Duelist had dealt in death most of her life. If there was such a thing as a soul, hers was blacker than night. What would another stain matter? It was said that when a person died, their souls were weighed. Perhaps love would grant her some forgiveness. Such a thing happened in stories, sometimes.

She did not wonder how the scales would weigh for the witch's soul.

There was a scandal, of course. Wild, torrid speculation that occupied the elite for years and had them looking over their shoulders at night, putting new locks on their doors, shivering in their underclothes with gruesome anticipation.

Not one of them had imaginations humble enough to conceive a woman such as Carmela abandoning of her own free will the most powerful man in the south. And then, simply, disappearing. Leaving behind a household. Taking nothing with her, save jewels and gold.

Everyone blamed that female beast that was her shadow. Such an ungodly creature, more man than woman. Gone, too. Not a trace. Probably a thief who had murdered poor beautiful Carmela and fed her dismembered body to the sewers. Or perhaps the man-woman was actually a secret agent of the north, bribed to murder the woman who had the Regent's heart, to unmake him; a most grievous attack that some called an act of war.

But war was coming anyway. It always was, always would be.

The Regent dispatched hunters. They never returned. He hired mercenaries. They never came back for their gold. He hired spies, oracles, sent letters to the Lord Marshals of cities a thousand miles away, asking them to listen for rumors of a woman who looked like a man, who bore a sword, who called herself the Duelist.

It made her chuckle, sometimes, when she'd hear tales of the Regent who had gone mad for the loss of a woman—only, the story changed, as stories sometimes do. It wasn't long before the impossible beauty he was to marry was entirely forgotten—but not the woman warrior who had defeated him, shamed him. She lived on in tales, grew in stature, prowess, mercilessness.

Even in beauty.

"But you *are* beautiful," Rose would say, tucking her scarf more closely around her throat, her silver earrings chiming in the wind. Faint wrinkles had begun to touch the corners of her bright eyes and mouth, deepening when she smiled. Which was often.

"But you love me," the Duelist would reply.

Years passed. Not many, but enough.

A rumor bloomed, with an unexpected origin; carried deep from the east, in wild lands never conquered, ruled by nomads on fast horses. Barbarians, they were called. Fur-wearing, slant-eyed mongrels.

Who also, it was said, guarded veins of gold thick as a dragon's neck, endless gold that blinded men in the sun, filled with healing powers; gold that would make a saint go mad with avarice. Deep in their mountains. Deep in the forests. Deep where no king had ever been able to send a single spy. Not without having his head returned in a handsomely embroidered velvet bag.

Only silk and spice merchants could buy passage through those barbarian lands. Escorted, watched, gently (and sometimes forcefully) guided. The smart merchants minded their own business. Respected rules of passage. Bartered, drank, made gestures of peace with those wild men and women. Without forgetting, ever, that they would never be one of them.

238 —

And so it was quite strange—impossible, really—when a spice merchant came home to his city telling a tale of two foreign women living amongst these barbarians—dressed in furs and silk, necks wrapped in loose scarves, riding fine horses. Seen with his own eyes, he swore. One of them huge, so broad in the shoulders he would have sworn she was a man until he saw the curve of her breasts beneath her jacket. Wearing a sword against her back, and her skin dark as a desert shadow.

And then, there was her companion.

"She was not human," protested the merchant. "No human woman could be so beautiful. I thought I must be mad."

"You *are* mad," said his colleagues. "No foreigners would ever be allowed to live amongst those horse-riding dogs."

"No," replied the merchant, incensed. "I *heard* them. The mannish one told that beauty, 'I would still kill the world for you.'"

"Stop," replied the others. "You're drunk."

But the merchant leaned forward. "They held hands even when they rode. It was the strangest thing. And that fair creature, that most beautiful woman, kissed that immense mannish paw and said, 'No. We are free, forever.'"

"Fool," they said. "Idiot."

It was beyond impossible. Offensive, even. Such lunacy.

But the tale spread. It made the storytellers laugh.

Once, they said, there was a witch who cursed a beautiful girl into a deep sleep. Until a warrior found and woke her, and together they killed the witch. A witch who had spread her curse through many lands—some, where her evil was still remembered. Where her killers would be welcome.

Storytellers have a long reach.

AUTHOR'S NOTE

Marjorie Liu: The problem of "Sleeping Beauty," for me, is that ultimately it's a story about a woman who is far more attractive "dead" than she is alive; a woman who has little agency, who is forced into an unnatural sleep, raped while she is unconscious, and then, when she finally wakes, must go and marry the man who took advantage of her. It's a grim story—if you'll forgive the pun—but not an unfamiliar one. It's also one of my least favorite fairy tales, which is why I wanted to reinvent it as a story about women, and the power of women, and how women save each other and themselves through sisterhood and love.

As most women I know will tell you, they don't always sleep a lot—but they fight plenty.

THE OTHER THEA

Theodora Goss

hea stared out the train window. Forest, more forest, and then a small town would flash by. And then more forest. She had taken this route many times while she was in school, although then she'd traveled with a large trunk filled with the clothes and books she would need for a semester at Miss Lavender's. This time she had a backpack, with just enough for a day or two. How long would it take? She hadn't really known what to bring. Should she even be going, in the middle of winter break?

But she hadn't known what else to do. She checked the text on her phone:

**Of course. Always pleased to see you, Thea. Let
us know when your train gets in. Love, Emily**

Then a smiling black-cat emoji. It was not one of the regular iPhone emoji, but Thea was not surprised that Miss Gray had somehow gotten into her phone. After all, she taught Magic and

Technology. Thea remembered her standing in front of the class-room: "Manipulating technology is no different from manipulating any other aspect of reality," she had said. And then she had put some complicated equations up on the board. Math was Thea's least favorite part of magic. The poetry part had always come more naturally to her.

And then her text in response:

Arriving Thursday 2 p.m. I'll walk from the station.

Miss Gray's response was another black-cat emoji. It winked at her.

"Next stop, miss," said the conductor. She looked up, startled. "Aren't you one of Miss Lavender's girls?"

"I was," said Thea. "I graduated last year."

He nodded. "Thought I remembered you, with that ginger hair." He pronounced it *jin-juh*. "If you need help with anything, let me know."

"Thanks," she said, and smiled. It was a weak smile; she knew that. She hadn't been very good at smiling lately.

"Hartfield, Massachusetts!" he called down the train corridor. "Next stop, Hartfield!"

Thea put her phone back in her backpack and zipped up her jacket. She made her way to the end of the compartment.

Forest, more forest. And then the first houses of Hartfield, with weather-beaten wooden siding. Suddenly they were in the town center, with its brick dental offices, boutiques, and coffee shops. The train slowed, then pulled into the station. The con-ductor put a metal bridge across the gap, and Thea walked over it. Here she was again, not for some sort of alumnae event, but because she didn't know where else to go.

From the station, she walked up Main Street, passing several antique stores, the food co-op, and Booktopia, where students from Miss Lavender's always congregated on Saturdays, ordering cappuccinos and egg or chicken salad sandwiches, reading Sylvia

Plath or Margaret Atwood or the latest Kelly Link. Should she stop in for a moment? Maybe . . .

Before she could reconsider, she had stepped inside, and there was Sam at the counter. She had not expected him to be, well, right there.

"Thea," he said, a wide smile spreading over his face. It was accepted wisdom at Miss Lavender's that Sam looked like a frog. Nevertheless, a respectable percentage of the students admitted to having crushes on him, despite or because of his rumpled hair, flannel shirts, and encyclopedic knowledge of literature. He had been a clerk at the bookstore through high school. During Thea's sophomore year he had left for college, but his mother had been diagnosed with cancer, and since his parents were divorced, he had returned to Hartfield to care for her. After her death, he had bought Booktopia with the insurance. As he reminded the town council on a regular basis, every town needed an independent bookstore. Now he was finishing his degree by taking night classes at UMass–Amherst. At least that was what it had said on the Booktopia blog, the last time Thea had checked.

"What are you doing back here? Don't you live in Boston now? Wait, I'll make you a cappuccino."

"No, that's okay; they're expecting me. But thanks. Yeah, Boston. I'm starting college next fall. I think. I mean, I am. I just took a gap year, that's all. I figured I'd stop in here for a minute, you know, to check out the writing books." There was a special section right up front, left over from National Novel Writing Month, with everything from *The Elements of Style* to Anne Lamott. "And to see where we used to hang out."

His eyes crinkled up at the corners. "Aren't you a little young to be getting nostalgic? You only graduated six months ago."

"Yeah." Thea laughed uncomfortably. "Way too young. Well, I'd better be going. They're expecting me. Maybe I'll come back . . .

for one of those books. I always meant to read John Gardner."

"If you have time, come back and tell me about your life in the big city. I'll give you a sandwich on the house. Or, to be more accurate, on the store."

"Yeah, all right, thanks." She turned, then pushed the door open again. Standing outside in the cold air, she thought, *God, I am such a dork.*

He hadn't changed at all. Of course, people didn't change that much in six months. Except her. She had changed, in ways she didn't understand. That was why she had come back here. She continued up Main Street, then turned down Oak and Maple (seriously, how unimaginative were the people who named streets in small New England towns?). And there, at the edge of town, were the brick main house and buildings of Miss Lavender's. And the familiar sign:

*Miss Lavender's School of Witchcraft
Founded 1812*

Thea had never seen the grounds looking so deserted. The last time she had been here, she had been graduating, and the town had been filled with students and their parents.

Not hers, of course. Her parents had died when she was a child, and her grandmother had been sick for many years—far too sick to travel for parents' weekends or even graduation. At those sorts of events, one or another friend's parents had always temporarily adopted her, and she had felt what it would be like to have a family, for a little while.

She walked up to the main house, which held the headmistress's office. She rang the bell and heard it echoing through the building.

"So you're back." She looked around, but saw no one. "Down here, idiot."

She looked down. "Oh, it's you, Cordelia. Hello." The tortoise-shell tabby stared up at her with yellow eyes.

"Hello yourself. I'm not at all surprised to see you again."

Before Thea could ask why, the door opened and there was Mrs. Moth, looking just as she always did, in a respectable wool skirt and cardigan, gray hair a little messy as though she had been running her fingers through it. The image of a headmistress.

"Thea, it's so good to see you," she said. "Do come in. I've just made tea. And you," she said, looking down at the cat. "You could have told us you would be out all night. You know how Lavinia worries."

"I was out on cat business, which is none of your business," said Cordelia. She slipped around Mrs. Moth's ankles and disappeared down the hallway.

"Cats!" said Mrs. Moth, shaking her head. "Come in, my dear. Let's go into the parlor. I've prepared one of the guest rooms for you. I'm afraid everyone's gone for the break—it's just me, Lavinia, and Emily right now. We always give teachers and staff two weeks for the holidays."

Sure enough, when Thea went into the parlor, where Mrs. Moth usually met with prospective students and their parents, there was Miss Lavender sitting on the sofa. Whereas Mrs. Moth was comfortably plump, Lavinia Lavender was thin and angular. She was wearing a soft gray dress, and the white hair escaping from her bun formed a halo around her face. It would have been intimidating, having tea with the founder of the school, but Miss Lavender looked so perfectly harmless. She was so forgetful that she sometimes accidentally walked through walls. It was a good thing that Mrs. Moth had taken over as headmistress, long before any of the alumnae could remember. But older students who had taken her seminar on Philosophy of Magic warned younger ones not to underestimate Miss Lavender. How could you be expected to remember the locations of walls when you

were contemplating the fundamental structure of reality?

And standing beside the fireplace was Miss Emily Gray. Thea was almost shocked to see that she was wearing leggings and a loose sweater, as though she had just finished doing yoga or something. Her brown hair hung in a neat braid over one shoulder. It made Miss Gray seem almost human, although as soon as she said, "Hello, Thea. It's so nice to see you again," Thea mentally panicked at the thought that she might have forgotten to do her homework. Did she look a mess? She was sure that she looked a mess. She took a deep breath.

"Cookies on the table, and I'll bring the tea," said Mrs. Moth, then disappeared down the hall toward the kitchen.

Thea quailed at the thought of having to make small talk with Miss Lavender and Miss Gray, but she should have known better. Witches don't make small talk.

"So what's the matter?" asked Miss Gray, sitting down on the sofa beside Miss Lavender. "You wouldn't have called if there was nothing wrong."

Thea put her backpack down and sat in one of the comfortable armchairs. While she was gathering her thoughts, trying to figure out what to say, Mrs. Moth came in with the tea things.

"Orange pekoe for Lavinia," she said. "Oolong for Emily, and Earl Grey for me. Thea, I'm guessing you want a chai latte. You'll have to add milk." There was nothing in the cups when she poured out, but out of the teapot came four distinctly different smells and colors of tea. Thea added milk and sugar to her cup, then stirred.

"The thing is, I'm not sure," she said. "You know my grandmother died last summer, just after graduation. Thanks for the wreath, by the way. She would have really liked getting a wreath from the school. That was tough, but at first I was all right. I mean, we were never close or anything. I had to meet with her lawyer, then catalog all her furniture for the auction. I sold almost everything,

except Mom's stuff. And then I had to sell the house. After that . . .
I was supposed to be at Harvard this fall. But I just couldn't—I
don't know, I was so tired. So I deferred for a year, and I rented
an apartment in Boston. I figured I'd write . . . you know, start
becoming a great writer." She smiled self-deprecatingly, in case
they thought she was being too grandiose, although all through
school that had been her talent: senior year, to her surprise, she
had been chosen editor in chief of *The Broomstick*. "But I couldn't do
that, either. So I've been living in the apartment, doing—nothing,
really. Some days I just wander around the city. Some days I don't
even get out of my pajamas." Thea put her head down in her
hands. "I don't know what's wrong with me."

Miss Gray took a sip of her tea. "When you went through your
grandmother's house, did you find your shadow?"

It was the question she'd been dreading. When she'd first
arrived at school, Mrs. Moth had sent a letter to her grandmother:

> *Dear Mrs. Tillinghast,*
> *Thea seems to have forgotten her shadow. Since she*
> *will need it to participate fully in school activities,*
> *could you please send it as soon as possible?*
> > *With best regards,*
> > *Wilhelmina Moth, Headmistress*

A week later, she had received a reply:

> *Dear Mrs. Moth,*
> *As Thea may have told you, several years ago Mrs.*
> *Tillinghast suffered a stroke. Although she has*
> *recovered a great deal, she lost some of her long-*
> *term memory and fine motor coordination, which*
> *is why I am writing this letter for her. She says she*
> *remembers putting Thea's shadow in a box, but*

*doesn't remember where she put the box. She says it
was a very troublesome shadow, and Thea is better
off without it. I'm sorry not to be more helpful, and
please give my love to Thea.*
Respectfully yours,

Anne Featherstone,
Mrs. Tillinghast's secretary

It had happened when she was six. After both of her parents
died when their small plane went down, Thea had been sent to
live with her grandmother. She had hated the gloomy old house
and the gloomy old woman who told her that her mother should
never have married that spendthrift, good-for-nothing Michael
Graves. If she hadn't, she would not be dead now.

One day, after her grandmother had forbidden her from
going out into the garden, she had shouted, "I hate you! You're
not my mother. I'm going to run away and you'll never see
me again, you old bitch!" Her grandmother had ordered the
butler to hold her, and with a pair of gardening shears she had
cut off Thea's shadow, *snip snip*. And that was the last Thea
had seen of it. By the time her grandmother had sent her to
Miss Lavender's, the third generation to attend, she had almost
forgotten it wasn't there. "Most people don't even notice," she
had said to Mrs. Moth when first asked about it. She had just
arrived at Miss Lavender's and was trying to figure out where
her room was, what classes she would be taking, whether she
would fit in or have friends. It was so different from her middle
school in Virginia.

"Most people aren't witches," Mrs. Moth had replied. "While
you're here, we'll work around it, but there will be certain kinds
of magic you can't do. And you'll need it eventually."

Sometimes new students had said, "What's wrong with Thea?
Why doesn't she have a shadow?" But at Miss Lavender's one quickly

learned that if one's roommate turned into a wolf at certain times of the month, or was faintly, almost imperceptibly green, or was missing a shadow, it was considered impolite to remark on it as anything extraordinary.

Before she had left for her grandmother's funeral, Miss Gray had said to her, "Find your shadow, Thea. It's time." Well, she had tried.

"No," she said now, in response to Miss Gray's question. "I looked everywhere"—from the attic to the cellar, with Anne and the butler and cook until they were all covered with dust—"but I couldn't find it. I have no idea what happened to it. Do you think that's what's wrong with me?"

"Of course, my dear," said Miss Lavender, speaking for the first time. "You could do without it as a child, but now that you're a grown woman—well, a grown woman needs her shadow. Without it, you're fading."

Fading? She was fading?

"It's part of growing up," said Mrs. Moth. "Children don't need their shadows, strictly speaking—remember Peter Pan. But adults are a different matter. Lavinia's right: without it you'll fade away. It will take some time, but I'm afraid the process has already begun. Eventually even ordinary people—well, not ordinary, of course, but not witches—will start to notice. Let's just see if we can find it, shall we? This didn't work the last time we tried—I suspect the box was shielded with a spell of some sort. But since your grandmother's passed away and the box has been lost . . . perhaps, just perhaps, it will work now."

How could she be fading? But Miss Lavender, more than anyone, could see things other people couldn't. In school, it was rumored that she could even see the futures—the multiple possibilities created by each moment.

Mrs. Moth leaned down and blew on Thea's tea. In the teacup, on the milky brown liquid, she saw an image form, in sepia like an

old photograph. A castle with strange, twisting spires, and mountains in the distance.

"I've seen that before," she said.

"Of course you have," said Miss Gray. "We went there on an eleventh-grade field trip."

Then it must be . . . "Mother Night's castle. Is that where my shadow went?"

"Yes," said Mrs. Moth. "And I'm afraid you'll need to go find it. You can't do without it much longer. When Lavinia says 'fading,' she doesn't just mean visually. Without it, you'll keep getting more tired. You'll start feeling despondent, as though you'll never accomplish anything. Eventually, it will seem too difficult even to try. One day you might not get up at all."

"But how can I find it?" asked Thea. "Mother Night's castle is in the Other Country. When we went, Miss Gray took us. Can you take me there again?" She looked at Miss Gray.

The teacher shook her head so that her brown braid swung around.

"Thea, my dear," said Mrs. Moth, "you are a graduate of this school. Like any witch, you should be able to find your way to the Other Country. By yourself."

The next morning, Thea woke to Cordelia patting her nose.

"Stop that," she said, and rolled over. That's right, she was at Miss Lavender's, in a guest bedroom on the second floor of the headmistress's house. Through the window, she could see the dormitory where she had spent six years of her life. It reminded her that Shoshana had sent her a Facebook message a couple of days ago, asking if Thea was all right and complaining about Chem 101. Of her two senior-year suite mates, Shoshana Washington was premed at Brown, and Lily Yu was in China working for a human rights organization. She would start an Asian literature and culture major at Stanford in the fall. She kept posting pictures of dumplings and rainy green hills on Instagram. Thea really should keep up with them, but it was hard when she was the only one who had nothing to say. *Binge-watched Netflix and ate ice cream for dinner* didn't make for a very inspiring Facebook post.

"Are you getting up, or do I have to sit on your face?"

She turned back over. "Cordy, how do you get to the Other Country?"

"How do I get there? I'm a cat—I just go. The question is, how do you get there?" All cats knew the way to the Other Country. That was one of the first lessons in Care and Feeding of a Familiar. If you couldn't find your cat, it was probably in the Other Country.

Thea scratched the cat behind her ears. "Can't you just take me there?"

"No, I can't take you. A little lower down . . . there. Now under the chin." For a moment, Cordelia actually purred. Then she continued, "You're a thick, clumsy human. You can't go the way cats go. We just slip between things. You need to go through a door."

"I remember!" said Thea. "When we went in eleventh grade, it was through a door. And the door was in this house. . . . But I don't remember which one it was. Cordy, can you show me which door goes to the Other Country?"

Cordelia swatted her hand away and looked at her with contempt. "Now you really are being an idiot. After six years in this place, you should at least know how to think like a witch."

Think like a witch? What did the cat mean? Suddenly she remembered a visiting lecturer, an alumna named Dr. Something Patel who taught physics at one of the local universities. She had come to talk to Miss Gray's class about magical physics. Thea remembered her standing in front of the blackboard, chalk in hand, saying . . . how did it go? "One of the most important things I learned in my time at Miss Lavender's, which has served me well as a theoretical physicist, is to think like a witch. If you can't find

the answer, a witch would say, you're probably asking the wrong question." Miss Gray had nodded emphatically.

Think like a witch.

"It's not *the* door. It's *a* door. I'm going to take a shower. I'll be ready in ten minutes. Wait for me, okay?"

Cordelia didn't answer. She stretched out in a sunny spot on the coverlet and started to wash herself.

Twenty minutes later, Thea was ready. In her backpack, she had a change of clothes, toiletries zipped into plastic bags, a notebook and pens, a battered copy of *A Wrinkle in Time* that she had been rereading, and half a chocolate bar.

"Are you coming?" she said to Cordelia. "Or did you wake me up this morning just because you felt like it?"

"I'm coming." The cat jumped down from the bed, then looked up at her. "Which door?"

"Kitchen. That way I can grab some breakfast along the way."

Thea walked quietly in case anyone else was still asleep, down the back stairs and to the kitchen. Last night, Mrs. Moth had shown her where everything was kept. "Just make yourself breakfast anytime you like," she had said. Thea found a bagel, then cream cheese to smear on both sides. She put them together to form a sandwich so it would be easier to carry. She put an apple into her backpack. That would have to do.

"All right," she said, holding the bagel in one hand, with the backpack slung over her shoulder. "Let's see if I'm right about how to do this."

She walked to the kitchen door. Standing in front of it, she took the notebook out of her backpack, scribbled a few lines. . . . Then she put her hand on the door handle and read,

> *"An entrance, entranced,*
> *you open into the brightness*
> *of summer and winter dancing,*

white snow on white blossoms,
in the country of my longing."

Not her best effort, but perhaps it would do. And she did like the pun: entrance, entranced. The trick was to tell the door what it was, what it could become. "The creation speaks two languages," Miss Gray had told them in Introduction to Magical Rhetoric. "Poetry and math, which are the same language to anyone who speaks them correctly. You must speak to the creation in its own language so it understands what you want it to do." Thea took a deep breath, hoping the spell had worked, and opened the door.

It was summer. It is always summer in the Other Country, or rather it is always no season at all: the apple trees are always blossoming, and in leaf, and bearing fruit at the same time. Sometimes it snows, and white flakes settle on the ripening fruit. But today seemed to be a perfect summer day. Thea and Cordelia walked down the sloping green hill toward the castle. Tall grass brushed against Thea's jeans, and the sun was warm enough that she stopped for a moment to take off her jacket and stuff it into her backpack. Beyond the castle was a lake, shining in the sunlight, and beyond the lake were mountains with forested slopes and snowy peaks. It looked like a postcard, or something that had been Photoshopped.

The last time she had been here, Shoshana had squealed in delight and Lily had said, "Seriously, are you making that noise? Because stop." Miss Gray had said, "Come on, girls. We're on a schedule." The castle looked just as Thea remembered—beautiful, but strange. As she and Cordelia walked down the hill and came to the gardens, she could see more clearly the stone towers, some going straight up and covered with small balconies, some spiraling like a narwhal's horn, some curled like a snail's shell. The buttresses, some of them supporting nothing but air, resembled a whale's skeleton. The whole structure was improbable, like a castle out of a dream, and reminded Thea of an Escher print. One of those towers, probably the largest, held the Tapestry Room, where gold spiders with jeweled eyes crawled up and down, weaving the threads of life into an enormous tapestry, whose front no person had ever seen. Her thread was somewhere in there. She wondered what it looked like, which part of the pattern it formed.

"And this," she remembered Miss Gray saying, in a voice like a tour guide's, "is the Library of Lost Books. All the books that are lost in the worlds are kept here. To our left, you will see the extension built specifically after the burning of the Library of Alexandria."

Thea stepped onto a garden path. Cordelia ran ahead and stood by the side of a long stone pool with yellow lotus flowers at its farther edge.

"Something interesting?" asked Thea.

"Fish," said the cat, staring down intently.

Thea sat on a stone bench beside the path and put her backpack beside her. She was starting to feel hot, and the bench was shaded by a linden tree, both blossoming and in leaf. "Anyway, I need a plan, you know," she said.

"Why?" said Cordelia, reaching a paw tentatively into the water.

"Well, because I need to find my shadow, and then I need to take it back with me, and I don't know how to do either of those things, is why." What she really wanted to do was stay here, in the warmth and sunlight, with the sound of bees buzzing in the linden flowers above her. After all, she had no idea how to find her shadow, or what to do after she had found it. She would sit, just for a little while. . . . At least it was better than sitting in her apartment, scrolling aimlessly through her Facebook news feed.

Cordelia leaned down and patted at the water, then jumped back, shaking her head from side to side.

"That's right, stupid cat!" came a shrill voice. "If you put your head down here, I'll spit at you again!" Thea leaned forward just enough to see an orange head sticking out of the water. One of the fish, looking rather pleased with itself. Thea heard a clucking sound and realized that it was laughing. Then it disappeared back beneath the green surface of the water. Cordelia hastily licked herself all over and then stalked off along the path, as though nothing had happened.

"Hey, where are you going?" Thea called, but the cat did not turn back or answer. She was alone in the still, sunlit garden.

"I want my ball back, and I want it now!"

She turned toward the voice. A girl about her own age was walking toward her, dressed in a bathing suit that looked as though it had come from the 1930s, with a frilled bathing cap on her head. "Where is it, Thea? I swear, if you don't give it to me right now, I'm going to turn you into a toad, or worse!"

Thea stared at her in astonishment. The girl pulled off her bathing cap, and down fell long black hair, with stars tangled in it. "Seriously, I don't know why my mother puts up with you. If I were her, I'd put you back in that box!"

"Lady Morgan?" said Thea hesitantly. This must be Mother Night's daughter. Was she supposed to curtsy or something? They had not met her on the field trip, but who else would be walking around the castle gardens as though she owned them, talking about her mother? And what was that about a box? "I'm not Thea. I mean, I'm the other Thea. I mean, she's the other Thea—I'm the real one."

"Oh!" said Morgan Morningstar, looking at her with astonishment. "Why, so you are. You're faded around the edges. Well, for goodness' sake, take her back with you—she's such a pest. You'd think being in a box for twelve years would have calmed her down, but evidently not. Last week, she almost started a fire in the library—there's a reason that fireplace is never used! She and one of those annoying satyrs thought it would be a good place to

toast marshmallows. Can you imagine? Now that you're here, you can take her—where are you from, anyway?"

"Miss Lavender's," said Thea. She stood up but decided not to curtsy. The time had passed for it, anyhow.

"Oh, how nice. Say hello to Emily and Mina and dear old Lavinia for me. You must be one of the students."

I graduated, Thea wanted to tell her, but Morgan had already taken her arm and was pulling her down the path toward the castle. "The problem is finding her. She stole my Seeing Ball, and now she can see me coming and hide. You know a shadow can hide in very small places, and the castle has lots of those. But now that you're here, maybe we can convince Mom to send her back. It's clear that Thea—the other Thea—should go home with you. I mean, look at you. . . ."

Thea didn't know how to respond, but she didn't have to. Morgan Morningstar was pulling her through the gardens: between flowering borders, and through a privet maze that Thea would surely have gotten lost in, and over a lawn laid out like a checkerboard, with chamomile forming the white squares. Where had Cordelia gone? Drat all cats. Then they were in the castle courtyard, with its Egyptian and Greek and Indian statues, and through the arched doorway.

The great hall was cool and dim after the sunlit courtyard. Just as she remembered, it had no ceiling: tall pillars ascended up to the blue sky. But the sun was already sinking toward the mountains, so the hall was mostly in shadow. It was empty except for a small group of people at the far end, close to the dais.

"Mom!" Morgan called. "Look who I found by the lotus pool." Several of the—people?—stepped back. Thea noticed a man with the head of a stag, a woman with ivy growing over her head instead of hair, and a woman who looked exactly like Dr. Patel, only what would Dr. Patel be doing here? A pirate, in a black leather coat and tricorne hat, took off his hat and bowed to her. But between them all was Mother Night. Today she looked like her daughter, black hair falling to her feet, a face as pale as the moon, unlined. She could have been Morgan's twin. The last time Thea had seen her, she had looked immensely old, with gray hair that wound around her head like a coronet. She had been sitting on her throne, and Miss Gray had introduced the Miss Lavender's students to her, one by one. They had bobbed awkward curtsies, having learned how to curtsy just the week before. Thea remembered what Miss Gray had told them: "Don't be nervous, but remember that she created the universe." It didn't matter what she looked like at any particular moment. You couldn't mistake Mother Night.

"Mom, this is—"

"I know, sweetheart. Hello, Thea. We've been expecting you. How are you feeling?"

"Pretty well, ma'am," said Thea, doing her best to curtsy, trying to remember how. This time she was sure she should curtsy.

"How do you think she's feeling?" said Morgan. "Look at her. Soon she'll be as transparent as a ghost. I could poke my finger through her, not that I want to. You need to make Thea—I mean shadow Thea—go back with her."

"Your mother doesn't *need* to do anything," said the pirate. But he said it so charmingly, with a grin and a wink at Thea, that she could not help smiling back at him. "I know you're in a bad mood, Morgan—"

"Don't you start with me, Raven," said Morgan, still gripping Thea by the arm. "You said the same thing when she stole your cloak of invisibility. You said, 'That shadow has to go.' Remember?"

So this was Raven! The famous, or infamous, Raven . . . Mother Night's consort.

"Stop, both of you," said Mother Night. "I can't make her go, for the simple reason that while she's separated from Thea, she's a person. Like any of you. Like Thea herself. I will not order her to leave here. I'm sorry, my dear," she said to Thea. "You need to

figure this out yourself." Which was just what Mrs. Moth had told her. Thea felt sick to her stomach. She had no idea how to find her shadow, much less convince her to . . . what, exactly? She still wasn't sure. And what had Morgan meant—as transparent as a ghost? Was she fading that fast?

"Remember there's a ball tonight," Mother Night continued. "The other Thea will certainly be there—she loves to dance. And now I have some things to attend to before the ball."

"I'll come with you," said Raven, taking her by the arm. The stag-headed man and the ivy-haired woman followed them out, as did Dr. Patel before Thea could say hello as a fellow Miss Lavender's alum.

"He always takes her side," said Morgan. "I guess I can't blame him. They've been together for what, a thousand years? But I really wanted Mom to just *do* something for once."

"So where do you think we'll find her?" asked Thea. "The shadow, I mean."

"Oh, Mom's right. She'll be at the ball. She wouldn't miss a party, and I have to admit, she is a good dancer. Come on, we need to find clothes to wear. We can't go to the ball looking like this—at least, you can't." Thea looked down at her jeans and gray Gap shirt. No, she couldn't. Could Morgan really have put a finger through her? She looked solid enough. Tentatively, she poked herself in the stomach. She felt solid. But both Morgan and Mrs. Moth had talked about her fading at the edges, slowly becoming transparent. She wished she didn't have to worry so much—about herself, and the shadow Thea. She was going to a ball in Mother Night's castle! Shoshana was going to freak out. Even Lily might be impressed. Which reminded her . . .

As she followed Morgan down a series of twisting stone hall-ways, she took out her iPhone. No reception here, of course, but she could take photos and share them later with Shoshana and Lily in their private Facebook group.

Morgan's room was the entire top of a tower. Out of a large wardrobe she drew dresses and suits of silk and velvet and lace, tossing them on her bed, which was shaped like a swan with its neck curved to form a backboard, while Thea walked around, looking through all the windows. Below she could see the castle and gardens. In one direction, hills and fields stretched away into the distance, until she could see a darkness that must be the sea. In the other, the lake reflected the setting sun, which was just beginning to touch the tops of the mountains with pink and orange.

"What else is there beside the castle?" asked Thea. "I mean, we only ever visited here. Are there—towns in the Other Country? If I went out there, what would I find?"

"All the stories you ever heard of," said Morgan. "And a whole lot you haven't. What about this?" *This* was a dress of green velvet that looked as though it had come from a museum exhibit or a Hollywood red carpet. "You can wear it with this." The second *this* was a mask of peacock feathers. Morgan rummaged among the clothes she had thrown on the bed.

"What are you going to wear?" asked Thea.

Morgan held up a black leather coat just like Raven's and put a hat just like his on her head. "With this," she said, holding a mask of black feathers to her face. The smile beneath it was mocking.

"You're still mad at him, aren't you?"

"I just don't like him telling me what to do. He's not my father. And he's, what, as old as civilization itself? That's nothing." Morgan shrugged. "That's like a moment in time."

"But your mother also said . . ."

"Well yeah, Mom. That's different. But Mom's never stopped me from doing anything I want to. She doesn't, you know— interfere. She knows what's on the front of the tapestry, the fate of every person in every world as it's being woven. Sometimes

I wish she would step in and act, especially when you other-worlders are doing something dreadful, like having another war. But she says that's what we're here for—you and me and Emily Gray. We're the ones responsible for changing things. That's why places like Miss Lavender's exist. Come on, it's getting dark. You can get dressed in the bathroom."

When Thea emerged from what turned out to be a surprisingly normal bathroom—but she figured people in Mother Night's castle needed to pee just like everyone else—she looked as though she had stepped out of a painting. Green velvet fell to the floor, covering her red Keds. Morgan's shoes had all been too small for her.

"I suppose you could magic your feet smaller," said Morgan, but at the beginning of junior year Mrs. Moth had told Thea's class, "If I discover that any of you have used magic for such a vain, trivial purpose as changing your physical dimensions, you will come to my office and have a serious talk with me." That had been enough to deter experimentation. Anyway, Thea wanted to feel at least a little like herself, underneath the dress and mask.

Before they left, she took two selfies in the wardrobe mirror: one by herself and one with the Morningstar, in which Morgan held up two fingers in a peace sign. What would Lily and Shoshana think of *that*? And then she followed Morgan back down through the castle corridors, passing what were obviously partygoers because they wore black tie or fantastical robes and gowns. Most of them wore masks, although sometimes she could not tell whether the masks were simply their faces.

In the great hall, it was twilight. The moon hung directly overhead, surrounded by constellations Thea did not recognize. The hall was illuminated by bubbles of light that floated through the air, seemingly wherever they wished. Earlier the hall had been bare stone, but now between the columns grew a forest of slender birch trees, with leaves that shone silver in the light of the floating bubbles. Thea reached up to touch a leaf and found that it was, indeed, made of pliable metal.

Beneath this forest moved the strangest, most fantastical people Thea had ever seen. There was the stag man, with flowers draped over his antlers. A woman with scaled blue skin was talking to what looked like a large owl. Three young girls with pig snouts were slipping in and out between the trees, playing tag. A satyr was bowing to a woman whose dress seemed to be made of butterflies—not just bowing but asking her to dance, because now the music was starting. The butterflies fluttered as she took his hand. In the center of the hall was a dance floor that looked like a forest glade, with mossy rocks at its edges to sit on. A small stream ran through it, so dancers had to be nimble to avoid stepping in the water.

"I'll take it as a compliment." Thea turned around. There was Raven, looking Morgan up and down critically. "You could be me as a beardless boy, a thousand years ago."

"I don't think I'll be mistaken for you tonight," said Morgan, then burst out laughing. But who could blame her? The dashing pirate of that afternoon now had the head of a fox, with the same expression of sly humor under the tricorne hat. "Are you showing your true face, Monsieur Renard?"

"One of them, at any rate. *Hola*, I hear a sarabande! Shall we dance, Lady Morgan?"

"I'll be back," said Morgan to Thea. "The refreshments table is over against the wall. You'll be all right, right?" Thea barely had time to nod before Morgan was swept away by the fox man. She took off her mask, which felt hot and strange. What was she doing here anyway? Suddenly, she felt lost and alone.

"How are you, my dear?" Thea turned toward the voice—it was Mother Night. She looked completely different than she had that afternoon. Now her skin was dark, almost blue-black, and she had a nimbus of short white curls around her head. She was wearing a silver dress, very simply cut, that could have come from ancient Egypt or a modern fashion magazine.

"I'm all right, I guess," said Thea. But she didn't feel all right. Instead, she felt as though she might throw up.

"You haven't eaten anything since breakfast, not even the apple in your backpack. You forgot about it, didn't you? You have half a chocolate bar in there too, in the front pocket. So of course you're going to feel sick. You need to take better care of yourself."

"I'm not very good at that," said Thea. "Taking care of myself, I mean."

"No, you're not. But you don't have anyone else to do it, so you'll have to get better at it. Why don't you practice right now? Go over to the refreshments table and get yourself some of the fish pie, which is very good. And there's asparagus with hollandaise, and ice cream. But meat and vegetables first! Not just ice cream, you know." Thea nodded. It had been a long time since anyone had told her to eat healthily, and the fact that Mother Night was doing it made her feel like laughing, despite her nausea.

"I'm serious," said Mother Night. She put her hands, cool and dry, on either side of Thea's face. Her eyes were black, with stars in them. For a moment, Thea felt as though she were floating in space. "Try to remember that you're also one of my daughters." And then, with a soft pat on the cheek, of both affection and admonition, Mother Night was gone. Thea shook her head as though to clear it, then walked around the dance floor, weaving between the birch trees and mossy stones, stepping over the stream, to the refreshments table.

She hung the peacock mask over her arm by its ribbons, then took a plate and some cutlery that looked like forks and knives on one end, and birch branches on the other. That must be fish pie—at least the crust was baked in the shape of a fish. She did not like asparagus but took some anyway, as well as some scalloped potatoes. A potato was a vegetable, right?

"What do you think that is?" asked the person ahead of her in line. Suddenly, she realized who she had been standing behind.

"Dr. Patel?" she said. The professor was wearing an ordinary black evening dress, with pearls. "I don't know, it looks sort of like a fern; you know, those fiddlehead ferns they sell at the farmers' market, except those aren't usually purple, are they? I'm Thea Graves. I graduated from Miss Lavender's last spring. I think you lectured to one of my classes. On magic and physics?"

"Oh, hello," said Dr. Patel, smiling the way people do when they're trying to remember who you are. "Call me Anita. It's always nice to see a fellow alumna. Have you tried those little cakes? The ones in all different shapes and colors. They have marzipan inside."

Thea took several of the cakes. She did like marzipan. "It's weird seeing someone I know—I mean, sort of know—here in the Other Country. Are you . . . just visiting?"

"Wouldn't that be nice!" said Dr. Patel. "Sometimes I think only students get real vacations. No, I'm afraid that I'm here on business . . . Mother Night's business, of course. And you?"

"Oh, um, yeah. Me too, business."

"Emily used to say, 'We are all on Mother Night's business, no matter what we're doing.' I bet she still says that to her students. How is everyone at Miss Lavender's? It's been so long since I visited—Homecoming, I think."

Suddenly, Thea had a vision of Miss Emily Gray, and Dr. Patel, and Morgan Morningstar, all going about Mother Night's business, whatever that might be.

"I'm really just here to find my shadow," she confessed. She didn't want Dr. Patel to think that she was taking too much credit, making her business out to be grander than it was. . . .

"Unless it finds you first!"

Thea turned around. There stood a girl, as tall as her, shaped like her, with her red hair. She wore a black catsuit and a mask that looked like a cat's face, with cat ears and whiskers.

"Asparagus? Seriously?"

"What?" said Thea.

"Asparagus? You like asparagus?"

"What . . . no. You're her. Me. You're me. You need to go home with me. We're supposed to be together." Could she sound any more inane?

The shadow took off her mask. Even though Thea had been expecting it, when she saw her own face she stepped back into the table and almost knocked over the tray of little cakes.

Dr. Patel was farther down the table now, and there was no one behind her in line. She and the shadow were as alone as they could be, in a ballroom.

"I'm not going anywhere with you," said the shadow. Her face was subtly wrong. Thea wondered why, then realized that for the first time she was looking at herself the way other people saw her, not reflected in a mirror. "Why should I? You put me in a box for twelve years! A shadow in a dark box—I barely existed. But here I'm as real as you are. Probably realer—you look sort of faded around the edges. In fact, why don't you stay here and be my shadow? That would be amusing!"

No, it wouldn't. "First of all, I didn't put you in a box for twelve years. My grandmother did. And second of all—"

"Well, you didn't take me out, did you? I'm not going anywhere with you, no way, nohow. I just wanted to see you in person. When I saw you in the Seeing Ball with Morgan Boringstar, I thought, *I wonder what she's like.* Well, let me tell you, I am *not* impressed. Except for the shoes—I do like the shoes, but that's it. And you can tell Morgan that she should find herself another Seeing Ball, because I'm not giving this one back!"

"Well, well, so you've found Thea, Thea!" The satyr Thea had seen dancing with the butterfly woman put his arms around the shadow. She laughed and yanked his long hair, then kissed him loudly on the mouth.

"Come on, Oryx," she said. "Let's go somewhere interesting. This party's lame!" He laughed and swung her onto the dance floor. As they capered away, over the stream and across the moon-lit room, Thea heard, "I saw you talking to her! Did she have my Seeing Ball?"

"No," said Thea. She turned around. Morgan was a little out of breath, still wearing her mask of black feathers. "She said to tell you that she wasn't giving it back."

"That little . . . When I find her, I'm going to put her back in a box. A sewing box—a cigar box—a matchbox. Let's see how she likes that!"

"I'm sorry, I need to sit down." How faint her voice sounded! Still clutching her plate, Thea turned away from Morgan and walked as steadily as she could to one of the doors, leaning for a moment against the frame, then down a torch-lit hall until she reached a stone arch through which she could see the garden. She stumbled out into the night and sat on one of the benches, putting her plate on her lap.

She could not eat. The nausea was even stronger than before. Was it because she had encountered her shadow? She looked down at the plate and almost cried out in fear. Its porcelain edges were visible through her hands. She held one hand up in front of her. Through it she could see the moonlit garden, with its topiaries black in the moonlight, its trellises on which white flowers bloomed in the darkness. Through her hand she could see the moon and constellations. Why was she fading so quickly? Mrs. Moth has said it would take time, but here in the Other Country, it was taking no time at all.

She had no idea what to do.

A small voice, her own although it sounded suspiciously like Mother Night's, said, *You must take care of yourself.* Step one: fish pie. Step two: scalloped potatoes. Step three: asparagus, ugh. But she ate every stalk.

"Finally you're doing something sensible," said Cordelia. The cat was sitting on the bench beside her, yellow eyes shining in the moonlight. "When you're done, I want to lick your plate. I mean the fish part of it."

"Where have you been all day?" said Thea, finishing the little marzipan cakes. She did not feel better, exactly. But at least she did not feel quite so hollow.

"On cat business, which is Mother Night's business, of course," said the cat. Thea put her plate on the bench, and Cordelia licked the remains of the fish and potatoes.

"I found my shadow, or she found me, but Cordy, it's hopeless." Thea looked down at her ghostly, almost transparent hands. "She blames me for putting her in that box. She doesn't want anything to do with me, unless I become *her* shadow. And everyone says this is something I have to figure out myself—Mother Night won't help me, and I don't know what to do."

"Well," said the cat, licking her paws and washing her face with them, "you can start by thinking like a witch instead of a whiny twelve-year-old. Remember the day you arrived at Miss Lavender's?"

"I'm not that girl anymore," said Thea. That small, scared girl, scarcely larger than the trunk she had lugged through the airport and then onto the train from Boston. She wasn't like that, was she?

"You could have fooled me."

Think like a witch. No, she wasn't that girl anymore. She was a graduate of Miss Lavender's, and even if she didn't know what to do right now, she would figure it out.

Thea took a deep breath. "Cordy, I bet she's still in the castle. She's the part of me that my grandmother cut away, the bad part. Or, you know, rebellious. Angry. She's teasing us now, showing us that she's smarter, better than we are. She likes doing that. So she's still here."

"Then let's go find her," said the cat.

"She stole Raven's cloak of invisibility. I think that's why Morgan hasn't been able to find her all this time. So we need another way to find her. Can you find her by smell?"

"How would I do that?" said Cordelia, looking at her incredulously. "Do you have any idea how big the castle is? I don't think even the castle itself knows! We could look for years."

"I think I know where to start. She's so confident, but it's all on the surface—she doesn't belong here any more than I do. She's lost, just like me. I think she's been hiding in the Library of Lost Books. That's what I would do, hide among the lost things. I think that's why she was toasting marshmallows in the library fireplace. Of course if she looks in the Seeing Ball, she can see us coming, in which case we're out of luck. But she didn't have it earlier—I would have noticed it on her, in that cat outfit. We have to take the chance that she's too occupied or distracted to check. Anyway, this is the only plan I can think of right now. Will you help me?"

"All right," said Cordelia. "I'll even let you carry me, as long as you don't turn me on my back. I'm not a human infant, you know!"

Thea put the cat over her shoulder. She didn't have time to return her plate and cutlery to the ballroom—hopefully someone would find them. "To a witch, any door is every door." Senator Warren had said that, speaking at her graduation. It was probably supposed to be a metaphor, but metaphorical language was poetry, right? And poetry was magic. She walked back to the stone arch that led into the castle. She stood in front of it, clutching Cordelia, and said,

> *"Ghosts of thoughts are lying*
> *on the shelves, rustling*
> *like a forest of dry leaves.*
> *Take me to them."*

See? Metaphor—or was that a simile? She was getting better at this. Thea stepped through the archway and into the Library of Lost Books.

The library was dark and silent, illuminated only by the moonlight that came through tall, mullioned windows. It gleamed on row upon row of books with gilt lettering on their spines. She put Cordelia down on the floor.

"All right," she said. "Look for someone who smells like me. I mean 'smell for.' You know what I mean."

Cordelia sniffed the air. Thea could see the shining circles of her eyes. Then she turned away and slunk into the darkness. This could take a while . . . but no, just a minute later Cordelia was back.

"Well, that was easy," she said disdainfully. "She may have gotten all the anger, but you got all the brains. They're asleep, right in front of the fireplace."

Thea followed the cat across the dark, cavernous room to a stone fireplace. On a carpet in front of the fireplace, there was . . . nothing. "Invisibility cloak," she said. "Show me where?"

Cordelia nudged the nothing.

Thea knelt down and felt the air . . . yes, it was fabric, scratchy like wool. She pulled it off. There, on the carpet, asleep and smelling distinctly of wine, were her shadow and Oryx the satyr. One of her arms was flung over his hairy chest.

"What now?" said Cordelia.

"I don't know." She had been doing the next thing and the next, as they occurred to her. Looking down at her shadow nestled against the satyr, she did not know what to do.

"Well, that's helpful," said the cat in her most disgusted tone. She sat on the stone floor and wrapped her tail around her feet.

Thea sat down beside her cross-legged, set the peacock mask on the floor, and put her chin in her hands. The green dress, black in the moonlight, puddled around her. How do you join a shadow to yourself after it has been snipped away? That was the question.

"If I could get her back to Miss Lavender's, I could ask Miss Gray to rejoin us—or maybe Mrs. Moth would do it? But I don't know how to get her back there without waking her up. And if I wake her, she'll never agree to go with me." The shadow had made that perfectly clear.

"Do you always wait for someone else to solve your problems?" Cordelia asked, as though posing a theoretical question.

Thea put her hands over her eyes, ashamed of herself. Yes, mostly, up to now she had. Her grandmother, and then the teachers at school. But she wasn't in school anymore, was she? She was an adult now, and adults solved their own problems. So did witches.

"Wait." She opened her eyes. Her hands were still in front of her face, but she could see right through them, to the bookshelves across the room. Both of her hands were completely transparent. Quickly, she put them in her lap, where she couldn't see them. She didn't want to know how much she had faded here, so close to her shadow. "Mrs. Moth said something—if only I could remember."

Cordelia yawned, pointedly.

"That's it!" Suddenly, it had come back to her—the conversation over tea, and a chance remark. "Magic is poetry. At least, poetry plus math. I always hated the math part, but all we need is for one plus one to equal one." Carefully, she leaned forward and turned the shadow over—the other Thea made a sound but did not wake up. Then she sat back and pulled out one of her long red hairs. "You'll have to be both needle and thread," she said to the red strand.

"Thread the needle, sharp as pain,
sew the fabric, strong as grief."

She put the soles of her feet right on the shadow's, her Keds to the soft black leather boots of the catsuit, and began to sew.

*"Join the twain, join them well,
bind them as a single soul,
so they cannot be unbound."*

Starting at the heel, up the outside and a few extra stitches at the toe, down the inside, knot. Then the other foot.

*"Sewing spell, join them soundly,
solidly and well."*

Once she had knotted the thread again, she stood up. The shadow lay on the floor, just where the moonlight would have cast Thea's shadow. Thea looked down at her hands. She could no longer see through them. They were completely solid.

"Well?" said Cordelia.

"I don't know. I think it worked. I remember being at Miss Lavender's and being in the box. If I'd been in that box, I would have hated me too! I think I do hate me. And my grandmother, and Anne Featherstone, and my parents for dying, and . . . Cordy, what's wrong with my face?"

"You're crying. You humans do that."

Thea could feel tears coursing down her cheeks. Suddenly, she started to sob—loud, heaving sobs that racked her as she leaned forward, hands on her stomach, then fell to her knees. She felt as though she were going to split apart again, this time from anger and grief. She had never felt anything so painful—the racking sobs continued—no, she had, she remembered now. But it had been long ago, when she was a child. And it all came flooding back—her mother's soft auburn hair, the sensation of riding on her father's shoulders, the day she had been told they would not, no never, come back. She couldn't bear it. She knelt on the cold, hard floor and sobbed.

"You have to get up," said Cordelia. "We have to go home. Look."

Thea looked up. Through her tears, she saw that it was brighter—no longer moonlight, but the soft blue light of early morning, beginning to come through the library windows.

"What's wrong with me, Cordy? Why can't I stop crying?"

"You're both of you now." The cat rubbed up against her, a rare gesture of affection. "Come on. You can do it, you know."

Thea stood up awkwardly and rubbed her hands across her face. They were slick with tears. She didn't want to ruin the green dress by wiping them on it, so she just rubbed them against each other, hoping they would dry. She took a deep breath that hurt her ribs. Her stomach was still queasy and there was an ache in her chest, but somehow she felt stronger than before. As though the world had stopped tilting around her.

"All right, give me a minute."

She knelt beside the satyr and kissed him on one cheek, despite his bad breath, then stroked his hair. "I liked you—a lot. And honestly, you're pretty hot for someone who's half goat." Then she picked up the peacock mask from where she had set it down.

"Can we go home now?" Cordelia yawned a wide cat yawn and blinked her eyes. This time, she seemed genuinely sleepy.

"One more thing. No, two." Thea found the Seeing Ball where she—the shadow—no, she as the shadow—had left it, behind Volume VII of *The Collected Poems of Sappho*. It was confusing, having two sets of memories. Going to school at Miss Lavender's—being in a box for twelve years, like a long, dreamless sleep—attending her grandmother's funeral—finding herself free in Mother Night's castle—sitting in her Boston apartment, watching anime on YouTube and eating takeout sushi, afraid of everything, college and what the future held for her—capering around the gardens with Oryx, hiding behind the giant chess pieces, teasing the fish. Which were her memories? All of them, she supposed. She felt around the floor next to the satyr—there, the invisibility cloak, with its scratchy wool. She put it over her arm so that her hand

looked as though it were floating in the air. Then she hoisted the soft, sleepy cat to her shoulder. Carrying cat and cloak and mask, she walked to the library door.

> *"Morning has come, and morning's star has risen:*
> *her chamber awaits its radiant messenger.*
> *Take me there."*

She stepped through the library door into Morgan's tower.

The Morningstar was, in fact, not there. Putting Cordelia on the bed, where she promptly curled up and fell asleep, Thea changed into her own clothes. Thank goodness she had brought extra. And Mother Night had said something about chocolate . . . yes, there it was, half a bar in the front pocket of her backpack. She broke off a square and put it into her mouth, chewing it quickly, automatically. But it was the best chocolate she had ever tasted—honestly, ever. Dark, sweet, bitter, creamy . . . had she never actually tasted chocolate before? Oh, for goodness' sake, she was starting to cry again, and her nose was starting to run. Hastily folding the green dress before she could get tears or snot on it, she put it on the bed with the peacock mask on top and the invisibility cloak beside it. Then she took the notebook out of her backpack, tore out a sheet of paper, and left a note, with the Seeing Ball on top to weigh it down:

> *Thank you so much for everything!*
> *I got my shadow and sewed it back*
> *on—very Peter Pan! Invisibility cloak*
> *is to the left ⟵ If you're on*
> *Facebook, friend me!!! ♡ Thea*

She slung her backpack over one shoulder and draped Cordelia over the other—drat the cat, why couldn't she wake up and walk?

She had to keep sniffing so her nose wouldn't drip. Somewhere in her backpack she might have a tissue, but she couldn't search for one while holding Cordelia and trying to come up with a poem. It didn't have to be long, right? Just effective.

> *"The greatest magic*
> *brings you home."*

She stepped through the tower door into the kitchen of the headmistress's house.

Mrs. Moth was in an apron, making breakfast. "Good morning, Thea," she said. "When we didn't see you yesterday, we figured you'd found your way to the Other Country. Why, look at you!" She said it in the tone of an aunt who has not seen you in a while and remarks on how much you've grown. "Emily, Lavinia," she called. "Thea's back! All of her, thank goodness." Then she held out a paper towel for Thea's dripping nose.

"Well, how do you feel?" asked Miss Gray. Thea had taken a shower and brushed her teeth, examining herself curiously in the mirror. She looked tired, and her eyes were red, and there was a shadow following her around, everywhere she went. She kept seeing it out of the corner of her eye and flinching. She could not get used to it.

"I don't know." She ate the last spoonful of her oatmeal. "Confused. Sad about my parents. Angry about being put in a box. Glad to be here. Any minute now I'm probably going to burst into tears again. Sometimes I feel like kicking things, and sometimes I feel like dancing around the room. Although I haven't actually done either of those things yet."

"Oh, but you will, my dear," said Miss Lavender. "It's very confusing, being all of yourself. You'll find it quite uncomfortable for a while. But you'll get used to it. We all do."

"Coffee, anyone?" asked Mrs. Moth.

"Not for me," said Thea. "I think I'll go to Booktopia for a latte. There was a book on writing I wanted to get—John Gardner." Maybe even the Anne Lamott.

"Good for you," said Miss Gray. "I always liked your pieces in *The Broomstick*, especially that article on Hans Christian Andersen. He really was a charming man, although terribly insecure."

"And Sam's quite attractive," said Mrs. Moth. "Though very young."

"This is about *literature*, not romance," said Miss Gray. "Anyway, you think anyone under a century is young. Have a good time, Thea."

"I'll try," said Thea. Miss Gray had read something of hers and actually liked it! Maybe she could write some poems or an article. That shouldn't be too hard, right? The novels could come later. . . . She smiled at herself, then sniffed again and wiped her nose with the balled-up paper towel.

On the way out, she scratched Cordelia behind the ears. The cat curled up more tightly on the parlor sofa, purring in her sleep. Thea put on her jacket and scarf, then stepped into the cold New England morning, her shadow accompanying her up the path and into the town, toward the bookstore and anywhere else she might want to go.

AUTHOR'S NOTE

Theodora Goss: I'm not sure which I read first, Hans Christian Andersen's "The Shadow" or Ursula Le Guin's essay "The Child and the Shadow," which is a Jungian interpretation of the Andersen fairy tale. Regardless, my own reading of the fairy tale was deeply influenced by Le Guin's, as well as by other stories I'd read of shadows or doubles, such as Edgar Allan Poe's "William Wilson," Robert Louis Stevenson's *The Strange Case of Dr. Jekyll and Mr. Hyde*, and Oscar Wilde's "The Fisherman and His Soul," which is partly a response to Andersen. One thing struck me about these stories: the protagonist is never female. There must be stories of women who are double, but if so, I haven't read them: traditionally in literature women *are* the other, so I guess they don't get an other? They have no shadows. . . . Therefore, in writing my own version of the Andersen story, I created Thea. Her other comes out of my sense that Jung is right about the shadow: it represents a dark, wild, but also vital part of the self that must be incorporated rather than rejected. Without her shadow, Thea can't be her complete adult self. The story also comes out of my understanding of depression: without her shadow, Thea experiences symptoms of depression, which include lethargy, loss of motivation, loss of a sense of self. I hope once she regains her shadow, Thea will go on to live a fulfilling, creative life. . . . And I believe we must all connect with our shadows if we are to live deeply and creatively, to our full potential.

WHEN I LAY FROZEN

Margo Lanagan

ell me again, Tommelise," Mrs. Markmusen wheezes from her great bed, "about the Mother and Father."

I open my eyes and glare into the darkness. I've spun thread since dawn, with those four hideous spider-sisters the Edderkops weaving and whispering around me. My fingers throb and my mind aches from holding off my revulsion. All I want to do is sleep.

"Well," I begin, as politely as I can manage, "it all started when the Mother kissed me alive—"

"Snik-snak, not that dull stuff!" The phlegm rattles in Mrs. Markmusen's angry throat. "You know what I want to hear. One night, you heard a sound . . ."

I wrap my blanket tighter. I hate that story. I wish I had never told it to her.

But this mousewife saved my life, I remind myself—and it

cost her. To share her food with me last winter, she went without. And because she did, she bore no young, either in spring or later in summer. The least I can do in return is satisfy her craving for these upsetting stories.

"I heard a sound, yes," I say. "I heard movements I could make no sense of, that were not any movement of sleep. And cries, from the Mother and then the Father, small cries but urgent, like warnings."

"You should have heeded those warnings and stayed where you were," Mrs. Markmusen growls.

"I should have! You are so right! But I rose from my bed, and I picked up my foxfire torch."

"Oh dear, oh dear . . ."

"I crept along the shelf to the corner and peeped around to where the Mother and Father slept."

The mousewife's bedclothes rustle, and the big wooden bed frame lets out a crack. "But they *weren't* sleeping, were they!"

"They were not." I shut my eyes tightly, but still I see, lit by torchlight and moonlight, the vast, peeled bodies surging out of the bedclothes. Their faces open and roam over each other like cattle desperately browsing. The Father, in agony, grows his extra, stunted leg, and the Mother takes fright and crushes it under her bottom in a frenzy, her bared breasts swinging, her hair a frizzled storm around the black hole of her mouth.

All during my telling, Mrs. Markmusen's bed cracks and cricks at the horror of it, ever faster and louder. Her promptings shrink to hisses and moans, of disbelief, of pity. She understands my discomfiture. She shares it, but she shivers and struggles where I can only lie and stare. She cries out in my stead, for the most I can do is coldly set forth the Mother's and Father's actions.

"I really feared for the Father's life," I say. "He lay so stiffly, and he gaped so widely. And the Mother, on top of him, looked so ill and unlike herself, all unbound and shaking without her clothes, her face and hair tossing about—"

"Oh!" cries Mrs. Markmusen. "Oh! Oh! How dreadful for you!" Her bed cracks hard and suddenly, fit to break with her writhing. As long as she doesn't begin to cough . . .

"Dreadful!" she says. "Terrible! Oh, you poor, poor—Oh! How you must have suffered!" Crick and crack and gasp and huff of bedclothes.

I wish I could writhe and shout like her and be done with it. Instead, I lie quiet, and the wrongness of it stays inside me, a stone in my belly. I fled the Mother and Father's house long ago—the spring before last, and now my second summer is waning—but I carry that stone with me still.

"What did it *mean*?" I plead into the darkness as Mrs. Markmusen subsides. "Why would they want to kill each other? During the day they went about so measured and civil, their clothes so neat, and their hair—"

"I cannot help you." Mrs. Markmusen sounds weary from giving voice to all my terrors. Then the coughing takes her, long and dreadful.

"It is a great mystery," she whispers when she's recovered, turning her face to the wall. "Sleep," she says. "The Edderkops will arrive early, and you must be up and spinning if they're to have thread for their work."

A few last gasps and jolts shake her, and then she sighs asleep. But I lie wide awake with memories moiling before me. When I flung myself into the grass from the Mother and Father's windowsill, I thought that I was leaving their madness behind. But then I found that the whole world was mad. Toads and fish, deer and cattle, birds and beetles—whenever I happened on new beasts, they would set to clambering and slithering over each other.

Worse, if they were not with another of their kind, they would turn on *me* and try to crush or drown me, or rub me out of existence. The terror and the formless shame of those memories still dog my every step. The fine unsettling rustle of Edderkop fingers at the loom fills my days, but the beasts' grunts and pants and mindless exclamations haunt all my nights.

Long ago, in the snow-time, I would rise and creep away from this noise of my mind. I would fetch a bowl and a bottle of water, and a small ration of grain from the mousewife's larder, and hurry to the tunnel where the bird-woman lay, thawed from the sleep that the snowstorm had put her in, yet trapped here by winter, just as I was.

I would feed her and give her water, and sit against her warmth and listen to her wise voice. So much of what she said is gone from me now, for I remember things poorly without nectar, but certain exchanges come back to me again and again.

Like the first:

Do I dream you, little glowworm? she said from above, as I cast about the piled earth that had been part of the tunnel roof before she came plunging through.

Eagerly I held up the lamp. There she was, against the ragged roof-hole aglitter with stars. She peered down, the icy air spiking up the feathers on the crown of her head. She was not frighteningly large. That pointed beak was for pinching insects out of the air, not snatching up mice or Tommelises from the ground.

You are revived, ma'am! I said, pleased.

Am I not in Danmark? she said.

Ma'am, you are in the tunnel that joins the house of Mrs. Markmusen to that of Mr. Muldvarp.

Ah, Danmark, then. But Markmus? Muldvarper? She shifted position on her earthen perch. *I am a flier! And you are no flower of Danmark. You have something of the Türk about you, I think. Yes, definitely you are warmlandish.*

Later I would wonder over those words, but for now I only clambered up the loose earth. The swallow was twice as big as me, but unlike Mrs. Markmusen she was smooth and dapper, her

body a single dark sweep out to tail-points in the shadows. She had picked apart the hay and thistledown I'd covered her with, and used it to line this draughty hollow of a nest.

I poured water into the bowl and laid it before her.

My name is Svale, she said. *Who are you, kindness?*

I am Tommelise.

She smiled. *Ah, I see. Brought here by giants, were you?*

I walked here myself, I said. *From the Mother and Father's house, where I was born.*

She nodded soberly. *Of course you did.* She dipped her beak into the water, lifted her head to tip it down her throat. *You must tell me all about that journey.*

And so I did. I told her everything—we had all winter for the telling, after all. When she left, she took my whole life story with her. And she left hers with me, so wild and bright and far-reaching and thickly patterned, my little dull year-and-a-bit seemed hardly worth recounting beside it.

Mrs. Markmusen comes to the weaving room to inspect the trousseau. The Edderkops bob and sway as she counts the items, their many eyes gleaming like polished black beads, their limbs fiddling and bunching. They are even more repellent idle than when they work—which must be why the mousewife has put them to weaving. She lets them live in a web-clotted corner of her entryway, pouncing on any insect that dares come near, wrapping and hanging the little corpses in their ghastly bower.

But however unnerving are the makers, the made things are sumptuously fine. If only I could use them *without* being imprisoned under the earth! I would delight in the broad, crisp bedsheets if Mr. Muldvarp, six times my size and larger, were not going to join me between them.

Mrs. Markmusen holds the fine linen nightgown up against me, so much softer than the little drugget shift I presently wear

at nights. "How small it is!" she says. "And as delicate as flower petals—as it should be, for such a little flower as yourself!"

But I hate this garment—it's the sort the Mother wore that night, the layer she shed before her night-game with the Father.

"I wish I did not have to wear it," I hiss.

The Edderkops skitter back from my outburst and clump in a corner.

Mrs. Markmusen leans down to me, and her watery eyes grow large. "You know how things stand, Tommelise. There is no discouraging Mr. Muldvarp. We've put him off all spring and right through the summer—who'd have thought we'd manage that? But he'll brook no further delay."

"But you know what he'll want. You know what he'll do. How can you deliver me up to such a creature?"

Mrs. Markmusen straightens, taking away her popping eyes and whiskery face. She shrugs up there, pulls out her handkerchief, trumpets into it, twice. Parceling up the nose-blowings in the cloth, she casts a cool eye down on me.

"I've done all I can for you, little one," she says. "But another winter like the last would kill me. A rich fellow like Muldvarp can easily spare a Tommelise's worth of food in the cold months. Much as I've enjoyed your company, we must be sensible about this."

How have you survived so long? said Ms. Svale.

I have learned to eat grain, I said. I was wonderfully warm, sheltered under her wing. Another storm raged above, and now and again a snowflake floated ghostly down, to melt on the rim of the nest. *And nuts too,* I went on, *from the mousewife's larder. None of it agrees with me, but it keeps me alive.*

She must be very old and spiritless, said Ms. Svale, *to let you make so free with her food.*

Oh no, she is quite strong and fierce, I said. *And clever. She has devised this whole matter of the trousseau to put off Mr. Muldvarp.*

Put him off from what? Ms. Svale fluffed up her feathers. I nearly swooned from the warmth.

From marrying me, I said. *But he won't be put off forever. At the latest we will marry in early spring.*

Ms. Svale bent her head around and regarded me a long time in the dimness.

What good can ever come of that? she said.

I know, I said dolefully. *Muldvarp's food is even worse than the mousewife's. But I dare say I will survive on it, just as I—*

How can you marry a Muldvarp, is what I mean, she said. *You are not only from a foreign clime but of a wholly other kind than him. He is beast, like the mousewife. You are blomst.*

Blomst?

I laughed, for how could I be one of those? Blomst were tiny, brittle creatures, spitting at me from the hedgerows or vanishing into meadow grasses. Or they were tall, gaunt, melancholy ghosts of lilies, stalking about the reed beds.

But Ms. Svale did not laugh with me. *Tut-tut,* she said. *The foreign smell of you has turned that poor man's head; that's all that's happened. You need to go away from here, to set both animals free.*

Fear choked my laughter off. *But where would I go?*

To the warm lands, of course, to marry among your own people.

I stared at her. *My own people?*

She laughed. *You didn't imagine you were the only "Tommelise" in the world?*

I have never met another, I said stiffly.

She shook her head, fluffed her feathers again. *Of course not, poor tiny. But you've seen every other creature pairing. Did you think that only you were meant to live alone?*

I sat very still in the feather-warmth. I had never asked myself that question. But now that she had uttered it, my whole life looked to me like a timid *Yes!* in answer to it. Now I could feel I was blomst, as hope sprang open in my head, splayed out its many petals, reminded me that there was color in the world beyond this black-and-gray winter, that there was light—and why should there not be love as well, blomst-love that would not hurt or revolt me?

But how can I ever find my kind, I said, *in a frozen world, without nectar?*

You must wait as I wait, Ms. Svale said, *for the world to warm again. To warm, and to blossom. Then, at the first opportunity, you must begin your search.*

Mr. Muldvarp leans forward intently. One hand strokes his velvet coat as if to say, *Note this quality! Could Edderkops ever make such as this?* He cannot see me well—he cannot see anything well. But he is as keen to hear me speak as Mrs. Markmusen ever is. "Her voice—so sweet, so small!" he often exclaims, interrupting my description of some mountain or mere I encountered in my travels.

If I turn my tale skyward, expounding on singular birds or butterflies or clouds I've observed, he will silence me with robust laughter. "Winged things—what kind of a life is that, flinging oneself about in the air? I should be afraid of flying apart, shouldn't you, Mrs. Markmusen, without the good earth on all sides of me? The deeper and darker the better, don't you think?" And I recall how he kicked—kicked!—Ms. Svale as she lay frozen in the tunnel on the night of that first snowstorm.

But his sensitive pink nose stays pointed my way, so I continue with my pretty ramblings, which he searches for disagreeable features of the outside world that he can enjoy pouring scorn on.

When his visit ends, Mrs. Markmusen and I accompany him, as always, through the tunnel to his home. Farewells said, and Muldvarp's front door closed, the mousewife turns to me with relief. "Well done, Tommelise! Another pleasant evening's entertainment! What a colorful life you have led. But not too colorful,

eh?" And up there in the dimness against the tunnel roof she taps her nose and winks down at me.

"And should I keep refraining," I ask her, "from telling him the more distressing tales, even after we are married?"

"Oh, then you may do as you please," she says carelessly.

She turns in a whisk of skirts and has gone several steps before she realizes I am not at her heels. She holds up her lamp. My troublement is written clearly on my face, I can feel. I hurry after her.

"Tell him the story of the fish," she suggests more kindly. "Yes, and then pay me a visit and tell me how that one takes him. Together we'll determine whether it's wise to go on."

Why the fish? Because the tale is quickly told? Because fish are so different from mice and moles and myself? I follow her, flinching at those memories: the bumps beneath the water-lily leaf I was seated on, the slithering turmoil as the fish grouped and tangled, the whitened water, those bubbles that did not burst, the smell that rose in the warm sun—strong, peculiar, wrong.

I cannot imagine Mr. Muldvarp being anything other than repelled by the story, as I and the mousewife are. If he scorns the sky and all flying things, how much more deserving of disdain will he find these other oddities!

But Mrs. Muldvarp is right—I should try a small oddity first and see how it moves him. He is so much larger than either of us and so will have larger passions. It's best to take care.

Come with me, Tommelise!

Ms. Svale's wings thrummed and trembled. I hung on tightly to the green shoot of an emerging snowdrop for safety.

We were above ground, a little way from the hole in the tunnel roof. All about us winter dripped from shrinking snow patches into the softening earth.

It's such a lovely time to fly about, the northern spring, she said.

And it doesn't last long—before you know it we will be off to the warm
lands, where your fellow blomsters' welcome awaits you!

I cannot leave Mrs. Markmusen, I said miserably. *She has been*
so kind to me.

A full winter on the mousewife's provisions had weighed me
down, body and spirit. I could not imagine climbing aboard the
bird-woman and leaping into the vast, overcast sky.

Well, you have been kind to me, *Tommelise.* Ms. Svale cocked
her head, fixing me with an eye as beady as any Edderkop's. *And*
yet I'm not spending the rest of my life with you!

But you are big and brave, I said. *And winged! I am tiny, and*
confined to the ground, stumbling from one alarm to the next. It is safer
for me here in the mousewife's warm burrow—

Safer? With that lust-addled Muldvarp hanging about, held off
only by an ailing mouse?

I clung to the snowdrop shoot. She was right. Yet I did not
have the courage to make my escape, to step outside what I knew.
However glowingly she described my future—and she had done
so many times during the snow months—I could not believe it
was mine to reach out and grasp.

She shook her head over me. *Don't decide now,* she said. *I'll*
stay nearby for the next little while—and I'll be back at summer's end,
on the way to the warm lands. Be above ground at any sunrise when
I first stretch my wings, and I will take a turn this way, in case you
change your mind.

How cruel I thought her, for forcing this choice upon me,
not just this painful once, but every sunrise! How often must
I face my own misery, my own timidity, and watch myself give
way before it? I only wished her gone, once and irrecoverably. At
the same time, I was in the utmost despair, for with her would
fly away all my hope of knowing who I truly was, and of living
among my own kind.

Ms. Svale spread her wings. I pulled the dust cloth from my

apron pocket and waved it over my head as she lifted herself from beside me. *Farewell, farewell!* I cried.

She flew twice around me, raising a wind that almost tore me from the snowdrop, wrenching my skirts and hair about. Then the wind died and she was a dark flourish shrinking to a fleck on the sky. And here I was, alone on the surface, the bare field around me patched with snow, the sky's untouchable heights above. No other bird or beast threatened me from any quarter of the still, wintry scene. And yet I ran to the tunnel-hole and dropped into the darkness as quickly as I could, as if all the monsters of spring were after me.

Mrs. Markmusen has often told me about Mr. Muldvarp's home, marveling at its size and luxury. One night he invites us both to view it. As he leads us through the many rooms, the mousewife nudges me to remark admiringly on their vastness, though even a creature as large as she must surely find so much space alarming after her own cozy home.

Some rooms are bare and full of nothing but our host's ambitious plans; in others, gigantic dark bureaus and sideboards stand about, or candelabra'd dining tables, or suites of couches and armchairs. Generations of Muldvarps have handed these furnishings down through the ages, and my betrothed is very proud of them. Here we will sit, when we are married and immured here together. I will trot out my threadbare tales of sunshine and butterflies, and he will snort in comfortable contempt of all the world above.

"This carving on the balusters, Tommelise—did you ever see such workmanship?" Mrs. Markmusen exclaims.

"I did not." I try to sound respectful, though this mole-craft looks lumpish and crude to my tiny eyes.

I cannot picture myself as the mistress of this mansion, with all its wearying halls and chambers. We are deeper here, and the

air is danker; I am destined to breathe it, day in and day out, for the rest of my life. The thought makes my heart shrivel.

But worse is when Mr. Muldvarp brings us down to his pantry. Mrs. Markmusen gasps as he flings wide the door, and I think for a moment that she must share my disgust, for the walls and floor are heaving with slow-crawling insects of the soil. All kinds stagger and wriggle and drop from the ceiling, the many-legged and the few, the armor-plated and the softer-shelled, and even an earthworm lashes its length about among the teetering carapaces and the blundering legs.

"What a feast, Muldvarp!" cries Mrs. Markmusen. "Tommelise, you will never go hungry here!"

"Forgive me," I say, my throat tight. "These are not my kind of foodstuffs."

"Oh, snik and snak!" she says joyfully. "That's what you said about grains and nuts when first you came to me, and look how you devour them now!" She reaches into the mass and pulls out something shiny black, with threads of legs whirling below. She thrusts it at me. "Try it!"

Mr. Muldvarp laughs. "Such a modest sample, Mrs. Markmusen! Give her one of these! They've a bit more meat on them." And he selects a beetle almost as big as one of his paws, all grimy shell and waving feelers.

He brings it to his mouth and bites away its head and half its body. Its back end spasms and stills. Muldvarp chews, a feeler poking out between his lips.

"Eat, Tommelise!" Mrs. Markmusen all but cuffs me.

Dazedly I push the smooth, scrabbling insect into my mouth and bite down. The thing dies with a crunch and its bitter insides fill my mouth. My throat rebels, but I swallow and swallow, keeping my face stiffly blank as the mousewife and the mole smile down on me.

"See? Delicious!" Mr. Muldvarp says heartily.

Mrs. Markmusen looks more severe. "You'll get used to them," she commands. Then she says more gently, "And they are richer than grains, so you need not eat so very many."

And I remember what a burden I was on her last winter. Right now she should be shooing her eighth litter from her door to gather their own store for the winter. She should be storing up food for herself, not wasting her energies arranging a marriage for a foreign interloper.

I force the last few shell fragments down my convulsing throat. "I'm sure I will come round to these," I manage to say. "In time."

I suffered every morning after Ms. Svale flew away, taking up my spindle under the cold, dim earth, trying not to think of the bird-woman wheeling and dipping in the sunshine above my head.

Mr. Muldvarp grew more spirited with the spring, arriving in a new coat one evening and pressing Mrs. Markmusen to set a date when she would release me to marry him.

"I cannot be precise," she said. "I've looked through her trousseau, and it seems to me that another set of woolens would be advisable, if Tommelise is to winter so deeply underground. Let me consult with the Edderkops."

Thus she put him off. And then summer came, and warmed the mouse-house right down to our workroom. The warm lands did not seem so seductive. Warmth made Edderkops weave and stitch faster and demand more thread. Their rustling grew furious, their scuttling sudden and alarming. I missed the cooler days when they were sluggish and predictable.

Now the grain above us is grown to its full height and gone from green to gold, and no sunlight touches even the mouth of Mrs. Markmusen's home, or slants in through the hole in the tunnel roof. The days cool and shorten, and I try not to think of the swallow.

I'll be back, she said, *on the way to the warm lands.*

Come with me, she said, so many times. *You must! It is a cruelty to these beasts for you to stay, let alone to your own misplaced self.*

Grimly I stay below, moving straight from bedroom to workroom and spinning there through the dawns. I have eaten nothing but beast-food for many months. I cannot even remember what nectar tastes like. Nectar fueled a different Tommelise entirely; who was that sprite who threw herself from the cottage sill so long ago, the blomst who had the energy to flee, one after another, the monsters that paraded toward her as she skirted lakes and swung herself, stalk to stalk, across meadows? That adventurer, that girl who ran outraged through the world, sure she deserved better, she is gone now, and in her place is this resistless half-person, spinning away her days, a stone at her center.

I am telling the mousewife, yet again, the story of the toad and the terrapin. The "foolish" toad, she calls him, though to my mind he is more appalling, how he jumped aboard the terrapin and pinned me to its shell, leaking toad-water between us and crooning about the toadlets we would make together.

Delving deep to retrieve his exact words and all those horrid details that she likes, I don't notice the moment when the cracking ceases from Mrs. Markmusen's bed. Only when I reach the end of the tale does it strike me that I have been speaking to a silent room for some time.

"Mrs. Markmusen?"

Not even her breath wheezes from that corner of the night. I sit up, hold still, listen.

"Ma'am?"

Not a sound.

I leap from my bed and across the room and shake her. She does not resist or revive. "Mrs. Markmusen!"

I uncover the foxfire lamp and hold it up. Her staring eyes see nothing. Her face-fur is damp from her sympathetic exertions,

but her warmth is already fading. No pulse beats in her; no breath comes or goes from her nostrils or mouth; not so much as a whisker of her trembles.

When I can move again, I drag my bedding into the passage—Edderkops may like to sleep among corpses, but I cannot.

I bundle myself tightly in blankets as the night opens—silent, spacious, terrifying—around me. The mousewife is dead. I owe nothing anymore to this house, to Muldvarp, to anyone. I could be that girl again, that running, swinging, monster-fleeing girl. I could throw off these wrappings, run along the passage, and there I'd be at the door. If only I had the strength—if only I had a bellyful of nectar instead of mouse-house stodge. If only I could direct my thoughts, instead of their trickling away like spring runnels from a snowpack. If only it were spring, with the promise of warmth outside, instead of chill autumn, when a person needs to shelter, needs to stay swaddled against the cold in blankets such as these, so soft, so familiar, so warm . . .

I wake to the tick and flicker of tiny Edderkop feet on the floor. The sisters' eyes shine and bob at me in the faint light filtering through the glass of the eastern door. I sit up, and we shrink to our opposite walls.

"We waited," says the eldest sister. "But the mistress did not come."

"No." I rise from the bedding, make a graceless gesture at the bedroom door. "And she won't *be* coming."

They shift like uneasy twig-brooms, all their eyes on the door, up and down. I push it wide for them, and they stare at me, then scuttle past. With ticks and taps and scrapes they take up positions around the mounded bed, and a silence falls, and extends.

And then they are in the doorway again, all four; two cling high on the doorposts. Recoiling, I am reflected eightfold in four sets of eyes as the first sunbeam strikes along the passage.

Spider-laughter vibrates them and sharpens their knees.

"She's dead, that mousewife," says a sister. They jump into the passage, herd me against the wall. "And do you know how much we care about your wedding clothes, trollop?"

"Your tablecloths, on and on, the finest damask, the most elaborate—"

"Your evening gowns, your housedresses, your winter coats—"

"Your *sheets*. Your endless wedding sheets where you'll disport yourself, with Mr. Mole under your spell—"

Tremendous thudding and scraping, and a muffled roar, shake the earth to the west of us, deep beyond the mousewife's house. I know those sounds, but before I can pin down the memory, the tunnel door shatters, the doorknob bouncing from the shadows and careening off my ankle.

"Speak of the devil!" The sisters pile on one another against the far wall.

"Yes!" The curve of the passage brings Muldvarp's whisper close, as if his mouth were right by my ear. "There *is* a change in the air! I'm a young man again, and my bride awaits!"

He barrels up the passage, shovel-claws and velvet with his pink nose leading.

"Come to my arms!" he cries out in joy, but I dive clear of his descending claw and roll to my feet, and run toward the light, and he is too big and clumsy to catch me.

I speed up the passage and across the vestibule, grasp the doorknob that will be too small and slippery for his claws, turn the heavy thing. His velvet weight is in the hall behind me. His claws scrape the floor. The sour insect-stink of his breath puffs over my shoulder.

I slip out the door and pull it closed against a blur of claw and velvet. He roars and throws his weight against it. It bows out, shaking in its frame, and its pretty glasswork cracks. It won't hold long.

I spin round to face the wreckage of the summer grain, every

stalk cut back to a stump, outlined in the sun's first gold. There is nowhere for me to climb and hide.

And rain has washed the ground overnight. What is not puddles is soft, sticky-looking mud—

The door crashes again. Splinters fly from its glass panels. Muldvarp pushes his nose through the broken pane, bloodying himself. "Mine!" he bellows. "You are mine. You are promised to me!"

I pick up my skirts and spring to the nearest stump, to the next, and the next, and onward.

"Mine!" Muldvarp bursts out of the house behind me.

Terror fumbles my feet, and I'm in water to my knees, ice cold, mud clamping my ankles. The water soaks the hem of my nightshift, pulls me down. And here comes Muldvarp, sloshing and splashing across the field.

My fists are in the mud. My breath sobs in my throat. I will never rise from here, never go on, never save myself. Do I have time to drown before Muldvarp reaches me? My reflected face blazes up at me, steeling itself to plunge into cold, blessed unconsciousness.

Something strikes my back and pulls me up from the puddle, suckingly free of the mud. Some dark, thrumming thing lifts me by my nightshift into the sun. The desolate field falls away. Spiders spill from the ruined mouse-house door. The maddened Muldvarp flounders through the mud, toward nothing now. His bellowing fades on the wide air, taking my terror with it.

And then they are gone and done with—spiders, mole, and mouse-house all too small for me to see. I swing myself around, catch hold of Ms. Svale's feathers, and scramble up to the warm, safe place between her steadily beating wings.

AUTHOR'S NOTE

Margo Lanagan: Hans Christian Andersen's "Thumbelina" is a tooth-dissolvingly sweet tale that speaks volumes about the gender divide of its time. Put this weeping, shivering moppet, always at the mercy of the giant creatures around her, up against the rambunctious adventurer Tom Thumb, and despair. But how to remake the story without simply giving the heroine a granite jaw, a weapon, and a big bag of agency? (I'll confess, in my first attempt, I did just that.) In the end I took Andersen's characterization of Thumbelina/Tommelise as a "spirit of a flower"—and a displaced flower at that, a tulip brought too far north—as my key. I gave her agency that she doesn't know about, a pheromonal cloud around her that arouses everyone she meets. Because she's exiled from her community, there's no one to explain what's happening to her, so the world becomes a bemusing place, and her journey one encounter after another with enormous, highly sexed creatures acting inappropriately. I guess I reached into the story and dragged out the elements that generally tend to set me off— the theme of tender young things being sent out into the world ignorant and powerless is one I've visited before and no doubt will again, it annoys me so. In the end it's education, a last skerrick of self-respect, and a lucky friendship that saves my Tommelise. May every innocent have a Ms. Svale crash-land in her life and help make it all comprehensible.

PEARL

Aliette de Bodard

n Da Trang's nightmares, Pearl is always leaving—darting away from him, toward the inexorable maw of the sun's gravity, going into a tighter and tighter orbit until no trace of it remains—he's always reaching out, sending a ship, a swarm of bots—calling upon the remoras to move, sleek and deadly and yet too agonizingly slow, to do anything, to save what they can.

Too late. Too late.

It wasn't always like this, of course.

In the beginning . . . in the beginning . . . his thoughts fray and scatter away, like cloth held too close to a flame. How long since he's last slept? The Empress's courtier was right—but no, no, that's not it. She doesn't understand. None of them understand.

In the beginning, when he was still a raw, naive teenager, there was a noise, in the hangar. He thought it was just one of the countless remoras, dipping in and out of the room—his constant companions as he studied for the imperial examination, hovering over his shoulder to stare at the words; nudging him when one of them needed repairs they couldn't provide themselves. And once—just after Inner Grandmother's death, when Mother had been reeling from the loss of her own mother, and when he'd come running to the hangar with a vise around his chest—he'd seen them weaving and dancing in a pattern beautiful beyond words as he stood transfixed, with tears running down his cheeks.

"Can you wait?" Da Trang asked, not looking away from the text in his field of vision. "I'm trying to work out the meaning of a line." He was no scholar, no favored to be graced with a tutor or with mem-implants of his ancestors: everything he did was like moving through tar, every word a tangle of meanings and connotations he needed to unpack, every clever allusion something he needed to look up.

A nudge then; and, across his field of vision, lines—remoras didn't have human names, but it was the one he thought of as Teacher, because it was one of the oldest ones, and because it was always accompanied by a swarm of other remoras with which it appeared to be in deep conversation.

>Architect. Need to see.<

Urgent, then, if Teacher was attempting to communicate—remoras could use a little human speech, but it was hard work, tying up their processes—they grew uncannily still as they spoke, and once he'd seen a speaking remora unable to dodge another, more eager one.

He raised his gaze, and saw . . .

Teacher and another remora, Slicer, both with that same look of intent sleekness, as if they couldn't hold still for long without falling apart—and, between them, a third one, looking . . . somehow wrong. Patched up, like all remoras—leftovers from bots and ships that had gone all but feral, low-level intelligences used for menial tasks. And yet . . .

The hull of the third remora was painted—engraved with what

Pearl

looked like text at first, but turned out to be other characters, long, weaving lines in a strange, distorted alphabet Da Trang couldn't make out.

>Is Pearl,< Teacher said, on the screen. >For you.<

"I don't understand," Da Trang said slowly. He dismissed the text, watched the third remora—something almost graceful in the way it floated, like a calligraphy from a master, suggesting in a few strokes the shape of a bird or of a snake. "Pearl?"

Pearl moved, came to stand close to him—nudging him, like a pet or favorite bot—he'd never felt that or done that, and he felt obscurely embarrassed, as if he'd given away some intimacy that should have been better saved for a parent, a sibling, or a spouse.

>Architect.< Pearl's lines were the same characters as on its hull for a brief moment; and then they came into sharp focus as the remora lodged itself on his shoulder, against his neck—he could feel the heat of the ship, the endless vibrations of the motor through the hull, like a secret heartbeat. >Pleased. Will help.<

Da Trang was about to say he didn't need help, and then Pearl burrowed close to him—a sharp, painful stab straight into his flesh; and before he had time to cry out, he saw—

The hangar, turned into flowing lines like a sketch of a Grand Master of Design Harmony; the remoras, Slicer and Teacher, already on the move, with little labels listing their speed, their banking angles; their age and the repairs they'd undergone—the view expanding, taking in the stars beyond the space station, all neatly labeled, every wavelength of their spectrum cataloged—he tried to move, to think beyond the confines of the vision the ship had him trapped in; to remember the poem he'd been reading—and abruptly the poem was there, too, the lines about mist over the water and clouds and rain; and the references to sexual foreplay, the playfulness of the writer trying to seduce her husband—the homage to the famed poetess Dong Huong through the reuse of her metaphor about frost on jade flowers, the reference to the bird from Viet on Old Earth, always looking southward. . . .

And then Pearl released him; and he was on his knees on the floor, struggling for breath. "What—what—" Even words seemed to have deserted him.

>Will help,< Pearl said.

Teacher, firmer and steadier, a rock amidst the turmoil in his mind. >Built Pearl for you, Architect. For . . . examinations?< A word the remora wasn't sure of; a concept Da Trang wasn't even sure Teacher understood.

>For understanding,< Slicer said. >Everything.< If it had been human, the remora would have sounded smug.

"I can't—" Da Trang pulled himself upward, looked at Pearl again. "You made it?"

>Can build others,< Teacher said.

"Of course. I wasn't doubting that. I just—" He looked at Pearl again and finally worked out what was different about it. The others looked cobbled together of disparate parts—grabbing what they could from space debris and scraps and roughly welding it into place—but Pearl was . . . not perfect, but what you would get if you saved the best of everything you found drifting in space, and put it together, not out of necessity, not out of a desire for immediate survival or return to full functionality—but with a carefully thought-out plan, a desire for . . . stability? "It's beautiful," he said at last.

>We built,< Teacher said. >As thanks. And because . . .< A pause, and then another word, blinking on the screen. >We can build *better*.<

Not beauty, then, but hope, and longing, and the best for the future. Da Trang found his lips twisting in a bitter smile, shaping words of comfort, or something equally foolish to give a remora— some human emotions to a being that had none.

Before he could speak up, though, there came the patter of feet. "Li'l brother, li'l brother!" It was his sister Cam, out of breath.

Pearl

Da Trang got up—Pearl hovering again at his shoulder, the warmth of metal against his neck.

"What—" Cam stopped, looked at him. "What in heaven is this?"

Pearl nudged closer; he felt it nip the surface of his skin—and some of that same trance rose in him again, the same sense that he was seeing the bones of the orbital, the breath of the dragon that was the earth and the void between the stars and the universe—except oddly muted, so that his thoughts merely seemed far away to him, running beneath a pane of glass. He could read Cam—see the blood beating in her veins, the tension in her hands and in her arms. Something was worrying her, beyond her usual disapproval of a brother who dreamt big and spent his days away from the family home. Pearl?

"This is Pearl," Da Trang said awkwardly.

Cam looked at him—in Pearl's trance, he saw her face contract; saw electrical impulses travel back and forth in her arms. "Fine," she said, with a dismissive wave of her hand. "You were weird enough without a remora pet. Whatever."

So it wasn't that which worried her. "What's on your mind?" Da Trang asked.

Cam jerked. There was no other word for it—her movement would have been barely visible, but Pearl's trance magnified everything, so that for a moment she seemed a puppet on strings, and the puppet master had just stopped her from falling. "How do you know?"

"It's obvious," Da Trang said, trying to keep his voice steady. If he could read her—if he could read people—if he could remember poems and allusions and speak like a learned scholar . . .

"The Empress is coming," Cam said.

"And?" Da Trang was having a hard time seeing how that related to him. "We're not scholars or magistrates, or rich merchants. We're not going to see her unless we queue up for the procession."

"You don't understand." Cam's voice was plaintive. "The whole Belt is scraping resources together to make an official banquet, and they asked Mother to contribute a dish."

Da Trang was going to say something funny, or flippant, but that stopped him. "I had no idea." Pearl was showing him things—signs of Cam's stress, the panic she barely kept at bay, the desire to flee the orbital before things got any more overwhelming—but he didn't need Pearl for that. Imperial favor could go a long way—could lift someone from the poorer, most outward orbitals of the Scattered Pearls Belt all the way to the First Planet and the Imperial Court—but it could also lead someone into permanent disgrace, into exile and death. It was more than a dish; it would be a statement made by Mother's orbital, by the Belt itself, something they would expect to be both exquisite and redolent with clever allusions—to the Empress's reign name, to her campaigns, to her closest advisers or her wives. . . .

"Why did they ask Mother?"

"I don't know," Cam said. Blood flowed to her face, and her hands were moments away from clenching. "Because there was no one else. Because they wanted us to fail. Take your pick. What matters is that we can't say no, lest we become disgraced."

"Can you help?" he asked, aloud, and saw Cam startled, and then her face readjusting itself into a complex mixture of—contempt, pity—as she realized he was talking to the remora.

"You really spend too much time here," she said, shaking her head. "Come on."

"Can you help?" Da Trang asked again, and felt Pearl huddle more closely against him, the trance rising to dizzying heights as the remora bit deeper.

>Of course, Architect.<

Days blur and slide against one another; Da Trang's world shrinks to the screen hovering in front of him, the lines of code slowly

Pearl

turning into something else—from mere instructions and algorithms to semiautonomous tasks—and then transfigured, in that strange alchemy where a programmed drone becomes a remora, when coded behaviors and responses learnt by rote turn into something else: something wild and unpredictable, as pure and as incandescent as a newborn wind.

Movement, behind him—a blur of robes and faces, and a familiar voice calling his name, like red-hot irons against the nape of his neck: "Councillor Da Trang."

Da Trang turns—fighting the urge to look at the screen again, at its scrolling lines that whisper he'll fix it if he can write just a few more words, just a few more instructions. "Your Highness." Forces his body into a bow that takes him, sliding, to the floor, on muscles that feel like they've turned to jelly—words surface, from the morass of memory, every one of them tasting like some strange foreign delicacy on his tongue, like something the meaning of which has long since turned to meaningless ashes. "May you reign ten thousand years."

A hand, helping him up: for a moment, horrified, he thinks it's the Empress, but it's just one of the younger courtiers, her face shocked under its coat of ceruse. "He hasn't slept at all, has he? For days. Councillor—"

There's a crowd of them, come into the hangar where he works, on the outskirts of the capital: the Empress and six courtiers, and bodyguards, and attendants. One of the courtiers is staring all around him—seeing walls flecked with rust, maintenance bots that move only slowly: the dingy part of the city, the unused places—the spaces where he can work in peace. There is no furniture, just the screen, and the pile of remoras—the failed ones—stacked against one of the walls. There's room for more, plenty more.

The Empress raises a hand, and the courtier falls silent. "I'm concerned for you, councillor."

"I—" He ought to be awed, or afraid, or concerned, too—wondering what she will do, what she can do to him—but he doesn't even have words left. "I have to do this, Your Highness."

The Empress says nothing for a while. She's a small, unremarkable woman—looking at her, he sees the lines of deep worry etched under her eyes, and the shape of her skull beneath the taut skin of the face. Pearl, were it still here, were it still perching on his shoulder, would have told him—about heartbeats, about body temperature and the moods of the human mind, all he would have needed to read her, to convince her with a few well-placed words, a few devastating smiles. "Pearl is gone, councillor," she says, her voice firm, stating a fact or a decree. "Your remora was destroyed in the heart of the sun."

No, not destroyed. Merely hiding—like a frightened child, not knowing where to find refuge. All he has to do is find the right words, the right algorithms . . . "Your Highness," he says.

"I could stop it," the Empress said. "Have you bodily dragged from this room and melt every piece of metal here into scrap." Her hand makes a wide gesture, encompassing the quivering remoras stacked against the walls; the one he's working on, with bits and pieces of wires trailing from it, jerking from time to time, like a heart remembering it has to beat on.

No. "You can't," he starts, but he's not gone far enough to forget who she is. Empress of the Dai Viet Empire, mistress of all her gaze and her mindships survey, protector of the named planets, raised and shaped to rule since her birth. "You—" and then he falls silent.

The Empress watches him for a while but says nothing. Is that pity in her face? Surely not. One does not rise high in the Imperial Court on pity or compassion. "I won't," she says at last, and there is the same weariness in her voice, the same hint of mortality within. "You would just find another way to waste away, wouldn't you?"

Pearl

He's not wasting away. He's . . . working. Designing. On the verge of finding Pearl. He wants to tell her this, but she's no longer listening—if she ever was.

"Build your remoras, councillor." The Empress remains standing for a while, watching him. "Chase your dreams. After all—" And her face settles, for a while, into bleak amusement. "Not many of us can genuinely say we are ready to die for those."

And then she's gone; and he turns back to the screen, and lets it swallow him again, into endless days and endless nights lit only by the glare of the nearby star—the sun where Pearl vanished with only its cryptic good-bye.

He isn't building a single remora but a host of them, enough that they can go into the sun; enough to comb through layer after layer of molten matter, like crabs comb through sand—until they finally find Pearl.

None of them comes back, or sends anything back; but then, it doesn't matter. He can build more. He must build more—one after another and another, until there is no place in the sun they haven't touched.

The first Da Trang knew of the banquet was footsteps, at the door of the hangar—Mother, Pearl's trance said, analyzing the heavy tread, the vibrations of the breathing through the hangar's metal walls. Worried, too; and he didn't know why.

"Child," Mother said. She was followed by Cam, and their sister Hien, and a host of aunts and uncles and cousins. "Come with me." Even without Pearl, he could see her fear and worry, like a vise around his heart.

"Mother?" Da Trang rose, dismissing the poetry he'd been reading—with Pearl by his side, it was easier to see where it all hung together; to learn, slowly and painstakingly, to enjoy it as an official would; teasing apart layers of meaning one by one, as though eating a three-color dessert.

Mother's face was white, bloodless; and the blood had left her hands and toes, too. "The Empress wants to see the person who cooked the Three Blessings."

Three Blessings: eggs arranged around a hen for happiness and children; deer haunches with pine nuts for longevity; and carp with fishmint leaves cut in the shape of turtle leaves, for prosperity and success as an official. "You did," Da Trang said mildly. But inwardly, his heart was racing. This was . . . opportunity: the final leap over the falls that would send them flying as dragons, or tumbling down to earth as piecemeal, broken bodies.

"And you want me to come."

Mother made a small, stabbing gesture—one that couldn't disguise her worry. It was . . . unsettling to see her that way; hunched and vulnerable and mortally afraid. But Da Trang pushed the thought to the back of his mind. Now wasn't the time. "You were the one who told me what to cook." Her eyes rested on Pearl; moved away. She disapproved; but then she didn't understand what Pearl could do. "And . . ." She mouthed silent words, but Pearl heard them, all the same.

I need you.

Da Trang shook his head. He couldn't—but he had to. He couldn't afford to let this pass him by. Gently, slowly, he reached for Pearl—felt the remora shudder against his touch, the vibrations of the motors intensifying—if it were human, it would be arching against his touch, trying to move away—he didn't know why Pearl should do this now, when it was perfectly happy snuggling against him, but who could tell what went through a remora's thought processes?

"It's all right," he whispered, and pressed the struggling remora closer to him—just a little farther, enough for his mind to float, free of fear—free of everything except that strange exhilaration like a prelude of larger things to come.

———✿———

The banquet room was huge—the largest room in the central orbital—filled with officials in five-panel dresses, merchants in brocade dresses, and, here and there, a few saffron-dressed monks and nuns, oases of calm in the din. Pearl was labeling everyone and everything—the merchants' heart rate and body temperature; the quality of the silk they were wearing; the names of the vast array of dishes on the table and how long each would have taken to prepare. And, beyond the walls of the orbital—beyond the ghostly people and the mass of information that threatened to overwhelm him, there was the vast expanse of space, and remoras weaving back and forth between the asteroids and the Belt, between the sun and the Belt—dancing, as if on a rhythm only they could hear.

At the end of the banquet room was the Empress—Da Trang barely caught a glimpse of her, large and terrible, before he prostrated himself to the ground along with Mother.

"Rise," the Empress said. Her voice was low, and not unkind. "I'm told you're the one who cooked the Three Blessings."

"I did," Mother said. She grimaced, then added, "It was Da Trang who knew what to do."

The Empress's gaze turned to him; he fought the urge to abase himself again, for fear he would say something untoward. "Really," she said. "You're no scholar." If he hadn't been drunk on Pearl's trance, he would have been angry at her dismissal of him.

"No, but I hope to be." Mother's hands tightening; her shame at having such a forward son; such unsuitable ambitions displayed like a naked blade.

The Empress watched him for a while. Her face, whitened with ceruse, was impassive. Beyond her, beyond the courtiers and the fawning administrators, the remoras were slowing down, forming up in a ring that faced toward the same direction—neither the sun nor the Belt, but something he couldn't identify. Waiting, he thought, or Pearl thought, and he couldn't tell what for.

"Master Khong Tu, whose words all guide us, had nothing to say on ambition, if it was in the service of the state or of one's ancestors," the Empress said at last. She was . . . not angry. Amused, Pearl told him, tracking the minute quirking of the lips, the lines forming at the corner of her eyes. "You are very forward, but manners can be taught, in time." Her gaze stopped at his shoulder, watching Pearl. "What is that?"

"Pearl," Da Trang said slowly.

One of the courtiers moved closer to the Empress—sending her something via private network, no doubt. The Empress nodded. "The Belt has such delightful customs. A remora?"

To her, as to everyone in the room, remoras were low-level artificial intelligences, smaller fishes to the bulk and heft of the mindships who traveled between the stars—like trained animals, not worth more than a moment's consideration. "Yes, Your Highness," Da Trang said. On his shoulder, Pearl hesitated; for a moment he thought it was going to detach itself and flee; but then it huddled closer to him—the trance heightened again, and now he could barely see the Empress or the orbital, just the remoras, spreading in a circle. "Pearl helps me."

"Does it?" The Empress's voice was amused again. "What wisdom does it hold, child? Lines of code? Instructions on how to mine asteroids? That's not what you need to rise in the Imperial Court."

They were out there—waiting—not still, because remoras couldn't hold still, but moving so slowly they might as well be—silent, not talking or communicating with one another, gathered in that perfect circle, and Pearl was feeling their sense of anticipation too, like a coiled spring or a tiger waiting to leap; and it was within him, too, like a flower blossoming in a too-tight chest, pushing his ribs and heart outward, its maddened, confused beating resonating like gunshots in the room.

"Watch," he whispered. "Outside the Belt. It's coming."

Pearl

The Empress threw him an odd glance—amusement mingled with pity.

"Watch," he repeated, and something in his stance, in his voice, must have caught her, for she whispered something to her courtier and stood.

Outside, in the void of space, in the freezing cold between orbitals, the remoras waited—and, in the center of their circle, a star caught fire.

It happened suddenly—one moment a pinpoint of light, the next a blaze—and then the next a blaring of alarms aboard the station—the entire room seeming to lurch and change, all the bright lights turned off, the ambient sound drowned by the alarms and the screaming, the food tumbling from the tables, and people clinging to one another as the station lurched again—a merchant lost her footing in a spill of rice wine and fell, her brocade dress spread around her.

On Da Trang's shoulder, Pearl surged—as if it was going outside, as if it was going to join the other remoras watching the star ignite—but then it fell back against Da Trang; and he felt something slide into him: needles with another liquid, which burnt like fire along his spine. At the next lurch of the station, his feet remained steady, his body straight, as if standing at attention, and his muscles steadfastly refusing to answer him—even his vocal cords feeling frozen and stiff. >Don't move.<

Da Trang couldn't have moved, even if he'd wished to, even if he wasn't standing apart, observing it all at a remove, high on Pearl's trance and struggling to make sense of it all—no fear, no panic, merely a distant curiosity. A star-wildfire; light waves that were destabilizing the station, frying electronics that had never been meant for such intensity—Pearl's readouts assured him the shielding held, and that radiation levels within the room remained nonlethal for humans, poor but welcome reassurance in the wake of the disaster.

In front of him, the Empress hadn't moved either; with each lurch of the station, she merely sidestepped, keeping her balance as if it were nothing. Of course she would have augments that would go far beyond her subjects', the best her Grand Masters and alchemists could design.

Abruptly, the station stopped lurching, and the lights slowly came back on—though they were white and blinding, nothing like the quiet and refined atmosphere of the banquet; and instead of the ambient sound there was only the low crackle of static. The Empress gazed at him levelly, and then went on, as if their conversation had been merely stopped by someone else's rude interruptions, "In all of the Dai Viet Empire, there is no one who can predict a star wildfire. We can determine when the conditions for the ignition are met, of course, but the scale of such predictions is millennia, if not millions of years. And yet you knew."

Da Trang shook his head. Pearl had withdrawn; he could still see the remoras outside, now utterly still, though Pearl's readouts assured him they were not broken—merely oddly, unnaturally still. Merely . . . content. Who knew that remoras basked in wildfire? "Pearl knew," he said. "You asked how it helped me. That's how."

The Empress watched him for a while; watched Pearl nestled on his shoulder, the remora's prow wedged in the hollow where his collarbone met his neck. "I see. I think," she said, slowly, softly, "it would be best for you to take your things and come back with us, child."

And like that—just like that, with two simple sentences, and a polite piece of advice that might as well be a command—Da Trang started his rise at the Imperial Court.

Da Trang is watching his latest remora, a sleek, small thing with a bent thruster—even as he does, he sees it move, and the thruster *flows* back into place; and the remora dips its prow, a movement that might as well be a nod, and is gone through the open doorway, following the path of the previous ones—pulling itself upward

into the sky, straight toward the sun. Toward silence.

>Architect. We are here.< Da Trang's head jerks up. The words are blinking, in a corner of his field of vision, insistent, and the remora saying this is close by too. It's not one of the ones he made, but it's one he's seen before, a vision from his past when he was still repairing remoras and studying for the imperial examinations—before Pearl, before the Empress. Pitted metal and those broken thrusters at the back, and the wide gash on the right side that he's never managed to patch; the nub on the prow and the broken-off wing, clumsily repaired with only a basic welder bot. . . .

"Teacher," he whispers, addressing the remora by the name he gave it, all those years ago. "I'm sorry."

Remoras don't have feelings, don't have human emotions. They lie somewhere halfway between ships and bots, outside the careful order of numbered planets; cobbled together from scraps, looking as though they're going to burst apart at any moment.

Behind Teacher is Slicer, and Tumbler, and all the rest of the remoras: the ones who were with him at the very beginning, the ones who made and gave him Pearl.

Teacher's image wavers in and out of focus, and Da Trang fights the urge to turn away, to go back to his code, because he owes Teacher that much. Because Pearl was given to him for safekeeping, and he has lost it.

"I'm sorry," Da Trang says again, though he doesn't even know if Teacher can understand him.

>New things are more easily broken,< Teacher says. Something very like a shrug, and the remora weaving closer to him. >Don't concern yourself, Architect.<

"Are you—are you building another?" Da Trang knows the answer even before he asks.

>Like Pearl? No.< Teacher is silent for a while. >It was flawed, Architect. Too . . . much vested into a single vessel. We will ponder how to build otherwise.<

Da Trang cannot wait. Cannot stand to be there, with the emptiness on his shoulder, where Pearl used to rest; to gaze at the remoras and the hangar and have nothing about them, no information about their makeup or their speed; all the things Pearl so easily, effortlessly provided him. If he closes his eyes, he can feel again the cold shock of needles sliding into his neck, and the sharpening of the world before the trance kicked in, and everything seemed glazed in light.

Slicer weaves its way to the first pile of remoras in the corner of the hangar: the flawed ones, the ones that wouldn't lift off, that wouldn't come to life, or that started only to crash and burn. It circles them, once, twice, as if fascinated—it never judges, never says anything, but Da Trang can imagine, all too well, what it sees: hubris and failure, time and time again. He's no Grand Master of Design Harmony, no Master of Wind and Water: he can repair a few remoras, but his makings are few, and pitiful, and graceless, nothing like Pearl.

"I have to try," Da Trang whispers. "I have to get it back."

>It was flawed,< Teacher says. >Will not come back.<

They know too, more than the Empress does, that it will take more than a sun's warmth to destroy a remora. That Pearl is still there. That he can still reach it, talk to it—make it come back.

Teacher moves, joins Slicer around the pile of stillborn remoras. >Architect. Use of this?<

No scraps of metal left unused, of course—they scavenge their own dead, make use of anything and everything to build. Once, Da Trang would have found it disquieting; but now all he feels is weariness, and impatience that they're keeping him from his algorithms. "I don't need them anymore. They're . . . flawed. Take them."

>Architect. Thank you.< He'd have thought they didn't know gratitude, but perhaps they do. Perhaps they've learnt, being so close to humans. Or perhaps they're merely doing so to appease

him—and would it really make a difference if that was the case? So many things human are fake and inconstant—like favors. >We will return. Much to ponder.<

"Wait," Da Trang calls, as the remoras move away from his discarded scraps, from the blurred, indistinct remnants of his failures. "Tell me—"

>Architect?<

"I need to know. Was it my fault?" Did he ignore Pearl—was there some harbinger of the things to come—were the odd times the remora fell silent, with its prow pointed toward the sun, a sign of what it secretly yearned for?

Could he . . . could he have stopped it, had he known?

Silence. Then Teacher's answer, slow and hesitant. >We built. We made, from metal and electronics to the spark of life. We didn't *determine*, Architect. It went where it willed. We do not know.<

No answer then, but why had he thought it would be so easy?

On the morning of the day he was to be raised to councillor, Da Trang got up early, with an unexpected queasiness in his stomach—fear of what would happen, of Mother and her dire warnings about Empresses' fickle favorites being right?—no, that wasn't it.

Pearl was gone. He reached out, scratching the callus on his neck, in the place where it usually rested—scanning the room and finding nothing, not even a trace of its presence. "Pearl? Pearl?"

Nothing under the sheets, nothing in the nooks and crannies of the vast room—he turned off everything, every layer of the Purple Forbidden City's communal network, and still he couldn't see Pearl.

Impossible. It wasn't human; it didn't have any desires of its own except to serve Da Trang, to serve the whims of the Empress and her endless curiosity about anything from stellar phenomena to the messages passed between remoras and bots, to the state of the technologies that underpinned the communal network—to be

shown off to scientists and alchemists and engineers, its percep-
tions and insights dissected and analyzed for anything of use to
the Empire. It couldn't just go wandering off. It—

Da Trang threw open the doors of his room, startling one of
the servants who'd been carrying a tray with a cup of tea—almost
absentmindedly, he reached out and straightened the tray before
moving on. "Pearl? Pearl?"

Courtiers, startled out of their impassivity, turned their heads
to follow him as he ran into courtyard after courtyard, finding
nothing but the usual bustle of the court, the tight knots of people
discussing politics or poetry or both—an endless sea of officials
with jade-colored sashes barely paying attention to him—and still
no Pearl, no trace of it or word on his coms.

It was only two bi-hours until the ceremony; and what would
he say to the Empress, if Pearl wasn't there—if he couldn't perform
any of the feats of use to her, and that distinguished him from the
mass of upstart courtiers?

"Pearl?"

He found the remora, finally, in the quarters of the Master
of Rites and Ceremonies. The Master was deep in discussion with
her students, pointing to something on an interface Da Trang
couldn't see. Pearl was in the small room at the end, where they had
gathered the necessary supplies for the ceremony.

"Pearl?"

It stood, watching the clothes on the mannequin in the center
of the room: the five-panel robe made from the finest brocade
with the insignia of the sparrow on the chest—not an official rank
attained through merit and examinations, but one reserved for
special cases, for emperors' and empresses' fickle favors. On the
shoulder was a rest for Pearl, with a small model of the remora.

"What are you doing here?"

Pearl didn't move, or acknowledge him in any way. It was . . .
that same particular intent stillness it had had, back at the time

ALIETTE
DE BODARD

Pearl

of the first star wildfire. Waiting—what for? "Is something going to happen? Pearl?"

>Architect.< The words were hesitant—letter after letter slowly materializing in his field of vision. And still Pearl didn't move, didn't head to Da Trang's shoulder, to fill the empty space he couldn't get used to. >Need. Time.<

"What for? The ceremony is in two bi-hours—"

Pearl shifted; and he realized then that it had been standing in a shaft of sunlight, its prow turned toward the heavens. >Not meant for this.<

"You were built for this," Da Trang said. Why the strange mood—fear or nervousness? But remoras couldn't feel any of that, surely?

But, then, Pearl wasn't just any remora. *We can build better,* Teacher had said. Better, or merely more unstable? "Come," Da Trang said.

Pearl hovered to the shoulder of the mannequin—nudging the small model they'd made of it, which looked nothing like a remora: bedecked with silk and scraps of translucent cotton. >Not meant for this.< Its prow rose again, toward the sun. >Space. The song of stars. The heartbeat of the universe.<

"We'll be going into space," Da Trang said. "Often enough. I promise." It scared him now—the Imperial Court wasn't a place to hear the song of the stars or the rhythm of the universe or whatever else it was going on about. "Come."

>Not the same.< Pearl made a small whirring noise.

"They built you to help me," Da Trang said. And, without Pearl, he was nothing—just another dull-witted poor boy, the Empress's favor soon forgotten. "Pearl. Come on." He fought an urge to bodily drag it from the room, like a disobedient child, but it would have been unkind. "Remember Teacher and Slicer and the other remoras? They said they'd built you for me. For the examinations. For understanding."

Come on, come on, come on—if Pearl left him, he didn't know what he'd do, what he'd become, what he could make of the shambles that would be his life—

>Understanding.< Pearl's prow dipped again, toward the mannequin. >Building better.< Again, the same slowness to the words, as if it were considering; and then, to Da Trang's relief, it flew back to him, and the familiar weight settled on his shoulder— the familiar ice-cold feeling of needles biting into his shoulder, the sense of reality becoming unbearably sharp, unbearably clear, everything labeled and parceled and analyzed, from the Master of Rites and Ceremonies' minute frown to the student fighting off sleep in the first row—from the cut and origin of the silk to the fluctuating intensity of the sunlight in the room.

>Can help.< But as Da Trang turned away, he felt Pearl's weight on his shoulder—felt the remora looking upward at the sun— the pull of the motors, barely suppressed; and he knew that he hadn't managed to quell Pearl's yearnings.

He doesn't sleep—only so many hours in a day, and there are ways to enjoy them all. Not for long, of course, not with the drugs he's pumped himself full of; but what does he care for more time? He *needs* Pearl back, so badly it's like a vise, squeezing his ribs into bloodied shards. Without Pearl, he's nothing: an ex-favorite of the Empress, fallen from her regard—an overambitious boy from the outer edges of the Empire, overreaching and tumbling over the waterfalls instead of soaring, dragonlike, in the wake of imperial favor. But it's Pearl that the Empress was truly interested in—its tidbits on stellar phenomena, on technologies, on ships and what made them work—what Pearl called the understanding of the universe, with an earnestness that didn't seem to belong in a remora: everything that they put into always moving, never stopping, it put into intent stillness, in that posture on his shoulder where its eyes, if it'd had any, would have bored holes into steel or diamond.

Pearl

It's still there, in the heart of the sun. Waiting. For him, or for something else; but if Pearl is there, that means he can find it. That means . . . He doesn't know what he will do when he finds Pearl, how he'll beg or plead or drag it from the sun—but he'll find a way.

It was a routine journey, a shuttle ride between the First Planet and the White Clouds orbital; and the Empress, of course, insisted her new Councillor come with her, to show her the wonders of space.

Da Trang came, because he had no choice—in spite of deep unease—because Pearl had been restless and distant, because he'd tossed and turned at night, trying to think of what he could do and thinking of nothing.

Halfway through the trip, the Empress called for him.

She was in her cabin, surrounded by her courtiers— they were all sitting on silk cushions and sipping tea from a cup as cracked as eggshells. In front of her was a hologram of space as seen from the prow of the ship. As Da Trang entered, the view blurred and shifted, and became the outside of the orbital—except that the stars were dimmer than they ought to have been.

"Councillor," the Empress said. "I thought you would enjoy seeing these."

Pearl snuggled closer to Da Trang—needles extended, the blissful cold spreading outward from the pinpricks, the trance rising—extending to the outside, narrowing until he could see the bots maneuvering nano-thin filaments, unfolding a large, dark shape like a spread cloth behind the orbital.

Void-nets. Da Trang had sat in nightlong sessions with the Ministry of War's engineers, describing to them what Pearl saw— what Pearl thought—how the remora could even analyze the dust of stars, the infinitesimal amounts of matter carried by the wind in the void of space—and how, in turn, those could be trapped.

He hadn't thought—

"Your Highness," Da Trang said, struggling to remember how to bow. "I had no idea this was such a momentous occasion."

"The Ministry of War has been testing prototypes for a while—but it is the first time a void-net is deployed in the vicinity of a Numbered Planet, to be sure." The Empress was almost . . . thoughtful. "All to your credit, and Pearl's."

Another nudge, but he had no need to see heartbeats or temperature to catch the anger of the courtiers. As if they'd ever be capable of matching him . . .

"Tell us," the Empress said. "What will we find in your nets?"

A brief moment of panic, as nothing happened—as Pearl didn't move, the thought that it was going to be today, of all days, when the remora failed him—and then a stab so deep under his collarbone it was almost painful—and the view shifting, becoming dotted with hundreds of pinpoints of colored lights, each labeled with a name and concentration. "Suffocating metal 5.3 percent," he whispered. "Frozen water 3 percent. Gray adamantine crystals 9.18 percent . . ." On and on, a litany of elements, labeled and weighed: everything the Empire would decant to fuel its machines and stations and planets, names and images and every use they could be put to, a flood of information that carried him along—such a terrible, breathless sense of being the center, of knowing everything that would come to pass . . .

He came to with a start, finding Pearl all but inert against him, softly vibrating on his shoulder. The Empress was looking at him and smiling—her face and body relaxed, her heartbeat slow and steady. "A good take. The Ministry of War should be satisfied, I should think." She watched the screens with mild curiosity. "Tell me what you see."

"Colors," Da Trang said. Even with Pearl quiescent, he could make them out—slowly accreting, the net bulging slightly outward as it filled—the bots straining under the pressure. "A dance of lights—"

Pearl

He never got to finish the sentence.

On his shoulder, Pearl surged—gone before Da Trang's flailing arms could stop it, tearing through the cabin—and then, with scarcely a pause, through the walls of the ship as if they were nothing more than paper; alarms blaring, the Empress and him thrown to the ground as the cabin sealed itself—but Pearl was already gone. Fumbling, Da Trang managed to call up a view from ships around the orbital—a slow zoom on Pearl, weaving and racing toward the stars, erratic and drunken, stopping for a bare moment, and then plunging toward the heart of the sun.

>Architect. Farewell. Must be *better*. Must show them.<

And then there was nothing—just emptiness on his shoulder like a hole in his own heart, and the memory of those words—and he could not tell if they were angry or sad or simply a statement of fact.

Nothing.

Days blur and slide against one another; his world shrinks to the screen hovering in front of him, the lines of code slowly turning into something else. He can barely read them now; he's merely inputting things from rote—his hands freeze, at odd intervals; and his vision goes entirely black, with whole chunks of time disappearing—everything oddly disjointed.

Except for his remoras.

They're sleek and beautiful and heartbreaking now, moving with the grace of officials and fighter-monks—one by one, pulling themselves from the floor, like dancers getting up and stretching limb after limb—still for a heartbeat, their prows turned toward him, and then gone toward the sun, a blur of speed he cannot follow anymore—as darkness grows and encroaches on his field of vision.

He must build more.

Remoras come and go: Teacher, Slicer, and all the others, taking from the pile of scraps, making small noises as they see a piece of metal or a connector; slowly, determinedly taking apart his earlier efforts—the tearing sound of sheets of metal stretched past the breaking point; the snapping of cables wrenched out of their sockets; the crackling sound of ion thrusters taken apart— his failures, transfigured into life—patched onto other remoras, other makings; going on and on and on, past Da Trang's pitiful, bounded existence—going on, among the stars.

"Tell me," he says, aloud.

>Architect. What should I tell you?< One of them—Slicer, Teacher, he's not sure he can tell them apart anymore; save for his own remoras, everything seems small and blurred, diminished into insignificance. Everything seems dimmer and smaller, and even his own ambitions feel shriveled, far away, belonging to someone else, a stranger with whom he shares only memories.

"Pearl wanted to be better than you. It said so, before it left. Tell me what it means."

Silence, for a while. Then letters, steadily marching through his darkening field of vision. >Everything strives. It couldn't be better than us, Architect. It is—<

"Flawed. I know."

>Then you understand.<

"No, I don't. That's not what I want. I want to—I need to—" He stops then, thinks of remoras, of scarce resources that have to be endlessly recycled, of that hunger to rebuild themselves, to build others, that yearning that led to Pearl's making.

And he sees it then. "It doesn't matter. Thank you, Slicer." He stifles a bitter laugh. Everything strives.

>I am Teacher.<

Its words are almost gentle, but Da Trang no longer cares. He stares ahead, at the screen, at the blurred words upon it, the life's blood he fed into his remoras, making them slowly, pain-stakingly, and sending them one by one into the heart of the sun. He thinks of the remoras' hopes for the future, and of things that

Pearl

parents pass on to their children, and makers to their creations. He knows now that Pearl, in the end, is like Teacher, like Slicer, no better or no different, moved by the same urges and hungers. He thinks of the fires of the sun, the greatest forge in the system; and of Pearl, struggling to understand how things worked, from the smallest components of matter to mindships and humans—he'd thought it was curiosity, but now he sees what drove it. What still drives it.

If you know how things work, you can make them.

Darkness, ahead and behind him, slowly descending upon the screen—the remoras dancing before him, scavenging their own to survive, to make others.

Yearnings. Hunger. The urge to build its own makings, just as it was once built.

Must be better.

Must build better.

And as he slides into shadows—as his nerveless fingers leave the keyboard, his body folding itself, hunched over as if felled by sleep—he thinks of the other remoras, taking their own apart—thinks of the ones he made, the ones he sent into the heart of the sun; and he sees, with agonizing clarity, what he gave Pearl.

Not tools to drag it back or to contact it, but offerings—metal and silicon chips and code, things to be taken apart and grafted, to be scavenged for anything salvageable—the base from which a remora can be forged.

As his eyes close—just for a moment, just for a heartbeat, he sees Pearl—not the remora he remembers, the sleek making of Teacher and Slicer, but something else—something *changed*, reshaped by the heat of the sun, thickened by accreted metal scooped from the heart of a star, something slick and raw and incandescent, looming over him like a heavenly messenger, the weight of its presence distorting the air.

Darkness, ahead and behind him—rising to fill the entire world;

and everything he was, his lines of code, his remoras, scattering and fragmenting—into the fires of the sun, to become Pearl's own makings, reforged and reborn, and with no care for human toil or dreams or their petty ambitions.

There is no bringing Pearl back. There is no need to.

And as his eyes close for the last time, he smiles, bitterly—because it is not what he longed for, but it is only fair.

>Farewell, Architect.<

And Pearl's voice, booming, becomes his entire world, his beginning and his ending—and the last thing he hears before he is borne away, into the void between the stars.

AUTHOR'S NOTE

Pearl

Aliette de Bodard: I don't remember where I first heard the tale of Dã Tràng and the Pearl, but it's been rattling around my head for a while. I was always struck by its final few lines: after the loss of the pearl, Dã Tràng exhausts himself looking for it, dies, and is reincarnated as a small sand-digger crab (which bears his name in Vietnamese). I've always had a weakness for metamorphosis tales, and this was a particularly dramatic one! I wanted to retell it as a space opera, because it's what I usually do: a lot of my science fiction has roots both in fairy tales and in science. It seemed pretty natural to me that the equivalent of animals in a fairy tale would be low-level AIs: the remoras, who have formed a parallel society on the edge of the human one; and that Pearl would be not a thing but a living being—a special remora made by a class of beings who kept remaking and modifying themselves as necessity dictated (there's more than a hint of the golem in Terry Pratchett's *Feet of Clay* in Pearl). Once I had that nailed into place, the story pretty much wrote itself. (Okay, no. There was blood, sweat, and tears, but that's business as usual!)

-THE TALE OF-
MAHLIYA AND MAUHUB AND THE WHITE-FOOTED GAZELLE

Sofia Samatar

his story is at least a thousand years old. Its complete title is "The Tale of Mahliya and Mauhub and the White-Footed Gazelle: It Contains Strange and Marvelous Things." A single copy, probably produced in Egypt or Syria, survives in Istanbul; the first English translation appeared in 2015. This is not the right way to start a fairy tale, but it's better than sitting here in silence waiting for Mahliya, who takes forever to get ready. She's upstairs staining her cheeks with antimony, her lips with a lipstick called Black Sauce. Vainest crone in Cairo.

She leaves her window open for the birds to fly in and out. If you listen closely, you'll hear the bigger ones thump their wings against the sash. The most famous, of course, is the flying feather-less ostrich. A monstrous creature, like something boiled. Mahliya adores it. She lets it eat out of her mouth.

——✿——

While we're waiting, why don't I tell you the Tale of the White-Footed Gazelle? I'm only a retainer, but I do know all the stories, for that's the definition of a servant, especially one in my position, the head servant, and indeed, in these lean times, the only one. Once I presided over a staff of hundreds; now instead of directing many people, I direct many things: I purchase shoes and bedding, I keep up with all the fashions, with advances in medicine, tax laws, satellite TV. If your purpose, as you say, is to produce a monograph on the newly translated *Tales of the Marvelous and News of the Strange*, including versions of the stories as told by people who experienced them, why not begin with me? I am perfectly familiar with the Tale of the White-Footed Gazelle, which lies enclosed in the Tale of Mahliya and Mauhub. You will be familiar with this narrative structure from *A Thousand and One Nights*, a collection of tales whose fate has been very different from that of Mahliya's story. One might ask: Why? Why should *A Thousand and One Nights* rise to such prominence, performed on stages in Japan and animated by Disney, while the very similar collection containing the Tale of Mahliya and Mauhub has moldered in a library for centuries? Well! No doubt all that is about to change. Just close the window for me, if you would; my bald head feels every draft. When I was a younger man—but that's not the story you came to hear! Listen, then, and I shall spin you a marvelous tale.

The Tale Of The White-Footed Gazelle

———◈———

I have condensed it for you because you are a researcher. In this story you will find:

1. Haifa', daughter of a Persian king, also a gazelle
2. The White-Footed Gazelle, also a prince of the jinn
3. Ostrich King

4. Snake King
5. Crow Queen
6. Lion

A love story. Haifa' and the White-Footed Gazelle fall in love, then separate, then move toward each other again, then apart, as if in a cosmic dance. We learn that the Ostrich King unites hearts while the Crow Queen divides lovers. These movements of attraction and repulsion also characterize the Tale of Mahliya and Mauhub.

An animal story. A prince of the jinn takes the form of a white-footed gazelle to follow Haifa' into her secluded garden. When he abandons her due to a misunderstanding (he thinks she's divulged his true nature), she tracks him through a country of marvelous beasts. In a wild green valley, ostriches graze in the shadow of the Obsidian Mountain, which marks the border of the land of the jinn. The Ostrich King herds his flock with a palm branch, flicking their tails with the spikes. That night, as Haifa' takes shelter with him, the Snake King passes with his retinue. A noisy party, jostling and laughing, quaffing great goblets of smoke. They ride upon snakes and wear snakes coiled round their heads like turbans. "Have you seen the White-Footed Gazelle?" Haifa' asks. "No," says the Snake King, flames flashing up in his mouth. "Ask the Queen of the Crows."

To reach the Crow Queen, Haifa' flies on a smooth-skinned, featherless ostrich, which covers a two-year journey in a single night. The Crow Queen is a scowling old woman with ten jeweled bracelets on each arm, ten anklets on each leg, and ten rings on each finger. She wears a golden crown studded with gems, carries an emerald scepter, spits on the floor, and has never shown pity to anyone. Fortunately, Haifa' bears a letter from the Ostrich King, and the Crow Queen owes him a debt. She reunites Haifa' with her beloved.

The story doesn't end there. Haifa' pines for her own country, and her new husband agrees to a visit as long as they both go as gazelles. Unfortunately, they are captured: Haifa' the Gazelle by Mauhub, and the White-Footed Gazelle by Mahliya. When we meet Haifa', she's just been turned back into a woman by a priest of Baal. Weeping, she tells Mauhub her story. Mauhub is astounded, but not as much as you might think. He's an animal intimate himself: as a child, he was suckled by a lion.

A few more interesting points about this story:

1. Feet

The White-Footed Gazelle is named for his feet and also seems to have a foot fetish. When he first transforms himself into a man in front of Haifa', he declares his love and immediately kisses her feet. In between kisses he speaks to her in a pure and elegant language, more delicious than honey and softer than clarified butter. "He said I was like a shoot of sweet basil. He kissed my feet and sucked them and by God I felt my heart fly into my throat."

2. Shivering

The gazelle shivers and turns into a woman. She tells the story of the White-Footed Gazelle, which shivered and turned into a man. A weird sort of shudder seems to precede transformation. The strangest thing, though, is the seizure suffered by our heroine's father. This happens early in the story, when Haifa' is living with her lover in an exquisite idyll: he's her pet gazelle by day, her lover in a locked room at night. Then one night Haifa' wakes to a cry of alarm: "The king! The king!" Terrified for her father, she rushes out half-dressed, leaving the door open. The White-Footed Gazelle doesn't wake up—perhaps he's a heavy sleeper, or perhaps, being a jinni, he's deaf to human sorrow. Whatever the reason, he only wakes at dawn. Finding himself alone, the door open, he thinks Haifa' has betrayed him and exposed their secret.

Out the window he goes on mist-white feet. Haifa' will come back soon, having left her father sleeping peacefully. She'll cry out over the empty bed. She'll dash out into the garden, slapping her face in her grief. She will begin her quest.

How strange that the source of the error that parts these lovers should be a seizure. An excess of trembling.

To shiver is to move rapidly from one place to another and back. From prince of the jinn to white-footed gazelle, from beloved to enemy. I think of this whole story as a long shudder.

3. *Lion*

I did say there was a lion, didn't I! Haifa' the Gazelle meets him shortly before she's captured by Mauhub. The lion has scraped out a hole in the ground, and he's squatting in it and crying. "Dark-eyed gazelle, fair as the moon, I, the red lion, have suffered a great sorrow. . . ." The story sort of drops him there. Later, of course, he'll turn out to be the long-lost mate of the lioness who suckled Mauhub. This fact won't redeem the lion, who remains throughout the story the same dirty, sniveling creature we meet in this scene. Forget about him. He's an asshole.

I think I hear Mahliya's feet on the stairs. It's either that or the shuffling and crowding of the birds on the perches in her bedroom. Mahliya's feet are so light they sound like wings. You'll notice, in a few moments, how graceful and regal she is, an incredible thing at her age. Even I, who have attended her for more years than I care to remember, and have therefore had many occasions to be annoyed with her tricks, admit this. Her queenly poise never shatters. During the revolution, while others cowered indoors, she watched the crowds from her balcony, smoking a water pipe.

Really, it's too bad that a foreign researcher like yourself, the first to visit her, should be kept waiting so long! If you like, I can tell you a version of her story myself. Just keep in mind that Mahliya will tell it differently.

The Tale of Mahliya and Mauhub

or

The Portrait

———✧———

My story begins with a portrait. The Egyptian princess Mahliya
fell in love with a portrait of Mauhub that was painted on the wall of
a church in Jerusalem, as was customary for princes of Mauhub's
line. The painting was fresh, the oil still gleaming; it was adorned
with red gold, and its eyes were a pair of topazes. Beside it glimmered a picture of a lioness suckling the infant Mauhub. A crystal
candle filled with jasmine oil illuminated both paintings. Mahliya
was enchanted. She embarked at once on a love affair conducted
entirely under the sign of the portrait.

Portrait One: Mahliya as a Young Man

When Mahliya first met Mauhub, she was disguised as a young
man. She introduced herself as Mukhadi', Mahliya's vizier. We must
suppose she did this in order to increase Mauhub's interest in the
real Mahliya, who was sending him gifts and letters at the same
time. A frantic existence: by day, hunting trips and conversation
with her beloved, seizing each chance to give him a brotherly punch
in the arm; by night, tender yet formal letters, the preparation of
splendid packages, sighs, poetry, fainting spells, and tears. You will
have noticed the shudder in this story, the same trembling motion
that shapes the Tale of the White-Footed Gazelle. Back and forth,
back and forth. Incidentally, it's a wonder Mauhub didn't suspect
Mahliya's pretty young vizier. Mukhadi' means Impostor.

Portrait Two: Mahliya as Mirror

On their last hunting trip together, Mauhub caught Haifa' in
her gazelle form and Mahliya caught the White-Footed Gazelle.
It was Haifa', restored to human shape, who informed Mauhub
that his hunting companion was also the mysterious princess who

kept sending him gifts and letters. Mauhub rushed to Mahliya's tent. They spent one glorious night together before their fathers recalled them to their respective kingdoms. The lovers continued to communicate through gifts, the most magnificent of which was certainly Mahliya's mirror.

This mirror was enchanted so that when Mauhub looked into it, he saw Mahliya sitting beside him. "Nothing was missing," the story tells us, "except the lady herself." Such an odd phrase; if she was missing, surely nothing else mattered.

I see Mauhub contorting himself, one eye on the mirror, embracing a lady who only appears to be there.

When Mahliya heard of the beauty of Haifa', who was staying with Mauhub, she got so furiously jealous she sent an eagle to snatch the mirror away.

Portrait Three: Mahliya as Anchorite

For the crime of arousing Mahliya's suspicions, Mauhub had to be punished. Mahliya tortured his messengers, crushed his armies, beguiled him across the sea with a magic bird. At last, worn thin from travel and near starvation, ugly with suffering, he stumbled to a hermitage on swollen feet. An anchorite peered down from the window, radiant in black wool. She made Mauhub swear to serve her, forced him to write the promise on his arm. All this so that when he reached the city, Queen Mahliya, in her true form at last, could yank up his sleeve and expose his inconstancy.

A love story. She forgave him.

An animal story, teeming with life. Mahliya's army of buffaloes tramples Mauhub's army of lions. Her army of wildcats destroys his army of elephants. She builds him a fortress in the land of the jinn, a place swarming with snakes and lizards. Above each door of this fortress, a brass falcon whistles in the wind. When the lovers have passed many years in delight, a sorceress transforms Mauhub into a crocodile. Mahliya recognizes him by his pearl earrings. She knows him, although he never recognized her: neither as Mukhadi' the vizier nor as the beautiful anchorite. He didn't know. He didn't know me. Of course it was me, what's the matter with you? Why are people so stupid? You're like Mauhub: rather than the real person in an unexpected shape, you prefer the magic mirror, which gives you the image you wish to see, although it leaves you grasping nothing but air.

THE WONDER CURSE

Now that we're being honest, let me ask you something. (A photograph? All right. Here, I'll blow some smoke. That's an old movie star trick. It'll make my mouth a delectable little beak, smooth my wrinkles, and impart an air of nostalgia.) My question is this: Why are you people so hungry for marvels? I mean here you are, braving a twelve-hour journey from JFK, one of the world's worst airports, plus a taxi ride through the afternoon traffic, only to sit in an elderly woman's apartment and listen to a story. Really, I felt I had to trick you to make it worth your while! (Hand me my wig, will you? It's under your chair. You'll want another photograph now, I suppose!) Of course there's a venerable tradition of marvel tales here, a tradition that harbors my own story. But lately it seems to me that there is such a thing as a *wonder curse*, like the literary version of a resource curse. As if, having once tasted the magic of the East, visitors become determined to extract it at any cost.

The link between marvels and money is quite clear. Fabulous tales, astronomical wealth: both are forms of fortune. Perhaps the story is a kind of treasure map. But there is more than one map of the world, my friend. Consider what this tale contains and what it does not.

This Tale Contains:
Yellow silk, red leather, white marble, red onyx, gilded copper, ambergris, topaz, emerald, amber, musk, ebony, gold, carnelian,

camphor, Indian aloes, Bactrian camels, pearls, rubies, Chinese steel, silver, sandalwood, slaves.

This Tale Does Not Contain:
Airports, cigarettes, Internet cafés, Chipsy potato chips in tiny packets, pineapple-flavored Fayrouz soft drinks, soap operas based on the works of Naguib Mahfouz, traffic jams, copy shops, subway trains shrieking down long black tunnels, subway trains so crowded you can't get in, schoolgirls fanning themselves with exercise books, schools, radios, the knife grinder's cry, wedding parties on barges, street murals of Umm Kulthum with her iconic glasses and handkerchief, the light through the windows of Mari Mina Church at precisely five forty-five p.m., broken china, makeshift tents, outdoor barbers, street musicians, street protests, cell phones, pictures of bruises taken with cell phones, barricades, security police, rooms where the lights are never turned on, tear gas, pamphlets, bullets, peaceful activists shot down on the street, a poet shot down on the street, the poet who wrote of the streets, who trembled, bleeding, her body transformed into something else, but what? There is no gazelle.

The Lion's Tale

There is, however, a lion. There's always a lion. This is his story:

The lion weeping in the dust was reunited with his mate, Mauhub's wet nurse. He promised to be faithful to her, as Mauhub had promised Mahliya. But just as Mauhub betrayed Mahliya by swearing to serve the lovely anchorite, even going so far as to write her name on his arm, the lion betrayed the lioness. Tempted by some delicious roasted game, he agreed that if the old woman cooking it would give him a taste, he would marry her daughter.

For the sin of inconstancy he was turned over to devils in

human shape, who docked his tail and cauterized the stump with fire. His nose and ears were cut off, his whiskers shaved, his body smeared with dung, his neck encircled by an iron ring. Fairy tales are inexorable, their ferocity divine. When the lion returned to his mate, he was so hideously deformed she wouldn't have him. His howls of anguish curl about the story, creating a beautiful border, a frame for Mauhub and Mahliya's wedding portrait.

Yes, it was Mahliya—that is, it was I—who sent the old woman to tempt the lion. You may suppose I did so in order to spare my beloved, to transfer his crime onto another body through which I could then enjoy, without suffering myself, all the pleasures of vengeance. Think what you like. Somebody has to pay. There's always an animal, a wonderfully absorbent material, capable of sopping up an ocean of cruelty. Go visit the Alexandria Zoo sometime—you'll see lions panting in a concrete hole, surrounded by mounds of trash.

The Crow Queen's Tale

———✦———

Things don't always work out in life. Somebody has to pay. This is my song.

Oh, come. You must have known I was also the Crow Queen. Didn't you read the story? Look how Mahliya holds back from Mauhub, hides from him, tricks him, fights him. She is the Queen of the Crows, who separates lovers.

In the end, it's true, I stayed with him. He died quietly in my arms. He had grown so small by the end, so shriveled, I could carry him like a child. The day before he died I flew with him over the tombs of Giza. He was half-blinded by cataracts, but he loved the air.

Sometimes I still can't believe I cast my lot with human beings. It's humiliating. Of Mahliya the story says: "Iblis captured her heart." It's true, I was captured and I was defeated. I can save a man who has been turned into a crocodile, but not a man who is growing old.

"Are you near or far, living or dead?" sings Mahliya in the story. "Oh that I were a cross hung around his neck, that I might taste his scent." She sings that she wants to cover his mouth with hers, trace the gaps between his teeth with her tongue. "Oh that I were a sacrifice, mingled with his spit." A love story, an animal story. All these animals in love. I understand the White-Footed Gazelle's desire for his beloved's feet. There is a place where we are all animal, even you. We flicker in and out of it. We can be terribly hurt there, but also comforted.

The Queen of the Crows falls from her window at dusk. She catches the air. An old woman, languid. She glides down Ramses Street toward Masarra. She doubles back toward the river. Masr al-'Adima. Everything's pink. In the gardens of Maadi they are hosing down the paths.

I am the spirit of ruined utopias and unrequited love. It's not my fault. You didn't recognize me—do you think I recognize myself? No! That face in the mirror: that's not me. I see myself only in motion, smoking, gripping my windowsill in the instant before flight. I only recognize the wings that flap. God, I loved Mauhub so much. He was a descendant of Nebuchadnezzar, you know—the king who lost his mind and ate grass like an ox, whose hair grew long like an eagle's feathers and his nails like an eagle's claws.

It's growing late. The Crow Queen always feels restless at this hour. She longs for flight. Tonight, however, she has a guest, a foreign researcher. The Crow Queen squawks like an impresario, preens before the camera. The photographs will show a bald old lady with snapping kohl-rimmed eyes.

I have cast my lot with human beings, even knowing what I know: that things don't always work out, that somebody has to pay.

I'll rise or fall with them. Dear beasts! Instead of scribbling down notes, why don't you let me fly you over the square tonight? You can ride the featherless ostrich if you prefer, though I warn you he's very slow these days, his belly scarred by rubber bullets. We'll weave through the ghostly lights around the Mugamma al-Tahrir and watch the city flicker like a broken bulb. In that stuttering glow the square is like a dirty yellow mirror, a magic mirror reflecting even the ones who are missing. Yes, even the lions. I call it my palace, for these beasts are my true subjects. Look at me: I can't stop shaking.

AUTHOR'S NOTE

SOFIA
SAMATAR

Sofia Samatar: I wanted to retell this story, first, because I love it: the role of animals fascinates me, as does the dynamic heroine Mahliya, who's almost an anti-heroine, a beloved witch. I also wanted to interact with the story as an event, as part of the medieval text *Tales of the Marvelous and News of the Strange*, which was released in English in 2015, translated by Malcolm C. Lyons. This book comes into a world that has been primed to receive it by more than three centuries of love for *A Thousand and One Nights*, which is probably the most influential collection of stories in the world. I wanted to look at that—the western passion for tales of a marvelous, medieval east. I wanted to set the wonder tale against scenes of contemporary Egypt, against stories we're less interested in reading. In doing this, I paid tribute to the poet and activist Shaimaa' al-Sabbagh, "the poet who wrote of the streets," as I call her in the story, who was shot and killed during a peaceful demonstration in Cairo on January 24, 2015.

REFLECTED

Kat Howard

hen I was a kid, I played with mirrors. I was convinced that if I was fast enough, stealthy enough, *something* enough, I could make it so the reflection was different from the reality on my side of the mirror. That I could trick the mirror into showing something that wasn't truth.

My fascination with mirrors continued as I grew up. I studied the way they were made, and the way reflections happened. The way the shape of the mirror could alter what was seen in it. The more I learned about them, the more I wondered if my early childhood games didn't hold some seeds of truth.

Which is how I wound up doing my graduate work on mirrors and the physics of reflections. Which is how I wound up in the lab when, well. Easier if I just tell you.

The experiment that changed everything started off as goofing around, the three of us playing "what if" with the kinds of ideas you get when you're a kid: What if there really is an opposite world behind a mirror? What if you can walk into its reflection, breaking the surface as easy as diving into a still pool? What if you can walk into one mirror and out of another?

What if becomes something more when you have lab space and a research grant, when you've spent grad school studying quantum entanglement and positing the existence of pocket universes.

So then it wasn't just goofing around, late-night discussions over one too many beers, spinning theories like telling stories; it was Lara and Zack and me in the lab, trying to see if there was anything on the other side of the mirrors and how we could get to it, to figure out how to reflect whatever might be there back to us.

I couldn't imagine Lara doing any other sort of work. She seemed almost as if she was made from mirrors. Glass-pale and sharp-angled, she was the kind of person it could be stressful to be friends with: her reflection of you was uncompromising, and always less flattering than you wanted it to be.

I stuck around anyway. There's something compelling about the discomfort of that sort of reflection, like the relief of picking a scab and seeing the healed skin underneath. Plus, she was a brilliant scientist, utterly driven. It was like she could see the constituent parts of the universe in the same uncompromising and sharp-angled way that she saw people.

Zack and I had been friends for what felt like forever, but was actually since our freshman year of high school. He was the person who knew me best, the person I could share anchovy pizza with at three in the morning, the person who also wanted to know how the small pieces of the universe fit together. The person I went to for everything, because I knew he'd help me see things clearly.

The mirrors weren't the hook for him. Zack wanted to know if there were other universes behind their reflective surfaces. If there were, he wanted to go to them. I didn't. I wanted to know if they existed, of course—I had a theory that you could modify the mirror equation to measure their location the same way we measured objects' reflected distances now—but I liked it here. There is comfort in known qualities.

Which was why it was going to be Zack standing inside the mirrors that day, and I would be on the outside of them, recording observations and making adjustments as Lara tried to capture his reflection. And yes, I mean capture, not just see. That was part of the idea: that if we could separate a reflection from the reflected object, it could more easily travel between the mirror universe and our own than a physical object could. We were hoping that if it worked, the connection between Zack and his reflection meant that he'd be able to provide us with specific observations of what that mirror universe was like.

"Are you worried about what might happen to your reflection?" I asked, ducking under his arm to turn on the lights as he held open the lab door.

"What, like it'll get caught in the mirror and never come back?"

"Or maybe that it likes it there so much, it decides to stay."

"Wouldn't happen," he said.

"You've been talking about how cool a mirror world would be since we started this. What do you mean, it wouldn't happen?"

"Well, my reflection might want to stay, but you would reach through the mirror and pull its ass out." He grinned, and we got to work.

Lara had been setting up the mirrors in increasing numbers. First, there had been two full-length mirrors, framed in wood that looked almost red, Zack between them. Then she put him at the center of an equilateral triangle.

"No good. I'm still catching bits of secondary reflections," I said. We were after a clear image, not a reflection of Zack, plus a spare reflection of one of his arms.

"Are you sure you don't need me to actually do anything?" Zack asked.

"Just stand there and look pretty," Lara said.

Zack struck an exaggerated runway model's pose.

I laughed and helped her turn the triangle into a square, the muscles in my back and shoulders grumbling as we rearranged the heavy mirrors.

"Remind me again what you're going to do with his reflection if you catch it," I said.

"I have some thoughts."

"She'll clone me and all my fabulousness."

"Wrong field, Zack," I said.

"Details, details."

But four mirrors wasn't the right number either, and neither was five.

Six, however.

Lara and I were moving opposite mirrors. Had we stopped and stood in front of them, I would have been reflected in hers, and she in mine. Then we set them, six-sided as a snowflake.

"I can see—" Zack began, his whole body taut, electric.

A great shattering. Particles of mirrored glass falling through the air like snow. When they settled to the ground, the space at the center of the mirrors was empty.

Zack was gone.

All the way gone. Disappeared.

I flung my arms up and shouted, my stomach knotted into surprise and delight. We had done it. We had really done it. Forget capturing his reflection, we had skipped that step completely, done what we'd only barely hoped might someday be possible, and sent Zack somewhere else, another world maybe, through the mirrors.

The mirrors.

They were destroyed. Shattered. Not one piece of glass left in a frame. Which meant that whatever there was to connect Zack to here, to us, was gone.

The knots of my emotions twisted from delight to concern. I stepped toward the broken mirrors.

Lara shouted from the other side of the room, startling me into stillness. "It probably can't happen again without the reflections, but." She pulled one of the mirrors to the side, breaking up the snowflake symmetry.

"Still," she said, face flushed, eyes shining, her excitement a heightened reflection of mine. "Look at what we did!"

"It is kind of amazing," I said. "Kind of completely amazing. But we need to bring him back."

"Right," Lara said. "It's no good to us if all we can do is make someone disappear. A stage magician can do that. So we need to figure out what happened here, exactly. That should give us some idea of where he is, and what to do next."

So we spent the day taking measurements, recording every factor of everything we could think of that might possibly be useful, and then, when we were as certain as we could be that we had the data we needed, gathering up the enormous piles of glass that sat at the foot of each mirror.

"Are you seeing the same thing I am?" I asked.

"All the pieces are broken in the exact same shape," Lara said. "A hexagon, just like the mirrors were."

"Any idea what it means?"

"Not yet. I want to run some basic tests." After those tests were run, we put the pieces in marked, labeled boxes.

"Are you okay?" Lara asked.

"Sure, why?"

"You keep staring at the center of the room."

Where Zack had been standing when he disappeared. "I guess I keep hoping that whatever we did will spontaneously reverse. That he'll just be . . . back."

"I don't think it's going to be that easy."

She was right, of course.

I dreamt about Zack that night. It made sense that I did—there were certainly reasons for him to be on my mind. But the whole thing was deeply unsettling. Memories appeared in still images like photos, then froze over and shattered: painting our faces blue and white for Spirit Day our freshman year of high school, making popcorn in a pressure cooker for our first-year physics lab in college, splitting a bottle of champagne the day we found out we'd both gotten into grad school here.

When the pieces fell, they fell like snow, one after another after another after another, gone, until I stood in a blizzard made from the pieces of our past. And while I could see his footprints, tracks clearly visible in the fallen heap of memories, I couldn't follow them, couldn't find him.

I woke up shivering.

I didn't get any warmer when I got to the lab the next day.

There was snow falling steadily in the center of the room where the mirrors had been, over the precise spot where Zack had disappeared. I held my hand underneath, to check and make sure it really was snow, not just falling pieces of mirrors. Flakes landed, chilled my skin, then melted away into small drops of water. I scrubbed my hand against my jeans.

"Lara," I called, coat still on. "You probably want to come here and see this."

I heard her footsteps stop when she saw it. "That's unexpected. Hang on. I want to record this."

Outside the lab, it was early fall. The day was predicted to be sunny and in the upper sixties. We hadn't even had a frost warning yet.

Inside the lab, there weren't any clouds or anything that might have given a clue as to where the snow was coming from. It was just there, starting about a foot above my head and falling to the ground. I hugged my arms around my stomach, chilled.

"Frozen in reflection," Lara said as she checked gauges, took samples.

"Reflection," I repeated, the word setting off a train of images in my mind. "Do you think the snow is coming from wherever Zack is?"

"I think that's the most likely possibility. We did ask him to send back any impressions. You know how he is. No matter how weird things were, he'd try to stick as close as possible to the plan of the experiment."

"And so he's sending us snow."

"Either that, or sending him through weakened the barrier between the mirror universe and ours to the point where we're experiencing their weather events. Either way, it's interesting," she said.

I stood in the falling snow, perfect six-sided flakes reflecting the light, and pushed the memory of my dream away. That hadn't been real, and dwelling on it wouldn't help. "It is interesting, but watching it isn't bringing Zack back."

"I thought we agreed the best way to do that is to figure out where he went—I'm running your modified mirror equations now—and determining the source of the snow could help do that. There may be trace elements in it that will offer some data."

"I'm not so sure that's the best way to find him anymore. I think I need to concentrate on him, not his location."

She shook her head, dismissing the idea. "You can't bring him back if you don't know where he is."

"I think I can," I said.

Lara looked at me.

"Spooky action at a distance. I re-create as much as I can of the circumstances of his departure, and see if by acting on the mirrors I'm able to act on him wherever he is now in a way that pulls him back through." It was the same sort of large-scale entanglement we'd hoped for with the original experiment—the captured reflection being held in the mirror, with Zack here to influence it and relate its experiences—just reversed. Well, reversed and complicated by the fact that it was a person, and not a reflection, that had been captured. Complicated by a lot of things, actually, not least of which was that spooky action at a distance hadn't yet been proven on anything larger than a particle.

Lara shook her head. "It's a stretch. Too much of one. I'm going to continue with the location work."

"I understand," I said, then went down the hall and got out the boxes of shattered glass. I did understand, and I felt better that we were coming at the problem from two different directions. It was more likely that something would work.

As I sorted through the pieces of the mirrors, I realized they weren't clear reflections anymore. They held color, lines, fragments of pictures that didn't change. It might not have been Zack's reflection that we'd caught, but we'd captured something.

I let myself hope.

I set the glass back into the mirrors, very carefully. I didn't want to glue it in, or introduce any material that might interfere with the mirrors' connection to Zack. The glass itself was cold, so cold my bones ached after ten minutes of work, and I had to take frequent breaks to rewarm my hands.

It took me days—days while Lara continued to run equations and tests, marking formulae on the mirror in her office in grease pencil, using her own theories to look for Zack—to sort enough pieces of glass to fully see it, but not only had we captured reflections, we'd captured six different images, one in each mirror. Pictures of Zack, frozen in crystals of time. Some of them I recognized—like the one of him disappearing, shock and delight reflected on his face.

Some of them I didn't. There was one that was him from the back, in the same clothes he had worn in the lab, faded jeans and a black sweater with a pull on the hem. He was walking through a snow-covered forest. In another, Zack knelt at the feet of a woman whose face wasn't visible, passing a small piece of glass into her hand.

There was a tiny piece missing from one of the mirrors. A thin shard of glass in one of the images of Zack that I did recognize, from the day we had all begun working in the lab. The missing piece was right over where his heart would be. I looked all over the tables, dumped the boxes where the pieces had been stored upside down, but nothing fell out.

Lara found me, what felt like hours later, knees bruised from crawling back and forth across the floor. "What are you doing?"

"There's a piece missing."

"It's not missing. I know exactly where it is."

I picked myself up off the floor and followed her down the hall.

The piece of glass was broken, cracked in two down the center. "I found it the day he disappeared. I set it aside because it was the only one broken differently from the others, and I wondered if that mattered—like maybe the shattering started with this piece. I've been running tests on it, checking baselines against the measurements we took of the other pieces the day they shattered. That's why I had it in here."

"Were you planning on giving it to me?"

"Once you needed it, of course."

The two halves fit together perfectly, but they didn't fit into the mirror. When I set it in place, all the pieces of glass from that frame fell to the floor. I looked around, making sure the other five mirrors were still intact, coils of tension releasing from around my stomach when they were. I dropped to the floor, searching with shaking hands through the pieces of glass to make sure none of the others were further broken or chipped.

"Did you do anything to the glass when you tested it?" I asked.

"Of course not, but that doesn't mean it's unchanged. We are working in fairly unknown territory here. If you don't mind, I'll run a few more tests while you put the mirror back together."

"Go ahead. Just . . . be careful." I couldn't shake the feeling that if something happened to the pieces of the mirror, we'd never be able to get Zack back.

Hours later, the rest of the mirror reassembled, I went to get the twice-broken piece from Lara. She looked puzzled. "There's something unusual about it. Nothing that should have changed its size or the way it fits into the image—I measured against the others—but there's a crystalline lattice inside its two halves, and I don't recognize the structure. It's not normally found in mirror glass, and it's not present in any of the other pieces."

The internal change shouldn't have made a difference, but it did. I placed the other pieces Lara had been testing in the frame without incident, but when I put the two broken halves in place, all the pieces of glass fell out of the mirror again.

It felt like something fell out of me with it. All those hours of work, lost again, meaning even more hours away from being able to even try to bring Zack back. I was terrified that one of these times, the strange luck that kept the other pieces from breaking further wouldn't hold, or the pieces would fall out of the five other mirrors, or. I didn't even know what other disaster to anticipate.

"What am I going to do?" I scrubbed the exhaustion from my eyes.

"Go home," Lara said. "Warm up—I can see you shaking from here. Start again tomorrow with a fresh eye."

Good advice. I hated taking it.

It was still snowing in the lab when I came in the next day. It had gotten colder, too. Measurably colder, cold enough to leave a rime of frost on things in the lab.

Though not the mirrors. The five that had all their pieces still stood, showing the captured images. I spent most of the day putting the glass back in the frame with the missing piece, my hands aching from the cold.

The snow fell faster as I worked, hard enough that it was difficult to see the mirrors through it.

"I want to set the mirrors back into place like they were when Zack disappeared," I told Lara. "See if it will bring him back, even with the missing piece. The rest of the mirror holds together without it."

"It's unlikely to work," she said.

"Then it doesn't. And we can try something else next. But we need to try this now. I'm worried about the obscuring effects of the snowfall, and if there's something important about their precise location, it's not like we can just set them up in another area of the lab." I could hear the desperation in my voice. So could Lara.

"Fine," she said. "Maybe the temperature shift is a signal of some sort. Let's see what happens."

Lara and I arranged them back into the standing pattern, six sides, like a snowflake. We set them in place so that with the final two, we would have been reflected in each other's, had there not already been images of Zack there.

We stepped back, and the temperature in the room plummeted. There was a great howl of wind and snow, and I could hear the shriek and groan of the glass in the mirrors.

The snow cleared, and Zack was there.

He was dazed and cold—blue framing his lips and edging his fingernails. His hair was rimed with frost, and snow coated his clothing. He blinked against the lights, rubbing hard at his eyes.

He was here. Safe and whole, for all that he stood frozen in my arms as I hugged him, tears of relief freezing in the corners of my eyes.

———◆———

But that wasn't the end of it. It soon became clear that while Zack had returned, he wasn't the same. It was like his personality had been left behind, or frozen out of him. He was flat, not all the way here, a blank stranger dressed up in Zack's clothes.

And there was nothing that stranger wanted more than to go back to where he'd been.

"Let me see the equations again," he said to Lara. "Maybe I can see where you're going wrong." He spent all his time in the lab—there before either Lara or I were in the morning, staying long past when we left, running numbers, poring over notes from the experiment that had disappeared him.

"Does he talk to you about it? Where he was, what happened?" I asked Lara. "Because he doesn't talk to me." Not about being there, not about anything. If I was lucky, he'd say hello. I'd asked him about the images in the mirrors, and he said that they already showed me all I needed to know, and walked away.

"He lets bits and pieces slip when we're working. Like, he said it was snowing there. But he won't answer direct questions about it. He thinks it was something in the mirrors themselves that helped him pass through."

"And that's why he couldn't come back until they were reassembled," I said. "There might be something to that. And the missing piece might explain why he's been so strange since he came back."

"He's not strange; he's just focused."

"The kind of focused where he doesn't remember to eat meals or leave the lab or interact with other humans. You know that's not like him. There's something different. I think something may have happened to him while he was gone. I mean, the other day, I brought him anchovy pizza, and he picked the anchovies off."

Lara looked at me out of the corner of her eye. "I don't think good taste in pizza is grounds for assuming there's something wrong with him. We sent him to another world, remember? People change for all sorts of reasons, and that's a pretty compelling one to me.

But it's nothing more than that. Stop trying to see something that isn't there."

I started staying overnight at the lab. Poring over all the notes the three of us had generated since we first started talking about the idea of a world behind the mirrors. Reading journal articles that theorized that time could be captured and crystallized, trying to see if I could find anything in them that would match up with the crystalline structure in the broken mirror piece. Staring at the frozen images of Zack in the mirrors, trying to parse the mysteries of the ones that were unrecognizable.

Trying to understand what had happened. To understand why all of Zack hadn't come back.

I wasn't the only one staying at the lab at all hours. Zack stood at the center of the mirrors, the puffs of his breath frosting the glass. That was the other thing that was different about Zack now—he was cold, all the time, as if the snow was falling inside him.

"What do you see?" I asked.

"I see a place I need to go back to, a place I should have stayed."

"Why?" I asked, my heart breaking over the question.

"Because I was myself there. My true self. Look in the mirror—you can see how I really am."

I couldn't, though—the mirrors no longer showed new reflections on their surfaces, only the images of Zack that had been frozen there when he disappeared. So all I saw was a flat copy of my best friend, a piece missing from his heart. This was someone so changed and cold that there was nothing left of the warmth I remembered.

Still. Maybe he could see something I couldn't. "How about me? What do I look like in the mirror?"

"I don't think I can see you," he said. "There's no part of you there."

Maybe not.

———◆———

Days had passed now, but snow still fell, in that space at the center of the mirrors. It felt like a door left open.

I was still trying without success to decipher the crystalline lattice in the twice-broken piece of mirror. It looked, I thought, almost like snowflakes, like a pattern of frost. Frozen in reflection.

I pinched the bridge of my nose, closing my eyes.

Maybe, I thought, maybe if I melted it. I put it on a plate and lit a Bunsen burner underneath it. After a couple of minutes, I heard Zack shout from the other side of the lab, crying out that he was burning, something in his shirt pocket, burning his chest.

I turned off the burner. Heard Lara ask if he was okay, heard him say it had stopped.

I looked at the pieces of mirrors again after they had cooled. There was no change. The heat that burned Zack from across the lab hadn't been enough to melt the crystals.

I put my head down on the lab table and cried.

It wasn't science, what I did. I couldn't replicate it in a lab. I don't know why it worked, and most of me didn't expect it to. But I was desperate.

I stood in the center of the room, where the snow fell, and I held the broken pieces of mirror in my hand, and I filled them with reflections.

I thought about the time, sophomore year of high school, when my period had bled through my jeans, and Zack hadn't said anything, hadn't even blinked, just shrugged out of his ever-present flannel shirt, giving it to me so I could tie it around my waist and hide my embarrassment.

About the time we had taken the railing off the wall to get the couch out of his floor of the rental house, and watched as it shot down the stairs, out of the front door, and across the street because both of us thought the other had a grip on it. How both of us had nearly fallen after it, we were laughing so hard.

The time I said I missed seeing the stars, and he drove me out of the city, into the Florida Keys, so I could find them.

I stood and reflected on all the things that were the way I saw him—his laugh, his enthusiastically off-key singing, the way he emptied his pockets for any homeless person he passed—and snow fell around me and froze my breath and my tears, and then I filled the small, missing piece of Zack's reflection with the mirror I held in my hand.

The image in the mirror changed—it became a woman's face, crystalline and beautiful as snow. She held out her hand, and on it, there was a piece of a mirror, six-sided, like a snowflake.

As I watched, it melted.

She closed her fingers over the emptiness, looked at me, and nodded. Her image faded.

The snow stopped falling.

I heard the door to the lab open and looked over to see Zack, standing outside the ring of mirrors. I walked back through them, to him. He smiled, really smiled at me, for the first time since he'd come back, and rubbed his hands across his eyes.

"Sophie," he said. "You've got to come see this. I'm working on location calculations, when one of the mirrors in my section of the lab decides it's like a slide show or something. It showed me all these old pictures of us."

"Really?" I asked.

"Like the day we met, and the day we started class here, and, oh, in undergrad, the day we were mad scientists for Halloween! Remember?"

I did. "That was fun."

But when we went into the lab, the surface of the mirror was clear of everything but the expected reflection.

Zack shook his head. "I guess I've been working too hard. I

must have fallen asleep and had a dream that seemed so real I needed to tell you about it."

"Stranger things have happened," I said.

"Right?" He grinned. "Hey, I'm starving. Want to go grab some pizza?"

"With anchovies?" I asked, hoping so hard for the right answer.

"Of course."

I glanced back at the mirror—now whole—as we left, and I saw the change in the reflection. Over his heart, on the pocket of his shirt, there was a fading spot of water, like what might have been left by melted snow.

AUTHOR'S NOTE

Kat Howard: Mirrors have always seemed sort of magical to me. When I was a little girl, I used to play the same game with my mirror as the narrator plays with hers in the story's opening. I would try to somehow outrun my reflection, wishing that if I just moved fast enough, I would be out of the frame of the mirror, and she would still be there. I wasn't quite sure what would happen after that, but I knew it would be amazing. Then, right before I got the invitation to write a story for *The Starlit Wood*, I read a physics article about the possibility of time crystals (which, sadly, almost certainly don't exist). So when I needed to think about rewriting a fairy tale, my brain mashed up mirrors and crystals and said, "Hey, let's try 'The Snow Queen' with science in it." My favorite part of "The Snow Queen" was always the mirror. That strange mirror that broke into pieces and fell like snow and changed what people saw, that melted like ice—I loved everything about it. I was shocked when I reread Andersen's original, at how little page space the mirror took up, because in my memory, it was this huge thing, the focus of the story. So this was also my way of altering the story's reflection to show my favorite pieces of it.

SPINNING SILVER

Naomi Novik

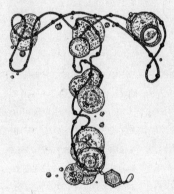 he real story isn't half as pretty as the one you've heard. The real story is, the miller's daughter with her long golden hair wants to catch a lord, a prince, a rich man's son, so she goes to the moneylender and borrows for a ring and a necklace and decks herself out for the festival. And she's beautiful enough, so the lord, the prince, the rich man's son notices her, and dances with her, and tumbles her in a quiet hayloft when the dancing is over, and afterwards he goes home and marries the rich woman his family has picked out for him. Then the miller's disappointed daughter tells everyone that the moneylender's in league with the devil, and the village runs him out or maybe even stones him, so at least she gets to keep the jewels, and the blacksmith marries her before that firstborn child comes along a little early.

Because that's what the story's really about: getting out of

paying your debts. That's not how they tell it, but I knew. My father was a moneylender, you see.

He wasn't very good at it. If someone didn't pay him back on time, he never so much as mentioned it to them. Only if our cupboards were really bare, or our shoes were falling off our feet, and my mother spoke quietly with him after I was in bed: then he'd go, unhappy, and knock on a few doors, and make it sound like an apology when he asked for some of what they owed. And if there was money in the house and someone asked to borrow, he hated to say no, even if we didn't really have enough ourselves. So all his money, most of which had been my mother's money, her dowry, stayed in other people's houses. And everyone else liked it that way, even though they knew they ought to be ashamed of themselves, so they told the story often, even or especially when I could hear it.

My mother's father was a moneylender too, but he was a very good one. He lived in the city, twenty miles away. She often took me on visits, when she could afford to pay someone to let us ride along at the back of a cart or a sledge, five or six changes along the way. My grandmother would always have a new dress for me, plain but warm and well made, and she would feed me to bursting, and the last night before we left she would always make cheese-cake, her cheesecake, which was baked golden on the outside and thick and white and crumbly inside and tasted just a little bit of apples, and she would make decorations with sweet golden raisins on the top. After I had slowly and lingeringly eaten every last bite of a slice wider than the palm of my hand, they would put me to bed in the warmest corner of the big, cozy sitting room near the fireplace, and my mother would sit next to her mother, and put her head on her shoulder, and not say anything, but when I was a little older and didn't fall asleep right away, I would see in the candlelight that both of them had a little wet track of tears down their faces.

We could have stayed. But we always went home, because we loved my father. He was terrible with money, but he was endlessly warm and gentle, and he tried to make his failure up to us: he spent nearly all of every day out in the cold woods hunting for food and firewood, and when he was indoors, there was nothing he wouldn't do to help my mother; no talk of woman's work in my house, and when we did go hungry, he went hungriest, and snuck food from his plate to ours. When he sat by the fire in the evenings, his hands were always working, whittling some new little toy for me or something for my mother, a decoration on a chair or a wooden spoon.

But winter was always bitter in our town, and every year seemed worse. The year I turned sixteen, the ground froze early, and cold, sharp winds blew out of the forest every day, it seemed, carrying whirls of stinging snow. Our house stood a little bit apart from the rest anyway, without other walls nearby to share in breaking the wind, and we grew thin and hungry and shivering. My father kept making his excuses, avoiding the work he couldn't bear to do. But even when my mother finally pressed him and he tried, he only came back with a scant handful of coins. It was midwinter, and everyone wanted to have something good on the table; something a little nice for the festival, their festival.

So they put my father off, and while their lights shone out on the snow and the smell of roasting meat slipped out of the cracks, at home my mother made thin cabbage soup and scrounged together used cooking oil to light the lamp for the first night of our own celebration, coughing as she worked: another deep chill had rolled in from the woods, and it crept through every crack and eave of our run-down little house.

By the eighth day, she was too tired from coughing to get out of bed. "She'll be all right soon," my father said, avoiding my eyes. "The cold will break."

He went out to gather some firewood. "Miryem," my mother

said, hoarsely, and I took her a cup of weak tea with a scraping of honey, all I had to comfort her. She sipped a little and lay back on the pillows and said, "When the winter breaks, I want you to go to my father's house. He'll take you to my father's house."

I pressed my lips together hard, and then I kissed her forehead and told her to rest, and after she fell fitfully asleep, I went to the box next to the fireplace where my father kept his big ledger book. I took it out, and I took his worn pen out of its holder, and I mixed ink out of the ashes in the fireplace, and I made a list. A moneylender's daughter, even a bad moneylender, learns her figures. I wrote and figured and wrote and figured, interest and time broken up by the scattered payments—because my father had every one of those written down; he was as scrupulous in making sure he didn't cheat anyone as no one else was with him, and when I had my list finished, I took all the knitting out of my bag, put my shawl on, and went out into the cold morning.

I went to every house that owed us, and I banged on their doors: it was early, very early, because my mother's coughing had woken us in the dark. Everyone was still at home. So the men opened the doors and stared at me in surprise, and I looked them in their faces and said, cold and hard, "I've come to settle your account."

They tried to put me off, of course; some of them laughed at me. Some of them smiled and asked me to come inside and warm myself up, have a hot drink. I refused. I didn't want to be warmed. I stood on their doorsteps, and I brought out my list, and I told them how much they had borrowed, and what they had paid, and how much interest they owed besides.

They spluttered and argued and some of them shouted. No one had ever shouted at me in my life: my mother with her quiet voice, my gentle father. But I found something bitter inside myself, something of winter blown into my heart: the sound of my mother coughing, and the memory of the story told too many times in the village square. I stayed in their doorways, and I didn't move. My numbers were true, and they and I knew it, and when they'd shouted themselves out, I said, "Do you have the money?"

They thought it was an opening. They said no, of course not; they didn't have such a sum.

"Then you'll pay me a little now, and again every week, until your debt is cleared," I said, "and pay interest on what you haven't paid, if you don't want me to send to my grandfather to bring the law into it."

Our town was small, and no one traveled very much. They knew my mother's father was rich, and lived in a great house in the city, and had loaned money to knights and once to a lord. So they gave me a little, grudgingly; only a few pennies in some houses, but every one of them gave me something, and I wrote down the numbers in front of them and told them I would see them next week. On my way home, I stopped in at Panova Lyudmila's house, who took in travelers when they stayed overnight. She didn't borrow money: she could have lent it too, except for charging interest. And if anyone in our town had been foolish enough to borrow from anyone but my father, who would let them pay as they liked or didn't. I didn't collect anything; from her I bought a pot of hot soup, with half a chicken in it, and three fresh eggs, and a bowl of honeycomb covered with a napkin.

My father had come back home before me; he was feeding the fire, and he looked up worried when I shouldered my way in. He stared at my arms full of food. I put it all down and I put the rest of the pennies and the handful of silver into the kettle next to our own hearth, and I gave him the list with the payments written on it, and then I turned to making my mother comfortable.

After that, I was the moneylender in our little town. And I was a good moneylender, and a lot of people owed us money, so very soon the straw of our floor was smooth boards of golden wood, and

the cracks in our fireplace were chinked with good clay and our roof was thatched fresh, and my mother had a fur cloak to sleep under or to wear. She didn't like it at all, and neither did my father, who went outside and wept quietly to himself the day I brought the cloak home. The baker's wife had offered it to me in payment for the rest of her family's debt. It was beautiful; she'd brought it with her when she married, made of ermines her father had hunted in his lord's woods.

That part of the story turned out to be true: you have to be cruel to be a good moneylender. But I was ready to be as merciless with our neighbors as they'd been with my father. I didn't take firstborn children exactly, but one week, one of the peasant farmers had nothing to pay me with, not even a spare loaf of bread, and he cursed me with real desperation in his voice and said, "You can't suck blood from a stone."

I should have felt sorry for him, I suppose. My father would have, and my mother, but wrapped in my coldness, I only felt the danger of the moment. If I forgave him, took his excuses, next week everyone would have an excuse; I saw everything unraveling again from there.

Then the farmer's tall daughter came staggering in, a heavy gray kerchief over her head and a big heavy yoke across her shoulders, carrying two buckets of water, twice as much as I could manage when I went for water to the village well myself. I said, "Then your daughter will come work in my house to pay off the debt, three mornings this week and every week you can't pay," and I walked home pleased as a cat, and even danced a few steps to myself in the road, alone under the trees.

Her name was Wanda. She came silently to the house at dawn, three days a week, worked like an ox until midday, and left silently again; she kept her head down the entire time. She was very strong, and she took almost all the burden of the housework in just her three mornings. She carried water and chopped wood, and tended the small flock of hens we now had scratching in our yard, and watered the new goats and milked them, and scrubbed the floors and our hearth and all our pots, and I was well satisfied with my solution.

For the first time in my life, I heard my mother speak to my father in anger, in blame, as she hadn't even when she was cold and sick. "And you don't care for what it does to her?" I heard her cry out to him.

"What shall I say to her?" he cried back. "What shall I say? No, you shall starve; no, you shall go cold and you will wear rags?"

"If you had the coldness to do it yourself, you could be cold enough to let her do it," my mother said. "Our daughter, Josef!"

But when my father looked me in the face that night and tried to say something to me, the coldness in me met him and drove him back, just as it had when he'd met it in the village, asking for what he was owed.

So in desperation my mother took me away on a visit when the air warmed with spring and her cough finally went away, drowned in soup and honey. I didn't like to leave, but I did want to see my grandmother, and show her that her daughter wasn't sleeping cold and frozen, that her granddaughter didn't go like a beggar anymore; I wanted to visit without seeing her weep, for once. I went on my rounds one last time and told everyone as I did that I would add on extra interest for the weeks I was gone, unless they left their payments at our house while I was away.

Then we drove to my grandfather's house, but this time I hired our neighbor Oleg to take us all the way with his good horses and his big wagon, heaped with straw and blankets and jingling bells on the harness, with the fur cloak spread over all against the March wind. My grandmother came out, surprised, to meet us when we drew up to the house, and my mother went into her arms, silent and hiding her face. "Well, come in and warm up," my grandmother said, looking at the sledge and our good new

wool dresses, trimmed with rabbit fur, and a golden button at the neck on mine, that had come out of the weaver's chest.

She sent me to take my grandfather fresh hot water in his study, so she could talk to my mother alone. My grandfather had rarely done more than grunt at me and look me up and down disapprovingly in the dresses my grandmother had bought. I don't know how I knew what he thought of my father, because I don't remember him ever having said a word about it, but I did know.

He looked me over this time out from under his bristling eyebrows and frowned. "Fur, now? And gold?"

I should say that I was properly brought up, and I knew better than to talk back to my own grandfather of all people, but I was already angry that my mother was upset, and that my grandmother wasn't pleased, and now to have him pick at me, him of all people. "Why shouldn't I have it, instead of someone who bought it with my father's money?" I said.

My grandfather was as surprised as you would expect to be spoken to like this by his granddaughter, but then he heard what I had said and frowned at me again. "Your father bought it for you, then?"

Loyalty and love stopped my mouth there, and I dropped my eyes and silently finished pouring the hot water into the samovar and changing out the tea. My grandfather didn't stop me going away, but by the next morning he knew the whole story somehow, that I'd taken over my father's work, and suddenly he was pleased with me, as he never had been before and no one else was.

He had two other daughters who had married better than my mother, to rich city men with good trades. None of them had given him a grandson who wanted to take up his business. In the city, there were enough of my people that we could be something other than a banker, or a farmer who grew his own food: there were enough people who would buy your goods, and there was a thriving market in our quarter.

"It's not seemly for a girl," my grandmother tried, but my grandfather snorted.

"Gold doesn't know the hand that holds it," he said, and frowned at me, but in a pleased way. "You'll need servants," he told me. "One to start with, a good, strong, simple man or woman: can you find one?"

"Yes," I said, thinking of Wanda: she had nearly paid off her father's debt by now, but she was already used to coming, and in our town there wasn't much other chance for a poor farmer's daughter to earn a wage.

"Good. Don't go yourself to get the money," he said. "You send a servant, and if they want to argue, they come to you."

I nodded, and when we went home, he gave me a purse full of silver pennies to lend out, to towns near ours that hadn't any moneylender of their own. And when my mother and I came again in the winter for another visit, after the first snowfall, I brought it back full of gold to put into the bank, and my grandfather was proud of me.

They hadn't had guests over usually, when we were visiting, except my mother's sisters. I hadn't noticed before, but I noticed now, because suddenly the house was full of people coming to drink tea, to stay to dinner, lights and bustling dresses and laughing voices, and I met more city people in that one week than I had in all the visits before. "I don't believe in selling a sow's ear for a silk purse," my grandfather told me bluntly, when I asked him. "Your father couldn't dower you as the guests who come to this house would expect of my granddaughter, and I swore to your mother that I would never put more money in his pocket, to fall back out again."

I understood then why he hadn't wanted my grandmother buying dresses for me, as he'd thought, with fur and gold buttons on them. He wouldn't try to make a princess out of a miller's daughter with borrowed finery, and snare her a husband fool enough to be

tricked by it, or who'd slip out of the bargain when he learned the truth.

It didn't make me angry; I liked him better for that cold, hard honesty, and it made me proud that now he did invite his guests, and even boasted of me to them, how I'd taken away a purse of silver and brought back one of gold.

But my grandmother kept her mouth pursed shut; my mother's was empty of smiles. I was angry at her again as we flew home in the warm sledge over the frozen roads. I had another purse of silver hidden deep under my own fur cloak, and three petticoats underneath my dress, and I didn't feel cold at all, but her face was tight and drawn.

"Would you rather we were still poor and hungry?" I burst out to her finally, the silence between us heavy in the midst of the dark woods, and she put her arms around me and kissed me and said, "My darling, my darling, I'm sorry," weeping a little.

"Sorry?" I said. "To be warm instead of cold? To be rich and comfortable? To have a daughter who can turn silver into gold?" I pushed away from her.

"To see you harden yourself like a stone, to make it so," she said. We didn't speak the rest of the way home.

I didn't believe in stories, even though we lived in the middle of one: our village had been cut out of the North Forest, a little too near the depths where they said the old ones lived, the Staryk. Children who ran playing in the woods would sometimes stumble across their road and come home with one of the pebbles that lined it: an unnaturally smooth pebble that shone in starlight, and got lost again very quickly no matter how much care you took with it. I saw them displayed in the village square a couple of times, but they only looked like smooth white pebbles, and I didn't think magic was needed to explain why children lost a rock again in short order.

You weren't supposed to ride through the woods dressed too fine, because they loved gold and gems and finery, but again, I didn't mean to be afraid of fairy lords when thieves would do just as well, to make it poor sense to go riding through a deep forest wearing all your jewels. If you found a grove full of red mushrooms with white spots, you were supposed to go back out again and stay well away, because that was one of their dancing rings, and if someone went missing in the woods they'd taken him or her, and once in a while someone would come staggering out of the forest, feverish, and claim to have seen one of them.

I never saw the road, or took any of it seriously, but the morning after my mother and I came back home, Wanda ran back inside, afraid, after she'd gone out to feed the chickens. "They've been outside the house!" was all she said, and she wouldn't go out again alone. My father took the iron poker from the fireplace and we all went out cautiously behind him, thinking there might be burglars or wolves, but there were only prints in the snow. Strange prints: a little like deer, but with claws at the end, and too large, the size of horses' hooves. They came right to the wall of the house, and then someone had climbed off the beast and looked through our window: someone wearing boots with a long pointed toe.

I wasn't stubborn about my disbelief, when I had footprints in snow to show me something strange had happened. If nothing else, no one anywhere near our town had boots that absurd, for fashion; only someone who didn't have to walk anywhere would have shoes like that. But there didn't seem to be anything to do about it, and they'd left, whoever they'd been. I told Wanda we'd hire her brother to come and guard the house during the night, mostly so she wouldn't be afraid and maybe leave her place, and then I put it out of my mind.

But the tracks were there again the next morning, though Sergey swore he'd been awake all night and hadn't heard a thing.

"If the Staryk haven't anything better to do but peer in at our

windows, I suppose they can," I said out loud and clear, standing in the yard. "We're no fools to keep our gold in the house: it's in Grandfather's vault," which I hoped might be overheard and do some good whether it was an elf or a thief or someone trying to scare me.

It did something, anyway; that night as we sat at our work in the kitchen, my mother doing the fine sewing she loved, and I with my spindle, my father silently whittling with his head bowed, there was suddenly a banging at the door, a heavy thumping as though someone were knocking against the wood with something metal. Wanda sprang up from the kettle with a cry, and we all held still: it was a cold night, snow falling, and no one would come out at such an hour. The knocking came again, and then my father said, "Well, it's a polite devil, at least," and got up and went to the door.

When he opened it, no one was there, but there was a small bag sitting on the threshold. He stepped outside and looked around to one side and the other: no one anywhere in sight. Then he gingerly picked up the bag and brought it inside and put it on the table. We all gathered around it and stared as though it were a live coal that might at any moment set the whole house ablaze.

It was made of leather, white leather, but not dyed by any ordinary way I'd ever heard of: it looked as though it had always been white, all the way through. There wasn't a seam or stitch to be seen on its sides, and it clasped shut with a small lock made of silver. Finally, when no one else moved to touch it, I reached out and opened the clasp, and tipped out a few small silver coins, thin and flat and perfectly round, not enough to fill the hollow of my palm. Our house was full of warm firelight, but they shone coldly, as if they stood under the moon.

"It's very kind of them to make us such a present," my father said after a moment doubtfully, but we all knew the Staryk would never do such a thing. There were stories from other kingdoms farther south, of fairies who came with gifts, but not in ours. And then my mother drew a sharp breath and looked at me and said, low, "They want it turned into gold."

I suppose it was my own fault, bragging in the woods where they could hear me, but now I didn't know what to do. Moneylending isn't magic: I couldn't lend the coins out today and have the profit back tomorrow, and I didn't think they meant to wait a year or more for their return. Anyway, the reason I had brought in so much money so quickly was that my father had lent out all my mother's dowry over years and years, and everyone had kept the money so long they had built heaps of interest even at the little rate my father had charged them.

"We'll have to take the money from the bank," my mother said. There were six silver coins in the bag. I had put fourteen gold coins in the bank this last visit, and the city was only an eight-hour sleigh ride away when the snow was packed this hard. But I rebelled: I didn't mean to trade our gold, *my* gold, for fairy silver.

"I'll go to the city tomorrow" was all I said, but when I went, I didn't go to the bank. I slept that night in my grandfather's house, behind the thick walls of the quarter, and early the next morning, I went down to the market. I found a seat upon the temple steps while the sellers put out their stalls: everything from apples to hammers to jeweled belts, and I waited while the buyers slowly trickled in. I watched through the morning rush, and after it thinned out, I went to the stall of the jeweler who had been visited by the most people in drab clothes: I guessed they had to be servants from the rich people of the city.

The jeweler was a young man with spectacles and stubby but careful fingers, his beard trimmed short to stay out of his work; he was bent over an anvil in miniature, hammering out a disk of silver with his tiny tools, enormously precise. I stood watching him work for maybe half an hour before he sighed and said, "Yes?" with a faint hint of resignation, as though he'd hoped I would go away instead of troubling him to do any business. But

he seemed to know what he was about, so I brought out my pouch of silver coins and spilled them onto the black cloth he worked upon.

"It's not enough to buy anything here," he said, matter-of-factly, with barely a glance; he started to go back to his work, but then he frowned a little and turned around again. He picked one coin up and peered at it closely, and turned it over in his fingers, and rubbed it between them, and then he put it down and stared at me. "Where did you get these?"

"They came from the Staryk, if you want to believe me," I said. "Can you make them into something? A bracelet or a ring?"

"I'll buy them from you," he offered.

"No, thank you," I said.

"To make them into a ring would cost you two gold coins," he said. "Or I'll buy them from you for five."

"I'll pay you one," I said firmly, "or if you like, you can sell the ring for me and keep half the profit," which was what I really wanted. "I have to give the Staryk back six gold coins in exchange."

He grumbled a little but finally agreed, which meant he thought he could sell it for a high enough price to make it worthwhile, and then he set about the work. He melted the silver over a hot little flame and ran it into a mold, a thick one made of iron, and when it had half cooled, he took it out with his leathered fingertips and etched a pattern into the surface, fanciful, full of leaves and branches.

It didn't take him long: the silver melted easily and cooled easily and took the pattern easily, and when it was done, the pattern seemed oddly to move and shift: it drew the eye and held it, and shone even in the midday sun. We looked down at it for a while, and then he said, "The duke will buy it," and sent his apprentice running into the city. A tall, imperious servant in velvet clothes and gold braid came back with the boy, making clear in every expression how annoyed he was by the interruption of his more important work, but even he stopped being annoyed when he saw the ring and held it on his palm.

The duke paid ten gold coins for the ring, so I put two in the bank, and six back into the little white pouch, and I climbed back into Oleg's sledge to go home that same evening. We flew through the snow and dark, the horse trotting quickly with only my weight in back. But in the woods the horse slowed, and then dropped to a walk, and then halted; I thought she just needed a rest, but she stood unmoving with her ears pricked up anxiously, warm breath gusting out of her nostrils. "Why are we stopping?" I asked, and Oleg didn't answer me: he slumped in his seat as though he slept.

The snow crunched behind me once and once again: something picking its way toward the sleigh from behind, step by heavy step. I swallowed and drew my cloak around me, and then I summoned up all the winter-cold courage I'd built inside me and turned around.

The Staryk didn't look so terribly strange at first; that was what made him truly terrible, as I kept looking and slowly his face became something inhuman, shaped out of ice and glass, and his eyes like silver knives. He had no beard and wore his white hair in a long braid down his back. His clothes, just like his purse, were all in white. He was riding a stag, but a stag larger than a draft horse, with antlers branched twelve times and hung with clear glass drops, and when it put out its red tongue to lick its muzzle, its teeth were sharp as a wolf's.

I wanted to quail, to cower; but I knew where that led. Instead I held my fur cloak tight at the throat with one hand against the chill that rolled off him, and with my other I held out the bag to him, in silence, as he came close to the sleigh.

He paused, eyeing me out of one silver-blue eye with his head turned sideways, like a bird. He put out his gloved hand and took the bag, and he opened it and poured the six gold coins out into the cup of his hand, the faint jingle loud in the silence around us.

The coins looked warm and sun-bright against the white of his glove. He looked down at them and seemed vaguely disappointed, as though he was sorry I'd managed it; and then he put them away and the bag vanished somewhere beneath his own long cloak.

I called up all my courage and spoke, throwing my words against the hard, icy silence like a shell around us. "I'll need more than a day next time, if you want more of them changed," I said, a struggle to keep trembling out of my voice.

He lifted his head and stared at me, as though surprised I'd dared to speak to him, and then he wasn't there anymore; Oleg shook himself all over and chirruped to the horse, and we were trotting again. I fell back into the blankets, shivering. The tips of my fingers where I'd held out the purse were numbed and cold. I pulled off my glove and tucked them underneath my arm to warm them up, wincing as they touched my skin.

One week went by, and I began to forget about the Staryk, about all of it. We all did, the way one forgets dreams: you're trying to explain the story of it to someone and halfway through it's already running quicksilver out of your memory, too wrong and ill-fitting to keep in your mind. I didn't have any of the fairy silver left to prove the whole thing real, not even the little purse. Even that same night I'd come home, I hadn't been able to describe him to my anxious mother; I'd only been able to say, "It's all right, I gave him the gold," and then I'd fallen into bed. By morning I couldn't remember his face.

But Sunday night the knocking came again at the door, and I froze for a moment. I was standing already, about to fetch a dish of dried fruit from the pantry; with a lurch of my heart I went to the door and flung it open.

A burst of wind came growling through the house, as cold as if it had been shaved directly off the frozen crust of the snow. The Staryk hadn't abandoned a purse on the stoop this time: he stood waiting outside, all the more unearthly for the frame of wood around his sharp edges. I looked back into the house wildly, to see if they saw him also; but my father was bent over his whittling as though he hadn't even heard the door opening, and my mother was looking into the fire with a dreamy, vague look on her face. Wanda lay sleeping on her pallet already, and her brother had gone home three days before.

I turned back. The Staryk held another purse out to me, to the very border of the door, and spoke, a high, thin voice like wind whistling through the eaves. "Three days," he said.

I was afraid of him, of course; I wasn't a fool. But I had only believed in him for a week, and I had spent all my life learning to fear other things more: to be taken advantage of, used unfairly. "And what in return?" I blurted, putting my hands behind my back.

His eyes sharpened, and I regretted pressing him. "Thrice, mortal maiden," he said, in a rhythm almost like a song. "Thrice shall I come, and you shall turn silver to gold for my hands, or be changed into ice yourself."

I felt half ice already, chilled down to my bones. I swallowed. "And then?"

He laughed and said, "And then I will make you my queen, if you manage it," mockingly, and threw the purse down at my feet, jingling loud. When I looked back up from it, he was gone, and my mother behind me said, slow and struggling, as if it was an effort to speak, "Miryem, why are you keeping the door open? The cold's coming in."

I had never felt sorry for the miller's daughter before, in the story: I'd been too sorry for my father, and myself. But who would really like it, after all, to be married to a king who'd as cheerfully have cut off your head if your dowry didn't match your boasting? I didn't want to be the Staryk's queen any more than I wanted to be his servant, or frozen into ice.

The purse he'd left was ten times as heavy as before, full of shining coins. I counted them out into smooth-sided towers, to try and put my mind into order along with them. "We'll leave," my mother said. I hadn't told her what the Staryk had promised, or threatened, but she didn't like it anyway: an elven lord coming to demand I give him gold. "We'll go to my father, or farther away," but I felt sure that wasn't any good. I hadn't wanted to believe in the Staryk at all, but now that I couldn't help it, I didn't believe there was a place I could run away that he wouldn't find some way to follow. And if I did, then what? My whole life afraid, looking around for the sound of footfalls in snow?

Anyway, we couldn't just go. It would mean bribes to cross each border, and a new home wherever we found ourselves in the end, and who knew how they'd treat us when we got there? We'd heard enough stories of what happened to our people in other countries, under kings and bishops who wanted their own debts forgiven, and to fill their purses with confiscated wealth.

So I put the six towers of coins, ten in each, back into the purse, and I sent Wanda for Oleg's sledge. We drove back to the city that very night, not to lose any of my precious time. "Do you have any more?" Isaac the jeweler demanded the moment he saw me, eagerly, and then he flushed and said, "That is, welcome back," remembering he had manners.

"Yes, I have more," I said, and spilled them out on the cloth. "I need to give back sixty gold this time," I told him.

He was already turning them over with his hands, his face alight with hunger. "I couldn't *remember*," he said, half to himself, and then he heard what I'd said and gawked at me. "I need a little profit for the work that this will take!"

"There's enough to make ten rings, at ten gold each," I said.

"I couldn't sell them all."

"Yes, you could," I said. That, I was sure of: if the duke had

a ring of fairy silver, every wealthy man and woman in the city
needed a ring just like it, right away.

He frowned down over the coins, stirring them with his fingers, and sighed. "I'll make a necklace, and see what we can get."

"You really don't think you can sell ten rings?" I said, surprised, wondering if I was wrong.

"I want to make a necklace," he said, which didn't seem very
sensible to me, but perhaps he thought it would show his work off
and make a name for him. I didn't really mind as long as I could
pay off my Staryk for another week.

"I only have three days," I said. "Can you do it that quickly?"

He groaned. "Why must you ask for impossibilities?"

"Do *those* look possible to you?" I said, pointing at the coins,
and he couldn't really argue with that.

I had to sit with him while he worked, and manage the people
who came to the stall wanting other things from him; he didn't
want to talk to anyone and be interrupted. Most of them were
busy and irritated servants, some of them expecting goods to be
finished; they snapped and glared, wanting me to cower, but I met
their bluster too and said coolly, "Surely you can see what Master
Isaac is working on. I'm sure your mistress or your master wouldn't
wish you to interrupt a patron I cannot name, but who would purchase such a piece," and I waved to send their eyes over to the
worktable, where the full sunlight shone on the silver beneath his
hands. Its cold gleam silenced them; they stood staring a little
while and then went away, without trying to argue again.

I noticed that Isaac tried to save a few of the coins aside while
he worked, as though he wanted to keep them to remember. I
thought of asking him for one to keep myself, but it didn't work.
On the morning of the third day, he sighed and took the last of
the ones he'd saved and melted it down, and strung a last bit of
silver lace upon the design. "It's done," he said afterward, and
picked it up in his hands: the silver hung over his broad palms

like icicles, and we stood looking at it silently together for a while.

"Will you send to the duke?" I asked.

He shook his head and took out a box from his supplies: square and made of carved wood lined with black velvet, and he laid the necklace carefully inside. "No," he said. "For this, I will go to him. Do you want to come?"

"Can I go and change my dress?" I said, a little doubtful: I didn't really want the necklace to go so far out of my sight unpurchased, but I was wearing a plain work dress only for sitting in the market all day.

"How far do you live?" he said, just as doubtful.

"My grandfather's house is only down the street with the ash tree and around the corner," I said. "Three doors down from the red stables."

He frowned a moment. "That's Panov Moshel's house."

"That's my grandfather," I said, and he looked at me, surprised, and then in a new way I didn't understand until I was inside, putting on my good dress with the fur and the gold buttons, and I looked down at myself and patted my hair and wondered if I looked well, and then my cheeks prickled with sudden heat. "Do you know Isaac, the jeweler?" I blurted to my grandmother, turning away from the brass mirror.

She peered at me over her spectacles, narrowly. "I've met his mother. He's a respectable young man," she allowed, after some thought. "Do you want me to put up your hair again?"

So I took a little longer than he would have liked, I suspect, to come back; then we went together to the gates and through the wall around our quarter, and walked into the streets of the city. The houses nearest were mean and low, run-down; but Isaac led me to the wider streets, past an enormous church of gray stone with windows like jewelry themselves, and finally to the enormous mansions of the nobles. I couldn't help staring at the iron fences wrought into lions and writhing dragons, and the walls covered with vining fruits and flowers sculpted out of stone. I admit I was glad not to be alone when we went through the open gates and up the wide stone steps swept clear of snow.

Isaac spoke to one of the servants. We were taken to a small room to wait: no one offered us anything to drink, or a place to sit, and a manservant stood looking at us with disapproval. I was grateful, though: irritation made me feel less small and less tempted to gawk. Finally the servant who had come to the market last time came in and demanded to know our business. Isaac brought out the box and showed him the necklace; he stared down at it, and then said shortly, "Very well," and went away again. Half an hour later he reappeared and ordered us to follow him: we were led up back stairs and then abruptly emerged into a hall more sumptuous than anything I had ever seen, the walls hung with tapestries in bright colors and the floor laid with a beautifully patterned rug.

It silenced our feet and led us into a sitting room even more luxurious, where a man in rich clothes and a golden chain sat in an enormous chair covered in velvet at a writing table. I saw the ring of fairy silver on the first finger of his hand, resting on the arm of the chair. He didn't look down at it, but I noticed he thumbed it around now and again, as though he wanted to make sure it hadn't vanished from his hand. "All right, let's see it."

"Your Grace." Isaac bowed and showed him the necklace.

The duke stared into the box. His face didn't change, but he stirred the necklace gently on its bed with one finger, just barely moving the looped lacelike strands of it. He finally drew a breath and let it out again through his nose. "And how much do you ask for it?"

"Your Grace, I cannot sell it for less than a hundred and fifty."

"Absurd," the duke growled. I had a struggle to keep from biting my lip, myself: it was rather outrageous.

"Otherwise I must melt it down and make it into rings," Isaac said, spreading his hands apologetically. I thought that was rather

clever: of course the duke would rather no one else had a ring like his.

"Where are you getting this silver from?" the duke demanded. Isaac hesitated, and then looked at me. The duke followed his eyes. "Well? You're bringing it from somewhere."

I curtsied, as deeply as I could manage and still get myself back up. "I was given it by one of the Staryk, my lord," I said. "He wants it changed for gold."

"And you mean to do it through my purse, I see," the duke said. "How much more of this silver will there be?"

I had been worrying about that, whether the Staryk would bring even more silver next time, and what I would do with it if he did: the first time six, the second time sixty; how would I get six hundred pieces of gold? I swallowed. "Maybe—maybe much more."

"Hm," the duke said, and studied the necklace again. Then he put his hand to one side and took up a bell and rang it; the servant reappeared in the doorway. "Go and bring Irina to me," he said, and the man bowed. We waited a handful of minutes, and then a woman came to the door, a girl perhaps a year younger than me, slim and demure in a plain gray woolen gown, modestly high-necked, with a fine gray silken veil trailing back over her head. Her chaperone came after her, an older woman scowling at me and especially at Isaac.

Irina curtsied to the duke without raising her downcast eyes. He stood up and took the necklace over to her, and put it around her neck. He stepped back and studied her, and we did too. She wasn't especially beautiful, I would have said, only ordinary, except her hair was long and dark and thick; but it didn't really matter with the necklace on her. It was hard even to glance away from her, with all of winter clasped around her throat and the silver gleam catching in her veil and in her eyes as they darted sideways to catch a glimpse of herself in the mirror on the wall there.

"Ah, Irinushka," the chaperone murmured, approvingly, and the duke nodded.

He turned back to us. "Well, jeweler, you are in luck: the tsar visits us next week. You may have a hundred gold pieces for your necklace, and the next thing you make will be a crown fit for a queen, to be my daughter's dowry: you will have ten times a hundred gold for it, if the tsar takes her hand."

I left twenty gold pieces in the bank and carried the swollen purse into the sledge waiting to carry me home. My shoulders tightened as we plunged into the forest, wondering when and if the Staryk would come on me once more, until halfway down the road the sledge began to slow and stop under the dark boughs. I went rabbit-still, looking around for any signs of him, but I didn't see anything; the horse stamped and snorted her warm breath, and Oleg didn't slump over, but hung his reins on the footboard.

"Did you hear something?" I said, my voice hushed, and then he climbed down and took out a knife from under his coat, and I realized I'd forgotten to worry about anything else but magic. I scrambled desperately away, shoving the heaped blankets toward him and floundering through the straw and out the other side of the sledge. "Don't," I blurted. "Oleg, don't," my heavy skirts dragging in the snow as he came around for me. "Oleg, please," but his face was clenched down, cold deeper than any winter. "This is the Staryk's gold, not mine!" I cried in desperation, holding the purse out between us.

He didn't stop. "None of it's yours," he snarled. "None of it's yours, little grubbing vulture, taking money out of the hands of honest working men," and I knew the sound of a man telling himself a story to persuade himself he wasn't doing wrong, that he had a right to what he'd taken.

I gripped two big handfuls of my skirts and struggled back, my boot heels digging into the snow. He lunged, and I flung

myself away, falling backward. The crust atop the snow gave beneath my weight, and I couldn't get up. He was standing over me, ready to reach down, and then he halted; his arms sank down to his sides.

It wasn't mercy. A deeper cold was coming into his face, stealing blue over his lips, and white frost was climbing over his thick brown beard. I struggled to my feet, shivering. The Staryk was standing behind him, a hand laid upon the back of his neck like a master taking hold of a dog's scruff.

In a moment, he dropped his hand. Oleg stood blank between us, bloodless as frostbite, and then he turned and slowly went back to the sledge and climbed into the driving seat. The Staryk didn't watch him go, as if he cared nothing; he only looked at me with his eyes as gleaming as Oleg's blade. I was shaking and queasy. There were tears freezing on my eyelashes, making them stick. I blinked them away and held my hands tight together until they stopped trembling, and then I held out the purse.

The Staryk came closer and took it. He didn't pour the purse out: it was too full for that. Instead he dipped his hand inside and lifted out a handful of shining coins to tumble ringing back into the bag, weighed in his other palm, until there was only one last coin held between his white-gloved fingers. He frowned at it and me.

"It's all there, all sixty," I said. My heart had slowed, because I suppose it was that or burst.

"As it must be," he said. "For fail me, and to ice you shall go."

But he seemed displeased anyway, although he had set the terms himself: as though he wanted to freeze me but couldn't break a bargain once he'd made it. "Now go home, mortal maiden, until I call on you again."

I looked over helplessly at the sledge: Oleg was sitting in the driver's seat, staring with his frozen face out into the winter, and the last thing I wanted was to get in with him. But I couldn't

walk home from here, or even to some village where I could hire another driver. I had no idea where we were. I turned to argue, but the Staryk was already gone. I stood alone under pine boughs heavy with snow, with only silence and footprints around me, and the deep crushed hollow where I had fallen, the shape of a girl against the drift.

Finally I picked my way gingerly to the sledge and climbed back inside. Oleg shook the reins silently, and the mare started trotting again. He turned her head through the trees slightly, away from the road, and drove deeper into the forest. I tried to decide whether I was more afraid to call out to him and be answered, or to get no reply, and if I should try to jump from the sledge. And then suddenly we came through a narrow gap between trees onto a different road: a road as free of snow as summer, paved with innumerable small white pebbles like a mosaic instead of cobblestones, all of them laid under a solid sheet of ice.

The rails of the sledge rattled, coming onto the road, and then fell silent and smooth. The moon shone, and the road shone back, glistening under the pale light. The horse's hooves went strange and quickly on the ice, the sledge skating along behind her. Around us, trees stretched tall and birch-white, full of rustling leaves; trees that didn't grow in our forest, and should have been bare with winter. White birds darted between the branches, and the sleigh bells made a strange kind of music, high and bright and cold. I huddled back into the blankets and squeezed my eyes shut and kept them so, until suddenly there was a crunching of snow beneath us again, and the sledge was already standing outside the gate of my own yard.

I all but leaped out, and darted through the gate and all the way to my door before I glanced around. I needn't have run. Oleg drove away without ever looking back at me. The next morning, they found him outside his stables, lying frozen and staring blindly upwards in the snow, his horse and sledge put away.

I couldn't forget at all, that week. They buried Oleg in the churchyard, and the bells ringing for him sounded like sleigh bells ringing too-high in a forest that couldn't be. They would find me
frozen like that outside the door, if I didn't give the Staryk his
gold next time, and if I did, then what? Would he put me on his
white stag behind him, and carry me away to that pale cold forest,
to live there alone forever with a crown of fairy silver of my own? I
started up gasping at night with Oleg's white frozen face looming
over me, shivering with a chill inside me that my mother's arms
couldn't drive away.

I decided I might as well try something as nothing, so I didn't
wait for the Staryk to come knocking this time. I fled to my grandfather's house behind the thick city walls, where the streets were
layered with dirty ice instead of clean white snow and only a
handful of scattered barren trees stood in the lanes. I slept well
that Shabbat night, but the next morning the candles had gone
out, and that evening while I sat knitting with my grandmother,
behind me the kitchen door rattled on its hinges, and she didn't
lift her head at the noise.

I slowly put aside my work, and went to the door, and flinched
back when I had flung it wide: there was no narrow alleyway
behind the Staryk, no brick wall of the house next door and no
hardened slush beneath his feet. He stood outside in a garden of
pale-limbed trees, washed with moonlight even though the moon
hadn't yet come out, as if I could step across the threshold and
walk out of all the world.

There was a box instead of a purse upon the stoop, a chest
made of pale white wood bleached as bone, bound around with
thick straps of white leather and hinged and clasped with silver.
I knelt and opened it. "Seven days this time I'll grant you, to
return my silver changed for gold," the Staryk said in his voice

like singing, as I stared at the heap of coins inside, enough to make a crown to hold the moon and stars. I didn't doubt that the tsar would marry Irina, with this to make her dowry.

I looked up at him, and he down at me with his sharp silver eyes, eager and vicious as a hawk. "Did you think mortal roads could run away from me, or mortal walls keep me out?" he said, and I hadn't really, after all.

"But what *use* am I to you?" I said desperately. "I have no magic: I can't change silver to gold for you in your kingdom, if you take me away."

"Of course you can, mortal girl," he said, as if I was being a fool. "A power claimed and challenged and thrice carried out is true; the proving makes it so." And then he vanished, leaving me with a casket full of silver and a belly full of dismay.

I hadn't been able to make sense of it before: What use would a mortal woman be to an elven lord, and if he wanted one, why wouldn't he just snatch her? I wasn't beautiful enough to be a temptation, and why should boasting make him want me? But of course any king would want a queen who really could make gold out of silver, if he could get one, mortal or not. The last thing I wanted was to be such a prize.

Isaac made the crown in a feverish week, laboring upon it in his stall in the marketplace. He hammered out great thin sheets of silver to make the fan-shaped crown, tall enough to double the height of a head, and then with painstaking care added droplets of melted silver in mimic of pearls, laying them in graceful spiraling patterns that turned upon themselves and vined away again. He borrowed molds from every other jeweler in the market and poured tiny flattened links by the hundreds, then hung glittering chains of them linked from one side of the crown to the other, and fringed along the rest of the wide fan's bottom edge.

By the second day, men and women were coming just to

watch him work. I sat by, silent and unhappy, and kept them off, until finally despite the cold the crowds grew so thick I became impatient and started charging a penny to stand and watch for ten minutes, so they'd go away; only it backfired, and the basket I'd put out grew so full I had to empty it into a sack under the table three times a day.

By the fifth day, I had made nearly as much silver as the Staryk had given me in the first place, and the crown was finished; when Isaac had assembled the whole, he turned and said, "Come here," and set it upon my head to see whether it was well balanced. The crown felt cool and light as a dusting of snow upon my forehead. In his bronze mirror, I looked like a strange deep-water reflection of myself, silver stars at midnight above my brow, and all the marketplace went quiet in a rippling wave around me, silent like the Staryk's garden.

I wanted to burst into tears, or run away; instead I took the crown off my head and put it back into Isaac's hands, and when he'd carefully swathed it with linen and velvet, the crowds finally drifted away, murmuring to one another. My grandfather had sent his two manservants with me that day, and they guarded us to the duke's palace. We found it full of bustle and noise from the tsar's retinue and preparations: there was to be a ball that night, and all the household full of suppressed excitement; they knew of the negotiations underway.

We were put into a better antechamber this time to wait, and then the chaperone came to fetch me. "Bring it with you. The men stay here," she said, with a sharp, suspicious glare. She took me upstairs to a small suite of rooms, not nearly so grand as the ones below: I suppose a plain daughter hadn't merited better before now. Irina was sitting stiff as a rake handle before a mirror made of glass. She wore snow-white skirts and a silver-gray silk dress over them, cut much lower this time to make a frame around the necklace; her beautiful dark hair had been braided into several thick ropes, ready to be put up, and her hands were gripped tightly around themselves in front of her.

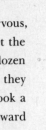

Her fingers worked slightly against one another, nervous, as the chaperone pinned up the braids, and I carefully set the crown upon them. It stood glittering beneath the light of a dozen candles, and the chaperone fell silent, her eyes dreamy as they rested on her charge. Irina herself slowly stood up and took a step closer to the mirror, her nervous hand reaching up toward the glass almost as if to touch the woman inside.

Whatever magic the silver had to enchant those around it either faded with use or couldn't touch me any longer; I wished that it could, and that my eyes could be dazzled enough to care for nothing else. Instead I watched Irina's face, pale and thin and transported, and I wondered if she would be glad to marry the tsar, to leave her quiet, small rooms for a distant palace and a throne. As she dropped her hand, our eyes met in the reflection; we didn't speak, but for a moment I felt her a sister, our lives in the hands of others. She wasn't likely to have any more choice in the matter than I did.

After a few minutes, the duke himself came in to inspect her, and paused in the doorway of the room behind her. Irina was still standing before the mirror; she turned and curtsied to her father, then straightened again, her chin coming up a little to balance the crown; she looked like a queen already. The duke stared at her as if he could hardly recognize his own daughter; he shook himself a little, tearing free of the pull, before he turned to me. "You will have your gold, Panovina," he said. "And if your Staryk wants more of it, you will come to me again."

So I had six hundred gold pieces for the casket and two hundred more for the bank, and my sack full of silver pennies besides; a fortune, for what good it would do me. At least my mother and father wouldn't go cold or hungry again, when the Staryk had taken me away.

My grandfather's servants carried it all home for me. He came downstairs, hearing my grandmother's exclamations, and looked over all the treasure; then he took four gold coins out of the heap meant for the bank, and gave two each to the young men before he dismissed them. "Drink one and save one, you remember the wise man's rule," he said, and they both bowed and thanked him and dashed off to revel, elbowing each other and grinning as they went.

Then he sent my grandmother out of the room on a pretext, asking her to make her cheesecake to celebrate our good fortune; and when she was gone he turned to me and said, "Now, Miryem, you'll tell me the rest of it," and I burst into tears.

I hadn't told my parents, or my grandmother, but I told him: I trusted my grandfather to bear it, as I hadn't trusted them, not to break their hearts wanting to save me. I knew what my father would do, and my mother, if they found out: they would make a wall of their own bodies between me and the Staryk, and then I would see them fall cold and frozen before he took me away.

But my grandfather only listened, and then he said, "Do you want to marry him, then?" I stared at him, still wet-faced. He shrugged. "Sorrow comes to every house, and there's worse things in life than to be a queen."

By speaking so, he gave me a gift: making it my choice, even if it wasn't really. I gulped and wiped away my tears, and felt better at once. After all, in cold, hard terms it *was* a catch, for a poor man's daughter. My grandfather nodded as I calmed myself. "Lords and kings often don't ask for what they want, but they can afford to have bad manners," he said. "Think it over, before you turn away a crown."

I was tempted more by the power my grandfather had given me than the promise of a crown. I thought of it: to harden my heart a little more and stand straight and tall when the Staryk came, to put my hand in his and make it my own will to go with him, so at least I could say the decision had been mine.

But I was my father's daughter also, after all, and I found I didn't want to be so cold. "No," I said, low. "No, Grandfather, I don't want to marry him."

"Then you must make it better sense for him to leave you be," my grandfather said.

The next morning I rose, and put on my best dress, and my fur cloak, and sent for a sledge to carry me. But as I fastened the cloak around my throat in the sitting room, I heard a high cold jangling of bells drifting faintly in from the street, not the bells of a hired harness. I opened the door, and a narrow elegant sleigh drew up outside, fashioned it seemed entirely out of ice and heaped with white furs; the wolfen stag drew it, legs flashing, and the Staryk held the reins of white leather. The street lay blanketed by a thick, unnatural silence: empty even in midmorning, not another soul or sledge or wagon anywhere in sight, and the sky overhead gray and pearled-over like the inside of oyster shells.

He climbed out and came to me, leaving long boot prints in the snow down the walk, and came up the stairs. "And have you changed my silver, mortal girl?" he asked.

I swallowed and backed up to the casket, standing in the room behind me. He followed me inside, stepping in on a winter's blast of cold air, thin wispy flurries of snow whirling into the room around his ankles. He loomed over me to watch as I knelt down behind the casket and lifted up the lid: a heap of silver pennies inside, all I'd taken in the market.

He looked maliciously satisfied a moment, and then he stopped, puzzled, when he saw the coins were different: they weren't fairy silver, of course, though they made a respectable gleam.

"Why should I change silver for gold," I said, when I saw I'd caught his attention, "when I could make the gold, and have them both?" And then I untied the sack sitting beside the chest, to show him the heap of gold waiting inside.

He slowly reached in and lifted out a fistful of gold and let it drop back inside, frowning as he'd frowned each time: as though he didn't like to be caught by his own promises, however useful a queen would be who could turn silver to gold. What would the other elven lords think, I wondered, if he brought home a mortal girl? Not much, I hoped. I daresay in the story, the king's neighbors snickered behind their hands, at the miller's daughter made a queen. And after all, she hadn't even kept spinning.

"You can take me away and make me your queen if you want to," I said, "but a queen's not a moneychanger, and I won't make you more gold, if you do." His eyes narrowed, and I went on quickly, "Or you can make me your banker instead, and have gold when you want it, and marry whomever you like."

I put my money in a vault and bought a house near my grandfather's; we even lent some of the gold back to the duke for the wedding. Isaac was busy for a month making jewelry for all the courtiers and their own daughters, to make a fine show at the celebrations, but he found time to pay visits to my family. I saw Irina once more, when she drove out of the city with the tsar; she threw handfuls of silver out of the window of the carriage as they went through the streets, and looked happy, and perhaps she even was.

We left the business back home in Wanda's hands. Everyone was used to giving her their payments by then, and she'd learned figuring; she couldn't charge interest herself, but as long as she was collecting on our behalf it was all right, and by the time everyone's debts had been repaid, she would have a handsome dowry, enough to buy a farm of her own.

I've never seen the Staryk again. But every so often, after a heavy snowfall, a purse of fairy silver appears on my doorstep, and before a month is gone, I put it back twice over full of gold.

AUTHOR'S NOTE

NAOMI
NOVIK

Naomi Novik: Since I've had my daughter, I've been reading and thinking about fairy tales a great deal. One of the things I love about them is the sense of justice at their heart: the cruel stepsisters don't get to marry the prince, and the witch doesn't get to eat Hansel and Gretel, but if Red Riding Hood strays from the path, the wolf gets his meal. I want that kind of satisfaction from a story, the feeling that the ending is not accurate but *true*.

But I'm suspicious of the Rumpelstiltskin story: the bragging rewarded, the awful king rewarded, promises broken, but it's all right because the miller's daughter is beautiful and the ugly little old man who helps her is devilish and cruel. There's something uncomfortable and not quite right about that, too much justice on Rumpelstiltskin's side, and it's hard for me to miss the sinister in the caricature of the hunched long-nosed man whose hands run with gold and who wants to steal golden-haired babies.

That feeling is at the heart of this story for me: that stomach-tightening moment when we see ourselves in a story, seen through a hostile eye, and understand that we aren't allowed to be the hero. Because of course, I *do* also want the miller's daughter to be victorious; to come out of the whole affair with a crown and a happy child, the accepted grand prizes of fairy tales. But I want to be her, with her in that victory; and I want the power to be in her hands, for good and evil.

ACKNOWLEDGMENTS

We'd like to thank several people who were instrumental in helping us pull this anthology together: Joe Monti and Ann VanderMeer for guidance and support; John Joseph Adams for advice and anthology expertise; Michael McCartney for making our book look beautiful with his brilliant and innovative art direction and design; Elizabeth Blake-Linn for making the book feel like a work of art; Jeannie Ng, Bridget Madsen, and Valerie Shea for making it perfect; Benjamin Carré and Stella Björg for their beautiful art; and Ellen Wright for taking awesome pictures of us. We'd also like to thank the rest of the team at Saga Press: Justin Chanda, Jon Anderson, Alexa Pastor, Catherine Laudone, Faye Bi, Audrey Gibbons, Ellice Lee, and Deane Norton. And a huge thank-you to the writers whose stories make up this book. Thanks as well to Ellen Datlow and Terri Windling for inspiring us with their many beautiful fairy tale books over the years. Dominik would like to thank friends and loved ones for their support, especially Derek Newman-Stille, Mike Allen, Kaitlin Tremblay, and his family. He would also like to thank Marianne LeBreton for always being there, Nicole Kornher-Stace for always having his back, and Kelsi Morris for a great many things. Navah would like to thank her family and good friends, and the members of the Feminist Book Club past and present, with a special shout-out to Liz Kossnar and Kristin Ostby for giant beanbag/couch support. She would especially like to thank Naftali Wolfe for far too many things to count, and the world's best tiny humans and fairy tale believers, Eliora and Ronen.

ABOUT THE EDITORS

NAVAH WOLFE is a Hugo and Locus Award–nominated editor at Saga Press. She is also the coeditor, along with Dominik Parisien, of *Robots vs. Fairies* and *The Starlit Wood: New Fairy Tales*, which was a finalist for the Locus Award and the Shirley Jackson Award, and contains a Nebula Award–winning story. Her books have been finalists for the Nebula, Stoker, and Locus Awards, and have won awards such as the Printz Honor, the Pura Belpré Award, the PEN/Faulkner Award, the Stonewall Book Award, the Lambda Literary Award, and the Schneider Family Book Award. In her past life, she has worked as a bookseller, a rock-climbing-wall manager, and a veterinary intern at a zoo. She lives in Connecticut with her husband, two tiny humans, and one editorial cat. Find her on Twitter at @navahw.

DOMINIK PARISIEN is the coeditor, with Navah Wolfe, of *The Starlit Wood: New Fairy Tales* and *Robots vs. Fairies*. Dominik edited the Aurora Award nominee *Clockwork Canada: Steampunk Fiction* and is the guest fiction editor-in-chief of *Uncanny* magazine's *People with Disabilities Destroy Science Fiction!* His fiction, poetry, and essays have appeared in *Uncanny* magazine, *Strange Horizons*, and *Exile: The Literary Quarterly*, as well as other magazines and anthologies. His fiction has twice been nominated for the Sunburst Award. You can find him online at dominikparisien.wordpress.com and @domparisien on Twitter.

ABOUT THE CONTRIBUTORS

CHARLIE JANE ANDERS is the author of *All the Birds in the Sky*. She's also a founding editor of the science fiction website io9.com and the organizer of the Writers with Drinks reading series. Her stories have appeared in *Asimov's Science Fiction*, the *Magazine of Fantasy & Science Fiction*, *Tor.com*, *Lightspeed*, *Tin House*, *ZYZZYVA*, and several anthologies. Her novelette *Six Months, Three Days* won a Hugo Award.

ALIETTE DE BODARD lives and works in Paris, where she has a day job as a system engineer. She is the author of the critically acclaimed Obsidian and Blood trilogy of Aztec noir fantasies, as well as numerous short stories. Recent works include *The House of Shattered Wings*, a novel set in a turn-of-the-century Paris devastated by a magical war, and *The Citadel of Weeping Pearls* (*Asimov's*), a novella set in the same universe as her Vietnamese space opera *On a Red Station Drifting*.

AMAL EL-MOHTAR is the author of *The Honey Month*, a collection of poetry and prose written to the taste of twenty-eight different kinds of honey. Her short fiction has received the Locus Award and been nominated for the Nebula Award, and her poetry has won the Rhysling Award three times. Her fiction has appeared most recently in magazines such as *Lightspeed*, *Strange Horizons*, and *Uncanny*, and in anthologies such as *The Bestiary* (edited by Ann VanderMeer) and *Kaleidoscope: Diverse YA Science Fiction and Fantasy Stories* (edited by Alisa Krasnostein and Julia Rios). She contributes articles and reviews to NPR Books, Tor.com, and the *L.A. Times*; is a founding member of the Banjo Apocalypse Crinoline Troubadours and a contributor to *Down and Safe: A Blake's 7 Podcast*; and edits *Goblin Fruit*, a quarterly journal of fantastical poetry. She divides her time and heart between Ottawa and Glasgow. Find her on online at amalelmohtar.com or on Twitter @tithenai.

JEFFREY FORD is the author of the novels *Vanitas*, *The Physiognomy*, *Memoranda*, *The Beyond*, *The Portrait of Mrs. Charbuque*, *The Girl in the Glass*, *The Cosmology of the Wider World*, and *The Shadow Year*. His story collections are *The Fantasy Writer's Assistant*, *The Empire of Ice Cream*, *The Drowned Life*, and *Crackpot Palace*. A new collection, *A Natural History of Hell*, will be out in 2016 from Small Beer Press. He lives in Ohio and currently teaches part-time at Ohio Wesleyan University.

MAX GLADSTONE has been thrown from a horse in Mongolia and twice nominated for the John W. Campbell Best New Writer Award. Tor Books published *Last First Snow*, the fourth novel in Max's Craft Sequence (preceded by *Three Parts Dead*, *Two Serpents Rise*, and *Full Fathom Five*) in July 2015. Max's game *Choice of the Deathless* was nominated for the XYZZY Award, and his short fiction has appeared on Tor.com and in *Uncanny* magazine.

THEODORA GOSS's publications include the short story collection *In the Forest of Forgetting* (2006); *Interfictions* (2007), a short story anthology coedited with Delia Sherman; *Voices from Fairyland* (2008), a poetry anthology with critical essays and a selection of her own poems; *The Thorn and the Blossom* (2012), a novella in a two-sided accordion format; and the poetry collection *Songs for Ophelia* (2014). Her work has been translated into ten languages, including French, Japanese, and Turkish. She has been a finalist for the Nebula, Crawford, Locus, Seiun, and Mythopoeic awards, and on the Tiptree Award Honor List. Her short story "Singing of Mount Abora" (2007) won the World Fantasy Award. She teaches literature and writing at Boston University and in the Stonecoast MFA Program. Her first novel,

The Strange Case of the Alchemist's Daughter, is forthcoming from
Saga Press in summer 2017.

DARYL GREGORY is an award-winning writer of genre-
mixing novels, stories, and comics. His most recent work is the
young adult novel *Harrison Squared* (Tor). The novella *We Are All
Completely Fine* won the Shirley Jackson award, was a finalist for
the Nebula, Sturgeon, Locus, and the World Fantasy Awards, and
is in development at the SyFy Channel. His SF novel *Afterparty*
was an NPR and *Kirkus* Best Fiction Book of 2014 and a finalist
for the Campbell and the Lambda Literary awards. His first novel,
Pandemonium, won the Crawford Award and was a finalist for the
World Fantasy Award. His other novels are *The Devil's Alphabet* (a
Philip K. Dick Award finalist) and *Raising Stony Mayhall* (a *Library
Journal* Best SF Book of the Year). Many of his short stories are collected in *Unpossible and Other Stories*, which was named one of the
best books of 2011 by *Publishers Weekly*. His comics work includes
the *Legenderry: Green Hornet*; *the Planet of the Apes*; and *Dracula: The
Company of Monsters* (cowritten with Kurt Busiek).

KAT HOWARD is an award-nominated short fiction writer
who lives and writes in New Hampshire. Her novella, *The End of
the Sentence*, cowritten with Maria Dahvana Headley, was named
one of the Best Books of 2014 by NPR. Her debut novel, *Roses and
Rot*, was published in 2016 by Saga Press.

STEPHEN GRAHAM JONES is the author of fifteen and
a half novels and six story collections. Most recent is *After the People
Lights Have Gone Off*, from Dark House. Up next is *Mongrels*, from
William Morrow. Stephen lives in Colorado with his wife and kids.

MARGO LANAGAN is the *New York Times* bestselling author
(with Scott Westerfeld and Deborah Biancotti) of the Zeroes trilogy.

Her solo novels include *Tender Morsels* and *The Brides of Rollrock Island*, and she has published five short story collections, including *Black Juice*. She has won four World Fantasy Awards and been shortlisted for the Hugo, Nebula, Tiptree, and Shirley Jackson Awards. Margo lives in Sydney, Australia.

MARJORIE LIU is an attorney and *New York Times* bestselling author of over seventeen novels. Her comic book work includes *Monstress*, *X-23*, *Black Widow*, *Dark Wolverine*, and *Astonishing X-Men*, for which she was nominated for a GLAAD Media Award for outstanding media images of the lesbian, gay, bisexual, and transgender community. Liu currently teaches a course on comic book writing at MIT—and a seminar on popular fiction at the Voices of Our Nation workshop.

SEANAN MCGUIRE was born and raised in Northern California, pinned between redwood trees and the towering shadow of Mount Diablo. She lives there still, in a crumbling farmhouse at the edge of a wildlife reserve, which she likes to cheerfully remind people is directly in the path of the tarantula migration. Seanan shares her home with two enormous blue Maine Coon cats, a terrifying number of books, and a steadily growing collection of creepy dolls. Really, all she's missing to be a horror movie is her own private corn maze. Seanan was the 2010 winner of the John W. Campbell Award for Best New Writer. Her first book was published in 2009 (*Rosemary and Rue*, DAW Books). She has released more than twenty-five books since then, under both her own name and the name Mira Grant, and she shows no signs of slowing down. Seanan doesn't sleep much. When not writing, she records albums of original science fiction folk music (called "filk"), travels, and continues in her efforts to visit every single Disney Park in the world. It's a relatively harmless hobby, so we let her have it. You can keep up with Seanan at www.seananmcguire.com, or on Twitter as @seananmcguire.

A full-time writer since 2001, GARTH NIX has worked as a literary agent, marketing/PR consultant, book editor, book publicist, book sales representative, bookseller, and as a part-time soldier in the Australian Army Reserve. More than five million copies of Garth's books have been sold around the world, and his books have appeared on the bestseller lists of the *New York Times*, *Publishers Weekly*, the *Guardian*, and the *Australian*. His work has been translated into forty-one languages.

NAOMI NOVIK is the acclaimed and bestselling author of the Temeraire series, begun with *His Majesty's Dragon*. Her latest novel, *Uprooted*, is a new fantasy inspired by stories of Baba Yaga and the Polish fairy tales and folklore of her childhood.

SOFIA SAMATAR is the author of the novel *A Stranger in Olondria*, winner of the William L. Crawford Award, the British Fantasy Award, and the World Fantasy Award. She is also a Hugo and Nebula award finalist and the recipient of the 2014 John W. Campbell Award for Best New Writer. Her new novel, *The Winged Histories*, was published by Small Beer Press in 2016.

KARIN TIDBECK is the award-winning author of *Jagannath: Stories* and *Amatka*. She lives in Malmö, Sweden, where she works as a freelance writer and creative writing teacher. She writes in Swedish and English, and has published work in *Weird Tales*, *Tor.com*, *Words Without Borders*, and anthologies like *Fearsome Magics* and *The Time Traveler's Almanac*.

CATHERYNNE M. VALENTE is the *New York Times* bestselling author of over two dozen works of fiction and poetry, including *Palimpsest*, the Orphan's Tales series, *Deathless*, *Radiance*, and the crowdfunded phenomenon *The Girl Who Circumnavigated Fairyland in a Ship of Own Making*. She is the winner of the Andre

Norton, Tiptree, Mythopoeic, Rhysling, Lambda, Locus, and Hugo Awards. She has been a finalist for the Nebula and World Fantasy Awards. She lives on an island off the coast of Maine with a small but growing menagerie of beasts, some of which are human.

GENEVIEVE VALENTINE is an author and critic. Her first novel, *Mechanique: A Tale of the Circus Tresaulti*, won the 2012 Crawford Award; her second, *The Girls at the Kingfisher Club*, was an NPR, *Washington Post*, and *Chicago Tribune* Best Book of the Year. Her short fiction has appeared at *Tor.com*, *Clarkesworld*, the *Journal of Mythic Arts*, and in *New Haven Review* and others; her nonfiction and criticism have appeared at the *Dissolve*, the *AV Club*, the *Los Angeles Review of Books*, and the *New York Times*. Her most recent novel is *Icon*, the second book in the Persona duology.